A DANCE OF FANG
AND CLAW

THE RANGER ARCHIVES: VOLUME THREE

PHILIP C. QUAINTRELL

Copyright © 2022 by Philip C. Quaintrell
First edition published 2022.

Cover Illustration by Chris McGrath
Book design by BodiDog Design
Edited by David Bradley

ISBN: 978-1-916610-20-0 (paperback)
ASIN: B0BLHSNQS7 (ebook)

Published by Quaintrell Publishings

For Henry... Welcome to the fold

ALSO BY
PHILIP C. QUAINTRELL

THE ECHOES SAGA: (9 Book Series)

1. Rise of the Ranger

2. Empire of Dirt

3. Relic of the Gods

4. The Fall of Neverdark

5. Kingdom of Bones

6. Age of the King

7. The Knights of Erador

8. Last of the Dragorn

9. A Clash of Fates

THE RANGER ARCHIVES: (3 Book Series)

1. Court of Assassins

2. Blood and Coin

3. A Dance of Fang and Claw

THE TERRAN CYCLE: (4 Book Series)

1. Intrinsic

2. Tempest

3. Heretic

4. Legacy

SEE THE **FULL MAP** AT PHILIPCQUAINTRELL.COM/VERDA

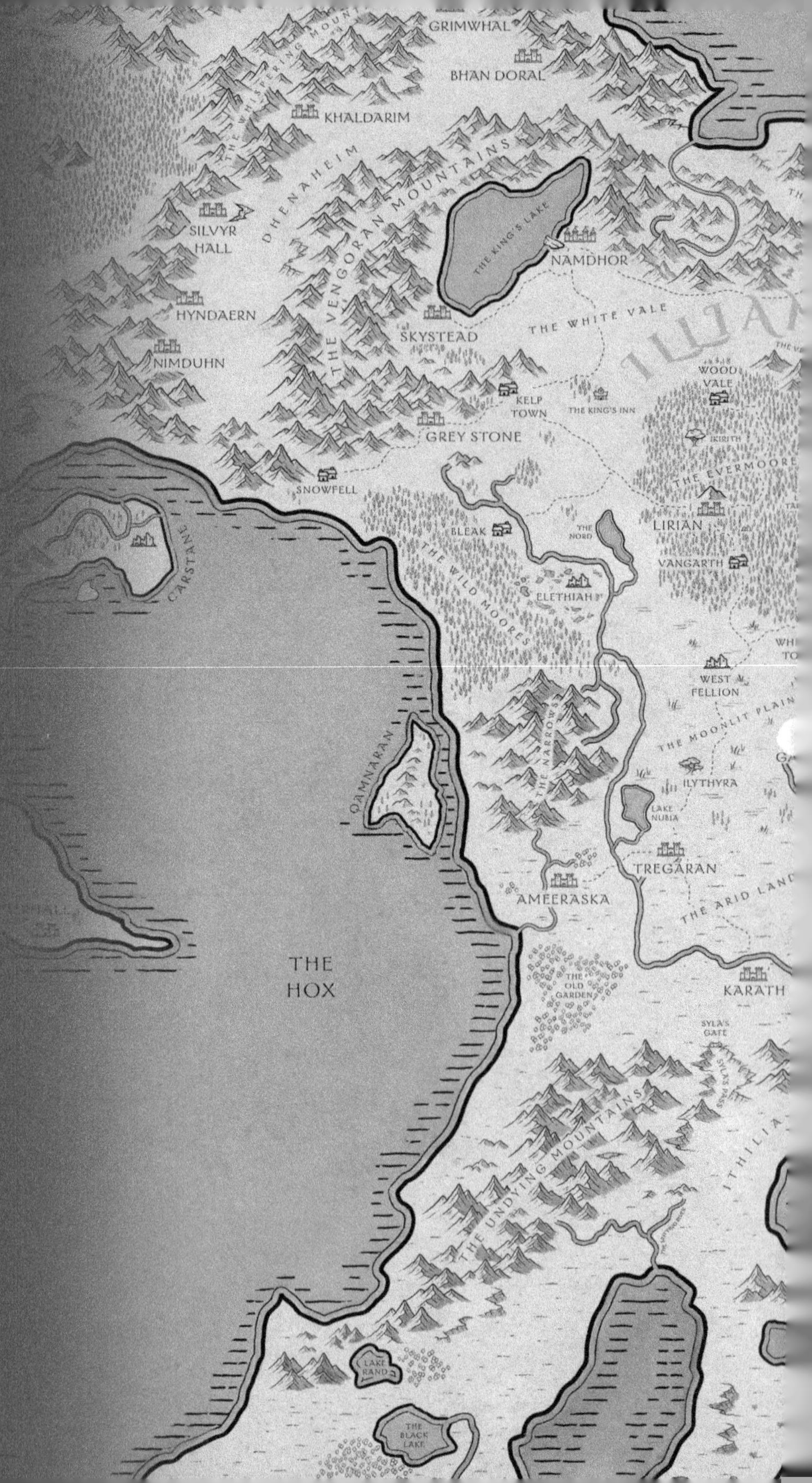

DRAMATIS PERSONAE

Asher
Ranger

Borvyn Murell
Lord of Dunwich

Captain Lonan
Captain of the Kelp Town Watch

Creed
Werewolf

Danagarr Stormshield
Dwarven smith

Deadora Stormshield
Child and daughter of Danagarr and Kilda

Doran Heavybelly
Ranger

DRAMATIS PERSONAE

Kilda Stormshield
Dwarven Healer

Lord Kernat
Lord of Kelp Town

Merith
Vorska

Nasta Nal-Aket
Father of Nightfall

Russell Maybury
Werewolf/Ranger

Salim Al-Anan
Ranger

Vouder Stould
Gang Leader

CHAPTER 1
CRYING WATERS

*Wretch - This might be the twelfth edition, but these monsters have
featured in every iteration of our fine bestiary. It's as if these creatures
have accompanied us from the very hands of the gods. There might be
some truth in that, as our oldest legends would suggest we humans came
from The Wild Moores. A humble ranger cannot say. What I can say is,
be it the damned Outlanders or the Wretches that blend in to the trees,
don't go anywhere near The Wild Moores without expecting a fight.
As for the Wretches themselves, they can blend in with their
environment. You're going to need Dovun Dust, let me tell you. Throw it
high in the air and let the beasts move through that red cloud. No
missing them then. Swing true and victory will be yours.*

***A Chronicle of Monsters: A Ranger's Bestiary, 12th Edition,
Page 5.***

Balor Ved, Ranger.

B leak was the sky, a cold twilight that reflected in the black waters of the lifeless swamp. Blacker still were the trees that rose from those waters, like the petrified fingers of Death itself. At disquieting angles, and with ne'er a branch nor leaf, they reached for that setting twilight, that insipid sky. Beneath the still surface, the shallow water was home to naught but a web of dark roots that knotted together the small wood of ominous pillars.

A ripple, a tsunami to those stilled waters, pushed between the trees.

A man followed in its wake.

His green cloak pressed upon the water behind him and fanned out across the mirroring surface. The water reached to just beneath his knees yet the muddy base was beyond sight. The roots wished to trip him, to bring him down into the swamp's numbing embrace. It was with the measured steps of a ranger that the man advanced, his feet shifting to fit precisely between the twisting snakes of gnarled wood.

Asher stopped.

Crouching, he ran two fingers over the slick bark of the nearest tree, an inch above the waterline. It was there that the trees were so black as to appear a void that swallowed all the light and colour from the world. Inspecting his fingers, he observed a glistening substance that clung to his skin as readily as it did the trees.

He was getting closer.

The ranger smiled.

The setting sun still offered some of its bleak light when he heard it, that distant call of distress he had been anticipating. The shout for help was garbled but the shriek of terror that trailed it was piercing, cutting through the lifeless swamp as a ray of sunlight might cut through rainclouds.

Asher changed direction and pursued the call for help and the sound of panicked splashing. He ventured beyond the barren trees and into a clearing where the swamp rapidly deepened into untold depths. Perhaps forty feet out, he spied the troubling

2

scene that had drawn the four missing people from nearby Kelp Town.

Like the ranger, they had seen the hand desperately clawing for life and the head, concealed by matted black hair, that routinely broke the water's oily skin to cry for help. Asher imagined them charging into the deep and swimming out to save the apparent girl before she drowned.

The ranger did no such thing.

To quiet the alarm in his mind, the instinctual part of him that felt urged to dive forward and save the girl, Asher retrieved his folded bow and thumbed the latch to snap the limbs to life. The sound of the taut bowstring's release filled the eerie atmosphere with more tension. Whistling across the glassy water, the arrow sailed directly into the girl's head, impacting with a wet *thud*.

Then he waited.

"Help!" came the laboured call, only a moment later.

Asher took a breath, his mind able to focus now on the irrefutable truth of the situation: it was a Hell Hag.

He had suspected as much when negotiating the terms of the contract, back in Kelp Town, and had pressed upon the town's watch the colossal task ahead of him were he to slay it for them. He didn't enjoy driving up his price in towns or villages, where the populations were smaller than the bustling cities and they relied so much more on their true grit to survive, but he hadn't been delusive in his description of the beast. Hell Hags didn't die easily.

Asher looked back at the way he had come, knowing that Hector remained tied to a tree at the swamp's edge. A Chronicle of Monsters: A Ranger's Bestiary was in his saddlebags, the leather-bound book the last of its kind. He had spent the previous day poring over the relevant archive only to discover that he knew it word for word. It was little comfort.

Turning back to the deeper swamp, he watched the girl's body rise as high as her shoulders, both hands dashing the water. How wretched a beast Hell Hags were, to use the ragged corpse of a previous victim only to lure in more. How the creature was able to puppet a human's terror so accurately Asher could not say, only

3

that it possessed the vile limb somewhere along its spine. It was an image beyond nightmares in which he envisioned the monster manipulating the body's vocal cords, likely repeating the victim's last words.

Since his bow was useless in the fight to come, he collapsed the limbs with a flick of the wrist and returned it to his back for now. He drew his two-handed broadsword. There was no better sound to the ranger than steel ringing free. The weapon was relatively new, having only rested on his hip for three months, but it was identical to the previous sword and the one before that. Its weight and balance were faultless, the blade a perfect companion in his expert grip. Inevitably, he was still likely to lose it or break it before the next winter blanketed Illian. The ranger always chalked it up as a hazard of the job and was always sure to keep some coin aside to pay for the replacement.

Considering the arena in which he was to fight this particular monster, Asher stepped across to a grassy knoll and spun the broadsword around, driving it into the firmer ground. Using the guard as he would a hook, the ranger proceeded to remove his quiver and bow and hang them on it. After unclipping his cloak, the bemired fabric was draped over them all. That left him with one significant weapon, its hilt of sandy brown leather protruding over his right shoulder.

The silvyr short-sword slid from its scabbard, the rare metal singing as it scraped against the hard leather and tasted air. So light was the weapon that it could have been mistaken for a child's toy, yet so strong was the hourglass blade that it could cleave steel with a measured application of strength. It would have no trouble passing through the hide of a Hell Hag.

The ranger needed no more than an upward glance to know that night was coming, and fast under winter's unyielding watch. He sighed. "Best be getting on with it then," he muttered, his voice as dry as brittle leaves.

Ignoring the Hag's foul puppetry, Asher prepped his silvyr blade, lathering it with a pre-made paste, awarding the weapon the venomous bite of a Luxun. He had slain the Luxun almost a year previously and had been awaiting a reason to employ the venom he had harvested from its glands. Having taken the water into consideration before setting off from Kelp Town, Asher had also prepared an insoluble paste to prevent the venom from being washed away.

All he had to do now was stab the fiend.

Leaving his broadsword and gear behind, Asher took deliberate steps into the deeper waters. Arcing ripples heralded his approach, reaching as far out as the dead girl who had once pleaded for her life. The water quickly rose about him as he descended the natural slope. The cold of those waters was bitter and raw, a seizing hand that sought to undo him, to hollow him out of all warmth and strength.

The touch of it cast his memories and instincts back to an earlier time in his life, when he had been no more than an initiate in Nightfall. How many times had he and others been weighted down with stones and thrown overboard, into the murky depths of The Adean? Survive or die. It was the Arakesh way. Only when he could hold his breath for a number of minutes and function suitably in icy waters could he progress. Not everyone had.

After twenty feet he ran out of ground and took to swimming. The ranger looked about him for any signs of the Hag's true limbs coming to claim him, but he failed to even see his hands pushing through the ink-black water. Coming to a stop only a few feet away from the putrid meat puppet, Asher began to tread water.

"Come on then," he rasped, growing impatient.

The girl sank unceremoniously into the swamp.

All was still and hushed but for Asher's continued treading. Knowing what was to come, he began to take successive large breaths, helping his lungs to fill his blood with more oxygen than it would usually hold. The coil about his left leg was barely felt before it pulled him under, returning the swamp's polished black top to its pristine condition.

Pitch-black was the vault beneath that sealed top, so capped by the monster's natural oils. Not a single sliver of light was permitted entry, creating a watery abyss. It was an environment all

Hell Hags knew instinctively was an advantage to them: they who had been born in the dark.

But now there was another monster down there with it, a monster that *fed* on the dark.

A part of the mind that lay dormant in all but the initiated of Nightfall came to life, fuelled by an elven brew that had been forced upon him since childhood. The Nightseye elixir, coursing through his veins, turned the black surroundings into an extension of his body, defining every aspect with the impossible reach of his senses.

The swamp was dead. Not even the plant life could survive a Hell Hag and its natural secretions. The monster itself dominated the ranger's mind, feeding all but his sense of smell with information about its macabre body. The shape that displaced the water around it gave Asher the impression that it was similar to a spider, with a bulbous body and large legs that rose up before sinking down into the mud. From that rounded torso, however, extended the abominable limb that worked the now limp corpse.

Asher could taste the rotting flesh of that body, just as he could feel the smooth bones that littered the glutinous ooze below him. It would have been enough to drive most to madness, to be thrown into hell *before* death. Instead, his mind had collapsed into a smaller space, a shapeless void that dragged him down, as surely as the Hell Hag did. It was an iron curtain of solitude, of absolute focus.

It was the realm of the *Assassin*.

There was no fighting that murderous part of him now, not when he needed it so. Rather than fight it, as he would, Asher let those old thought patterns take over, comforting him, reminding him that *he* was the apex predator.

It wasn't the only thing he was allowing to happen. Had he wished, he could have slashed at the tentacle that pulled him ever deeper, but the Hag was saving him precious energy and bringing him to it. Soon, he knew, the worming limb that gripped him would be accompanied by more, and they would seek to entangle him and draw him into the jaws of that watery perdition.

He could feel them, unfurling towards him. Their every movement secreted more of the black oil that rose to collect at the surface. One came for his arm but he raised his free leg and it gladly coiled around it. He could hear the parting of small fangs and ringed suckers as the Hag prepared to strip him to his bones, sucking in the meat and all else with ferocious proficiency.

The creature lacked any eyes to see the silvyr blade in Asher's hand. The acute senses it possessed likely didn't know what to make of the mineral, only that it was to be discarded as waste. Perhaps with that in mind, another tentacle prowled about his arm, intending to wrap around his wrist and squeeze it from his fingers.

But he was close enough now, and so he was done playing the victim.

Ignoring the probing tentacle, the ranger tensed his bound legs and tucked his upper body in. A single swipe sliced through the organic bindings and spilled inky blood. The beast recoiled, sending ripples that disturbed the coated top. The remaining tentacles ceased their subtle approach, floating about him like seaweed, and came for him with a vengeance.

The ranger cut down two more before a third tugged on his ankle and cast him down like an anchor. His impact disturbed the ossuary of broken skeletons, filling his ears with their rattle and the resounding knock of his short-sword biting into a discarded femur bone. The tentacle around his ankle contracted and he was yanked through the debris and up, returned to the monster.

Again, he found the angle and severed the tentacle. Asher floated before the Hell Hag and sensed its increasing agitation. The Luxun venom would be slowly spreading through its wretched system, though he would need to deliver a greater sting if he was to bring the monster down for good.

Before departing Kelp Town, Asher had questioned his use of the Luxun venom. He knew the bite of an Arkilisk could bring down a grown man in minutes and would certainly have killed the Hell Hag by now. The Basilisk's smaller cousin, however, would have taken far longer to track down, distant as it was in The Evermoore. Deciding the monster needed slaying sooner rather than later, the ranger had settled for the Luxun venom he already possessed.

Feeling the burn in his chest, he began to regret his decision.

With so many tentacles now useless to it, the fiend adjusted its stance and raised its front half, there to reveal previously hidden claws. They unfurled and came for him, snapping as a crab's would.

Asher had no intention of engaging those claws, each capable of cutting him in half. Perfectly aware of his surroundings, the ranger made his evasion by grasping at one of the retreating tentacles and letting it pull him out of harm's way. Indeed, the nearest claw fastened shut only a moment later, chopping through the water and his previous position.

By the time the Hell Hag realised what its prey was doing, Asher's momentum was enough to bring him and the creature together. The ranger slammed into its smooth eyeless head and rolled over the top, silvyr blade angled to stab down. It would be done in a single stroke. He could already taste the air that awaited him.

Be that as it may, the final blow proved beyond his abilities as the Hell Hag flexed its bent legs and pushed its body up. The force of it was enough to flatten Asher, plastering him across the top of its body. It was also enough to rob him of the poisoned blade, the hilt snatched from his grasp.

There came a rush of water when the Hag's rounded back broke the sable top and Asher was returned to the world above. He gulped the air, quenching the fire that had started in his lungs. The sky above had yet to succumb to true darkness and the meagre light that existed banished the effects of the Nightseye elixir. The transition was distracting at best and threatened to stupefy the *Assassin's* sharp focus. But it was not to last.

The creature beneath him was already descending, preparing to leave him on the surface. Death would surely follow, for the beast had only to reach up with one of its claws and end it all.

The instinct to not only survive but slay the monster moved his hand to the back of his belt, where a curved dagger awaited it. Before the Hag disappeared into the ink, Asher stabbed its back and twisted the blade so that he might be pulled down with it. A moment later and he was submerged into the world of the *Assassin* once more.

The silvyr's pureness was as bright to his senses as the flame of a candle in a dark room. Using the dagger to find purchase along the Hell Hag's cumbersome body, the ranger pulled himself to its edge. The short-sword was standing proud amidst the bones, not two feet from one of the monster's pointed legs. As soon as he swam for it, however, he would be at the mercy of those savage claws. But what choice did he have?

Kicking off and down, he dived for the blade and its promise of victory.

The Hell Hag shifted, scattering bones and kicking up mud. One of its legs knocked into Asher ribs, its sharp ridges cutting through the leather of his cuirass and sawing through skin and bone. The ranger's cry of pain was stymied by the engulfing water, but human blood was flowing now, exciting the Hag. It shifted all the more, trying to find the right angle to ensnare its wounded prey. In doing so, it dislodged the silvyr blade and cast it further away.

In pain, dismayed, and feeling the loss of blood, Asher fell out of tune with his heightened senses and missed the incoming claw. Swatted by the hard appendage, the ranger struck another of the fiend's armoured legs and had his back lacerated by the razored protrusions. Bolts of agony ran through him, pressing upon him the need to get out of the swamp and abandon the contract.

Survive, his instincts hissed, and always using the voice of Nasta Nal-Aket, his old mentor, would-be father, *captor*.

Asher gritted his teeth until it hurt. He was sick of hearing the old man's voice in his head. Pushing off from the leg, he swam down, homing in on the metallic taste of silvyr. Towering over him, the behemoth moved one way then the next, its bulk proving too troublesome to tackle prey that dwelled beneath it. Using the advantage while he had it, the ranger closed the gap and finally reclaimed the short-sword.

There came no hesitation from the *Assassin*—it meant to destroy, as it had been bred to do.

Rooted as the Hag's legs were, their rigidness only aided Asher's attacks. Slowed by the water, two strikes were required to sever a portion of the hard limb and unbalance the beast. Its pain reverberated from somewhere deep in its chest, sending waves of vibrations through the murky water.

The ranger wasn't nearly done.

Pushing up from the bottom, he launched himself by the point of his blade into the crevice where the damaged leg joined the bulbous body. He stabbed again and again before hacking at the top of the barbed limb. Inevitably, it fell free of the main body and the Hag reeled, reduced now to five legs. Still the ranger attacked, plunging the Luxun venom into its dark hide.

Only when it succeeded in turning did he have to swim to evade the legs. But he was soon faced by the monster's claws again, and behind them its ravening jaws. The right claw came for him first. Fighting against the water, Asher was only able to avoid it snapping closed, the sharp edge still slicing a line across his hip and adding more blood to the swamp.

Then came the next claw. It snapped once, twice, a third time: the last attack clamping around his leg. That should have been it, the mortal blow that saw him bleed out profusely and die before the Hag could even consume him. But he did not die. He did not bleed out. He didn't lose the leg.

Wracked by spasms, the Hell Hag did no more than break the bones and lacerate the skin. The claw opened, leaving Asher with the leg still intact but with new depths of crippling pain.

Marred and mangled as he was, the ranger tasted blood in the water, though it wasn't his own. The Hag was spewing its insides out, vomiting internal organs into the swamp.

Some distant part of Asher's mind, untroubled by the pain and broken leg, conjured a sense of relief. *Finally*, the quiet voice thought. The Luxun venom was slow, but it could not be denied, even by a Hell Hag.

Soon, the creature's remaining legs failed to support it and the bottom rose up to meet it. More spasms rippled through its muscles and its mouth sat ajar, twitching in death.

His lungs desperate for air, Asher swam up, his left leg no more than a useless weight. He broke the surface and inhaled life, his hair and face coated with the Hag's oils. Night had finally come to the world and a clouded one at that, carrying a threat of snow about it. Asher couldn't care less about the weather. Everything hurt, his blood was adding to the Hag's, and he could barely organise his thoughts.

When, at last, the swamp shallowed and he was able to crawl on his good leg, the ranger made his way back to his sword and gear, where he might sit back against one of the petrified trees. A long groan escaped his wet lips.

"I should have charged more," he grumbled, glancing over the canvas of wounds he had amassed.

None was so bad as his leg. Splinted by his hands, the injured limb was raised from the water where he could better examine it. There was a bone protruding through his skin and trousers, just above the boot. Were he to present to any healer in the land, even a king's physician, they would recommend amputating the leg as quickly as possible, before the blood could be spoiled.

Asher had no intention of losing his leg.

Leaving the limb to rest in the water, the ranger peeled off the fingerless glove on his right hand. Sitting quiet but proud on his index finger was a ring of simple iron and within its claws a black gem. Where it had come from, or how it had become his, lay so far in his past that Nightfall's brutal training had scrubbed the truth from memory.

All he knew was the power it granted him.

Clenching his fist, Asher willed the magic therein to bathe him, to renew his body. Pain always came first, but it was fleeting and bearable for its time. The bone in his leg retracted back into place, eliciting a clipped yell from the ranger. The gashes to his torso and back knitted together, revealing healthy skin through the tears in his leathers. Lastly, his energy returned with the replenishing of his blood.

Rising from the swamp, the ranger stood—a man made whole again.

Looking back at the deeper swamp, all was calm, the smooth surface imparting no hint of the battle that had just taken place. Asher reached for his cloak and gear when a thought occurred to him, giving him pause. He looked back at the water again, reluctant to grant his thought any credence. Yet, he knew the people of Kelp Town would demand proof of the monster's demise before coin left their purse.

The ranger sighed and left his gear where it was. With the silvyr short-sword in hand, he waded back into the swamp and dived into the watery graveyard.

CHAPTER 2
RANGER BUSINESS

Hell Spores - If you've got this far into the bestiary, you're probably expecting another monster with claws or talons and a hide of scales or spines. Not all monsters are so easily identified, nor do they hunt as you would expect.

Hell Spores are often found near damp caves (See A Charter of Monsters, Page 86, for known locations). They also like to grow around tasty mushrooms. Some poor soul comes across the mushrooms, picks them, and ends up breathing in the Hell Spores. What follows ain't pretty.

It might take seconds or hours but the end is the same: death. In death, the spores really get to work. They appear to take control of the body and violently attack anyone and anything to spread more spores. Don't worry, you'll know an infected person when you see one. They're wild and covered in what can only be described as fungi.

Burn them. Burn them all.

A Chronicle of Monsters: A Ranger's Bestiary, 12th Edition, Page 91.

Cal Vornan, Ranger.

. . .

Both light and sound broke through the trees, guiding the ranger back to civilisation, if Kelp Town had ever been called such a thing. Hector breached the outer edge of the marshland that surrounded the Hag's swamp and trotted onto the road of slush and mud.

Asher brought the animal to a stop, giving way to the horses and carts that ferried dozens of miners in and out of the large town. Some were being taken west, towards the Demetrium mines for the night shift, while others—begrimed and dishevelled—were being brought back to rest.

Some of the miners took note of the ranger, whose appearance was equally unkempt and fouled after his encounter with the Hell Hag, though, in addition, the swamp had lent him a loathsome odour. Of course, most were drawn to the monstrous limb being dragged behind Hector, bound to the horse by a length of rope. It was only a portion of the Hag's already severed leg, but it was big enough to convince the town's watch that he had, indeed, slain the beast.

The way clear, Asher guided Hector onwards. Coming in behind the last wagon of miners, the ranger entered Kelp Town under the arched framework of dark wood, upon which its name had been carved. Old wind chimes and tired bunting showed where they had, sporadically, been hung from it, and now blew in the light breeze that cast the falling snow at a slanted angle.

For the most part, the townspeople had retired for the night. Only here and there came the ruckus of merriment, drifting through the streets on the wind. Asher considered the town's central square, where so many taverns and inns were situated. His stomach growled at the thought of a hot meal and he dared to dream of a cold cider to go with it. Catching his own scent, the ranger had to wonder which, if any, establishment would grant him entry.

Steering Hector away from the central square for now, Asher made his way through the north-east district. He caught glimpses of people inside their homes, warmed by fires and comforted by family. Stray dogs and lone cats cut through it all, stalking in alleyways and sniffing out scraps along the edge of the street. More than one of them approached the Hag's leg to investigate the separated limb's unusual smell. None so much as licked it.

Arriving at the largest building in the neighbourhood, its third floor rising above the rooftops around it, Asher dismounted and secured Hector to the post outside, pausing only to offer the horse an apple from his saddlebag. "I'll find you somewhere for the night soon enough," he promised.

Untethering the rope from the back of the saddle, Asher proceeded to drag the Hag's leg up the short steps. Beyond the small porch, the door remained closed and resisted the ranger's attempt to enter. Stepping back, he read the sign nailed to the wall: *Town Watch, established under the reign of King Jard of house Orvish.* The date was no longer legible, though Asher imagined it was likely centuries ago. More importantly, it said nothing about being closed.

Three times the ranger's fist hammered the door.

Forgettable was the best description of the watchman who answered his knock, though he did open the door wide rather than peer out through a crack as most would do after sunset. It was a testament, no doubt, to the confidence his title instilled in him. "We're closed," he stated gruffly, turning his nose away from Asher.

The ranger did little to conceal his indignation. "You're the *watch*," he pointed out.

The watchman's nose twitched and he furrowed his brow. "All the same; we're closed. Off with you now." Without waiting for a response, he ended their brief interaction by closing the door.

The door, however, failed to shut.

The watchman jumped back and with an undignified yelp at that. "What in the gods..."

Asher used the Hag's leg, the same leg he had jammed into the closing gap, to push the door open again. "I don't think the gods had anything to do with this," he said dryly. "Captain Lonan," he added expectantly.

His large eyes fixed on the monstrous leg, the lawman's naturally blank expression was pinched by something close to disgust.

Asher kicked the leg, stealing his attention. "Captain Lonan," he repeated.

The watchman licked his lips. "Captain's in the... in the back," he managed. The ranger grunted and moved past the young man. "Oi! You can't go back there!" came his trailing call, a sense of urgency about him.

"Ranger business," Asher replied, moving through a narrow corridor and into a small foyer with a surprisingly high ceiling. Activity sounded from the adjacent room, where shadows danced across the visible wall, and voices collided in quiet argument. Then there was the smell emanating from within, so odorous that it overpowered the filth plastered to the ranger.

How familiar it was, the scent of blood and death.

Intrigued and forgetting where he was, Asher made to investigate before the young watchman caught up with him and blocked his path. "I told you, fella, we're *closed*. I could have you bound in irons for the intrusion."

Asher looked the man in the eyes, and with enough steel in their blue to put a lump in the watchman's throat. "What is it you boys are always saying in the vales? *The watch never blinks*," he recalled, thinking little of the inflated motto.

The lawman swallowed the knot in his throat and shrugged his shoulders in an effort to straighten his back without notice. "That's right," he said, voice breaking.

"How can the watch be *watching* if you're closed?" Asher asked him bluntly.

"What in the hells is going on out there?" The demand came from the adjacent room, from a voice many years older than the man standing in Asher's way, and too old to be Captain Lonan. It carried true authority, though the ranger knew well that had nothing to do with experience.

Joining them in the foyer, a man smaller than them both

planted himself before Asher, narrowed eyes scrutinising him. It wasn't long, of course, before he detected the swamp clinging to the ranger and, like the younger watchman, he steered his nose in a different direction. Unlike those of the town's watch, he wore civilian clothes and fine they were too. Indeed, his plum cloak and dyed furs were likely worth more than any man of the watch earned in a year.

His greying beard and slicked back hair were immaculately trimmed, a standard of grooming favoured by the wealthier class who could afford such attention to detail in their appearance. Given the authority being exuded by the older man, Asher was leaning more towards the ruling class than mere wealth.

It was then that the torchlight kissed the bronze brooch pinned to his right lapel, the metal forged into a bloody hand gripping a rose. The sigil pierced Asher's memory, dredging up distant lessons in Nightfall. He failed, however, to recall the name behind the plucked rose before the man spoke again.

"Why is there a beggar dripping all over my boots?" he fumed, his articulation and fervent sense of drama confirming, beyond doubt, that he was connected to the lord of these lands. Of course, he wasn't nearly dripping in enough gold to be *the* lord of Kelp Town. He was also an unobservant fool if he thought common beggars wore two-handed broadswords on their hip.

"Apologies, Secretary Royce," the young watchman proffered with a short bow. "I did try to—"

"I don't care what you *tried* to do, boy!" the secretary interrupted. "Just get him out of here! And quick about it before the smell of him strips the paint!" Before he could return to the room from which he came, Captain Lonan filled the doorway, his cool eyes locking with Asher's.

"Apologies, Secretary," the captain offered, stepping fully into the foyer. "This man has business with *me*."

Secretary Royce briefly glanced back at the ranger, as if his eyes could not stand the sight of him for too long. "You have business *tonight*?" he questioned, subtly gesturing at the adjacent room. "And with the likes of this... vagabond? What *business* is it then?"

17

"*Watch* business, Secretary," Lonan replied vaguely.

"*Ranger* business," Asher corrected, pushing the Hag's leg at the captain's feet.

The secretary deigned to lay eyes on Asher again, though his derision remained all too clear. "Ranger?" he echoed, suspicion in his tone.

Beside him, Captain Lonan had crouched down to examine the limb. "You killed it," he said, incredulous. "I don't believe it," he whispered, one finger running over the barbed ridges.

A strain of revelation crossed Royce's face. "Please tell me this has nothing to do with that mess in the marshlands, Captain." When Lonan failed to respond, the lord's secretary cursed. "Atilan save me! The watch was to take care of that..." He waved a hand at the severed leg. "Whatever it was! Who gave you permission to use watch coin, *good* coin, on a blasted hunter? I know I didn't! Lord Kernat certainly didn't!"

Kernat... The name probed the depths of Asher's mind all the more and he finally recalled Lord Aren Kernat—if, indeed, he was still the sitting lord. The Kernats had lorded over Kelp Town for all of human memory, granted nobility by one of The Ice Vale's earliest kings. The word *insignificant* felt appropriate to the ranger.

"What credit can be taken for the slaying of the fiend now?" the angry secretary went on. "What are we to tell the people? That we couldn't kill the beast so we out-sourced it to some vagrant with a sword? Do I have to remind you of the pressures we're under from Grey Stone? Of the eyes that are upon us?"

"I require no such permission, Secretary, on the spending of the watch budget. This..." He returned his attention to the black limb, stumped.

"Hell Hag," Asher announced gruffly, drawing all eyes momentarily.

"*Hell Hag*," Lonan repeated, the name catching in his mouth, "has killed four townspeople that we know of. But what I know for sure, Secretary, is that not a single watchman employed under the banner of house Kernat is trained to slay monsters in swamps."

"Mind your tone, Lonan," came the clipped response. "It is only tradition that sees you titled as captain, a *soldier's* rank. One word in my lord's ear and you will find yourself bereft of such grandeur, perhaps even position."

Tension filled the void between the two men, fuelling Asher's boredom and returning his thoughts to hunger and need of a soft bed. "I'll be taking my *good* coin now," he said bluntly, inserting himself into that palpable void.

His statement was directed at the captain, but it was the secretary that took umbrage, eliciting a mocking laugh that rippled up from his gut and stopped in his throat. Perhaps it was his lack of decorum. Perhaps it was the obliviousness he displayed towards his betters. Propriety or ignorance—the ranger didn't much care which he was being accused of so long as he got what he was owed.

Captain Lonan stood, towering over the secretary by a whole head, and returned his attention to Asher. "You appear unscathed," he observed, notably perplexed by the lack of blood and gore that should accompany the damage to his leathers.

"*You* appear light of coin," Asher replied without missing a beat.

Looking to be between a rock and a hard place, Lonan's jaw tensed in what was clearly an attempt to suppress a sigh. "Your work is appreciated, Ranger, and will not be forgotten," he declared, though it was perhaps said for the secretary's benefit more than Asher's. The captain retrieved a key from his pocket and tossed it to the young watchman who had stood statue-still for the entire exchange. "You'll find the coin in the top drawer of my desk," he instructed. "See the man paid and escorted out."

"Good riddance," Royce commented, already returning to the adjacent room and the death that surely lingered therein.

Captain Lonan gave no more than a nod before trailing the secretary and disappearing inside the room. Curious, the ranger thought, but damned if he wasn't starving now.

His belt weighted with coin again—and absent the Hag's razored limb—Asher mounted Hector and directed the horse to the main square. By the time he had haggled a good price with the stable master and seen Hector fed and bedded for the night, the snow had arrived in force, sticking to everything pile upon pile.

Accustomed to camping in the wilds, Asher was never fussy when it came to choosing somewhere to eat and sleep inside the walls of men. Dandy's Inn was the closest source of food and a potential bed, and so he quickly found himself standing amidst the small crowd that had gathered around the bar.

"Room?" the Dandy's owner repeated, her eyes roaming over the unsightly ranger, nose crinkling.

Asher glanced down the bar, at the bowls of food waiting to be served. "And a hot meal," he reiterated, dreaming of the moment his face might bath in the hot steam of chicken stew.

Those around the ranger began to disperse, complaining of the stench coming off him in waves. Some went so far as to say the smell had put them off their food. Asher maintained his usual demeanour, not one to be disturbed or embarrassed by the grievances he might stir.

"You're not to be eating here," the owner told him. "Not smelling like that. You'll sicken my customers. You can wash first," she quickly instructed. "There's a bath upstairs. It'll cost you *extra*," the owner added with a haughty smirk.

Though the ranger disliked being leveraged, and for coin no less, he had already planned on bathing to rid himself of the swamp. He had only hoped it might come *after* a hot meal.

"And the room?"

The Dandy's owner slapped a key on the bar. "Room two." Asher reached for the key only to find the woman's hand covering it. "You got the coin?" By her tone, she clearly believed their negotiation was about to come to an abrupt end.

The ranger planted his newly-weighted coin purse on the counter and lorded a smirk of his own over the short woman.

What followed was a gloriously hot bath, a change of clothes, a quick scrub down of his leathers, and a seat in a gloomy booth while he waited for his bowl of steaming chicken stew. By then, of course, there were few left in Dandy's Inn. From those who left while he was waiting, Asher heard them speak their fears of walking the streets under a full moon—the night of monsters, they all called it; a colloquial title the ranger had not heard before.

He paid them little heed. He wished to eat, drink, and sleep. Nothing more. The ranger began to tap his fingers against the table top, his hunger driving his impatience.

Asher's needs were briefly forgotten when the Dandy's door opened and an icy draft invaded the tavern. Late was the hour for new patrons. Too late. It set the ranger's instincts off, making a raw nerve out of him. Heavy boots pounded over the old boards—three men, he counted without looking. The sound of scraping metal—armour if ever he had heard it.

Soldiers was the logical conclusion.

To the ranger's rationale, they had either come through the town on their way elsewhere—unlikely given the hour—or they were part of the company permanently stationed in Kelp Town to guard the Lord.

"Can I help you, boys?" the Dandy's owner enquired, in a light tone that Asher had yet to hear from her.

"We're looking for the ranger," one of the soldiers informed her, his clipped voice that of a man accustomed to a world of commands.

The owner gave no verbal response, but Asher caught her shifting eyes as she directed the trio to his booth. It became painfully obvious then that he was without his leather armour and weapons, all resting in his room. Instead, he sat there attired in a clean but simple cotton shirt—his only spare—a pair of dark trousers, and his usual travelling boots.

The soldiers didn't hesitate to approach him, a wall of armour and steel. Asher considered the tankard in his hand. It still had some of his cider in it—good for momentarily blinding at least one of them. The tankard itself was tin, and with enough force could prove quite the weapon if used appropriately. Then there were the things he could do with his bare hands, things that could maim a man for the rest of his life. Or worse.

That was, of course, if these soldiers had come for his life or his freedom. Why they would seek to take either remained to be seen, but Asher was always one to assume the worst of his fellow man.

"You the ranger then?" grunted the lead soldier.

Asher tilted his head enough to run an eye over the trio. Soldiers indeed. They were encased in iron cuirasses and matching gauntlets, all emblazoned with the sigil of the bear, the animal long associated with the ruling family in The Ice Vales. Black cloaks hung from their shoulders, forming a dark curtain between Asher's booth and the rest of the tavern.

"I suppose I am," the ranger replied wearily, his nose catching the appetising aroma of the chicken stew as it was brought out of the kitchen.

"By the order of Lord Aren Kernat, king-appointed governor of Kelp Town, you are to accompany us to his lordship's hall."

Asher couldn't fathom the reason for such a summons, though, since meeting Secretary Royce, it wasn't a stretch to believe some form of threat was coming his way regarding the Hell Hag. "If Lord Kernat wishes to give credit to his watch for the Hag's death, I will happily take my coin and move on without a word." The ranger felt he had said all that needed to be said, and gestured for the distant barmaid to continue her journey and deliver his stew.

"You're not required to speak," the lead soldier snapped, his response halting the barmaid. "But you *will* come with us. *Now.*"

Asher's knuckles began to pale around the tankard's handle.

"There's no need for concern," came a familiar voice from the door.

One of the soldiers shifted to track the speaker, allowing the ranger to see Captain Lonan of the town watch. He approached the booth with lighter steps than his soldier counterparts, his demeanour more agreeable. In his far simpler cuirass of dull grey and black cloak, the captain addressed the ranger without so much as a glance at the brutish trio.

"Nor is there need for violence," he intoned, his gaze flashing over Asher's tight grip. "Lord Kernat *requests* an audience with you at my recommendation. His lordship has interest in your... *skills*. Nothing more, I assure you."

"Well if you *assure* me," Asher quipped dryly.

The lead soldier was visibly ruffled by the response, so much so that his hand fell onto the pommel of his sword. Again, Captain Lonan interfered, stepping closer to the booth so that his physical presence might cool the soldier's ire.

"It could prove a *profitable* meeting," Lonan inferred.

Asher glanced at the captain, acknowledging his efforts to persuade him. "Will there be chicken stew?"

A glint of confusion and surprise crossed the captain's eyes. "No," he said succinctly.

The ranger sighed.

CHAPTER 3
THREE NIGHTS OF FRIGHT

Clackers - What interesting creatures these beasties are. Rare too. I say that with a prayer of thanks to Atilan. Clackers are blind monsters who rely on sound to find their prey. It is my belief, though, that they also use their incessant clacking to understand their environment as we might use our eyes.
As for the threat they pose: it is extreme. They move in nests of at least a hundred, but you will find just one Clacker is fight enough.

A Chronicle of Monsters: A Ranger's Bestiary, 12th Edition,
Page 236.

Nessa, Ranger.

Permitted no more of his gear than his forest-green cloak, Asher stood in what passed for a grand entrance hall in that part of the realm. Like his forebears, Lord Kernat called Stormwood Manor his home. It was a palace to the lord's subjects, each room comparable to a house for the average family in Kelp Town.

Asher was unimpressed, though his increasing hunger was likely colouring his view of everything.

Numerous rugs, long past their opulent best and thick with dust, dotted the floors from room to room. The imposing staircase of rich wood, rising up from the centre of the hall and branching left and right, was in need of repair, with several steps splintered and warped. Overseeing it all were portraits wider and taller than any man. They each displayed a small plaque that named Lord Kernat's ancestors, but the brass letters were obscured by tarnish and old smudges.

Then there was the smell. It was not nearly as rank as the stench inside the watch building, but it was damned close with notes of decay and general neglect.

Asher spared the soldiers a glance, the trio having taken up positions behind him, blocking the door. Creaking boards drew his attention away, leading the ranger to Captain Lonan who was returning with Secretary Royce by his side.

"We meet again, Ranger," Royce declared, fingers clasping in front of him so that his myriad rings and fine gems might catch the torchlight.

"You sound as happy about that as I am," Asher remarked caustically.

The secretary raised his chin at the ranger. "You were certainly not *my* recommendation," the older man disclosed, directing a ripple of annoyance Lonan's way.

"And what, exactly, have I been recommended for?"

Royce whipped up a single finger to silence the captain. "That's his lordship's business. Speaking of which," he went on, moving to stand before the ranger, "have you ever been in the presence of a lord?"

Asher's mind drifted to Lord Borvyn Murell of Dunwich and to his daughter Esabelle.

To his son.

Thomas Murell.

The ranger had certainly been in the presence of a lord, as he had crept through a manor grander than the one he now stood in. His conduct, however, had been nothing short of monstrous, his crime greater than any of the monsters he had since slain.

Asher swallowed and took a breath to compose himself. "Can't say I have," he lied.

"Hmm," the secretary voiced, his eyes dissecting the ranger from head to toe. "Conversing with his lordship is no mundane thing—this is not a *tavern*. You will speak when spoken to and you will address your better as Lord Kernat or your Lordship. You will sit if his lordship offers you a chair. Failing this, you *will* remain standing." Royce flicked his head up, a thought suddenly occurring. "And mind your words. His lordship has the authority to bind you in irons or worse and he has *not* been a patient man in recent times."

The secretary's clipped instructions were cut short by a strident voice. "Royce!" came the call, resounding from the room beyond. "What am I bloody waiting for?" the voice added vociferously.

Secretary Royce stood a little straighter and smoothed out his robe as a way of regaining his composure. "Follow me," he commanded quietly, turning on his heel.

Falling into step beside the ranger, Captain Lonan leant in so that Asher alone could hear him. "He's not wrong about his lordship. He lost his wife last year, to the red pox. Since then he has been burdened with grief. I tell you this so you might tread carefully in there," he added, gesturing to the room ahead. "Do not negotiate with his lordship as you did with me. I strongly urge you to take his offer. Atilan knows we need the help," he muttered lastly, though more to himself.

Asher's curiosity was surely piqued by the unfolding events and would have intrigued him all the more if only he wasn't so damned hungry. Even now he could smell the lingering scent of recent cooking, the food having been carried through the manor.

The room was well proportioned, with a great table of rich wood at one end and a collection of sofas and armchairs at the other, and with generous space throughout. The walls and ceiling were lined with exposed beams and displayed frescos in between. At the far end, where the seats offered a place around the sizeable fireplace, a figure stood as no more than a silhouette against the flames, a glass of dark wine in hand as he leant against the mantel.

While Secretary Royce and Captain Lonan were permitted to walk freely about the room, the guardsmen brought Asher to an abrupt halt before he could pass beyond the end of the table.

"Lord Kernat—" Royce began, before his master let loose a stentorian roar.

"GRENSON!"

Nobody moved, rooted to the spot by the lord's apparent wrath. Moments later, the quick footsteps of a younger man preceded a servant's arrival. "Your Lord—"

"What is this?" Lord Kernat interjected, raising his glass of wine.

Young Grenson licked his lips nervously. "Wine, my Lord."

"What kind of wine, you *pillock*?" came the biting retort.

The servant swallowed. "Velian Redhouse, my Lord."

"VELIAN!" Lord Kernat bellowed, and directly into Grenson's face. "Why is there *Velian* wine in my cellar? I can taste their inflated egos with every drop of the swill! Get rid of it!" He tossed the contents of his glass into the fire, the hiss punctuating his last command, before shoving the empty glass into Grenson's unsteady hands.

"Perhaps something a little closer to home, your Lordship," Secretary Royce suggested, moving to the cabinet on his left. As the servant hurried from the room, Royce took his place and offered his master a small glass of what looked like Gold Mountain Brandy by its amber hue.

"Very good," the lord of Kelp Town uttered, quick to bring the rim of the glass to his lips.

His features caught in the torchlight now, Asher could see the man that belonged to such a fiery temper. He had, perhaps, been blond before age sank its teeth into him, leaving his beard and unkempt hair with naught but echoes of his youth. His clothes, though mostly concealed within the folds of a red velvet cloak, appeared to hang off his frame, suggesting he had lost considerable weight. Likely due to grief, Asher deduced.

Secretary Royce held out an arm to encompass Asher. "Lord Kernat, might I introduce—"

"The *ranger*," his lordship announced, beating his man to it.

Never one to feel the need to prove himself, Asher remained just as he was, a sentinel of stoicism like so many of the portraits he had seen.

Lord Kernat drank him in as he did the brandy—all in one. "So you're the one then? You slew the beast that's been claiming the fools too *stupid* to stay out of the swamp. I can't help but wonder if we should have allowed the fiend to live, if for nothing more than weeding out the idiots."

Something between discomfort and embarrassment crossed the secretary's expression, though he offered no remark to the contrary. "My Lord," he said, instead, "I still don't think the slaying of one beast qualifies this *ranger* to slay another. Particularly if it's... Yes well, perhaps it would be best if we dealt with this ourselves. Captain Lonan could—"

"What was it?" the lord demanded of Asher, as if Royce had said nothing at all. "This creature you bested in exchange for my coin. Tell me about it." It seemed only then that he noticed the guards either side of the ranger. "I have invited this man into my home!" he pointed out, a long finger shooting out from its grip around the glass. "Go and do something useful, cretins!"

Showing a degree more self-assurance than the servant Grenson, the soldiers excused themselves at once. Captain Lonan remained, close to the wall. Though the commander of the watch had definitely inserted himself into the vicinity of his lord, he had yet to be recognised. With a hawk-like gaze, Secretary Royce kept Asher in his sights at all times, monitoring him for any lapse in decorum.

Second to none in all of Kelp Town, Lord Kernat simply waved at Asher to come closer. "Tell me of this monster."

Since his lordship remained on his feet, so too did Asher as he moved into the heat of the fire. "It was a Hell Hag," he stated. A look from the secretary prompted him to add, "My Lord."

Lord Kernat chuckled at the name. "Hell Hag. Sounds like my mother-in-law—Atilan rest her soul." He held out his glass to Royce who, in turn, looked to Captain Lonan to refill it. "Are they large fiends, these Hell Hags?"

Asher looked about. "As big as this room, perhaps."

The lord of Kelp Town tasted his new glass of brandy before replying. "*Unnecessarily* big then," he commented. "Yet you—*one man*—defeated this Hag. How?" he asked sharply.

The ranger looked away, momentarily enraptured by the dancing flames, his answer straddling the line between truth and omission. "I poisoned it, my Lord," he revealed.

"Poison?" Lord Kernat questioned, displaying his aversion to such a dishonourable method. "What ever happened to meeting monsters with steel? Were I a younger man I might have taken to that swamp myself."

"Not all monsters can be slain with steel, your Lordship," Asher countered, garnering the secretary's silent ire. "But if it pleases you to know, I used my sword to deliver the venom. Multiple times," he added, unaware that he had been summoned to entertain the lord with a tale.

A crooked smile stretched the lord's face. "Ingenious," he complimented, eyeing the ranger. "You have no drink," he noted. "Why does a guest in my house have no drink?" he fumed, turning on Royce. "Come, come, get the man whatever he wishes. This is the same man who rid our lands of a Hell Hag!" he declared, as if he now had a greater understanding of the foul creature.

Secretary Royce ruffled on the spot. "We have *paid* him for those services, my Lord."

Lord Kernat, taller than them all, looked down on his man. "Royce, can you imagine facing a monster equal in size to this room?"

The secretary tensed his jaw, eyes flashing from Asher to his master. "No, your Lordship," he answered meekly.

"Then get a drink for the man who did," he simply commanded.

With no more than a bow of the head, Royce turned to face Asher expectantly, if reluctantly.

Asher hadn't predicted the offer of anything, but the amber tone of Lord Kernat's drink caught his eye. Gold Mountain Brandy was a highborn potation if ever there was one, worth a whole keg of Hobgobber's Ale. "I'll take one of those," he said.

"Of course you will," the secretary retorted dryly.

By the time he was holding a glass of very expensive brandy, Lord Kernat had taken to one of the armchairs and gestured for Asher to join him in the adjacent chair. Sitting in an armchair of plush red wine leather, and with a glass of Gold Mountain in hand, gave Asher a taste of the other life, known only to highborns and royalty. It was almost too comfortable, an ease of living the ranger had never known and—now that he was sampling it—not one that he would ever choose. Such finery made one soft, and easy to kill.

"How did you know this venom would work?" Lord Kernat went on, his temper sedated while entertained.

"I possess an archive of sorts. A bestiary, my Lord."

"A book?" the lord questioned, disbelief in his eyes. "You can read? Very good," he added without a hint of mockery. "So, you researched the beast and sought out its *weaknesses*," he summed up, looking at Secretary Royce all the while. "What was it you suggested again?" he asked of his man. "Ah yes, arm the king's men with spears and send them into the swamp."

"That was a *suggestion*, my Lord. My *original* suggestion was to send in Captain Lonan and his men to scout first, so we might have a better understanding of the monster."

"And we did," Captain Lonan confirmed, speaking in the presence of his lord for the first time. "We didn't have to scout for very long before coming to the obvious conclusion that a… *specialist* was required. Hence my employment of the ranger, my Lord."

Lord Kernat patted the air with his hand, silencing the bickering he no longer cared for. "It seems to me that you are quite qualified," he acclaimed, his attention returned to Asher.

The ranger brought his glass away from his lips before taking the intended sip. "With respect, your Lordship, what is it you believe I'm qualified to *do* exactly?"

Unlike Asher, Lord Kernat finished his glass before answering. "To hunt a monster far worse than some backwater Hell Hag," he replied ominously, a shadow forming over his eyes.

Asher's mind cast back to the scent of death that had permeated the office of the watch. Such macabre thoughts were cut through by the smooth brandy that bathed the ranger's tongue and throat with its rich taste. Fighting the urge to drink it all there and then, Asher let his hand rest on the arm of the chair, where the firelight played through the motes of golden dust that whirled within the glass.

Lord Kernat was staring out of the arched window, his gaze taken by the glow of the moon. "Every month—three nights of full moons," he began. "Three nights of fright, my grandmother called it. Three nights of fang and claw."

Asher had a sinking feeling in his gut.

His lordship glanced at the other men in the room before speaking again, and quietly so. "Do you know what creature hunts in the light of a full moon, Ranger?"

Motionless, as if he was part of the very chair he was sitting in, Asher stared at the lord of Kelp Town. "There is only one of renown," he answered, conjuring the image sketched into the bestiary. "The Werewolf."

Lord Kernat licked his lips, his old fingers rotating the empty glass in his hand. "The Ice Vales has a history with the beasts. Do you know of this?"

Asher shook his head, his lips sealed for the moment while he recalled the litany of warnings inside the bestiary.

Sinking further into his armchair, the lord sighed, his chest rattling. A single look at Captain Lonan impelled the man to walk over and refill his lordship's glass. "Nearly two centuries ago, they plagued our ancestors. *Werewolves*," he intoned, as if the very name was a curse. "They spread like a disease. Or they certainly did back then. Whole villages—gone. Snowfell was almost left a ruin. Even Grey Stone felt their bite." One swig of his drink nearly drained it again. "Nasty business."

"But they were defeated," Asher stated, as there could be no other conclusion.

Lord Kernat held on to his answer a moment longer. "Not exactly," he finally replied. "They simply vanished." His lordship chortled into his glass. "A damn near army of the buggers and they just... left. Who can say what happened? What remained, however, was a kingdom of people, of *survivors*, who passed on their fear of the wolf. Were such a beast to reveal itself in these parts it would have to be dealt with in a swift but *quiet* manner, lest we suffer a great panic."

The ranger indulged himself in another mouthful of brandy. "And *has* a Werewolf revealed itself in these parts, my Lord?"

A trickle of Gold Mountain Brandy escaped the lord's final gulp, running through his beard to the end of his chin. "We believe so." He gave Lonan a look but, this time, it had nothing to do with his empty glass.

The captain of the watch stepped inside the circle of the sofas and armchairs, where he might better feel the heat of the fire. "Not long before you arrived back from the swamps," he began, "one of my men was patrolling in the north-west quarter, near the outskirts of town." Lonan swallowed before carrying on. "He claims to have seen something drag Fen Underson—the local butcher in that quarter—from the alley beside his shop."

Asher could feel his stomach rumbling from hunger and spoke to drown it out. "*Something* doesn't sound like a Werewolf."

"I assure you," the captain responded, somewhat irritated, "the description my man gave was that of a Werewolf. He said it dragged Mr Underson from his shop and beyond the town, into the woods."

"I'm assuming your man gave chase," Asher reasoned, "given his duty to protect the citizens of Kelp Town. How did he survive an encounter with a wolf?"

Captain Lonan shifted uncomfortably on the spot. "He did not pursue," came the expected answer. "You show me a man who will follow a Werewolf into the night. They are feared for good reason."

Rare as Werewolves were, Asher maintained his steady level of scepticism. "One cowardly man sighting a tall beast attack a man in the dark of night is not proof of Werewolves."

"My man is no coward," Lonan fumed, stepping closer to loom over the ranger.

"Tell that to the butcher's family," Asher retorted, his eyes on the distant moon.

Lonan firmed his jaw and straightened his back. "And I do not doubt his eyes," he continued, moving past the comment. "Nor my own."

Asher looked up at the captain. "*You* have seen it?"

"No," Lonan admitted. "But I *have* seen Fen Underson. Or what's left of him at least."

"That was the smell in your office," the ranger said, though mostly to himself.

Lord Kernat waved a lazy hand through the air before the captain could reply. "You doubt," he stated, looking at Asher. "I pray to all the gods that your doubt is well founded, and that this is simply another monster of the night. It doesn't change the fact that it needs dealing with and quickly so. Kelp Town has been plagued by that Hag for some time. To suffer a second creature would do our reputation no good, no good at all."

The lord's final comment returned Asher's mind to the watch house, where Secretary Royce had berated Lonan about the pressures Kelp Town was under from Grey Stone and the eyes upon them. The politics of man meant little to the ranger, though he suspected the current authority in Kelp Town was under threat. Whatever that might be, it was no threat when compared to a potential Werewolf.

Asher returned his gaze to the moon, the first full moon of three. For the first time in his career as a ranger, he was hesitating. Worse still, he knew *why* he was hesitating. Fear. Not of the beast itself, for he had yet to meet a monster that incited that primal emotion within him. It was fear of *death*, a far greater probability when fighting the likes of a Werewolf. Why should he fear death now, after so many years of walking hand in hand with it, after so many years of yearning for it even? It was no more than he deserved for his past deeds.

And yet...

Had the prospect of life finally latched itself to him? Or did he feel as if he was actually atoning with the monsters he put in the ground? Asher couldn't find the answer there and then. He knew only one thing: the *Assassin* still had a foothold in him. A monster of his own. A monster that none but himself could slay. And how long before it reared its head again and added more lives to the tally of death? Perhaps the Werewolf would rid Verda of the *Assassin's* threat after all.

"Well man?" Secretary Royce challenged, irked on behalf of his master. "What say you?"

"Two thousand," Asher announced, his mind made up.

Royce looked down at him with the hint of a smile pinching his cheeks. "Two thousand is your price? Very good."

"Two thousand to *investigate*," Asher corrected. "Should the beast prove anything but a Werewolf, I will require a further thousand."

"And if it is a Werewolf?" Lord Kernat interrupted, his amusement sustained where the secretary's had dissipated.

"A further *three* thousand," the ranger declared boldly.

"You can't be serious?" Royce countered.

"Very good," his lordship acknowledged, ending his secretary's disapproval. "Find the beast—whatever it may be—and kill it. Quietly."

Asher finished his drink, savouring the rare taste, before standing up and handing the empty glass to an unimpressed Secretary Royce. "I will begin at dawn," he informed them.

"Dawn?" Royce echoed, his incredulity reaching new heights. "A man is already dead. You can start right now—Captain Lonan will accompany you to the scene."

"Hunting a Werewolf under a full moon is a good way to get

yourself killed," Asher insisted. "You hunt them in the day, when their flesh and blood is no different to ours."

Lord Kernat was wagging one finger at him, a wry smile cutting the expression he trained on Secretary Royce. "Weaknesses..." he quietly applauded.

Royce's mouth twisted into resignation. "Very well," he conceded.

"Oh," the ranger added, detecting once again the aromas drifting from the kitchen. "I also require a chicken."

The secretary's eyebrows shot up. "A chicken?"

Asher looked him dead in the eyes. "A *cooked* one."

CHAPTER 4
THE INVESTIGATION

Werewolf - 'Tis a curse, simply put. How this began is up for much debate, though talking about it makes little difference. Werewolves are real and they are among us.

Contracts concerning these beasts should be left to the most experienced of our kind. I don't just say that because these beasts are seven feet tall with claws as long as your fingers. I urge the young among our ranks to leave these contracts because a wise ranger knows you don't hunt the wolf. You hunt the poor soul who received the cursed bite. Be warned though, they're still stronger than the average person in their human form. It's going to feel like killing a person. A deed like that will weigh on a good man.

Oh, and don't stock up on silver, it's a myth most likely started by a Werewolf. You can kill it the same way you kill anything - with a good swing of steel.

A Chronicle of Monsters: A Ranger's Bestiary, 12th Edition, Page 49.

Arnathor (the old hunter), Ranger.

. . .

Apallid dawn brought a cold light to Asher's room at Dandy's Inn. It would have roused the ranger had he not already awoken. By then he had pushed aside the chicken carcass that sat on the bedside table and retrieved his bestiary, which he had been perusing in candlelight.

Again and again he had been distracted by the sketch committed to parchment by Arnathor, the ranger who had scribed the section pertaining to Werewolves. There was something about it that spoke to Asher's primal self, as if man and wolf had been natural enemies since the dawning of the world. And to see a wolf so mutated by evil's hand that it stood at seven foot tall, and on two legs no less, was disturbing at best.

He returned to the words, running a finger down the page that concerned hunting the person rather than the beast.

Now, when it comes to hunting down the afflicted man or woman, there are certain signs you can look for, especially if they're newly bitten. The new Werewolves, while in their human form, will exhibit emotional outbursts, typically violent ones. They're quick to anger and their new-found strength can make them dangerous.

If you're lucky, you might even witness one using their strength accidentally. While I was hunting one in Vangarth, I happened to witness a woman pick up her tankard in the local tavern and crush it without meaning to.

Outside of accidents, you're going to have to put the legwork in. If it's a small town, try and meet everyone. If they've been afflicted for some time, they'll have amber eyes. If they're newly afflicted, you might see it in firelight. Besides their eyes and strength, they have physical advantages that stop them from feeling the cold as we do. And they hardly sweat. Keep that in mind if you're observing folk at work.

When it comes to killing them—and I can't stress enough the importance of doing so while they're in their human form—you're going to naturally try and surprise them. Don't bother. Full moon or not, they have senses beyond the norm. If they don't smell you coming, they'll hear you coming. The best advice I can offer is to lie your way into striking distance—and make sure the first blow does the deed—or set a trap that allows you to kill them from afar.

Asher closed the book. He could already feel the *Assassin* snaking its way through his mind, awakening to thoughts of the hunt, the hunt for a *person*. That other part of him, that other self, was animated now, driven by the need to stalk and kill.

The ranger spared a moment to dwell on the poor butcher who had, himself, been butchered by the Werewolf. His family too, now bereft. Whether the wolf had a human side or not, the monster within could not be allowed to roam freely.

Rather than consider the parallel that stared him in the face, Asher donned his leathers, weapons, and cloak—all physical extensions of the *Ranger*. He felt his true self in those trappings, and with all the accoutrements of an expert monster hunter. To that end, he strode from Dandy's Inn and made for the offices of the watch.

Asher was satisfied to find Captain Lonan already there, waiting for him, just as he had said he would be. There were other members of the watch present, some of whom were in the process of removing their gear from the nightshift and preparing to go home for the day. Such work patterns were more commonly seen in the cities, a testament to Kelp Town's size.

"I'm assuming you've seen all manner of death, Ranger," the captain began, absent the usual formalities.

Asher decided the man was a little salty after the accusation regarding his cowardly staff. Asher didn't care. He actually preferred it that way. "After you," he simply replied, gesturing to the room.

They alone entered the rotting stench of death, the door closed behind them. The only window, on the far side of the room, had been shuttered to keep out prying eyes, leaving the room to be lit by torch and candle. In the gloom lay a single body, the corpse placed upon a table that took up most of the available space. Asher was glad he had been informed of the victim's identity for, at a glance, he would not have been certain it was even a man.

What remained of the head was only attached to the body by a few strands of flesh and muscle, the spinal column completely severed. The face was simply gone, be it the work of fang or claw, revealing the damaged skull beneath.

The right hand was missing while the left had been collected with most of the arm and laid on the table where it should have been attached to the shoulder. Asher moved round the table to better investigate the dismembered limb.

"It was torn off," he uttered into that thick musk.

"What's that?" the captain enquired, a kerchief covering his mouth and nose.

"The arm," Asher explained, one finger gliding through the air above the jagged shoulder. "It was ripped off by brute strength. This is neither the work of steel nor claw. It was just... *yanked* off."

"Is that typical of a Werewolf?"

The ranger wasn't quite ready to believe it yet. "It's typical of any monster with great strength, of which there are many."

Removing one of the small knives from the strap on his thigh, Asher used the blade to adjust the butcher's shirt, revealing his torso—or what was left of it. The beast in question had devoured all the organs and eagerly so judging by the gnawed and shattered ribcage.

"I assume there are plenty of monsters who consume organs too," the captain remarked.

"There are..." Asher replied, lost to thought as his mind sifted through page after page of the bestiary. "Though," he eventually added, scrutinising the eviscerated corpse, "most that do have characteristics that aid them, allowing them to take either the specific organ or all of them with proficiency. This..." Here the ranger took a breath, choosing his words carefully. "This was savagery."

Moving on to the legs—or what was left of them—Asher observed the bite marks that had shredded much of the man's clothes and skin until there was naught but broken bone. It was clear to see that the bite itself easily encompassed the entire left thigh, suggesting the beast had a considerable set of jaws. This too suggested the rest of its body to be equally large. Seven foot perhaps...

Much like the severed arm, the right leg displayed signs of brute force where everything from the knee down had been pulled free. What remained, however, had identical bite marks that had gone on to shatter the victim's hip.

"They are bite marks, yes?"

Asher spared the captain no more than a glance. "Yes," he said gruffly.

"Have you seen bites such as these before?" Lonan enquired.

"Yes," the ranger said again, inspecting the butcher's hands.

Shouldering his annoyance, the captain pursued his line of questioning. "And what monster was responsible?"

Asher knew exactly where he had seen similar bite marks, though they had certainly been smaller. "Wolves," he admitted. "Dogs even."

"Wolves?" the captain echoed, a hint of victory in his tone.

"You sound pleased," Asher commented.

Captain Lonan shifted his shoulders to adjust his cloak. "Make no mistake, Ranger, I pray to the gods that this beast is anything *but* a Werewolf. I simply believe *this* to be a waste of time. I told you what my man saw and, so far, I would say your findings are proving him right. We should be out there, right now, while the sun is up, trying to find the monster."

"If this is a Werewolf, there is no monster to find right now," Asher told him, satisfied with all he had deduced. "While the sun's up we hunt the person which, in a town this size, will be difficult. It's more likely that the full moon will rise before we identify them."

"All the more reason to be out there now," Lonan argued, "finding out what we can. Hunting the beast at night would surely be even harder."

Asher shook his head. "We don't hunt it at night," he warned.

The captain looked offended. "Then we are just to let it roam freely, to *kill* freely? You might only care about the coin, Ranger, but

I care about the people under my watch. I have a sworn duty to them."

"Is your man available?" Asher asked him, ignoring the sharp comment. "The one who witnessed this."

Lonan puffed out his chest and took a composing breath. "He can be."

"I need to question him."

One of the captain's fingers tapped incessantly against his thigh. "Very well. Watchman Elias isn't on shift today. He's likely at home."

Asher looked to the door. "After you."

Steaming vapour filled the cold air around the ranger's face as he crossed the town, Captain Lonan in step beside him. The hour was still early, marked by the large wagons that arrived and departed with exhausted and rested miners, pick-axes held between their knees. For some, their future held food and sleep while others were to be taken into the gloom of the Demetrium mines.

Most of the shops and stalls were already open and with customers too. On the main street it was a sea of dark furs and bound scarves, all interspersed with the playing of children or scavenging dogs. There wasn't much that could stop the world from turning, though it seemed an odd sight having just left what remained of the butcher.

Fen Underson.

Asher reminded himself of the name. It felt an important detail. To think of him as nothing more than a victim, made him no better than Geron Thorbear and the rest of his ilk. They, the first rangers he had ever met, had seen every victim as a means to an end where coin was concerned. It had never sat well with Asher and he had no intention of slipping into their mindset. He was better than that. At least he wanted to be, and that had to count for something.

"This is him," Lonan announced, gesturing to the narrow house wedged between a shop and a tavern.

Rising from his contemplation, Asher absorbed his surroundings. "This is the north-west quarter?"

"Yes," the captain agreed. "Mr Underson's shop is just round the corner. I'm assuming you will want to *investigate* there as well."

"We'll get to it," Asher assured, nodding at the door.

Two keen knocks followed. "Elias! It's Captain Lonan!"

Small as the house was, it didn't take the watchman long to reach the door. "Captain?" Young and nervous eyes took in the ranger.

"This is a conversation best had indoors," Lonan said, prompting an invitation.

Indeed, the house was cramped, an observation made all the more obvious after visiting Lord Kernat in Stormwood Manor. Yet it was four more walls than Asher had and contained many times more belongings than he could claim. The furnishings and such were not the only thing Watchman Elias had that Asher did not.

"Papa?" The little girl that gripped to Elias's leg was a timid thing, her copper ringlets spilling out and over one shoulder.

"Captain Lonan," came a lighter voice from the only room that led off from the one they were standing in.

"Good to see you, Saski," Lonan replied, a touch of genuine fondness in his voice.

Imagining the family of three huddled together by the fire, Asher couldn't help but think about another family of three, and with a girl no less. It had been too long since he had seen the Stormshields, since he had seen little Deadora. He had parted ways with them in The Black Wood near on two years ago and succeeded in visiting them only once in all that time. And all too brief it had been.

"Perhaps we could talk privately?" Captain Lonan proposed to his subordinate.

Saski didn't hesitate to guide her daughter by the shoulders and disappear into the other room, the door closed softly behind them.

"You recall the ranger," Lonan began, half turning to Asher. "We brought him in to deal with that swamp fiend."

"Aye, sir."

"Well now he's been brought in to deal with the... *other* fiend. The one you saw, Elias."

"I have questions," Asher said, inserting himself before there could be any more talk of him as if he wasn't in the room.

Elias glanced at his superior before his attention homed in on the ranger. "Of course."

The watchman gestured to the round table and three chairs. Asher hadn't intended on seating himself, always more comfortable on his feet in new settings, but he found himself sitting down as offered. Without asking, Elias poured them all a cup of water from a ceramic jug that appeared to have his daughter's hand imprinted on the side.

"What did you see?" Asher asked him directly, eager to progress.

Elias licked his lips. "It was dark. Quiet too. I always like to make one last patrol of the quarter before the end of my shift. I was passing Fen's place—Mr Underson that is—when I heard something smash. I went to investigate of course and that's when..." The watchman swallowed, sparing a moment to glance at the talisman of Atilan, king of the gods, that hung from a nail on the wall. "That's when I saw it."

"It?"

"The *wolf*," Elias specified. "It was taller than any man I've ever seen. I saw its fur in the light of my torch. And its claws... Like blades they were. It stood on two feet, with legs like a dog."

"What was it doing when you disturbed it?"

Again, Elias licked his lips, his gaze drawn distant to that gruesome scene. "As I rounded into the alley, it had just ripped one of Mr Underson's legs off. The sound of it," he agonised, swallowing his disgust. "I heard it before I saw it—the leg just lying there. Fen didn't even make a sound. I think he might have already been dead by then."

"Why didn't it attack you?"

At this, the watchman could only offer a shrug.

"The fire perhaps?" Lonan posed. "Monsters and animals alike tend to fear the touch of fire, yes?" When Asher didn't disagree, the captain added pointedly, "I would say Werewolves fit into both categories.".

"It barely noticed me," Elias went on, his voice little more than a whisper. "It was so fast. It was already dragging the body into the trees before I could even grasp my sword."

Dumb luck then, Asher surmised, a thought he kept to himself. "Show me where this happened," the ranger instructed.

Returned to the chill of winter, the three men rounded the corner and walked up half the street before arriving at the butcher's shop. The door was locked with a chain and there was no sign of activity inside, the family grieving elsewhere most likely.

"This is it," Elias announced. "Fen's place."

Asher noted the alley beside the shop. "Down there?"

The young watchman responded with a tentative nod, still haunted by the memory of it. The ranger made no delay, leaving the shop front to enter the alleyway. A handful of empty crates lined one side, those closest to the side door splattered with blood. That was only the beginning of it. The doorway had already been boarded up, but the brick around it was stained a dark red and Asher fancied he could see more blood soaked into the mud between the patches of snow.

Beyond the alley was a small clearing that separated the outskirts of town from the forest that clung to the base of The Vengoran Mountains. "How were you able to recover the... Mr Underson's body?"

"Elias here came straight to the watch house and roused the others. They woke me up on their way back here. Together, we entered the trees with swords drawn." The captain sighed. "We didn't get very far before we discovered Mr Underson. The wolf had left him only a few hundred yards beyond the tree line. No sign of the beast itself."

Asher acknowledged every detail before slowly walking towards the snowy clearing. Turning back, he could see some of

Kelp Town through the alley, as well as the back of several shops and homes.

"What are you doing?" the captain asked.

"Seeing what the wolf saw," the ranger answered.

"So you believe this *is* the devilry of a Werewolf," Lonan noted, a shadow of apprehension creeping over him now.

Asher regretted his choice of words but decided to plough on. "The *creature*," he intoned, "would have come from the trees. This was its view."

Again, the ranger scrutinised all that a monster could see from his current vantage. It would have been quiet at the hour Elias reported, with little to no foot traffic in the area. Except for Elias himself that is. If it was, indeed, a Werewolf that had emerged from the forest, its keen senses would have likely taken note of the watchman over all else. Such prey, tired and alone, walking through deserted streets, would have been far easier than breaking through a door and snatching a man from his own dwelling.

Asher eyed the young watchman.

"Your thoughts, Ranger?" the captain probed.

Asher wasn't of a mind to share them yet. Instead, he turned on his heel and strode towards the trees, ignoring Lonan's calls. It wouldn't take an expert hunter to find the spot where the creature breached the tree line with a body in tow. The low hanging branches had been snapped and were moving in the morning breeze. Fallen twigs lay broken where something heavy had trodden on them. Then there was the muddy snow, which had been dragged from the clearing and under the cover of the foliage —undoubtedly created by Mr Underson's corpse.

A few more steps into the forest, following a trail of gore, Asher came across the telltale sign of many a monster. Placing one hand to the bark of the tree, the ranger traced the deep claw marks that would forever scar the wood. Five there were, each scored line slightly too far apart to match Asher's hand. It was a small detail, but there were few monsters who could claim to possess five digits as a human did.

"By the gods," Captain Lonan cursed under his breath.

The ranger turned to see the section of intestines strewn over a protruding root. Over the captain's shoulder, he sighted Watchman Elias on the other side of the tree line, reluctant, it seemed, to follow them in.

"Come along, Elias," the captain cajoled, noticing the same thing.

"If it's all the same, Captain," Elias replied, and timidly so, "I'd prefer to stay out here."

Lonan frowned. "Sun's up, watchman. There are no wolves in here."

"All the same..."

The captain took a breath and cleared his throat, turning to see Asher's knowing look. "He is not a coward," Lonan insisted quietly. "Not every man was made to see such a monster."

"Hmm." Asher's guttural response preceded his departure and advance into the forest.

A couple of hundred yards in, just as Lonan had said, the ranger came across the area where Fen Underson had been turned inside out. The ferns had been flattened and darkened by blood. There were more claw marks on the surrounding trees as well as deep impressions in the mud, where the snow had been displaced.

Captain Lonan remained by the edge of the area, one hand cupping his razored jaw. "This is where we found him, gods rest his soul."

Asher didn't thank him for pointing out the obvious but, instead, crouched down, drawn as he was to a single detail. Jutting out from a shallow puddle of blood was a gnarled twig. Who could say what chaos had situated it there, but the tuft of fur caught in the splintered wood was less of a mystery. It had belonged to the monster.

Tearing it free, Asher felt the wiry strands between his fingers before bringing it up to his nose. Having never crossed a Werewolf before, the ranger couldn't say that the fur aided him in identifying it. He couldn't, however, identify any other creature by it, and he had fought numerous monsters covered in fur.

"Your findings, Ranger?"

Asher stood up and let the fur be taken by the breeze. "I need to speak with your man," he reported, leaving the captain in his wake as he retraced his steps.

Elias was right where they had left him, if not a little further away from the tree line. He was staring at the alleyway, one hand gripped to his left shoulder, as if he wanted to make himself small and unnoticeable. Asher had already determined that the young man wasn't built for the life of a watchman, though that revelation was something he would have to discover on his own.

"You knew Fen Underson," the ranger began, his abrasive voice yanking the watchman from his waking nightmare. "He was your local butcher," Asher continued. "You must have known him, if not everyone in the quarter."

Elias swallowed and attempted to stand a little straighter. "I knew him, yes. Everyone knew Fen. His family have been butchers for generations."

"So you'd know if anyone didn't like him," Asher pressed.

"Didn't like him?" Elias repeated, looking to his captain for support.

"Did he have any enemies?" Asher clarified. "People who might have vendettas against him. People he slighted. People he owed."

Elias couldn't get the words out, his shoulders rising higher and higher into a shrug. "Everyone knew Fen could be a little short-tempered. I don't wish to speak ill of the dead."

"You can't do any worse than what has already been done to him," Asher reminded.

Elias looked at the captain again, who urged him to answer the ranger's questions. "He wasn't always the easiest man to get along with, I'll admit. He was always getting into some argument or other."

"What's all this about?" Lonan asked of the ranger.

Asher backed off from the young watchman and let his eyes roam over the boarded side door again. "Hmm. There's a good chance this *is* a wolf," he told them gravely, unable to deny the evidence he had found so far.

Despite the ranger finally agreeing with him, the captain failed to muster an ounce of satisfaction. "What does that have to do with Mr Underson's temperament? He's just a victim in this."

"A victim, yes, but, potentially, a *targeted* one."

The watchmen shared a look but it was the captain who voiced their question. "Targeted? You mean the wolf chose Mr Underson specifically?"

"The obvious target would have been you," Asher replied, his gaze finding Elias. "It could have attacked you without making a scene. Instead, it went to the trouble of breaking through a door and dragging Fen Underson outside."

Lonan raised an eyebrow. "Aren't we talking about a mindless monster?"

Asher didn't have the bestiary to quote directly from and so he had to paraphrase. "For most of its life, yes," he agreed. "That's not the case for the young. For those recently bitten, their mind and that of the wolf bleed together for a time. Young Werewolves have been known to kill those their human counterpart considered foes, and even loved ones who have slighted them. At the same time, the infected human might display animalistic tendencies."

"Loved ones?" Elias spoke up.

"Yes. I will need to question Mr Underson's family. It could easily be his child or wife."

Elias was slow to respond, shaking his head. "His daughter died an infant, sir. His son is a man now—lives in Grey Stone."

"And his wife?" Asher asked.

"I heard she left him not long after their daughter died," the watchman replied. "She doesn't live in Kelp Town anymore."

Asher sighed, his shortlist of potential suspects a dead end. "Has there been anyone new to town? In the last month," he specified. "Before the new moon but after the last."

Captain Lonan was shaking his head. "Kelp Town borders the north. Everyone travelling north and south stops here."

The ranger turned back to Elias. "And there was no one who might have held a grudge against him?"

"In truth, sir, you won't find many who spoke highly of Fen,

48

but I wouldn't say any of them held a..." Elias drifted into thought, his attention drawn towards the street.

"What is it?" Captain Lonan asked.

"There was one *incident*, quite recently," the watchman reported. "I wasn't on duty but I heard them from my house."

"Heard who?" Asher pressured.

"Fen was arguing with some fella and it spilled out into the street I suppose. I came out because it sounded like it might come to blows, but by the time I rounded the corner it was all over. The fella was running away. I only saw the back of him."

Asher's investigative mind was absorbed. "Did you speak to Mr Underson?"

Elias nodded. "Told me the fella had walked into his shop and..." Revelation illuminated his young features. "He said the fella started eating one of the other customer's steaks from the counter. A *raw* steak."

"When was this?"

"Two days ago maybe."

"Just before the first full moon," Captain Lonan remarked.

Asher had already made that connection and moved several steps ahead. "What can you tell me about the man? Would you recognise him?"

The expression on Elias's face didn't give Asher much hope. "He was already running away when I got there."

Asher took a breath to quash his frustration. "What about the customer?"

"Customer?"

"The one in the shop," the ranger replied impatiently. "They must have seen this man."

"I didn't go inside," Elias admitted. "I never saw them."

Asher's frustration demanded its voice be heard. "And you recall nothing of the man who fled?" With naught but a sheepish shake of the head from Elias, the ranger snapped, "You're supposed to be a man of the watch! Is it not a basic skill to remember what you see?"

"He said he didn't see the man," Lonan interrupted, rising to the defence of his man.

"A miner," Elias blurted. "I think he was a miner."

Asher whirled on him. "Explain."

"His boots," the watchman began. "They all wear the same boots; big chunky things they are. And his clothes, they were filthy black."

The ranger turned away from the younger man, considering his list of suspects again. It had just been reduced from the entire town to the miners alone, though that might well be half the town. Still, it was a better starting point.

"How many miners live here?" he demanded, all too aware that winter's sun was against them.

Captain Lonan considered his answer. "Five hundred. Maybe six hundred. We have the biggest Demetrium mine in Illian."

Asher sighed, exhausted by the thought of interrogating that many men. He gripped the hilt of his broadsword, his thoughts always clearer with a weapon in hand. "How many are in the mine at any given moment?"

By the captain's physical reaction he had been posed a much harder question. "Overseeing the mine isn't typically in my remit —the king's men see to its security."

"Your best guess will do," Asher replied, his tone clipped.

"A hundred and fifty perhaps."

The ranger moved to the end of the alley, where it met the street. "So there are around four to five hundred men out there," he reasoned. "Four to five hundred men who I need to look in the eyes."

Lonan was quickly beside him. "You want to meet them *all*?"

"If one of them is the wolf," Asher told him, thinking back to the bestiary, "I'll know it when I see them."

The captain appeared overwhelmed by the idea. "That's a *lot* of men. And a good number of them will likely be sleeping, ready for their night in the mine. They won't be best pleased to be woken."

"Damn their sleep," Asher retorted. "You said you care about the people under your watch." The ranger nodded his head at the dull sky. "When the moon next rises more people will die."

Lonan was rocked back into deliberation, his thoughts clearly arriving at the only conclusion. "I will need to speak with Secretary Royce to see the charter," he replied, his voice catching. "Every miner is registered."

"Good. I need a torch," the ranger added, thinking of the fire-light. "And you're coming with us," he instructed, looking to the young watchman.

Elias paled. "I'm... I'm not on duty today."

"You are now," Asher commanded, despite his lack of authority in the matter. "You might recognise him."

Elias turned to his superior, who agreed with Asher's judgment. "Go to the watch house and be ready to meet us outside the manor."

The watchman swallowed. "Yes, sir," he answered reluctantly.

Asher was already striding towards Stormwood Manor. "Time is against us, gentlemen," he called back, and gruffly so.

The hunt was upon him.

CHAPTER 5
AMBER IN THE DARK

Ratikan - Who can say where these monsters came from. Some would point at mages and their magic and they might be right. Mages have been known to conjure wicked fiends and lose control. But, Ratikans could just as easily be another monstrous part of the natural world. Whatever their origin, it does not change the fact that they are dangerous. Growing to eight feet and capable of standing on their back legs, Ratikans will easily tower over their prey. And their name is well earned thanks to their rat-like appearance. There are numerous legends surrounding them, as there are for all things, I suppose. The prevailing mythos, though unproven, is that Ratikans are men by day and monsters by night. I see no truth in this, but we already know of other monsters who are bound by similar laws.

A Chronicle of Monsters: A Ranger's Bestiary, 12th Edition, Page 431.

Do Harcken, Ranger.

Hastened by winter's relentless whip, the day was fading fast. Asher had lost count of how many miners he had stood before, his torch brought to bear so he might scrutinise their eyes. Stepping out of the latest house, the torch was quickly becoming a necessity in the growing gloom. Worse still, a subtle fog had swept over Kelp Town, robbing the world of its sharp edges.

"How many more?" the ranger asked, turning to the captain of the watch.

Lonan ran a cursory eye over the parchment in his hands. "Just over a hundred, perhaps."

The response elicited a low growl from deep in Asher's throat. "It's taking too long," he complained, irritated by the time required travelling from house to house.

"They're too dispersed," Elias agreed, now attired in the leathery cloak of the watch, a sword on his hip.

"Or not at home," Lonan added, dourly.

Their complaints sparked an idea in the ranger. "How many did you say would be in the mine?"

"Around a hundred and fifty," the captain reiterated.

"That's a lot of men in one place," Asher pointed out.

Lonan didn't appear pleased by the proposal. "You want to go to the mine? Surely that's the last place to find our man. Think about what he's gone through. Hells, there's a good chance he's not even home. We should probably be searching in the woods."

Asher disagreed. "He won't believe what's happening to him," the ranger explained. "He likely woke up somewhere in the woods, naked, cold, alone. Covered in *blood*. The whole thing will feel more like a nightmare that he can't understand. He'll be in denial. Craving normality. He'll try and convince himself that it'll all go away if he just keeps to his routine."

Captain Lonan was watching him closely, perhaps a little impressed by the insight. "I thought you hadn't hunted Were-wolves before," he commented with curiosity more than anything else.

"I haven't. But I have hunted people." His response intensified the captain's curiosity, inflicting an edge of caution in him even. "Comes with the job," he quickly added, laying any fears to rest while avoiding the truth of his past.

Nodding along, Captain Lonan gestured to the road ahead, hazily visible through the growing fog. "To the mine then."

~

Deepening twilight was upon the trio by the time they arrived at the Demetrium mine. The entrance sat at the base of a tall cliff, its jagged edges illuminated by the torches fixed to the stone.

To the left, nestled between the trees that spread out from the cliff wall, there appeared a barracks of some kind, possibly for the soldiers who guarded the mine. Dotted about were a number of ancillary buildings and all with soldiers wearing the sigil of the royal bear moving between them.

Using the document Secretary Royce had given them, bearing Lord Kernat's seal, Captain Lonan led the three beyond the soldiers who had called up the miners from their work.

Asher's attention was increasingly drawn to the closing night. The full moon was already visible and would soon exert its power over the infected miner and bring out the wolf within.

"Come on!" the soldier in charge barked at the men. "Line up! The quicker we get this done the quicker you can get back to work!" That same soldier turned to Lonan and, tone lowered, asked, "What is it Lord Kernat wants of these men exactly?"

Without an answer the soldier would take seriously, and the need to keep the whole affair as quiet as Lord Kernat had decreed, Captain Lonan simply replied, "Ranger business."

Asher would have been amused were he not standing before a hundred and seventy-five men, among whom there was a possible Werewolf. The ranger made his way to the end of the first line, where bewildered miners tried not to look too nervous. Since there wasn't time to reassure them they weren't in trouble, Asher got on with the task and began his examination of every man.

Face after face, the ranger held his torch to them all as he studied their eyes. The men were of all ages, though they all boasted the same solid physique that came with wielding a pickaxe for years. In the first line there were none who raised suspicion in Asher and only one halfway along the second line, though it proved to be no more than a trick of the light on closer inspection.

Approaching the last miner on the second row, the ranger was beginning to lose hope, his concern growing that the real wolf was back in town and on the cusp of transforming.

Such concern might have crested into frustration had the miner on the end of the row not fled.

And he was damned quick on his feet. Sprinting back down the line, the miner cleared the entire row while Asher had only claimed two steps in pursuit. One of the soldiers yelled at the man and defiantly stepped in his path, one hand gripped threateningly to his resting sword.

He simply flew, shoved by the miner and sent crashing into one of the ancillary buildings. There came more shouting from the soldiers and calls for his capture, but the miner was already up and over the small embankment and lost to the forest. The rest of the miners naturally huddled together, anxious and confused, and almost closed the ranger in.

But escape the panic he did, rushing past the soldiers and over the embankment himself. He heard Captain Lonan shout out his name but the ranger had abandoned any thought of aid just as he had his torch.

While the soldiers organised themselves, Asher was easily a hundred yards in already, following the sound of beating feet. His eyes had adjusted to the dark quickly but his mind remained fixed on the rising moon, tendrils of its light piercing through to the mist-veiled forest floor.

How long did he have? How long until he was on his own in the forest pursuing not a man but a Werewolf? He had to find him swiftly and kill him.

But the sound of heavy boots fleeing into the gloom had disappeared. Asher stopped in his tracks, chest heaving, while he listened. The soldiers made a ruckus trampling through the dense foliage, the clatter of their chainmail and swords cutting through the night. In a bid to put some distance between him and the clamorous horde, Asher advanced at pace, though wary of the various trip hazards.

To his left, the ranger heard the distinct sound of a twig snap, yet to his right he heard the rustle of leaves. It was the laboured breathing, however, that urged him forwards. Past more trees and through the rising mist he pressed on, determined to find the man before he became the wolf.

Nothing.

There was no trace of the miner and no sound to hunt down. Making matters worse, Captain Lonan and Watchman Elias arrived with a torch between them, dispelling Asher's night vision and filling his senses with their presence.

"Asher!" Lonan hissed, dropping the formality he had been using all day.

"You shouldn't be here," the ranger warned. "Fall back to the mine and take the soldiers with you."

The captain gripped him by the arm. "You said hunting the wolf under a full moon was a good way to die," he reminded. "We should all retreat and take up the hunt again at dawn. We can get his identity from the others. We can find him *tomorrow*," he urged.

Asher brushed the hand from his arm and opened his mouth to protest but the words caught in his throat and went no further. Instead, his attention had drifted beyond Lonan's shoulder, to Watchman Elias. Despite the winter chill, they were all sweating beneath their leathers and cloaks after the recent exertion.

Elias was dry as a bone.

His gaze had grown hard, as if his face had been transfigured into marble. Motionless, he appeared to be looking right through his captain's chest. Gone was the nervous young man who had seen the accursed wolf in all its nightmarish glory.

"Elias?" Asher uttered.

The sound of his name shot those big doe eyes up into the light

56

of the torch he held so perfectly still, only they weren't so inno-cent-looking anymore.

Now they were amber.

Taking note of the ranger's sudden alarm, the captain jumped back and drew his sword in one smooth motion. Instinctively, Asher's right hand reached up for the hilt of the silvyr short-sword protruding over his shoulder, though his fingers only grazed the weapon, halted by the distant and harrowing call of a howling Werewolf.

"There's two of them," he breathed.

"I'm sorry," Elias managed through a clenched jaw, his hands shaking by his sides. Pain erupted from nowhere and drew out an agonised wail from the young man, who dropped to his knees. "I'm sorry," he said through it all, as veins began to bulge beneath his skin. "It bit me," he confessed, one hand unconsciously touching his left shoulder. "I didn't know... what to do." His last word turned into a scream, and that scream morphed into something bestial.

Something monstrous.

Seeing the window of opportunity shrinking before his eyes, Asher left his short-sword where it was and opted for the larger broadsword. One good swing, and from a safer distance, would end Elias's threat. And his suffering.

"Please!" the watchman blurted, the remnants of his humanity fighting through. "Tell my family... I love—" His language degener-ated into a roar as the structure of his skull was remoulded by the beast within.

Asher adopted a stance he had assumed many times before—feet apart and legs braced to root him. His two hands anchored to the hilt of his sword, making the weapon a part of him as it curved round over his shoulder. One swing. That's all it would take. Casting all thought of the wife and daughter he was about to rob of their husband and father, the ranger did what he had come to do.

Asher's inexperience with Werewolves, however, was his undoing. That window of opportunity, as he had seen it, was considerably smaller than he had anticipated.

The blade only made it halfway through its arc before Elias

lashed out, his arm in two worlds but undeniably strong. And fast. Asher's feet had departed the ground before he realised what had happened and before he felt the pain in his chest. The ground soon found him again and he tumbled over the forest floor with no more control than a rag doll.

When next he looked up, through the strands of hairs that draped over his face, Lonan's sword was spinning through the air —cast from his grip by Elias—only a second before the captain himself was launched in its wake.

Asher was sure to keep his attention on Elias—Lonan would survive his impact. The infected watchman, however, was under-going the last of his vile mutation. The curse broke his bones and stretched his muscles as it transformed his human skin into a thick, dark hide.

It was then, before the wolf could claim its true form, that the king's soldiers arrived, drawn by Elias's inhuman cries. While shock and terror might have dominated any one of them, as a mob their mentality was bold enough to see the men attack the creature.

They would all die.

The Werewolf was on the precipice of having wiped out any trace of the man it had once been, his height and limbs extended beyond the norm. Asher was returned to his feet when the first of the soldiers took a clawed hand to the face, mutilating him beyond recognition.

"Get up!" the ranger snapped, his hands yanking Captain Lonan up.

The soldiers weren't without some skill, their blades and axes swinging in and swiping chunks from the wolf as it grew ever larger. But the beast had only to lash out the once and take a life, its claws penetrating their chainmail. Another found his end inside the jaws of the monster, his blood gushing between those terrible fangs.

"Run!" Asher shouted, shoving Lonan away.

Together, they hurtled through the forest, putting as much distance between them and the gnashing wolf and the screams of the men. Eventually the captain slowed, his laboured breathing getting the better of him.

"We need to keep moving," Asher insisted.

Lonan was shaking his head. "We should never... have left them. We should have stayed... and fought the creature."

"They died so we might survive. That won't happen if we don't keep moving."

Perhaps it was the captain's sense of honour or moral code that saw him disagree, but disagree he did. "If they are to die fighting the beast then I would die with them." He reached for the sword he no longer had, his eyes cast back into the dark from whence they came.

"Go back if you wish," Asher said, turning in the opposite direction. "But you'll find naught but death that way."

"An honourable death is a good death," the captain snapped back, able to stand tall again.

"There are no *good* deaths," the ranger told him gruffly, moving branches aside to progress.

"You would run?"

"Didn't you?" Asher retorted, pointing out the obvious.

Lonan made to speak again and again, each time managing no more than, "I was..."

It was shock, Asher knew, and a good helping of justified fear that had put the captain's legs to work. But shock and fear were two emotions a man of honour could hardly conceive, let alone speak of.

"If you want honour," Asher posed, "start by *surviving*. Hunt the monster tomorrow and kill it. What use is honour in death?" he finally muttered to himself.

Lonan began to answer with more defiance when the distant sound of battle ceased as suddenly as it had begun. As predicted, the soldiers were dead. Worse still, to Asher's assessment, neither he nor the captain had used their sacrifice to ensure their escape.

Now *they* were the prey.

"Run," the ranger whispered, leading the way.

There came no argument from Lonan this time—his fear

winning out over any misguided sense of duty or honour. One behind the other they hurried through the forest, leaping over fallen logs, slipping down muddy slopes, and scaling short embankments. But the wolf still gained, its angry snarl tearing through the quiet night and drowning out the sound of their own heavy breathing.

Lonan cried out as he fell, his foot having caught an unseen root in the dark. Asher doubled back and pulled him to his feet. "Move!" he growled, forcing him on.

It wasn't long, however, in the softening ground underfoot, before the captain tripped again. The ranger would have aided him had he not heard the *splash* caused by his companion's fall. Where he had remained on firm ground, Lonan had accidentally discovered water.

Moving beyond the man, leaving him to pick himself up this time, Asher stepped over the gnarled and snaking roots and into cold bog water. His brow pinching in contemplation, the ranger advanced a little further. As the water rose around his legs, the trees appeared stripped of their foliage and branches.

He knew immediately where he was, just as he knew there was a dead Hell Hag a hundred feet out and down.

A wild and savage roar turned Asher back to the heart of the woods, beyond the swamp's touch. The Werewolf knew exactly where they were and it was coming for them.

The ranger turned back to the swamp, to its black water, the surface still thick with the Hag's inky secretions. "Quickly!" he instructed, his voice forcing Lonan to wade between the disfigured and lifeless trees.

The captain managed a few desperate questions between the splashing, though not a one stopped him from accompanying the intent ranger into deeper waters. As it had the first time he had entered the swamp, the ground beneath that obsidian surface sloped until the water could claim them whole.

There was no time to reach that depth, the Werewolf already breaching the healthier trees, its legs striding into the swamp's water.

Asher snatched Lonan's tunic with both hands and plunged beneath the inky surface. It was then, in that watery crypt, that the Nightseye elixir came to life within Asher's veins.

Captain Lonan's entire body was pulsing, his heart beating to the tune of fear. Through the water, Asher could feel the cold corpse of the Hell Hag slowly rotting atop its victims' bones. It was all background noise to the ranger, his focus pulled to the four powerful limbs ploughing steadily through the swamp towards them.

Quite naturally, a slave to oxygen, Lonan tried to push up from the slope and feed his starving lungs. Asher gripped the root he had discovered looping through the mud and used it to anchor him while he pulled hard on the captain, keeping him similarly anchored.

They had to wait.

The wolf would seek them out but only for so long. Its need to hunt and run and feast would be burning in its veins, just as the elixir was burning in Asher's. His heightened senses easily picked out the beast's heart, its slow but powerful beats emanating like thunder through its limbs and across the water. Its claws scraped over the small pebbles buried in the mud as it stalked ever closer.

Again, Lonan tried to break for the surface but Asher held him firm. It did little good, of course, the captain's thrashing more than enough to send bubbles rising to the viscous top. That certainly explained why the wolf had continued so confidently towards them.

One more step and it would surely find Asher's hand fastened around the old root. Fighting the monster in the water would be even more disastrous than on land.

But he would *survive*. It wasn't so much a thought as a driving force, an edict that had been scribed into his every bone.

And so he acted.

In one smooth motion, the ranger released Lonan and drew the silvyr blade from over his shoulder. He had only to pause a moment, allowing the captain of the watch to surface, thereby gaining the wolf's attention first. As Lonan broke the water with an almighty gasp for air, the beast snarled, its head swivelling to the right, unaware that a monster hunter lay just beneath it.

Asher sprang, lest the captain feel the bite of fang and claw.

Shooting up, the silvyr cut through the surface before the ranger followed in its deadly wake. He was acutely aware in that moment, brief as it was, that he must slay the beast with his first attack or he would join the Hell Hag in the swamp's depths.

In the ranger's favour, however, was the dwarf-forged blade of Danagarr Stormshield, and it knew no equal.

The short-sword entered the Werewolf where the base of the jaw met its broad neck and did not stop until it tasted air again. Quick as the kill was, and there was no denying the blade lodged through its skull, the wolf still managed to bring up one clawed hand and pierce Asher's leather cuirass and the skin beneath.

While his senses were readjusting to their normal parameters, and Captain Lonan was still gulping down air, the ranger let the weight of the wolf collapse into the water, taking his weapon with it. The effect of its claws was immediate and potentially worse than he had first thought given the tightness he felt around his chest. With the water a little below his waist, Asher took a moment to call on the power of the black gem and heal his wounds before Lonan became aware.

As the initial pain of the magic pinched around the individual injuries, something dark and substantial caught the ranger's attention, something so dark and massive that even the shadows could not hide it. Chest heaving, he set his gaze to the trees that met the swamp. It was only then that he recalled his recent revelation.

There had been *two* of them.

Before his eyes settled on that shadowy mass, he was transfixed by two gleaming dots of amber in the dark. From that shadowy place, the wolf's head deliberately moved into the cool light of the moon, its menacing features and hot breath laid bare.

Asher stood fast under that blazing glare. He could feel the monster's wrath. Even from a distance its dominating height was apparent. It had but to bound ahead and it would be upon him in seconds. The ranger considered his defences, severely aware that his broadsword was lying far away amidst a gruesome scene of death.

The ranger snapped to action and retrieved his silvyr short-sword from its place in Elias's skull. It had taken him no more than a second, yet the Werewolf had managed to advance ten feet into the swamp, sending ripples across the black water. Then the wolf took another deliberate step, as if it was enjoying the fear its presence elicited.

Mid-step, the beast froze.

Its paws pressed down into the swamp, fixed among the gnarled roots. Its pointed head whipped to the left and its nose crinkled before a low rumble escaped from deep in its throat.

Then it was gone, lost to the trees and foliage beyond the swamp in a blur of black on black.

Asher blinked, dumbfounded.

In the beast's wake there came more sounds of rushing feet and snapping branches as something gave chase—several *things* in fact. A dash of white against the dark drew the ranger to the trees a little beyond the bog. There a man looked back at him, his face as chiselled as any statue and, perhaps, just as pale. Long hair, so blond it could have been pearl, framed that perfect face and hung over his chest.

Each man beheld the other for a moment longer, neither betraying what lay beneath their stoical facades. Then the stranger too was gone, vanishing between the trees as the wolf had.

"What happened?" Lonan asked between breaths, emerging from behind the dead Werewolf. "Where did the beast go?"

Asher remained where he stood, struggling to piece together what had happened. Clearly the captain had missed the stranger and whoever his companions had been. Deciding to keep things simple where Lonan was concerned, the ranger only made mention of the wolf's flight.

"Why would it run?"

Asher didn't have the answer to that, though he still conjured a lie with ease. "The dead wolf," he said, gesturing lazily at the beastly body protruding from the water like a giant stone.

At least it had been. The dead wolf began to melt away before their very eyes, its hulking musculature shrinking beneath the water.

"What's it doing?" Lonan sounded concerned, scared even, that this was some insidious development.

The ranger was of a different mind. He reached into the water and felt for the body, not surprised to find the naked human form of the dead watchman.

"Elias..." Lonan uttered, his hand never quite reaching the young man's face.

"We should see him returned to his family," the ranger said, his voice the only sound in that quiet swamp.

Lonan agreed though he was drawn to the trees, back the way they had come. "Word of the wolf will spread now—even the *king* will not be able to ignore what has happened here."

Asher considered the great number of dead soldiers littering the forest and was inclined to agree. Fear would set in to Kelp Town and with it there would be unbridled chaos.

The ranger looked back to the spot where the pale stranger had emerged. It seemed there was more than just the wolf to consider...

CHAPTER 6
AFTERMATH

Marrow Wolf - Easily identified by their hard exterior of bone. It's this same exterior that makes them quite hard to kill. They're as fast and agile as a wolf and they each possess a keen predatory mind, so striking true with axe or blade can be difficult enough without hitting that natural shielding.

My recommendation, dear ranger, would be the use of poison. That said, I am yet to find a poison potent enough to actually kill a Marrow Wolf. Ghast Gut or Hyron's Bane, however, is powerful enough to slow the beasts. Once sluggish, you can move in and locate one of the gaps between its bony armour and put it down for good.

A Chronicle of Monsters: A Ranger's Bestiary, 12th Edition, Page 78.

Kat Orteeze, Ranger.

Not long after daybreak, chaos had indeed overcome Kelp Town, spread by a wildfire of gossip and fear. From the steps of Stormwood Manor, Asher watched the mob swell as news continued to draw in people from every corner, word brought by the miners and the few soldiers who had not been allocated to the initial hunt. The latter had discovered their dead comrades and reported it to Lord Kernat who, subsequently, had been obligated to send a missive to Grey Stone, to King Gregorn of royal house Orvish.

In a matter of days there would be armoured soldiers patrolling the region.

Secretary Royce raised his arms to call for silence before his master replaced him. Lord Kernat had not taken kindly to the news of so many witnesses, particularly after his orders to keep the job quiet. Quite manic, he had at one point ordered Asher be put in irons and even escalated the order to one of execution for the situation, regardless of the dead wolf.

News of a second wolf had sobered the older man. He had looked to Captain Lonan, the more trusted of the pair, for the truth, though the watchman had naught but hard facts for his lordship. After a brief spell of shock, Lord Kernat had demanded to know why they had even bothered returning without completing the job.

He was just as afraid as everyone else.

When his threats inevitably returned to taking Asher's freedom away, the captain had stepped in and pointed out that there was only one man in all The Ice Vales who had slain a Werewolf. Again, Lord Kernat's temper had been restrained. His next command had been to Asher himself, demanding that he hunt down the elusive wolf if he wanted to see a single coin beyond his investigation, his fee for slaying Elias apparently forfeited.

Coin or no coin, Asher felt invested now, spurred on all the more by Elias's distraught wife, Saski. Fetching her pre-dawn to see her husband's body had been the work of a nameless watchman, but she had been met at the watch house by Captain Lonan and the ranger, their haggard appearance more than enough to inform her the worst had happened before being told so. Their daughter had been left with a neighbour, sparing her the nightmare that had awaited her mother.

While Asher felt nothing for slaying the beast, a labour he could have performed again and again without remorse, he had been left with an aftermath of guilt that he wasn't accustomed to experiencing in his line of work. Killing monsters had always felt an act of atonement, and deeply satisfying at that. Putting Werewolves in the ground had proven to be a double-edged sword.

"Yes!" Lord Kernat began, his voice ragged from grief and excessive drinking. "Yes," he cried again. "The rumours are true! Those brave souls of the king's men, those who defended our mine, were taken from us in the night. Taken from us by... by a wolf of the old stories!"

A ripple of unease and hushed whispers ran through the mob, along with calls for the creature's death. Pitchforks, pick-axes, and aged swords were thrust into the air to punctuate their demands. Beside Asher, on the steps of the manor, Captain Lonan subtly directed a pair of his watchmen to the western flank of the mob, where he had likely identified potential anarchists.

"I stand here, before you," Lord Kernat continued, "not just to tell you of the beast, but to tell you of its demise! The wolf is dead!" he exclaimed, fists balled in the air.

"Lies!" one man in the crowd dared to hurl.

Lord Kernat patted the air to beg for calm, aware that one word more was adequate kindling for the fiery mob. "'Tis true!" he insisted. "Standing with me is the very man who put his blade to the wolf and laid it low!"

Those on the steps turned their eyes to Asher, and the masses with them. The ranger had already felt exposed on the steps, elevated above the people. Now he felt as if he had been put to a pyre for his crimes.

"Captain Lonan of the watch!" Lord Kernat broadcast, his long arm sweeping out to find the man.

Master of his own emotions and expressions, Asher gave

nothing of his surprise away, though he was more surprised with himself for not expecting the deception. The captain, however, shifted where he stood, an uneasy glance thrown the ranger's way, before Secretary Royce ushered him on to speak.

He cleared his throat. "Lord Kernat speaks the truth—the beast has been slain!"

"What of the other?" came a hidden response, their voice laden with suspicion.

Asher caught the ire that flashed across his lordship's face. He had damn near howled when informed of the fact. His anger now seemed tenfold since word had obviously spread to the people. The most likely source was the miners, who knew the man who had fled the line-up was not the body they had carried back from the swamp.

Again, Lonan cleared his throat. "The second wolf yet lives," he answered honestly.

This sent another ripple of discord amongst the townspeople, their hubbub quickly rising to unmanageable levels. "But there's another full moon tonight!" one woman cried out.

Lord Kernat almost shoved the captain down a step as he replaced him before his subjects. "Fool," he hissed.

Secretary Royce puffed out his chest and bellowed a solitary command for silence, an impressive feat for a man of his age. The mob only calmed after Lord Kernat had delivered a handful of words.

"...enforce a curfew! I say again: it is for this reason that I must enforce a curfew beyond sundown tonight! Anyone seen outside their home will be subject to the king's law!" Here the lord of Kelp Town took a breath and surveyed his people. "Make no mistake, the evil we face is very real! It plagued our ancestors! It will *not* plague us! We have already slain one of the beasts! We *will* slay the other!"

The mob was mostly appeased by this, with only a few groups here and there that clearly doubted their lord's confidence. Still, they were dispersed by the watch easily enough, returned to what normality they could manage until sunset.

Lord Kernat ascended the steps before pivoting on the ball of his foot and looking down on Lonan and Asher. "By tomorrow," he seethed, "Kelp Town will be swarming with the king's men. Whomever his grace sends to oversee the situation will likely be given authority over me until the wolf is dealt with. I will not be *silenced* in my own town. Therefore, you have until tomorrow to find and kill the beast. Fail me, Captain Lonan, and you will find yourself stripped of more than your office."

Secretary Royce moved in after Lord Kernat stormed away. "Get it done," he fumed.

Captain Lonan swallowed his pride as well as his retort. Instead, he turned to Asher. "I apologise for..." He couldn't find the words to describe his master's betrayal and deception—because he was a loyal man as well as a good man, Asher decided.

"The people need to know they're safe under *your* watch," Asher replied, unfazed by his lack of credit, "not *mine*. Now, we just need to..." The ranger trailed off upon sighting a small group of men approaching from the scattering crowd.

Following his distracted gaze, Lonan sighed. "Leave this to me," he said.

Asher had no intention of getting involved in town politics, but there was something about this particular group of men that spoke to the ranger's sixth sense, the one that informed him of imminent violence. Of the six, there wasn't one who didn't have a weapon of some description resting on their belt; though it was more than that. Asher just knew a thug when he saw one.

"Who are they?" he enquired, following Lonan down the steps to meet them.

"Local gang," the captain reported. "The one leading them is Vouder Stould. Considers himself the real lord of Kelp Town. He and his boys run all the illegal fight pits in the area."

"You haven't shut them down?" Asher asked, his tone free of judgment.

"If only it were that easy," the captain muttered before they arrived within earshot of the gang. "Vouder," Lonan addressed, coming face to face with the lead thug. "What can I do for you?"

"I'll take the truth for starters," Vouder replied, his round head and squat neck sat firmly on broad shoulders. "We both know you don't have the stones to kill a Werewolf." At this accusation, the thug's eyes shifted to Asher. "Him on the other hand... I've never seen him before, so he can't be from round these parts. My best bet —and you know I'm a betting man," he added with a sly wink at the watchman, "is that he's a hunter. One of them *ranger* folk you hear about." Vouder scrutinised Lonan's reaction to this and a wry smile spread his thick cheeks. "Thought so," he concluded.

"What do you *want*?" the captain asked again, a little more force behind his words now.

"*I* want this town to be safe," the thug stated. "And I don't think you and your boys can do that. So I'm here to tell you, quite simply, to stay out of our way. We'll see to this."

Lonan took a breath that seemed to make him that much taller. "No one is to take the law into their own hands, Vouder. If you break the law I will—"

"What?" came the challenge. "What will you do, Captain Lonan? I have more support in this town than you do, more than our dusty old lord even."

The captain advanced a step, displaying his superior height. "Do not mistake loyalty for fear, Vouder Stould. And do not doubt the reach of my authority. If you break curfew, you will find yourself in irons."

The thug offered a toothy grin, thumbs hooked into the belt that hid beneath his gut. "If your authority was worth spit, you'd already have Russell Hobbs in those irons you speak of. Better yet, you'd have his head on the block."

Mention of the name caught Lonan off guard. "Russell Hobbs?"

Vouder looked back at his men, his amusement spreading to them all. "He doesn't even know the fella's name! Looks like you're a little behind, Captain." The thug laughed as he turned away. "Good hunting, boys. Be seeing you, Ranger."

Lonan waited until the gang had faded from earshot before swearing and cursing Vouder Stould's name. "Tigg!" he called, beckoning one of the watchmen overseeing the clearing mob.

Old and lean was the man who responded to the name. "Sir?" His mouth was almost completely concealed by the white moustache that dominated his upper lip.

"I sent Yosuf and Corban to question the miners for the suspect's identity. Where are they?" he barked.

If the older watchman was flustered by the abrasive captain he didn't display an ounce of it. "They're working through the list, sir. I believe there's quite a lot of them."

Lonan was already shaking his head. "Find them and recall them—Vouder Stould has already got the name we're looking for," he added, his disappointment and frustration plain to hear. Tigg prepared to move away until the captain touched his arm. "Get me the address for *Russell Hobbs*."

Within the hour, Asher was standing outside the lowly dwelling of one Russell Hobbs. The man lived on the outskirts, not far from the town's main entrance in the south-east. It was just as rundown as those either side, if the smallest of the three.

The watchman Asher had identified as Corban approached his captain, sword in hand. "There's a back door, sir. Yosuf and Falad are covering it."

"He's not in there," the ranger told them, one wrist resting lazily on the hilt of his broadsword.

Lonan looked at him, his expression still racked by strong lines of determination. Then he looked away, jaw shifting. "He's right. Hobbs has to know we're looking for him. He wouldn't come back here."

The muscles around Asher's eyes pinched as he narrowed his gaze on the door. "That doesn't mean there's nothing to learn here," he replied, moving for the entrance. "It's broken," he reported, indicating the handle resting at an awkward angle. Proving his word, the ranger pulled the handle free of the door and tossed it to Corban.

Captain Lonan sighed. "Vouder's already been here," he deduced.

Asher didn't agree but he kept his opinion to himself and lightly pushed the door open. No more than a glance was required to know that Russell's home had been ransacked. The miner couldn't claim to own much but what he did own was on the floor. The table had been upturned, the cupboards opened and drawers pulled out, their contents spilled amongst the debris. What few clothes he owned had been removed from the splintered wardrobe and scattered.

More interestingly, there were a handful of floorboards that had been torn from their place, exposing the hollow space below. The same damage could be seen in the ceiling.

"What a mess," Lonan muttered on his way inside. "Vouder's boys have a heavy touch."

The ranger crouched down and investigated one of the discarded floorboards and the empty space left in its place. "This wasn't Vouder," he said quietly, just catching the captain's attention.

"Then who else?"

Asher discarded the board and resumed his full height. "Vouder and his men are looking for Hobbs." The ranger gestured to their dishevelled surroundings. "Whoever did this was looking for something considerably smaller than a man."

"Something smaller?"

"No one could hide in here," the ranger pointed out.

Lonan agreed by expression alone. "Then what?"

The *what* gnawed at Asher, but it was the *who* that absorbed his curiosity. He naturally thought of the man on the edge of the swamp and those who had, apparently, chased off the wolf.

With nothing to offer on the matter, Asher responded with a question of his own. "What do we know about Russell Hobbs?"

Focused by the name of their assailant, Captain Lonan moved past the ranger's musings. "Corban?" he summoned. "Tell me you know more about Hobbs than where he lives."

The younger watchman licked his lips. "Aye, sir. From the

records we know he's lived here for three years. Moved from Snowfell when they closed the copper mine."

"Family?" the captain pressed, though Asher felt the answer was obvious given their environment.

"None, sir. He moved here alone and, according to the miners that knew him, he lived alone. We could send a raven to Snowfell requesting any further details they might have."

Lonan pinched the bridge of his nose. "It won't help us find him in time. We need to know where he would go if he isn't here."

Corban raised a finger in the air. "Them we questioned said he frequented The Gauntlet, sir."

"A tavern?" Asher echoed incredulously. "You won't find him there. You won't find him anywhere—he's not in Kelp Town anymore."

"You can't know that," Lonan countered.

"Your friend Vouder has likely told the whole town who we're hunting," Asher argued. "And they already knew *what* we're hunting. There's nowhere he can go, no one he can trust."

Lonan appeared visibly disheartened by the assessment. "So how do we find him then?"

"We don't," the ranger said simply enough. "He's out *there* somewhere. If he's new to being a Werewolf he'll have taken himself into the *wilds*, beyond civilisation, where he thinks he won't be a danger to anyone. If he's had years with the wolf, he'll know how to survive situations like this, and the outcome remains the same—he's not here."

The captain of the watch was clearly struggling now to maintain his fortitude. "You know we can't take that explanation back to his lordship."

Asher thought about the coin he had already made; more than enough to see him to the next town or city. Unlike Lonan, he wasn't tied to Kelp Town and could walk away if he wished to. It would be the sensible thing to do—it's what a *survivor* would do. He had been damned lucky fooling the first wolf in the swamp. What were the chances his luck would hold out for the second?

The Arakesh that lurked in the shadows of his mind urged him to collect Hector and leave. He nearly even convinced himself that the second wolf would never return and that he had already saved lives by slaying Elias. The *Assassin* was nothing if not cunning, well aware of the Ranger's desire to do good, a characteristic it considered a weakness to be exploited.

But Asher could still hear Saski's wails as she fell into Lonan's arms. They will have been echoed by her daughter that very day, and all the families of the slain soldiers.

No, he told the *Assassin*. He was to hunt the wolf that had done this to Elias, that had forced him to kill the young watchman. The young *husband*. The young *father*.

Asher met Lonan's expectant gaze. "We're going to bait it."

CHAPTER 7
SECRETS IN THE WALLS

Weadle - Fascinating creatures! And proof that not all monsters require a blade to deal with them. Weadles, on the whole, are not to be feared, though I caution against getting in their way. At twelve foot tall and with a jagged exterior akin to mountain stone, these lofty walkers will squash you without care.

It should be archived that this is not done maliciously. From observations, it seems Weadles simply don't notice humans, as if we are just another part of the mountain environment in which they live. They spend their days walking across the highest slopes of The Vengoran Mountains doing no more than moving boulders around, as if they are curating the mountains themselves. Who can say why they do this. Like everything else about these lithe creatures, it is a mystery.

A Chronicle of Monsters: A Ranger's Bestiary, 12th Edition, Page 221.

Maynar Phal, Ranger.

T he night was still, with a light mist clinging to the ground, reminding Asher of the swamp where he had slain not one but two monsters now. For the third night, the moon hung over the world in its full and luminous glory, though glory it would not bring.

Equally still was the town itself, and with hardly a speck of light amongst its many windows. In the distance, Stormwood Manor sat atop its rise as no more than a dark box against an even darker backdrop.

After an early evening of snowfall, Captain Lonan's boots crunched through the fresh powder as he approached the ranger, the door to The King's Arms closing behind him, taking its promise of warmth with it. The senior watchman joined him by the corner of the tavern, where they could survey the town's main square and central well. Tied to the post of that well was a cow, its patchwork of black and white smothered in goat's blood.

The bait.

Asher remained leaning against the tavern, arms crossed. He rarely had much to say and was often content to wait until the other person spoke first.

Lonan didn't disappoint. "I feel it my duty to remind you of your own words again, Ranger."

"Too much ground to cover hunting the man," Asher put forth, and not for the first time that day. "Can't lure the man either. But the wolf..." Here, the ranger looked at the red cow, its hot breath collecting in the frigid air. "The wolf can be persuaded."

"That still leaves the wolf to fight," Lonan pointed out, his hand reflexively reaching for the hilt of his sword.

The ranger couldn't argue with that, though he did spare a moment to spy the groups of watchmen secreted in the shadows of the surrounding buildings. It would hardly be a surprise, but an ambush would be their only chance, an attack from all sides that *might* overwhelm the wolf. Asher didn't fancy their chances, believing their best hope to be in the swing of his silvyr blade before too many fell to fang and claw.

Peering out from under the overhang of the tavern, he laid eyes on the moon. Somewhere out there, Russell Hobbs had been replaced, swallowed whole, by the beast that lived within.

Asher sympathised.

"You should go inside for a while," Lonan suggested. "You've been out here for hours now. Your arms and legs will be stiff and slow. Either or both will get you killed this night."

The ranger agreed with the assessment but he didn't feel like going inside. Instead, he made for the side street.

"Where are you going?"

"For a walk," he called back. "Just keep your eyes on that cow."

Leaving the captain and his men in position, the ranger took to the muted streets of Kelp Town, his boots creating the only sound. He hadn't made the conscious decision to visit Russell's home, yet that was where he eventually found himself. Since the lock was still broken, he opened the door without obstruction and entered the abandoned dwelling.

With no inhabitants and no fire, the still and quiet room was illuminated by no more than the cold light of the moon, and it was just as frigid inside as it was outside, keeping Asher's breath visible in the air. A sheen of frost clung to every surface. Remaining close to the door, the ranger contemplated his reasons for being there at all. It was the mystery that hung over the place, he decided. He was confident Vouder Stould and his men hadn't been the ones to ransack the house, just as he was confident that those who *had* turned the place upside down hadn't been looking for Hobbs.

So what had they been searching for? And who were *they*?

If the answer to any of those questions truly lay inside the house, there was only one way he was going to find it. Before the ranger had even arrived at that logical conclusion, his right hand had already removed the red strip of cloth from his belt. Trying to quash his enthusiasm, Asher tied the blindfold at the back of his head, dropping his mind into darkness, where the *Assassin* lived.

The *Ranger* fought for control, reminding himself that the Nightseye elixir was a necessary investigative tool and nothing more. It didn't stop the *Assassin* from baring its teeth, recalling images of stalking from the rooftops, steel in hand.

Asher took a breath and steadied himself. His focus sharpened, aiming to root him to no more than that room. He had a job to do.

Initially, his senses absorbed the room and much beyond it. Foot by foot, he pulled back his awareness of the world outside of Russell Hobbs' home, closing himself off to the slow and steady heartbeats of the families sleeping on the other side of the walls.

Inside the main room of the small dwelling, his nose was assaulted by a plethora of scents and stinging aromas. That wasn't unusual in a home, a place where food, both fresh and old could always be found. He was soon drawn beyond them and the damp wood and the open bottle of ale. There was something different about the single bed in the corner, specifically its rumpled sheets.

Sweat. The lingering sweat of Russell Hobbs was unlike any Asher had encountered. He had, however, come across the smell in certain monsters, their sweat laden with elements of their prey.

In this case, the ranger detected Fen Underson, the butcher.

Moving further into the room, Asher displaced the still air. It brought more to his attention, giving him pause. He could feel the specks of dust bombarding his skin and filling his lungs, each a messenger of the past.

There were two things that instantly stood out to the ranger. The first was quite simply *old*. Something very old had passed through Russell's home, carrying with it notes of decay. The second was *death*. Asher tilted his head, questioning his findings. Something very old and dead had recently been inside the room. His initial conclusion was a corpse, but the deathly smell was not so rotten as an old corpse.

The mystery surrounding the home thickened all the more.

Moving past the broken table, where a flat arch in the wall separated the bedroom from everything else, the ranger tasted something that halted him again.

Metallic. Bronze in fact.

Along with the taste he quickly discovered the smell of it, the dual senses homing him in. Rubbing his fingers and thumb together, Asher could feel the object's smooth surface as if he was actually holding it. The *it* in question was small, he knew. Small enough to fit in the palm of his hand and as light as an apple.

But where was it? He detected wood between himself and the curious object, as well as empty space around the ball of bronze. Crouching in the archway, one hand running down the frame of wood that separated the two areas, Asher found the hollow he was looking for, close to the floor. He tapped it twice with one finger, using the subsequent vibrations and sounds to learn all of its secrets. There was no mechanism or feat of engineering that kept the object hidden—just a removable piece of wood that appeared seamless at a glance.

Using two hands, he carefully dislodged the piece of framework and set it aside. Wishing to see the object with his own eyes, Asher removed his blindfold and braced through the disorientating transition. And there it was, nestled in the hollow of the frame, a solitary sphere of bronze. The ranger scooped it up and rose to his full height to better examine the ball.

It wasn't entirely smooth, ringed by three ridged bands at its centre. Inquisitive as he was, Asher fiddled with the rings and discovered they moved silently left and right.

Asher held the object in a shaft of moonlight, scrutinising it as a whole. He had no idea what he had found, though he didn't doubt it was the source of *someone's* investigation. But how Russell Hobbs was tied up in it all still lay beyond his understanding.

Like a spider detecting a vibration in its web, a shadow crept across Asher's mind, his warrior's sixth sense warning him of unseen danger.

He was not alone.

There were eyes on him, and so close he could likely reach out and touch the stranger. How the individual had come to occupy *any* space in the small house without alerting Asher was unfathomable. How had he not heard them? They must have entered the house after he removed his blindfold, only seconds ago.

These questions ran through the ranger's mind in the time it took him to turn on the spot and locate those watching eyes. They weren't the amber of a wolf but the black of death, devoid of soul. Those deathly eyes of onyx belonged to a man a few inches shorter than the ranger, though the shadows clung to so much of him that there was no more to see than his chestnut hair, scraped back into a ponytail, just as his features appeared scraped back into sharp angles.

Asher was instantly reminded of the pale figure on the edge of the swamp, though he couldn't say exactly why. What he did know, what seemed inexplicably clear to him, was that the man before him was no man at all.

And so, for the third time since arriving in Kelp Town, Asher found himself faced with a monster.

The man-shaped creature suddenly ploughed into him, moving just fast enough to take even the ranger by surprise. Asher felt the framework of the arch and a portion of the wall give way behind him, his body forced through it and beyond, until the far wall of the house held him. He fell onto the bed, saving him from another hard impact, and looked at his attacker—who had already turned from the ranger to pick up the bronze sphere.

Asher launched himself from the bed and threw all of his weight into the tackle, his arms wrapping around the stranger's waist. The sphere skittered across the dusty floor and rebounded off another wall while the two combatants wrestled through the debris. The ranger came out on top and immediately dropped a swift punch into his enemy's pale face. He might as well have flicked the man with his finger for all the harm it apparently inflicted. The next punch came up from the fiend and caught Asher across the jaw, the fist hurled with utter abandon.

Hitting the floorboards, Asher glimpsed the sphere rolling about as blood trickled from the corner of his mouth. Beside him, his foe was rising, dark eyes similarly fixed on the orb of bronze. The ranger whipped his legs out and created a snaring trap with them, bringing the monster down to his level again. He watched the man's face slam into the floor, an impact that would have broken bone or simply knocked the sense from a normal person.

Instead, those black eyes snapped open and he began to rise for a second time—not even a hint of pain about him.

Already on his knees, Asher thrust an uppercut into the monster's human gut, doubling it over, though with force rather than pain apparently. A cold hand clasped the ranger's neck and shoved his head down into the floor, before an abrupt boot landed in his stomach and rolled him away. The sound of metal scraping across the floor filled the room as the fiend retrieved the bronze sphere. Through strands of hair, Asher watched the monster examine the object. It took the ranger another moment to realise how perfectly still his foe was standing, while he lay there, chest heaving.

No doubt in his mind that he faced a monster, Asher picked himself up and prepared to slay the thing. Close as they were, the ranger had no problem snatching the fiend's wrist and snapping its elbow in one smooth motion. The sphere was released, left to fall and tumble across the floor once more. The monster hardly reacted to the bone protruding from the inside of its arm, its attention centred on the mysterious sphere.

Never one to give an inch, Asher followed up his attack with a second, throwing his elbow at the fiend again, this time landing it across its face. The monster's human head was forced one way before it swivelled back an instant later, a determined rage blazing behind its eyes. Using its uninjured arm, the ranger's foe began a barrage of wild punches, no care given to any wound it might inflict upon itself.

Asher received three of those blows before his mind turned to steel, specifically the steel at the base of his back. The dagger was freed of its perch in a flash of moonlight and brought up to spear the creature's incoming fist. Again, it gave no cry of pain or distress at the new injury but simply continued to hurl attack after attack, bringing its legs into the melee. The ranger defended himself with the blade and lashed out with numerous counter attacks that scored new gashes across his enemy's body, yet still it came.

Despite the unbelievable amount of damage it could take, it became clear to Asher that the creature lacked any kind of training where fighting was concerned. It simply attacked as any monster might lash out, though it benefited from the singular advantage of being unable to experience pain. The ranger decided to use this advantage to his own, his disciplined mind orchestrating the required steps to ensure a clean kill.

Moving one way then the next, he batted aside the wild attacks and moved into his enemy's space. The dagger was plunged neatly into its chest, carving through heart and lungs until the guard met flesh. Asher paused there, ready to watch his foe's final moments unfold. Perhaps in death it would reveal its true self.

With a bloody hole in its hand, the creature grasped the ranger's wrist, their eyes locked together. It seemed the beast was just as good at eluding death as him. Inch by inch it forced Asher's hand back and the dagger with it. Caught in an instance of surprise, the ranger failed to block the knee that shot up and bolted into his stomach. He was stopped again by one of Russell's walls, both impacts enough to drop him to the floor this time.

What in the hells was this thing?

Again, the creature ignored the ranger and moved for the sphere and it was soon clasped between those bloody fingers. Asher's seasoned mind began to fray, and that dark void began to suck him in. He was done with whatever monster he faced. Now he could only think of carving the thing up, tearing it to pieces until he stood the victor, drenched in its blood.

The *Assassin* knew how to kill, and efficiently too.

With barely a sound, Asher rose to his feet, his cloak of moss green draped to the floor. The dagger that had clattered to the boards beside him was returned to a white-knuckled hand concealed beneath a dark fingerless glove.

His first step was purposeful, the sound deliberate. It made the creature turn, its instinct to lash out with its good arm. Asher had predicted it and ducked under the swing, his own arm rising to meet his enemy's head. As the dagger drove through skull and brain, the monster's good arm sent the sphere flying through the window and into the snow.

The ranger released his grip on the hilt, letting his foe topple to the floor with the blade still lodged in its skull. "Let's see you get up from that," he muttered, his jaw aching with every word.

Manoeuvring into a crouch so he might better examine the creature, a distant howl cut through the night and turned Asher to the broken window. The bait had been taken.

Leaving the dead creature and his dagger where they were, the ranger hurried from the house and into the street. There came no second howl but an almighty roar that pierced the town's calm. Then came the shouting and screams of death. Asher drew his broadsword, the monster's call granting him a second wind.

Against the white of the snow, however, the metallic sheen of the bronze sphere caught his eye, halting his departure just long enough to retrieve it. He desperately wanted to take more time investigating it, the cause of so much mystery, but his sword was needed elsewhere.

How much longer the journey back to the main square felt, even at a run. When, at last, he turned the final corner, he was just in time to see the back half of the cow being hurled across the square. That considerable bulk rammed two watchmen through the window of Dandy's Inn, a trail of blood and gore in its wake. Retracing the carcass's flight path, Asher laid eyes on the wolf itself.

It was bigger than the one he had slain.

Two arrows had found their home in its hide of leathery flesh and dark fur, though neither troubled the Werewolf. It snarled at the three soldiers and two watchmen that advanced, its fingers splayed to display those ferocious and ebony claws. The soldiers attacked first, and with spears. One succeeded in piercing the wolf's shoulder, the thrust having glanced off a backhand from the beast. It wasn't a killing blow but it brought out a howl from its terrible jaws. That was the last thing the soldier ever heard.

The claws that raked across his throat penetrated so deep he lost the ability to utter a sound as he slipped into death. His comrades tried to avenge him but they weren't nearly quick enough to bring the wolf down. One took a hand of claws directly to the face while the other suffered a bite across his neck and shoulder, his blood gushing out either side of the fiend's head.

In their stead, the two watchmen dashed in, each scoring red lines across the wolf's torso and back, matting the fur with its own blood. One of them received a backhand in retaliation, the blow strong enough to break his neck in the process. The other was saved when Captain Lonan charged into his side and brought them both down under the swing of claws. Heroic as it was, the captain of the watch had only succeeded in prolonging their lives by mere seconds.

On two legs, the Werewolf looked down at them, thick saliva and blood drooling from between its canines. It had only to bring its claws to bear and both men would perish, butchered by a rage that could never be quenched. But those claws never came for them, occupied as they were by a ranger of the wilds.

Asher swung his broadsword in a wide arc, the tip scraping a gory line across the wolf's shoulder and chest. It naturally retreated from the steel, where it met that of another. Vouder Stould's to be exact. The thug's axe chopped into the beast's thigh, producing a pained growl from the creature. His men were already there to back him up, their axes, swords, and hammers bearing down on the monster.

Taking what time he had been given, Asher turned away and helped Captain Lonan up. The man was sporting a vicious claw mark to his left leg, an injury that must have been inflicted before the ranger's return. It might have sparked a fire of guilt within him had his mind not been on the fight.

"Get back!" he urged, ushering the captain and his man towards the taverns.

Turning back to the battle, two of Vouder's men lay dead in the shadow of the wolf, their bodies mutilated beyond recognition. The thugs deserved some credit, however, having riddled the beast with wounds that soaked the snow with blood. But it wasn't enough. For all their grit and determination, they lacked the skill required to put the monster down for good.

Asher lacked no such skill.

Breaking into a dash, the ranger used the low wall that ringed the central well to gain some height and give his downward swing more momentum. Using the distraction Vouder and his men had unwittingly granted him, Asher came down at the wolf's back and opened a grisly line from shoulder to hip. The beast roared and forgot about the thugs in an instance of searing pain. It turned wildly to lash out at the one who had hurt it so, but the ranger wasn't there, having dropped into a roll.

Coming up, he did so with his broadsword swinging out wide. Again, he scored a crimson gash—this time opening up the wolf's hip. It succumbed to the pain and staggered back a step, giving Asher ample manoeuvring space to rise and swing his blade up with two hands. A third wound was wrought upon the beast, drawing a blood-soaked tear from jaw to brow. It fell this time, its body crushing the dead soldiers.

"Kill it!" Vouder bellowed, his axe lifted high.

And they would have, had the wolf not made its escape. Propelled by its strong arms, the beast was beyond their reach in a single bound. Despite its wounds causing it so much suffering, it was a creature of supernatural stamina and resolve, and so it found the will and the strength to carry on, making for the tree line beyond the northern edge.

"We've got it on the run!" Vouder cheered, leading his men after it.

"Stop!" Asher's warning fell on deaf ears. "You can't hunt it out there!" But they were gone, claimed by the trees as the wolf had been.

Despite the Werewolf's departure, the square was not left in silence. Men cried out in pain from the sides while others crawled through the snow to reach the light and warmth of the surrounding taverns. Healers that Lonan had kept on standby, hidden behind stone, rushed out to aid them all. Even injured, the captain of the watch hurled orders to confine the chaos.

In the midst of it, and one of few still to be on his feet, Asher was ignored by those who rushed past him. Having ever relied on the black gem to heal his ailments, the ranger could offer little in the way of medical aid. Just the thought of it made him consider the injuries he had taken on in Russell Hobbs' home. He decided against healing them for now—he wanted to feel the pain for a while. To do otherwise felt more akin to an insult where the injured and dying were concerned.

Fading away, the ranger vanished from the square of disfigured corpses and severed cow, from the cries of men and the blood they lay in. Walking through the streets of Kelp Town, he was infuriated by the wolf's escape and narrowly avoiding death. And though he was annoyed by the recklessness of Vouder and his men, he cared little for their wellbeing. They would all be dead by dawn.

Ultimately, the damage had been done and the Werewolf would have to be tomorrow's problem. While he gave some consideration to hunting Russell Hobbs down—difficult as that would prove to be—his more immediate concerns went to the other creature he had fought. With more forethought than his previous wanderings, the ranger went confidently to Russell's house, to the body he had left there.

The room was just as he had left it—minus the corpse.

It had left a good volume of blood behind, most of which could be found smeared across the floor, leading to the back door. Asher couldn't imagine the creature had crawled out of the house, not with his dagger still in its head. Nothing survived a dagger to the head.

It seemed more likely then that someone else, an ally of the creature, had retrieved the body. The obvious conclusion returned Asher's mind to the swamp, where he had seen the blond man surveying from the tree line. Whatever they were, they had the numbers.

And his dagger.

CHAPTER 8
THE WOLFMAN

Hook Hands - Aptly named I should say. The skin about their arms narrows to a bony protrusion that rounds into sharp hooks. So too do their four legs. These hooks are perfect for disembowelling their prey, so they might feast on the preferred organs (liver and kidneys), but the hooks are also excellent for lending these fiends great speed and agility. Like Sandstalkers, you will find subtle variations of these creatures in different environments (See A Charter of Monsters, Page 101, for known locations).

Personally, I have always found the ilk that dwell in caves harder to kill than those which inhabit woodland areas. Be that as it may, every variation of the Hook Hands species is vulnerable to bright light. Combine this vulnerability with fire and you have the perfect weapon.

A Chronicle of Monsters: A Ranger's Bestiary, 12th Edition, Page 32.

Horis of The Vales, Ranger.

"Where in the hells have you been?" Lonan spat, flustered by the chaos in the main square and pained by the bloody grooves in his thigh.

Asher looked from the brightening sky to the captain of the watch. He was sitting on a bench outside The Gauntlet, his injured leg propped up on a stool, while an aged woman crouched by his side and prepared a healing balm. He was one of a few now, others having succumbed to their injuries, their bodies covered by blood-stained cloaks.

Other townspeople had dared to enter the square, some to witness the aftermath and others to offer help in the early dawn. So much death and injury would only incite more fear, an emotional virus that could spread without check.

And yet the Werewolf was only one side of the mystery that had beset Kelp Town. Asher met the captain's expectant gaze, wondering whether to inform him of the other violent affair that had taken place in the night. The ranger thought better of it. The captain had more pressing matters to deal with—chiefly the monster that posed a genuine threat to the town. As long as the pale men remained on the periphery, Asher was content to narrow his focus.

For now.

"It won't be long before Secretary Royce arrives," the ranger said, his response skirting obtusely around Lonan's question. "He will translate Lord Kernat's wrath and likely remove both of us from the hunt."

The captain looked to have a sharp retort, though he never voiced it, his mood sobered as his eyes roamed over the dead that lay in the square. "Perhaps they would be right to," he lamented. "Perhaps the army will fare better. How many have died while I have been in charge of—" Lonan's question was transformed into an agonised grunt as the balm was applied to his wounds. "Either way," he finally managed, his hands fixed hard to the arms of his chair, "I don't think you're going to get the rest of your coin. If his lordship's disposition is dire enough, he might even consider irons for you."

"Let him consider," Asher quipped, more than confident that the lord of Kelp Town lacked the necessary resources to not only bind him, but capture him first.

"You tried, Ranger," the captain offered, his voice strained. "Hells, you might even have finished the beast had Vouder and his boys not interfered."

"I don't think Lord Kernat cares for those who *try*," Asher opined.

"In truth," the captain responded, and quietly so, "I'm not sure there's *much* his lordship cares about anymore. He was all wrath on those steps because he hadn't had a drink…" Lonan eyed the healer beside him and let his speculation trail off.

Asher stood there for a moment, unsure what to say. It felt as if the captain had made himself vulnerable, creating an opening for some level of emotional interaction, but the ranger couldn't muster the appropriate response. He considered him a *good* man—not a title he accorded everyone he met—but a night of violence and intrigue had a way of preventing his mind from translating his feelings into words.

Instead, he opted for, "There can be no punishment for anyone if the wolf is hunted down before the army arrives."

Lonan frowned up at him and not because of his pain. "We tried that," he said, taking in the gruesome scene around them. "Lord Kernat will not give either of us permission to try again—too many have died."

"I wasn't looking for permission," Asher remarked, turning away from the captain of the watch.

"Where are you going?" he called after him.

The ranger paused and looked back. "To catch the man."

"The man…" Lonan uttered. "You said it would be impossible to find him out there." The captain eyed him. "Why are you still here? Your pockets have been lined with enough coin already to see you from here to Velia. Why would you stay and face this terror?"

Asher glanced at the healer, who was busying herself with

preparing a new balm, before meeting Lonan's eyes and the anticipation that sat behind them. "It's the job," he said, combining the truth with a lie.

The captain hadn't been convinced but he appeared content to leave it there. "You seem to have a habit of ignoring your own advice, Ranger," he commented, looking off to the northern tree line.

Asher shrugged, with nothing to add, though he did look back to offer the captain one last piece of advice. "Burn the bodies."

Banishing the horrors of the night, a clear dawn pushed through the trees that blanketed the base of the mountains. Rays of clarity filled the forest with an atmosphere of serenity, and all to the call of birdsong.

Yet, earlier, a Werewolf slathered in the blood of its victims had sped through this same place, and pursued by violent thugs. How quickly nature forgave such intrusion.

But it did not forget.

Asher crouched low to the forest floor and rifled through fallen leaves spotted with blood. Further on were boot prints in the disturbed snow and broken branches where the thicket closed the gaps between trees. Moving on, he soon discovered the wolf's prints—two large hands and hind paws. For the first mile he covered it seemed the creature was struggling with its gait, no doubt feeling the sting of Asher's blade. Its struggles, however, appeared to have abated by the second mile.

"It heals quickly," he mused, checking the distance between hand and paw prints. "You're not the only one," he added under his breath, rising from his crouch.

The ranger made to take his next step but his mounting frustration gave him pause. He could likely follow the clumsy tracks of Vouder's men until he came across them and, perhaps, even the wolf, who would now have returned to his human form, but it was taking too long. Here and there, where the snow fall had been lighter or the forest opened up, the tracks were harder to find, slowing him down. He needed to know where to go and he needed to get there now.

Be it a growl or a sigh, it forced its way out of Asher's mouth. He knew what he needed to do. His hand was already on his belt, one finger touching the red cloth that hung there. It was an advantage, he knew, a tool to be utilised. Was it not a waste to ignore it, shun it even? Already it had proven useful. Useful to the *Ranger*. Was it not a twist of fate that the greatest weapon of the Arakesh could be used for good? Perhaps, Asher considered, if he believed in fate.

And yet...

He could feel his heart picking up speed at just the feel of it. Tuning into the environment, mastering it, was near divine. It energised the *Assassin* within, urging him to press the hunt and kill Russell Hobbs. And if Vouder and his men got in the way, they could join the cursed miner. No one would ever know—they would say it had been the wolf. At least that's what it would look like by the time he was finished with them.

Asher recalled the words of Arnathor from the bestiary. While the old ranger advised hunting and killing the person cursed by the bite of the Werewolf, he also warned of the toll killing a person would take on one's conscience if not one's soul. Arnathor had never met a man like Asher though.

With the blindfold free of his belt, Asher had to wonder if this wasn't the perfect time to rely on the *Assassin*. Let the monster shoulder the burden.

Unsure of himself, the ranger focused on the task—finding and killing the Werewolf plaguing Kelp Town. And so he bound his eyes behind that strip of red cloth and absorbed the world. The natural world, beyond the discord and clutter of civilisation, had just as much to say for itself as any one of those cities. There seemed an order to the bugs and critters scurrying about their lives, and all between the droplets of ice water that ran down the pines and splashed against the forest floor. Branches creaked in the breeze and woodland animals, far from sight, darted and snuffled their way through the morning.

His nose pinched to the scent of blood on the air. It wasn't human. Tuning in to the sounds from that same direction, he discerned an adolescent fox making a meal of an old rabbit.

Turning his focus elsewhere, he couldn't help but detect the dried blood left in the wolf's trail. Using that trail as a general direction, the ranger homed his senses in and waited for the feedback. There was certainly more blood in that direction, though it veered to the west.

Then he heard it, the telltale sound of humanity's mark on the world. Violence.

He first heard the swing of steel before feeling it between his fingers. Laboured breathing from multiple sources. Sweat permeated the clean air.

"Kill him, Vouder!" one of the men shouted.

Asher broke into a sprint no man could manage in a forest of hazards. He flowed through it, skipping over awkward boulders, hopping over jutting stones, slipping effortlessly between the reaching trees, and avoiding the hidden roots. The ranger could feel it all, as if the world itself was telling him where to plant each boot.

At great speed he covered the land that lay between him and the fight, and with barely a sound to accompany him. Before revealing himself, the ranger came to rest behind a tree and removed his blindfold. The image before him matched perfectly with what his senses had perceived, though it was his first laying of eyes on Russell Hobbs in the light.

Standing naked, the miner was half a foot taller than Vouder and his men—though who could speak of the two already laid flat to the ground? So too were his shoulders broader than any of the remaining thugs, his thick arms chiselled by years of handling a pick-axe. At a glance, Asher deduced the man had a decade on him, though his grizzled face was well masked by a thick beard and long draping hair.

Vouder lunged forward, his axe curling through the air and

missing Russell by a whole foot. The thug was anxious, fearful even, to get too close. Hobbs must have put his men down with some brutality. The other three began to circle the naked man they had construed as prey. How wrong they were.

Proving himself braver than Vouder Stould, one of the three thugs charged Russell with a short-sword and axe, one following the other. Hobbs stood his ground and simply snatched a wrist in each hand, holding the weapons at bay with ease. This immediately gave Asher some indication as to the man's supernatural strength.

Russell squeezed the wrists he had locked in his vice-like grips and the thug yelped as he dropped the blade and axe. A solid push kick to the man's chest sent him from his feet and flying into a tree. He didn't get back up.

Vouder took his chance again and chopped his axe down, intending to drive his blade deep in Russell's back. The steel of his weapon cut through no more than air, missing its target by inches. Asher blinked, unsure how he had missed Hobbs' movements. But moved he had. One strong hand grabbed Vouder by the collar and twisted him round, where a closed fist was waiting for his face. The lead thug went down and with a mouthful of blood.

The last two came as one, hoping to use their boss's distraction to their advantage. Like those before them, their efforts were futile. Hobbs evaded the swings of their blades with such ease the ranger might have assumed he had received training. It was unlikely given his job and background. It was more likely that the curse of the wolf had heightened his reflexes, making the thugs appear sluggish.

A swift backhand sent one down, his head driven to collide with the trunk of the nearest tree. The final among Russell's pursuers was lifted to his toes by a gut punch so fierce it forced vomit from his mouth. The next fist caught him about the eye and laid him out flat, there to join his companions.

Asher remained where he was, concealed for now. Damned if he wasn't impressed.

Continuing to watch him, he was intrigued as Russell turned

one of the men over and tugged free the length of rope that had been bound over his shoulder. The ranger frowned at the event unfolding before him. What was the miner doing? It soon became clear, however, as a noose was formed from the loose rope. After making sure his head fitted through the loop, Hobbs tossed the end of the rope high and over a thick branch that extended from the nearest trunk.

How curious, Asher thought, that he would again meet a man in the throes of suicide. He naturally thought back to meeting Salim Al-Annan on Dragorn, a true man of honour. And, of course, he himself who had once attempted to end his own life, and not far from this very spot.

He looked again at Russell Hobbs, sure that he knew what was going through the man's mind. He had seen the monster within, could feel it writhing under the surface, a threat to all. With the noose he hoped to end it, to end the killing and bloodshed. More than that, to end the *thrill* of it. In that moment, Asher had never felt more connected to another soul.

"They're going to feel it when they wake up," he announced without preamble, departing his hiding place. He couldn't say why he did such a thing, not when the man he intended to kill was about to save him the trouble.

Still working to secure the rope, Russell didn't so much as flinch, casting Asher no more than half a glance through the wild strands of his grey hair. "I thought you were just going to watch," he replied gruffly. "Take my body back to town and get your reward."

"My reward?" Asher enquired, using their reasonable conversation to close the gap.

"I know what you are," Hobbs said. "*Ranger.* You're here to hunt down the beast." He looked up at the hanging rope. "Give me a moment."

Asher opened his mouth to protest but quickly closed it again. He knew he shouldn't interfere. Unlike Salim, Russell Hobbs was a monster. The fact that he, the man, knew that about himself and wished to do something about it afforded him the kind of honour

Salim was always striving for. He should be allowed to see it through.

After Russell had piled three of Vouder's men atop each other —carrying each as if they were naught but a sack of potatoes— using them as a makeshift stool, he secured his neck within the noose and prepared to kick the bodies from under him. Again, Asher made to speak, to stop what he was beginning to feel was a waste of life. But Russell didn't show the same hesitation that he had, so long ago, when the point of his dagger had been pressed to his chest.

The bodies displaced, the cursed man dropped until his throat took the brunt of his weight. How many times had the ranger observed death? How many times had he looked a man in the eyes from no more than inches and watched his life fade like the dying flame of a candle? Yet he turned away from the hanging, his gaze left to roam over Vouder and his men.

Asher knew what he wanted to do, could feel his body fighting his mind to make it so. *Don't do it*, he told himself.

As he had moved away from the tree without thought, so too did his hand retrieve the folded bow from his back. Muscle memory did the rest, launching an arrow at the taut rope. The sharp tip sliced through half of the rope, uncoiling the strands and its overall integrity. Unable to take Russell's weight for another second, the rope split and the miner fell to his feet, face flushed red.

"What are you doing?" Hobbs demanded, his voice unnaturally strong following the recent strain.

The ranger returned his bow to its folded state and clipped it to his quiver. "You're a good fighter," he remarked, taking in the unconscious forms about them.

"You wish to test your mettle?" Russell questioned in disbelief. "You should have let me finish it."

Asher didn't miss the man's fists knotting into clubs by his side. He wondered if the monster in him had similar instincts to his own, demanding that he survive any and all threats. Suicide was likely his only way to beat the monster after all.

"My name is Asher," he began again, hoping to dispel some of Russell's unease. "You're right, I am a ranger."

"That doesn't explain why we're talking," Hobbs retorted.

"I suppose it doesn't," Asher agreed, confused by his own actions. "How long have you been a... a Werewolf?"

Somewhere beneath the mess of hair, Russell's brow pinched. "You want to know if there are more like me."

"That's not—"

"I am alone," Hobbs declared. "The one who bit me didn't stick around. There was only that poor soul in town, the man of the watch."

"Elias," Asher named.

Russell's features softened. "I didn't mean for... I have no control when the beast emerges."

Deciding he had found a line of dialogue, Asher pulled on the thread. "You remember biting him?"

Hobbs looked away, his attempted suicide put aside for the moment. "I can see pieces," he confessed. "It's like looking in a broken mirror." His eyes flashed amber in the light as he found Asher again. "You killed him."

"Yes," the ranger admitted.

"Then why do *I* still live?" With his question, Russell indicated the dried blood plastered to his bare skin. "I am twice the monster he was. I deserve your sword more than he did."

"I had no choice but to kill him," Asher replied honestly. "He was under the thrall of the moon. He would have killed me and the captain of the watch had I not acted first."

Hobbs raised one human hand. "Do not think my lack of claws ensures your safety, Ranger."

His anger was easy to see, as if a molten wave of rage overcame him without warning. When it flared, when the wolf bared its teeth in Russell's mind, it brought out the fight in him.

How akin they were.

"You say you remember pieces," Asher continued, using his words to distract rather than provoke. "Do you recall the men from the swamp, from the night I killed Elias?" It was all too clear that the man had no idea what he was talking about. "They chased you from the area. There isn't much that can give flight to an uninjured Werewolf."

"I don't know of these men," Hobbs breathed, seemingly pained by any effort to recall the wolf's memories.

"They know you," Asher went on, being so bold as to take a step closer.

"I said I don't know!" Russell fumed, his rage boiling over again.

The ranger held out his hands, palms up to beseech calm. He considered revealing the bronze sphere but the subject felt like a rabbit hole he couldn't afford to go down while the man was so obviously on edge.

Russell shook his head. "What business is any of this to the likes of a ranger?"

"My job is to root out the monsters terrorising Kelp Town, but I can't do my job if I don't know what all the pieces on the board are."

"Monsters..." Russell echoed, examining his own blood-soaked hand. "The word doesn't seem real. None of it does. Like it's someone else's life."

The ranger tilted his head, scrutinising the man before him. "You're new to this, aren't you? These were your first moons."

Hobbs could only nod his head.

"And the wolf that bit you," the ranger probed, "you're sure he's gone?"

Russell swallowed, somewhat dazed by his own introspection. "Yes."

Asher wanted to explore his new origins further but he could feel the precipice upon which they stood. "You didn't want to hurt anyone," he stated softly.

"Of course not!" the miner was quick to reply. "I didn't want any of this to happen!" His anger was spilling out again. "It isn't right! I was just walking home..." He trailed off as his breathing increased and his chest rose and fell with the steady hammering of a dwarven smith.

"When were you bitten?" Asher asked, hoping a specific question would focus the man.

Russell's eyes darted left and right. "Sixteen days ago," he replied, his voice ragged now.

Asher shifted his position so the man couldn't see the hand he had slipped to the dagger at the base of his back. The ranger managed to hide his irritation when he discovered no such weapon, the blade lost to the monster he had slain with it. There were other knives about his person but none that he could comfortably grip without being noticed. If the wolf inside Russell Hobbs decided to rear its head, he would have to reach for the silvyr short-sword and hope he retrieved it before it was too late.

"Sixteen days ago?" he questioned, doubt in his voice. "You weren't bitten by a... It wasn't a *wolf?*"

Russell shook his head. "It wasn't a full moon. He was human. At least, he *looked* human."

The ranger suddenly felt like throwing the bestiary away—it made no mention of Werewolves being able to pass on their curse while in human form.

Putting that aside for the moment, Asher began anew. "It isn't an easy thing to do," he said, looking to the noose still tied around Russell's neck.

"It's harder when someone breaks the rope," Hobbs snapped, his anger now subsided a notch.

"You took to it without hesitation," the ranger continued.

"What of it?"

"Easy," the ranger bade, his fingers flexed and clearly away from any of his weapons. "That you would take to it so easily speaks of your character. The monster may dwell within but it does not rule you. There are not many who can boast of such a thing."

Russell took a threatening step forward. "What is your point, Ranger?"

Asher called on all his discipline to keep his hands away from the hilts of his blades. "I was like you once. I tried to end it to keep my own monster from killing again. I failed," he added, arms outstretched to acknowledge the obvious. "But I use that monster now," he went on, exaggerating the extent of his control. "I use it for good."

Russell's nose crinkled. "Whatever your monster, Ranger, it is not the same that claws under my skin. Nothing good can come from what I am. *Nothing.*"

"*My* monster," Asher countered, inflating the truth to get his point across, "could fill Kelp Town with the dead that already lie at its feet."

Hobbs didn't respond for a breath, his gaze running over the ranger from head to toe. "What *are* you?" he queried, his senses evidently informing him that Asher was no more than a man.

"A ranger."

The answer didn't satisfy Russell, his jaw moving beneath his unkempt beard. "And you... You tried to take your own life?"

"I tried," Asher reiterated. "But in failing I have come to save lives and... avenge those I could not. I see that in you," he avowed. "That potential."

"Then you are blind," Hobbs asserted.

"Sometimes," the ranger admitted humbly. "But there are very few in this world who would take their own life to save others, to save *strangers.*"

Something about the man-made-wolf softened then, his surging rage dampened to a whisper. "Good for you," he replied. "And good for those you have helped. But the monster cannot be stopped. For three nights, *every month*, it will tear its way out of me and kill again. It would already be a safer world if you had left me to swing."

"*I* stopped the monster," Asher stated, referring to poor Elias. "I could stop it again if I had to."

"There is no *if*, Ranger." Frustration ruled the miner's tone. "The wolf will come as surely as the moon itself."

"The next full moon is a month off—we can cross that bridge when we get to it. Between now and then, you could put the wolf to work: do *real* good."

Russell shuffled where he stood. It was only then that Asher realised how incredibly still the man could stand, his every muscle under impeccable control. "*Real good?*" he repeated, as if the words were a fiction. "Even I don't know what real good is, never mind the wolf. For whatever your reasons, Ranger, you're trying to save the wrong man. The wolf cannot be put to work, only unleashed."

"That's not what I saw," Asher commented, sparing the unconscious bodies a glance. "You're stronger than the average man. Faster too. I bet you can smell and taste things even now that you couldn't before. Those are all skills any ranger would kill for. They can be used *against* the monsters of the world."

Hobbs was shaking his head. "You are suggesting what? That I hunt monsters as you do?"

"Well I'm not suggesting you use that strength of yours to mine for Demetrium," the ranger quipped. "If there is a way," he continued, seeing the doubt in Russell's eyes, "then we *will* find it."

"And if there isn't?"

Asher took a breath and slowly lowered his left hand onto the hilt of his broadsword. "I give you my word the wolf will not kill again."

Russell turned away, chewing over the branching decisions that would determine his future—one of which was no future at all. Asher thought he could see it in him though, that spark of life that lived in everyone. The ranger had seen and experienced enough of life to know that everyone wanted to live, no matter how dire things had become. To some, however, the thread was simply more tenuous and harder to grasp. Perhaps, Asher hoped, he had offered Russell something more substantial to hold on to, as Geron had once done for him.

"I've had my fair share of fights in the pits," Hobbs said, "but I know nothing of monsters."

There it was—the spark.

A crooked smile cut Asher's bristled jaw. "You will."

CHAPTER 9
RUSSELL HOBBS IS DEAD

Ice Troll - I am aware that the bestiary has an archive regarding Trolls and their various breeds, but I feel it prudent to give the Ice Troll its own piece of parchment.

Unlike its kin, the Ice Troll possesses a unique exterior that makes them much harder to kill. Most would describe it as jagged ice but, on closer inspection, it is something more akin to crystal. This strange armour seems to grow quite naturally from their skin and is entirely random, creating a distinct appearance for each Troll.

With most believing it to be ice, the majority of hunters have brought fire to tackle the beasts. Do not rely on fire. Their crystal-like hide will not melt to flame.

They have but one universal weak spot: their face. No Ice Troll has ever been seen with the natural armour on their face. A well-placed arrow, if you have the skill, could put the monster down in a single shot.

A Chronicle of Monsters: A Ranger's Bestiary, 12th Edition, Page 39.

Leah Norst, Ranger.

. . .

Seated quite casually atop a smooth boulder, its top dusted with snow, Asher tasted the arakan spices on his tongue before blowing out a cloud of smoke. The ranger thought of Doran Heavybelly every time he lit his long pipe, the habit instilled in him by the surly dwarf. It wasn't often he felt the need for a second opinion, if ever, but the son of Dorain had a way of cutting through the fog with his blunt opinions.

Asher wondered if Doran might have made a different choice. His wonder was soon replaced by the utmost confidence that the dwarf would have slain Russell Hobbs. In fact, he would likely be drunk already, his every coin spent on the finest ales.

Such thoughts led the ranger's attention to his broadsword, resting upright against the rock. From there he found Russell himself, up to his waist in the stream. Big and strong were the two words that came to mind, the muscles in his back akin to the boulders dispersed amidst the stream. His grey-white hair was plastered back and, like his skin, now free of blood.

Damned if it wasn't cold in there. Yet Hobbs had taken to it without any indication that he had even felt the temperature. If they truly could find a way to make this work, the ranger thought, then Russell Hobbs had the potential to be the greatest monster hunter to ever live.

If they could find a way...

Something occurred to Asher then, turning his gaze to the midday sky in contemplation. Despite the ever-lasting chill of The Ice Vales, a clear ocean of pleasant blue had settled over the world. Vouder Stould and his men were some miles away, left to their slumber and inevitable waking pain. But when they awoke, and they would, they would return to town and fan the flames. No one would rest until Russell Hobbs was captured and beheaded.

It all tied in to Asher's musings, leading him back to the behemoth in the glacial stream. "You're going to have to leave your name behind!" he called, turning the man back to him. "Russell is common enough in The Ice Vales, but anyone with the name Hobbs will be investigated by the king's men when they arrive."

Russell shrugged. "It's the only name I have."

Asher drew on his pipe and exhaled again before replying. "What was your mother's maiden name?"

The big man looked away. "I barely knew her," he uttered, his words just audible over the rushing water. "Maybury," he eventually announced.

The ranger took the pipe from his mouth and pointed it at him. "Russell Maybury. That'll do."

There was a distant look in Russell's eyes, a sadness behind them. He had already lost so much about himself and now he had lost something else, a crucial part of his identity.

"Russell Hobbs was a miner from Kelp Town," Asher began. "A poor man from poor beginnings who was unfortunate enough to be bitten by a Werewolf. Russell Maybury was the man who defeated the wolf and walked into the future on his own two feet. Be the latter. Let the past die." It was blunt, but it was all the advice the ranger had for him. It wasn't that long ago, he contemplated, that he wouldn't have said anything at all.

"Russell Maybury," the big man repeated to himself, testing the name in his mouth. "The man who defeated the wolf..."

Asher left him to his thoughts for a moment before adding, "And we're going to have to do something about..." The ranger hesitated before simply waving a hand over his own face and hair. Russell ran a hand through his beard as if he was just noticing it for the first time. "If you're going to *be* someone else, best to *look* like someone else."

Russell was nodding slowly. "As you say."

The water splashed about him as he made his way back to the southern bank of the stream, there to collect the clothes and boots he had taken from the tallest of Vouder's men, though no item fitted him too well. Asher looked away, just as his thoughts wandered away, drifting to his past. The morning's events had played out in a similar fashion to those that took place after his own attempted suicide, six years previously. Only then *he* had been

Russell and Geron Thorbear had been the one to show him a different path.

After dressing himself, Russell sat as still as the dead while Asher took a small blade to his hair and beard. It wasn't perfect but, when he was done, the man behind the mane was revealed, and how different he looked. His jaw was just as strong as the rest of him, and dusted with white bristles. His hair had been cropped almost to the scalp, giving his head more definition and, again, lending to his chiselled features. Besides his stature, there was nothing left of the man he had been.

Asher retrieved the cloak taken from Vouder's man and tossed it to his new companion. "Put this on."

Russell stopped stroking his jaw to catch the cloak. "I don't need it," he said, perhaps unimpressed with its length.

"Yes you do," the ranger insisted. "It's winter in The Ice Vales," he pointed out, his every word bringing forth more vapour. "Consider this your first lesson in living *with* the wolf—you need to blend in. Anyone walking about these parts with naught but trousers and a cotton shirt is going to arouse suspicion."

Russell made a face but he didn't argue. Having tied the cloak about him, a grey and muddied thing, it came to a stop just below his knees. Still, it was better than no cloak at all.

"So, what now?"

Asher met that question with his usual stoical expression. In truth, he was feeling like he had bitten off more than he could chew. The man before him was no man at all. And what a monster he was! Werewolves were creatures of pure devastation, capable of spreading their curse with a simple bite. And when he wasn't the beast he was a damned strong man prone to surges of violence.

Had Geron Thorbear known as much about *him* all those years ago, he might have left him beside that dead Skalagat. Then, what potential would have been wasted. How many lives had Asher impacted since donning his green cloak? With the right guidance, Russell had the potential to do just the same, if not more.

There was an argument to be had, however, that the right guidance would be better coming from someone else. Asher considered his own demons, dark things he hadn't exactly got under control. Why was *he* qualified to guide Russell?

The simple answer—he *wasn't.*

Asher looked to the sky again, his mind calculating the date. There was time, he concluded, if they made tracks that very day. Perhaps that second opinion wouldn't hurt after all.

"Now," he said, answering Russell's question, "we go to Lirian."

Russell looked to the east. "Lirian? In Felgarn?"

"Do you know another Lirian?" Asher asked sarcastically, strapping his broadsword back to his belt.

"It's just... I've never been beyond The Ice Vales."

To a man who had been everywhere and seen everything, that seemed an inconceivable statement. It was, of course, the norm for most of Illian's inhabitants, the merchants of the world being the few known for travelling the furthest.

"There's a lot out there," Asher reported, nodding his chin to the east. "But most of it's just... the *same*. Stay north of The Arid Lands and you won't need to concern yourself with languages. Take a care in the northern kingdom—they think they don't have to pay as much for our line of work. And *never* go to Dragorn. There's nothing there for good men. Or bad men for that matter. Only the worst of the worst thrive on that island."

Russell was nodding along, taking it all in. "Why Lirian?"

"Because it's not Kelp Town," Asher replied bluntly. "Or anywhere in The Ice Vales. We need to leave this region and before the king's men arrive." The ranger started for the tree line, beyond the stream. "Besides, Lirian's winter is better than summer here. You'll love it," he added dryly.

When Russell made to follow him, the ranger stopped and turned to face him. "Your path is that way," he instructed, pointing to an opening in the trees that went further east than the more southern route before them.

"*My* path? We are not to travel together?"

"I have to return to Kelp Town first. My horse is stabled there. Make for the east. When you break the tree line, keep east and make sure The Selk Road stays on your right. Kelp Town should be behind you. Keep it there. I'll catch up on horseback."

A flash of panic crossed Russell's face. "I must return," he uttered, his eyes drawn over the ranger's shoulder. "There's something... I need to go home."

Asher's gaze narrowed on the man. "There's nothing in that house worth your life."

Honest as he was, the lie Russell's mind was formulating was all too easy to see on his face. "I have savings in there, years' worth! I can't abandon it. I had plans..."

"Not anymore," Asher told him. "Those were Russell Hobbs' plans. Hobbs is dead. If you're to make a future for yourself, you have to leave everything behind."

"No." The word was expelled from Russell as a mighty wind might herald a brewing storm. "I *must* return."

"Is it truly coin you seek?" Asher asked him outright, sure that he knew the truth. "Or is it something else?" he pressed, one hand retrieving the bronze orb from his belt.

There was recognition in Russell's eyes, a yearning even. "That belongs to me," he said immediately.

"The creature that tried to kill me for it didn't seem to think so."

Now there was confusion in the man's eyes. "Creature?"

"It might have looked like a man," Asher said, "but it was not one. Something besides *me* has been hunting you. And I get the feeling *this*," he emphasised, raising the sphere, "is the *real* reason for Kelp Town's recent troubles. The creatures I speak of are the same that chased the wolf away and ransacked your home."

"I have no memory of them."

"But you know what they're after," Asher stated, twisting the metal ball with his fingers. Indeed he must, for the man was transfixed by the sphere, as if its bronze exterior held him under some spell. "What is this?"

Russell swallowed, still unable to look away from it. "I don't know," he said flatly.

The ranger took a breath, using the time to analyse the

response. He wasn't lying to him, but he hadn't said the whole truth either. "I don't believe you," he replied, testing the limits of Russell's patience.

"I don't know," he repeated, frustration overruling his even tone now. "I'm telling you the truth. I have no idea what it is. I only know..." his words shuddered to a stop in his mouth, his jaw clamped by some unseen force.

"You only know what?" Asher probed.

Russell's jaw tensed and relaxed and tensed again before he finally managed, "I only know it's important."

"How can you know that?"

Again, Russell fought something Asher couldn't see or hear. "It's important to... *him.*"

Asher paused, absorbing the word and the emphasis Russell had given it. "Him," he echoed, almost reverently. "You mean the one who..."

"Yes," Russell blurted, sweating for the first time.

Seeing how much effort only a few words had on him, the ranger decided to leave the subject of the sphere there. For now. "And the creatures that were looking for it?"

A sigh not dissimilar to a bull's forced its way out of Russell's nose. "I told you, I don't—"

"Know them," Asher finished, hoping to get in front of Russell's anger. "But *they* know *you.* And besides the mob waiting to pull you limb from limb, those creatures are likely still in town, waiting for you to be so foolish as to return." The ranger pointed at the gap in the trees. "So go that way and keep walking. Don't look back. I'll find you. You get this back *after* we meet up," he added, before concealing it within the pouch on his belt.

The moment it was out of sight, Russell Maybury, as he now was, returned to the present. "It isn't yours to keep," he uttered, sounding exhausted.

"It's mine until I say it's yours. Consider it leverage to make sure you're out there, heading *east.*" Again he pointed at the gap in the trees before turning to make his own way. After they had each taken a few steps in their appointed directions, the ranger paused to relay one last, but crucially important, piece of information. "Russell," he called, waiting for the man to stop and face him. "If you're *not* out there, I will hunt you down and finish what you started." In case the point was missed, Asher gripped the hilt of his broadsword.

∽

With a population numbering well into the thousands, re-entering Kelp Town unnoticed was easily done. For the most part, life had gone back to normal, as things must if people were to continue putting food on their table. That didn't stop the talk that had permeated every corner of the town.

Fear had them all in its cold grip.

From the snippets of chatter that Asher overheard, no one had the full story, but everyone had heard something of the night's grim events. It seemed word had also got out that King Gregorn was sending an inquisitor along with a contingent of soldiers, though the number of each varied from street to street, with some claiming half the army was marching to Kelp Town.

Asher kept moving. The only stops he made were to buy supplies from a handful of market stalls and a couple of shops— just enough to see them both to Lirian. Navigating the occasional watchman here and there, the ranger lastly found himself at the stables, where he settled his bill and saddled Hector, adding his fresh supplies.

Leading the horse out by the reins, Asher turned immediately right, taking the street that led to the town's arching entrance and from there access to The Selk Road. He soon found his way blocked, however, and by a single man that stood in the middle of the street, supported there by a dark cane.

"So that's it then?" Captain Lonan demanded, his warm breath breaking the frigid air. "Did you even try to hunt Hobbs down? Or did you just wait a while before doubling back?"

Whatever strange companionship or alliance had been struck between the two men—a bond Asher hardly recognised—it was clear to see that Lonan was taking his quiet departure as a betrayal. The captain of the watch wobbled where he stood, still unsure of his footing while his injured leg protested.

"You've got enough coin to see you on, is that it?" Lonan continued, his stern expression invaded by disappointment. "I thought you were..." The captain looked away, reassessing his choice of words. "I thought you were going to see this through."

"I have," Asher stated gruffly, eager to be on an easterly heading. The wolf was now his responsibility after all.

Confusion and revelation both pinched and illuminated Lonan's face. "You found him? He's dead?"

"I've seen the job through," Asher reiterated, taking purposeful steps, Hector in tow.

Lonan moved to block him all the more, though his wounded leg was slower to follow him and the pain showed through. "What does that mean, Asher?" he spat. "If you have killed Hobbs then why aren't you collecting your reward?"

Asher stopped rather than barrelling the captain over. "I'm not risking another audience with the man who threatened to put my head on the block. It's done. Russell Hobbs is dead. The wolf won't be bothering Kelp Town again."

"I don't believe you!"

"You don't have to," Asher retorted. "But I'm leaving all the same."

"Something isn't right. I know it!"

"Like you said—I've all the coin I need to move on." Asher punctuated his words by nodding at the street beyond the captain.

"What have you done, Ranger?" came the question in his wake. "What have you done?"

"Finished it."

CHAPTER 10
A LONG WAY TO GO

Pixlet - Where the name came from I cannot say, for these little buggers are better known as Kilits in The Arid Lands, where they originate. Still, the name has stuck amongst us northerners.

Now, the first thing you're going to do is underestimate a Pixlet. No taller than your knee and relatively rotund, they are seemingly harmless. Do not be fooled. Their jaws are capable of over-extending and when they do, you won't be able to count all the fangs inside. If you come across one on its own, you might be able to cut it down before it inflicts serious harm, but seldom are they alone. Their packs number in the dozens and they will strip you to the bone.

A Chronicle of Monsters: A Ranger's Bestiary, 12th Edition, Page 96.

Han Gorson, Ranger.

To Asher's relief, Russell had been easy to find, a lone figure beyond The Selk Road and upon the frosted moorland that stretched to the horizon. If anything, he had covered more ground than the average man in the time he had had, a testament to his new stamina.

The ranger had handed over the bronze orb, just as he had said he would. Russell gave it no more than a glance before tucking it away into the satchel he had taken from one of Vouder's men. From there, they travelled on, putting more miles between them and Kelp Town, before deciding to camp within a small patch of trees.

Seeing to the fire, Asher refrained from using whatever magic the black gem gifted him and started it with the flint he had long left in the bottom of his saddlebags. Across the growing flames, Russell sat on the cold ground, awkwardly still, gaze lost to the fire. There was unmistakable amber in those eyes.

Despite Asher's curiosity regarding the orb, which had grown like the flames of the fire since giving it to Russell, the ranger decided to open a different dialogue. "If you're going to make a life of hunting monsters for coin, you're going to have to convince people *you're* not the monster they should be afraid of."

Russell frowned, the muscles in his brow the first to move in some time. "What does that mean?" Already his tone was laced with hostility.

"You don't move enough," Asher told him, stoking both the literal fire and the one within Maybury. "You're so still it's noticeable. Remember your first lesson—"

"Blend in," Russell said, snapping the words off.

Asher didn't react, keeping a calm aura about him. "And you hardly blink," he added.

Russell looked at him with a hard and supernatural gaze before deliberately blinking. "Anything else?"

The ranger didn't flinch away from those steadfast eyes, the eyes of the wolf. "We need to work on your anger."

Maybury's jaw tensed and he finally looked away, one hand clenched into a fist and pressing into the ground. "How am I not supposed to be angry? My whole life has been..." He looked about, as if the words to describe the horrors that had unfolded around him would be there to be found. "I'm not even Russell Hobbs anymore. Or a miner! I've been working mines since I could hold a pick-axe. My home's gone. Hells, I can't even stay in The Ice Vales! And then..." Again, he looked left and right, those amber eyes glassy now. "The people I've killed. The lives I've ruined. That watchman's family." That hard gaze returned, its edges sharp as it homed in on the ranger. "I've got plenty of reasons to be damned angry," he fumed. "And if you could see my thoughts you'd get on your horse and flee."

Asher maintained his posture and peaceful composure a moment longer. "You have a lot to overcome," he admitted. "But if you are to make something of your life, you're going to have to see more clearly the distinctions between you and the wolf."

"What are you talking about?" Russell demanded, looking for a fight.

"Unlike most who have to deal with their monsters, yours has a physical manifestation—its own life that is. You cannot hold yourself accountable for its actions. You are, however, accountable for containing it every month and maintaining control of your impulses in-between."

Maybury was shaking his head. "You don't understand. I can feel it *moving* inside me. Even now I can feel it reaching out, through me, to get to you." He shook his head again and threw a small stick into the ground. "This is pointless. What am I doing here? You should never have interfered! If I was swinging from that tree the wolf would be dead!" He was on his feet now, pacing up and down. "I'm just a miner, a damned miner! What am I doing?" he muttered over and over, his sight regularly going to the trees, searching for a strong branch.

"You're surviving," Asher announced, cutting through the chaos of Russell's mind. "For now that will suffice, but you'll need to learn how to live if you're going to... well, *live*. That will come more easily in time—I can teach you ways to quiet the wolf's voice, its impulses."

Maybury advanced towards the fire. "And what of the beast itself?" he imposed. "Do you have ways to domesticate it too? A leash perhaps? Or maybe you could teach it some tricks!"

Asher looked up at him and sighed. The man had too much fire in his veins and too much noise in his head for the meditative technique he had in mind. There was only one way he was going to burn the fight out of him, rid him of the explosive energy. After that, they could get to real work.

Standing up, the ranger collected his broadsword on the way and tossed it to Russell, over the flames. Before he caught it, Asher had already drawn the silvyr blade from his shoulder and held it casually by his side.

"What's this?" Maybury asked, his irritation increasing all the more with confusion.

"It's a sword," Asher pointed out, using his response as a jibe. "Take it from the scabbard," he instructed, rounding the fire to face him.

His anticipation on the rise, Russell removed the steel with verve. The blade caught the light and flashed as his eyes did. It also looked smaller in his grip.

It was a clear and icy night, but the surrounding pines gave some shelter from the light of the moon, which perched lower to the horizon than its inevitable apex. This protected the shortsword's secret, though Russell seemed hardly the type to care about silvyr.

"We are to fight?" Maybury enquired, and eagerly so.

"We are to spar," Asher specified. "There's a difference."

Russell hefted the sword with ease. "What is the point of this?"

"Many things can be learnt from the practice of combat," Asher went on, moving further away from the fire. "We'll get to all of them in time. Tonight, its only purpose is to run some of that fire out of your blood."

Maybury looked at the sword in his hand. "I think it's going to take more than this."

"I just need you calm enough to use your ears. You need to listen to learn the next lesson."

Russell gripped the broadsword with both hands and braced himself into what felt to him like a natural fighting stance. It was all wrong, of course. His feet were too close together and his weight too firmly planted on his legs, rooting him to the spot. There was every chance, obviously, that his supernatural strength and speed could compensate.

"There are rules," Asher stated, interrupting the man's initial lunge.

"Rules?"

"You cannot loose your grip," the ranger informed him. "You cannot draw blood. You cannot break bone. And you cannot lose your temper."

Maybury appeared more disheartened with every edict. "Then what *are* we to do?"

"It ends when you yield," Asher said pointedly.

"You mean when one of us yields," Russell made to correct.

The ranger gave no response but to square himself against his opponent, short-sword still held low. It was an invitation that Russell gladly accepted.

The distance between them seemed like nothing at all with the speed Maybury used to close it. Asher's own broadsword was coming down on him in no time, a heavy two-handed strike that would do far more than merely draw blood. Still, the ranger wasn't there to greet it, his side step more than enough to see him removed from harm's way.

Strong and fast as he was, Russell's second attack appeared as if it was part of the first, swinging horizontally for Asher's hip. The ranger retreated a step and brought the flat of his short-sword around to bat the steel end away. A quick and calculated backhand had the silvyr blade tap Maybury's arm, alerting him to the wound that could have been inflicted.

"In a real fight," Asher explained, "you would have just lost the use of that arm."

Russell growled and came at him with three successive attacks, the broadsword sent high, low, and wide. Asher dodged the first and deflected the subsequent two, careful not to damage his own sword with the superior silvyr. It infuriated Maybury, and his rage forced him to abandon the sword and thrust out a solid boot. The ranger had seen it coming, the man's footwork all too obvious, and pivoted on one heel while manoeuvring the flat of the short-sword to come up under Russell's ankle. An upwards thrust was all the effort required to push his leg beyond the limits of his balance and flip him onto his back.

To his credit, those unrelenting fingers, so accustomed to wielding a pick-axe, held the broadsword firm. Even his recovery was at an enviable speed and he was swinging the blade round low as he rose to his feet. Asher lifted his right leg instinctively, evading the swipe, before pressing his own attack, and pushing Maybury into retreat.

Quite deliberately, the ranger exposed a gap in his form and baited Russell into thrusting at his chest—an opportunity to overcome his retreat. Somewhere between muscle memory and tactical strategy, Asher's sword arm moved to roll the incoming blade towards his opponent's centre mass before slamming the pommel into the man's wrist. It was a jarring attack designed to flex the fingers and release the weapon.

The broadsword fell through the air, where the ranger's waiting hand caught it.

A swift flick sent the flat of the broadsword into Russell's face, knocking him back a step and into Asher's sweeping kick that took his legs out from under him. Again, the man found himself on his back looking up at the ranger.

The solid blades of grass crunched as the broadsword was plunged into the ground beside Maybury's head. "Again," Asher commanded.

Four more times they collided in what was supposed to be simulated battle. Had any one of Russell's blows actually landed, however, Asher would have been carved in two. There was much work to be done, but the man's fighting techniques and self-control would only improve after mastering his own mind. That began with meditation. And it would have to begin that very night if he was to make progress in the time they had.

"Get up," Asher said for the sixth time.

Russell did so and with notably less anger than previously. "Who taught you to fight?" he questioned, his curiosity surpassing his frustration.

"The same man who taught me to master my mind," Asher replied, and with all the information he deigned to give on his past. "We're done with these," he added, one hand held out for his broadsword.

"But I didn't yield."

"Physically, no," the ranger agreed. "But your head is no longer in it—and that was the point of this exercise." He flexed his fingers in anticipation. The sword returned to him, he sheathed it and returned the silvyr blade to its place on his back before placing both on the ground beside Hector. "Sit," he instructed, gesturing to the fire.

"I can teach you to fight," he began, the two now seated opposite each other, the fire beside them. "But first, I would teach you to fight the wolf. Once you've overcome that, you can learn everything else."

Russell appeared far more uncomfortable now than he had when the sword had been put in his hand. "How do I fight the beast?"

"Have you ever meditated before?"

Maybury made a face. "What's... *meditation?*"

Asher took a breath and took a step back in his plans. Of course the miner from Snowfell had never heard of the elven technique for mindfulness—the wizened scholars of The All-Tower likely hadn't either.

"It's a breathing exercise that will allow you to focus your thoughts," he explained as simply as he could. "This," he continued, one finger pressed to his left temple, "is the only weapon you'll ever have against the wolf. Like your sword arm, it needs training."

Dubious as he appeared, Russell adjusted his position to mirror Asher's, legs crossed. "How does it work?"

The question transported Asher to his earliest years in Nightfall, when he had asked the exact same question of Nasta Nal-Aket. Echoing his old mentor, the ranger said, "Close your eyes. Take deep breaths. With every new breath, you're going to shut off your senses one by one until sound alone is all that remains of the world."

This command took Russell some time, his heightened senses refusing to be silenced. All the while, the moon rose higher and higher and the night colder and colder. Still Asher persisted, keenly aware of the importance of the lesson. One bout of anger in a crowded tavern would end in death for those around the man.

"It's no use," Russell hissed.

"Quiet." Assuming the role of the teacher, Asher couldn't help but think of Nasta again, his master's words returning to him with ease. "Focus your thoughts to that of a pinhead. When you arrive at that point, you realise the pinhead is the top of a well. You must fall into the well."

"What *are* you talking about?" Maybury asked. "How's this nonsense to help me?"

Asher sighed, his fatigue demanding his attention. "We'll try again tomorrow," he announced, suddenly moving to retrieve his bed roll.

"We have to do this again?"

"Every day," Asher replied, "until you don't need me to help anymore."

"I thought you were going to show me the ways of the ranger. Killing monsters and the like."

"You have to walk before you run," the ranger told him, repeating more of Nasta's words from so long ago. "You're no good to anyone if you can't control your rage. And when it comes to *killing monsters and the like*, rage won't help you. From here on out, your life is one of discipline and unwavering control."

Russell remained seated, head bowed in silent contemplation. "I'm just a miner from Snowfell. What if I can't do that?"

Asher lay down on his roll, a blanket added to the cloak he had draped over him. "The day you give any less... will be the day I come for you."

CHAPTER II
WHERE IT ALL BEGAN

Skab - Once referred to as the children of the forest, Skabs are impish creatures that move about the forests via burrows. It has been pointed out to me by my fellow rangers that the latter is merely a theory. Though burrows have been found near Skab sightings, they have never been seen to use them.

There are few reports of these little beasts harming folk. More often than not, travellers complain of belongings being stolen and farmers report missing livestock. Having seen Skabs up close, I am thankful they do not require the blade, for they bear an uncanny resemblance to human children.

A Chronicle of Monsters: A Ranger's Bestiary, 12th Edition, Page 371.

Delken Phen, Ranger.

How history repeated itself, Asher dwelled.

For near on a week he had travelled with Russell Maybury, traversing the cold and dull moorlands of The Ice Vales, and quietly so. Russell was a man of few words, just as *he* had been when making this same journey alongside Geron Thorbear, years earlier. Maybury offered up as much information as Asher had, though Geron's questioning and general chatter had been incessant, a tumultuous barrage of words compared to the few he had voiced since departing Kelp Town.

Still, he was intrigued by the miner from Snowfell and asking questions was the only way to forge ahead. There was every chance, of course, that there wasn't much to learn about him. In any case, Asher had decided early on that it would be better to leave the past where it was and keep their interactions concerned with the future. It was also a good way to avoid any questions regarding his own past.

The days were short by winter's accounting, but each one felt an eternity beside the man, his silence a noticeable void. And he never stopped nor asked for a break or a turn in the saddle. He just kept walking.

Russell should have been the perfect travelling companion as far as Asher was concerned, yet the ranger found himself uncomfortable in the midst of it. He didn't mind the silence when journeying on his own, but an equally stoical companion was hard going it seemed.

More than once Asher found himself wondering if he would have preferred Doran Heavybelly and his testy Warhog.

How the dwarf would bawl with laughter if he knew of such a thing!

And the ranger felt all the more the fool for even pondering it.

Every night, by the fire, the ranger attempted to continue Russell's learning in the art of meditation. Progress was slow, unlike the man's anger, which bubbled up more often than not. Asher had hoped to see better results as they approached civilisation but, as usual, his hope was good for naught.

"How long have you been a ranger then?" Russell asked, breaking the hours of quietude, as they hugged the tall trees of The Evermoore's western edge.

It took Asher an extra moment to register the question. He had been taking in the colour of the great forest and soft moss that clung to their trunks, the tone not unlike his cloak. There was still a world of snow about them, but the realm was truly a different place outside of The Ice Vales and its cursed lands of never-ending cold. The rest of Illian experienced the turning of the seasons, seeing and feeling nature's transitions as they were meant to be. Having spent numerous months in The Ice Vales, entering Felgarn's winter was most welcome.

Russell seemed not to have noticed, a telling thing in itself. Considering he had never left Illian's western lands, Asher had expected him to have some reaction to The Evermoore, a forest that dominated the view from north to south. Or the patches of grass here and there, with shades of green so full of life compared to that which survived The Ice Vales' snows. How deep his mind must dwell to miss the differences.

The wolf was ever-present.

"A ranger?" he echoed, giving himself some time to consider the simple question. "Six years or thereabouts," he estimated.

Russell made a face. "Doesn't seem so long," he remarked.

Asher laughed quietly to himself. "In years perhaps. But the life expectancy of a ranger is half that."

The response actually turned Maybury's gaze up to him. "It sounds like a hanging might be the more peaceful way out," he muttered.

In Asher's experience, there was no peaceful way out, but he kept his pessimistic opinion to himself. "You need to brace yourself for Lirian," he warned, changing the subject.

"How's that?"

The ranger nodded at the road ahead, the worn ground cutting in from the west and intruding on The Evermoore. "It's not like Kelp Town, or Snowfell for that matter. Lirian's a city, a *capital* city in these parts. There's going to be people everywhere, all the time.

Your senses are going to be overwhelmed." Asher thought of the scene Elias had spoken of, when Russell had tried to eat the butcher's raw steak. "Right now," he continued, "the wolf is close to you. We don't know what might set you off."

Maybury shrugged those rounded shoulders. "What am I supposed to do? Stick corks up my nose and in my ears?"

Asher would have given that some consideration if it wouldn't make Russell stand out. "Just stay close to me," he instructed.

"Where exactly are we going in the city?" Maybury asked.

"The quietest place I know," the ranger replied.

Another day was required to follow the winding road through The Evermoore, bringing the companions to Felgarn's capital well into the night. It wasn't quiet. Taverns were plentiful in Lirian and provided the city with almost as much activity as it experienced during the day.

Still, winter as it was, this activity was confined to the taverns themselves, packing them out wall to wall with only a few spilling out into the streets. Asher hadn't planned this for their arrival but was certainly thankful for it. He had envisioned arriving during the day and Russell being pulled in every direction by the scent of food or disorientated by the sheer noise of it all.

As it was, a few drunkards invited the duo to drink with them while a couple of others took deliberate offence to their mere existence. There were no fights to be had, nor drinks for that matter, as both Asher and Russell boasted a gaze few could withstand, even the inebriated aggressors.

Walking beside Hector, reins in hand, Asher spared a glance at Russell as they entered the eastern district. His composure was commendable, better than anything the ranger could have hoped for. Perhaps, he considered, he shouldn't be so quick to underestimate others, but the man had a lot more to prove. Tomorrow would be a very different day.

"What is this?" Maybury asked, his tone relaying just how unimpressed he was.

Asher thrust his chin at the tired door, its green paint in need of a new coat. "Somewhere quiet," he said, taking to the steps that led up to the long porch.

With two hands, he yanked the three boards that had been nailed across the threshold and tossed them aside. The door was locked, likely done so by the notaries—the only people with a spare key. The original key belonged to none other than Asher. Using it now, the ranger opened the door and pushed his way through the cobwebs.

"You have a key?" Russell enquired, following him inside. "Is this yours?" Now he sounded impressed.

"I suppose it is," Asher answered, his eyes cast low to the dark patch that had stained the floorboards for six years.

The ranger waited for Russell to move past him before closing the front door and locking it. Through the dusty square glass, fixed at eye-level in the door, he looked at the stables across the street, where Hector had been secured for the night. Asher had paid the stable master twice the fee by way of an apology for the late hour as well as his discretion.

"What was this place?" Maybury asked, exploring the open area that spread to the right. "It's enormous. You could fit four of my homes in here."

Thinking of the basement and the courtyard out the back, Asher felt that four was a low number. Realistically, they could have fitted double that, if not more, inside. Asher made no comment about this. Historically, his only interest in property regarded his ability to break in and out of it—he couldn't care less about owning it. In this instance, however, it had its uses.

"We can stay here while we wait. It won't cost us anything and there's a fireplace downstairs we can use to stay warm." The ranger gave Russell a second look. "So *I* can stay warm," he specified.

"There's a *downstairs*?" Maybury began to pivot, searching for access. He moved for the first door he found, his steps too quick for

Asher to halt him. Paused in the open doorway, Russell took in the smaller room that sat behind the main area.

Asher knew what he had discovered.

"What is all this?" came the inevitable question.

Asher trailed him into the room, pausing himself to survey the untouched armour, gear, and cloaks, all layered in dust and cobwebs. Without waiting for an answer, Russell picked up one of the vambraces, stretching the cobwebs beyond their limits.

"It's exactly what it looks like," the ranger said wearily. "It's a store room for armour and such."

He had half turned back to the main area when Russell dropped the vambrace on the table and made for the door on the other side of the room. Asher tried to tell him it would likely be locked but Maybury's new-found strength forced the door open, breaking the lock in the process.

The larger man looked back over his shoulder, an apology etched into his expression. The damage done, he walked out into the open-top courtyard with its surrounding roof that extended from the main building. Again, he was taken aback by the size of it, his arms opening wide to take it all in under a starry night.

"You own a damned palace!" he exclaimed, hot breath pluming into the cold air.

Asher hadn't known what to expect, but the empty courtyard had surprised him as much as it had Russell. The last time he had seen these walls they had been lined with all manner of weaponry. Now they were bare, leaving naught but a neglected forge. The ranger chalked it up to the Graycoats, who had overseen the investigation at the time. They had likely decided that a great number of idle weapons were best not left unattended. Who could say what they had done with them?

"Come on," he bade, returning to the interior.

The walls of the staircase were just wide enough to accommodate Russell's wide shoulders. The basement was even grubbier than the main floor and the odour that had taken to the place was nearing on foul. Again, Asher was first drawn to the dark stains that could be found almost everywhere, including the ceilings. That foul stench was old death.

"This is incredible," Maybury complimented, continuing his streak of awe.

He moved out from the stairs to walk among the armchairs and tables that spread out in disarray from the fireplace. It was illuminated by the pale gloom that spilled in through the high and narrow windows on the left-hand wall. A small number of the tables and chairs were broken; simply left where the wood had splintered under the duress of battle and all just as filthy as everything else.

"We can move these," Asher suggested. "Lay our rolls out by the fire."

"What's down there?"

The ranger didn't need to look to know that Maybury was gesturing at the lone corridor off the seating area. It was dark down there, an abyss of death and bad memories where the light of the moon could not tread.

"More rooms," Asher said, his interest diverting to the fireplace.

"*More* rooms?" Russell let his satchel and roll fall to the floor, his sharp eyes taken by that corridor.

Asher wondered if he could see through that thick shadow. Then he saw the man's nose crinkle and knew what his next question would be.

"Is that blood?"

The ranger was amazed it had taken him that long to get the scent. It seemed the miner from Snowfell was completely absorbed by the place. It was also good to know his senses could be distracted.

"It used to be known as *The Ranch*," Asher began, seeing now how naive he had been to believe the topic could ever be avoided. "It belonged to the rangers." He stopped there, suddenly aware that such a tale would require an explanation as to why the rangers no longer inhabited the place. That road led to Nightfall and to the Arakesh who had seen to their demise.

"It feels like there's more to it than that," Russell remarked, glancing at one of the many blood stains.

Asher tossed his bed roll onto the floor. "It's mine now. That's all that matters. Let's get the fire going. You need to work on your meditation before we sleep."

Eventually, the smell of the smoke overpowered the general, and repugnant, odour of the basement and the crackling of the flames offered some ambience to the deathly silence. To Asher, that stillness had felt like the deafening quiet after an execution, and he was all the more thankful for the fire.

"You said wait," Russell pondered, delaying the start of his meditation techniques—deliberately so perhaps. "What are we waiting for? I thought we came here to get away from The Ice Vales for a time."

"Not for a time," Asher corrected, picking up on his wording. "It would be best if you never returned to that part of the world."

"Never?" he repeated, clearly dismayed.

"Trust me," Asher said. "There's more to Illian than The Ice Vales. In time, you won't *want* to return."

Maybury didn't appear convinced. "The Vales have always been home," he breathed.

"Home isn't a place, it's a feeling." No sooner had the words left Asher's mouth than he surprised himself. He didn't know where that reply had come from, though it was obviously a reflex, a reflection of his true feelings.

Russell was quiet for a time, his thoughts his own as usual. "What are we waiting for?" he asked again, recalling the question Asher had sidestepped.

The ranger gave his response some thought, though not because he didn't have an answer, but because he was unsure how to categorise those they were waiting for. "Allies..." he led with, before rephrasing with, "...friends." It felt the more uncomfortable of the two words, but the latter would work better on Russell's nerves.

"Why don't you strike me as a man with *friends*?"

"They're fellow rangers," Asher explained, navigating the question and its obvious answer. "We can trust them."

Maybury's eyes narrowed on him. "Trust them to do what?"

Asher licked his lips and decided to keep some of the truth behind them. "You need more training than the average ranger, more than I alone can give. They will provide other... *perspectives.*" Whether one or both of those perspectives was that Russell Maybury should be slain on the spot remained to be seen.

"More training? I thought you said I was well suited to the job."

"You are, but those natural talents need *honing*. You can't just throw yourself at a monster and hope your strength and speed will prevail."

Russell retreated again as he chewed over his forming future. He definitely possessed that spark to live and, perhaps, more. He had been a different man walking into The Ranch, more animated and intrigued where before he had displayed all the characteristics of a cart being towed. It was a little easier to see now why he had accompanied Asher in the first place. He wanted something more from life, more than a miner's humble life.

"These allies, friends... *rangers*. They're in Lirian?"

Asher removed his fingerless gloves and placed them in front of the fire, where the light of the flames was absorbed by the black gem revealed on his finger. "They will be soon."

Some shadow of alarm crossed Russell's face. "Soon?"

Asher didn't have to ask to know the man was already thinking ahead to the next trio of full moons, three weeks hence. "We agreed to meet in Lirian every second week of Dunfold," he went on, naming the second month of Illian's winter.

"What are we to do in the meantime?"

"You're getting ahead of yourself," Asher told him. "Tonight there is meditation and sleep. Tomorrow will come in its own time." The ranger assumed the familiar position, legs crossed, opposite Russell.

~

Asher awoke to glowing embers, alone in the basement. Alarmed by Russell's absence, the ranger forced aside any grogginess and rose quickly to his feet, one hand reaching out and smoothly collecting the silvyr short-sword as he did so. It was only then that he realised how close to his thoughts the *creatures* were, those who sought the bronze sphere and would kill for it.

Those who even a Werewolf feared.

Noise from the ceiling led Asher up the stairs and into The Ranch's ground floor. His sense of rising dread was immediately dispelled at the sight of Russell Maybury sweeping the dusty floor with a broom. He had even taken down the boards from the windows and cleaned the glass with what was now a black cloth draped over one large shoulder.

"Morning," he said cheerily enough. "I couldn't sleep," he added with a shrug of the broom.

Asher was impressed by the transformation of the long room, though he would have preferred the man to have taken the time to work on his meditation, which was still severely lacking. "Put the broom down. I want to show you something."

After returning to the basement, the ranger claimed one of the long-abandoned candlesticks and lit it using what remained of the burning embers. With Russell in tow, he entered the dark corridor in which there were numerous doors to choose from. The first on his left he walked past, disinterested by the room and its bunk beds. The next had belonged to Rolan Vask, a ranger twisted by his own vision for what their order of monster hunters could amount to. The third door opened into a room he had been more acquainted with. In fact, the ropes that had kept him bound to the wall were still there to be seen in the candle-light. That and the large black stain, the remains of Dunkan the ranger.

"*This* is what you wanted to show me?"

Asher entered the room and held up the candle to the wall on his right, where a thick iron loop had been fastened by bolts. Its twin was equally fixed in place on the adjacent wall. The ranger moved from one to the other, giving them both a strong tug. They would do, he thought, though the ropes would need replacing with chains instead.

"We've got less than three weeks to transform this room," he said.

Maybury studied the three walls he could see from the doorway. "Transform it? Into what?"

Asher looked back at him and saw the amber in the man's eyes. "A prison."

Russell took a moment to absorb the word before looking at the room with a fresh perspective. "It's not particularly big. Isn't the wolf big?"

Having had the opportunity to compare the wolves of both Russell and Elias, Asher wanted to tell him that his own monster was on the larger side. "We need to contain it," he said instead. "The less room for manoeuvring the better. What we need to work on is the structure." Here, Asher rapped his knuckles against the boards that lined the walls. "Behind the wood," he continued, "it's solid enough, but it might not hold against an angry Werewolf." The ranger couldn't help but think back to The Mer Seed, one of Viktor Varga's ships that had been outfitted with a monster hold. "We're going to need to bar the walls with iron. The door too. In fact," he said, having a second thought, "it's likely going to need replacing altogether. Or reinforcing at the very least."

Russell was staring at him intently. "You're serious? You mean to let the beast out in here, in the heart of the city?"

"You'd be just as dangerous out there," the ranger stated, cocking his head to the door. "A Werewolf would be drawn to somewhere as loud and chaotic as Lirian from miles away. At least in here I can keep an eye on you."

Maybury was shaking his head. "Why bring me here at all?" he growled and walked out of the room. "I shouldn't be here. I shouldn't be allowed anywhere *near* here! If I could make a life of this curse—*if*—then surely it could only be in the middle of nowhere, somewhere the beast can be let out and hunt no more than animals!"

Asher followed him out, his face lit from below by the candlelight. "I told you, Russell," he said calmly, "the day you give any less will be the day I come for you. I meant that. You're either going to make this work or I finish the job I was paid for. There's no isolation. No cabin in the woods. No third option."

Maybury looked over Asher's shoulder, his sharp sight cutting through the gloom and shadows to see the details that lay hidden to ordinary eyes. "Three weeks isn't a lot of time to get all that done," he finally said.

"Less than three weeks," the ranger corrected.

～

Beyond The Ranch, the city had awoken just before the late winter dawn and the sounds of coursing civilisation permeated the walls. The business of buying and selling, haggling and trading, was the life blood of anywhere humans put down roots and Lirian was no exception.

Using The Tower of Gadavance—a lesser-known school of magic—as a navigational point, Asher was sure to keep Russell close to his side as they moved through that hustle and bustle. The buzz of it all was clearly overwhelming for the man, his frown seemingly etched permanently into his brow, his eyes darting from face to face, and his hands clenched into knots. It reminded the ranger of his earlier years, a time when his younger self had suffered through the Nightseye elixir.

The wolf, however, was an animal that followed its nose and, right now, that nose was detecting *everything*. Asher caught Maybury licking his lips numerous times, sampling delicacies on the air that the ranger could neither see nor smell. That particular sense was going to get him in trouble.

"Over there," Asher said, tapping the back of his hand against Russell's arm. "The blacksmith's. Go and talk to him, see if he can provide us with the materials we need—we can come back with the correct measurements later."

Seeing the ranger move in the opposite direction, Maybury called out, "Where are *you* going?" Asher turned to face the man but continued moving as he thumbed at the shop wedged into the junction of two branching streets. "Apothecary?" Russell voiced over the general hubbub.

"Just speak to the blacksmith," Asher instructed, turning his back.

The shrivelled old man who ran the apothecary's made several enquiries as to the purpose of the ranger's visit, only meaning to help no doubt, but Asher knew what he needed and found it soon enough. The old man held up the glass vial of safida and pinched his nose at just the memory of the smell. Again, he enquired as to why Asher sought to purchase it and, again, Asher gave no response but to slide the required coins across the counter.

The ranger paused on his way out, taking note of multiple ingredients that he already needed to restock. The bestiary called for every ranger to carry the equivalent stock of an apothecary—an impossible task for a natural nomad—and so Asher did his best to keep a healthy supply of those regularly used ingredients. His fingers danced over a handful of vials and he would have purchased them had he not heard the abrasive neighing of a horse and a subsequent kerfuffle outside. The fork in the road was a busy area, yet he just knew that Russell was somehow involved.

Striding out from the apothecary's, Asher used his hands to gently navigate the passers-by that had stopped to gawp at the commotion. On the other side of the street, outside the black-smith's, a horse and cart had come to a stop, only the horse was far from still, rearing up on its back legs and kicking the air. A collection of sundries appeared to have spilled from the cart and littered the road. Worse still, the owner of the horse and cart—and his two large sons—were confronting Russell, who had been backed up to the wall of the blacksmith's.

With all three men shouting in Maybury's face, Asher was none the wiser as to what had provoked the scene. He gave the irate horse a wide berth and approached the group from the side, again being forced to shove people aside to reach them. Closer now, he could see the veins bulging against the side of Russell's face and up to his temple, his skin flushing. Though still at his sides, his hands were splayed and ridged, reminding the ranger quite specifically of the Werewolf. How long would it be before the monster reared its head?

Asher had barely considered the question when one of the burly sons thrust his palm into Maybury's chest. It was hard to say whether he was moved or not, but the bold young man certainly moved when Russell grabbed him by the throat and spun him round to pin him against the wall. Naturally, his father and brother immediately grappled the man, though neither succeeded in freeing their kin.

The ranger threw himself into the fray, one hand clamping around Russell's arm while the other fumbled for the vial he had recently secured in a pouch on his belt. "Russell!" he snapped, inches from his ear.

"Get off him!" the father yelled fiercely, one hand thumping Maybury's broad back.

All the while, the young man pinned to the wall was turning an unhealthy colour. Asher finally had the safida spices in hand and he quickly removed the small bung with a flick of his thumb before placing the open tube beneath Maybury's sensitive nose. Russell's powerful sense of smell was blasted by the astringent vapours. He blinked once. Then twice. Then he took his first breath for some time. The moment his hand relaxed, Asher tore it from the young man's throat and barrelled his way through the lot of them until he and Russell were further down the wall.

Dazed by his own temper, Maybury wiped his brow and looked about. "What... What happened?"

"Are you alright, lad?" the father was asking of his son, who had slumped down the wall.

"I'm getting the watch!" the other son declared.

Under the scrutiny of so many, Asher could feel his own rage rising to the surface. "What happened?" he demanded, grabbing Russell by the shirt.

Maybury scratched his head and licked his lips. "I was just... I was just saying hello to the horse."

Asher regarded the restless mount, easily the loudest thing in the street. The ranger could picture the scene—Russell reaching out to pet the horse, which, in turn, could sense what he was. A predator. Asher had to wonder if the horse had a better idea of what Russell Maybury was than he did.

Russell was shaking his head. "I didn't... I didn't mean for..."

Asher growled, shoving him back while simultaneously turning to the father and son. "I'm sorry for the trouble," he offered, his feet retreating to trail Maybury.

"Where do you think you're going?" the father fumed, and rightly so. "The watch is going to deal with you!" The man abandoned his son to confront them, stop them even.

For the father's sake and any who arrived to support him, Asher gripped his broadsword and freed the blade just enough to reveal the steel within. It had the desired effect, putting just enough fear in the man to subdue some of his fury and see him advance no further. Wasting no time, the ranger turned on Russell and forced him down the nearest alley, where they could cut through and get lost in the city.

A thick and heavy tension had permeated The Ranch's basement. The crackling fire and Russell's tapping foot filled Asher's ears. In place of Maybury's anger, the ranger's had risen from the depths and threatened to rule him. It was in his silence that Asher fought for control of his emotions, lest he do something rash himself.

"I don't know what happened," Russell muttered, taking to his feet and pacing the room. "It was as if... It was as if I stepped back, beyond my own body. I had no control." His voice was laden with shame and underscored with fear. "What was that, that *thing* you put under my nose?"

The ranger took one last steadying breath before conjuring words, his lips dry. "Safida spices," he managed, to which Russell raised a grey eyebrow. "They're from Karath. Down there they use it to flavour food."

Now the man raised both eyebrows. "Damned strong stuff."

"It's temporary," Asher corrected. "You'll eventually get used to it and, in the heat of the moment, it won't have the same effect. You *need* to learn control," he implored, his own rage cooled somewhat now. "If you can't tame the beast between moons you can't..."

Maybury stopped pacing and turned to look at him. "Say it."

"You can't live among them," the ranger finished, rather than telling him he couldn't be allowed to live.

Russell's hands came to rest on the top of a chair, its wood creaking between his fingers until it splintered. "Just do it," he whispered. "Take me upstairs, out back, and cleave my head from my body. We both know that's where this ends anyway. It was a fool's hope to think I could make something of this. I'm *cursed*."

Asher remained still where he sat, one hand wrapped around the hilt of his broadsword. Had he too not been cursed? The moment his lips first tasted the Nightseye elixir he was doomed to the darkness. Earlier still, he had been cursed to a life of murder from the moment Nasta Nal-Aket found him. For all the life Asher had known, he had been fated to die by the edge of a blade, be it in service to Nightfall or, as the Father himself, being overthrown by some younger, stronger Arakesh who sought his title.

The ranger sighed. Damn the *ends* thrust upon them, he thought. He was living proof that it was possible to forge a new future, to scratch out one's fated end. Yet he knew of only one way to get there and he resented it so.

"Sit," he instructed, the word brimming with all the authority he could muster.

Russell hesitated, perhaps wondering if the ranger meant to execute him right there and then. Still, he moved to sit opposite him, mimicking Asher's folded legs.

"There are many paths to control," he began, closing his eyes and releasing his hold of the broadsword. "I have spent years, decades, learning them all and mastering them, mastering my mind. You do not have that kind of time," he pointed out, though Maybury was already shaking his head.

"Not *this* again. It doesn't work. I'm a miner, not a priest."

"You possess a brain," Asher stated, his frustration seeping in. "That's all you need."

"I'm telling you—" Russell began to reply before Asher cut him off.

"Quiet." The word came out short and sharp. "Begin your breathing exercises." He gave the man a moment before opening his eyes to see that he was doing no such thing. "Master the mind, master the wolf," the ranger explained as simply as he could. He closed his eyes a second after Russell did and dwelled on the mantra, replacing the wolf with the *Assassin*. He was preaching something he couldn't even do himself.

"Now what?" Russell asked irritably, snapping Asher back to the problem before him.

"Quiet," he ordered again, one hand grasping Maybury's wrist, where he might monitor the man's pulse. "Control your breathing. Listen to my voice. I'm going to guide you. Whatever happens," he warned ominously, "you must not lose your focus."

The moment stretched into seconds, then minutes, all to the sound of the fire beside them. Asher knew what must be done—the shortest route to that island. He had hoped to avoid it, that same technique Nasta had employed so long ago. But he could not argue with the results and, ultimately, Russell's life depended upon total control.

"You exist before a darkness," he finally voiced, echoing his own past. "You do not stand, you do not sit. You simply are. Beyond the confines of that darkness exists the body, but you cannot see it, you cannot feel it." Here he paused, allowing Russell the time to fully envision such a thing, to believe it. "Inside that darkness there is something darker still, an abyss that sinks deep down into untold depths. You begin to sink with it." Here came another pause except, this time, Asher snapped his free arm out and slapped Maybury's face. The man grunted, pain and surprise gripping him, sparking that rage.

"Focus," the ranger commanded, feeling Russell's pulse rate increase. "*Use* the pain."

As Maybury exhaled through his nose and closed his eyes again, Asher struck him once more across the face.

"*Use it.* Ride the pain down that well into the depths—take it with you. As you journey down it will lessen."

Slap.

The man's pulse was thundering beneath the ranger's fingers now. "The pain incites anger," Asher continued, "but where you're going there is no anger. Keep clinging to the pain. Hold it tight. You try desperately not to let it go but the deeper you travel down that abyss the more distant the pain becomes."

Slap.

Russell's subsequent grunt turned into a rumble in his throat, the beginnings of a growl.

"Focus," he said again. "You're still dropping down that well, further from your body. Keep sinking."

Slap.

"You're so deep now there exists only conscious thought. You're in a place that does not know pain or fear or anger. You're on an island. Only *you* can exist there."

It wasn't much, but Russell's pulse assuredly began to slow.

"This island will always be there. You must retreat to it in times of need."

Slap.

Asher had expected, if not hoped, that this particular slap would have little to no effect on the man, his island fully realised. Unfortunately, Russell didn't have years in Nightfall behind him and the pain that accompanied every day and night in its black halls. Pain was relatively new to him, though not nearly as new as meditation or the concept of separating his mind from body.

And so he leapt at the ranger.

Indeed, it seemed Russell's mind had retreated, just as it had when confronted outside the blacksmith's. Now, he was all wrath and violent retribution as he collided with Asher and the two wrestled across the floor. While the miner wasted time throwing punches—though the ranger certainly felt them all—Asher used their rolling tangle of limbs to find the right angles. With these angles, he was able to get behind Maybury and wrap his arms around the man's throat, deducing that what both man and wolf equally needed was air.

Clenched in that vice-like grip, Russell lashed out with his thick arms, clawing at Asher's face and head. A tug here and twist there, however, was all that was required to keep any retaliation at bay. He remained, however, exceptionally strong. The ranger was pushed and shoved across the floor in every direction, swept through chairs and tables alike. At one point, Maybury's hand reached out and found Asher's broadsword in its scabbard, the metal guard clattering against the fireplace. The ranger simply kicked out a foot and parted the two before the weapon could be brought to bear.

The conclusion to their brief yet explosive tussle was inevitable. Russell's thrashing limbs slowed as the colour in his face transitioned from flushing red to damning purple. He had held on longer than most. But like all men and beasts, he faded without air.

Asher released the tension in his muscles and let his head fall back to the floor, his face glistening with sweat. He swore profusely. And loudly.

CHAPTER 12
A MONSTER WALKS INTO A BAR

Tilly Wig - These monsters are located in the north east, specifically Longdale. These are the only beasts known to have ever been domesticated. Where they used to be a danger, they are now used to plough fields and cart goods about.
You'll easily spot them, being slightly larger than a bull. That and their horn, a protrusion that shapes most of their head.
It's rare, but these can go wild. When they do, it's guaranteed someone will die. Most of the time, the folk up there know how to deal with them but, just in case, see below for the best traps.

A Chronicle of Monsters: A Ranger's Bestiary, 12th Edition, Page 335.

Hestor, Ranger.

I t was only minutes before the cursed man awoke, and with a thumping headache by the way he was clutching his forehead. He rubbed his throat before his attention landed on the ranger.

Asher was seated on a chair, close by, with his short-sword spinning between his fingers, the silvyr tip worming into the floorboard. For those precious minutes, he had contemplated what to do with that deadly weapon. Whether he was to run him through or not, the ranger had decided he would wait until the man was awake. Seeing him now, he was still conflicted.

"What... what happened?" By the look on Maybury's face, his memories quickly rose to the surface and answered his own question.

"You lost control," Asher articulated for him anyway. "*Again.*"

Russell's jaw tensed. "I told you—"

"I know what you told me," the ranger calmly interrupted, his spinning blade coming to a swift halt, the hilt now firmly gripped in the palm of his hand.

Its movement—or lack thereof—hadn't escaped Russell's attention. "I'm sorry," the miner offered, if half-heartedly. "The pain..." He shook his head as if to clear it of the mess. "When the beast comes, under the moon I mean, there is so much pain. When you hit me it... it was like transforming all over again. It awoke the wolf."

That made so much sense to Asher, though he wished such a revelation could have come to him prior to the attempted meditation. Where pain triggered detachment between mind and body in him, it triggered detachment between man and wolf in Russell. Once he was removed from the equation, there was nothing to stop the wolf from taking over.

A revelation it might be, but it offered no obvious solution to their ongoing problem.

"You're not saying anything," Russell pointed out.

The ranger collected himself, unaware that his thoughts had been carrying him away. "We keep moving forward," he said, the only direction he knew anymore. "I will go to the blacksmith's and see what can be done before the next full moon."

"What shall I do?" Maybury asked, watching Asher rise to his feet and replace his short-sword over one shoulder.

"You should keep your mind and body occupied for now." The ranger looked about their surroundings. "Clean this place up. We're going to need the space if we're to continue your training."

"Continue?" Russell echoed, halting Asher's departure. "So we are to continue then?"

"For now," came the only response Asher could muster.

Winter soon swallowed the day, replacing light with dark. The hours of transition, however, had done nothing to replace Asher's doubts with conviction. He had met with the blacksmith and found little but excuses for why the work would take longer than three weeks and prove more costly than predicted.

Since then, he had walked the streets of Lirian, his feet lost to the by-ways, avenues, and alleyways of the capital city. So too did his mind wander, rarely settling on anything tangible. More than anything, he kept returning to his failures. It had been a mistake to attempt Nasta's techniques, especially on the uninitiated, but more so because they were simply wrong. They were the brutal techniques of killers and though Russell had blood on his hands, he was no true killer.

Despite being a specialist in always finding the best angle, the ranger had failed to see it. Without a viable solution, what life could Russell hope to have? Wallowing as he was, Asher decided to take the next left, well aware of the establishment that sat halfway down the street. There was Sable's Tavern, a perfectly good place to buy food and drink and, if one was so inclined, to find good company, yet to the ranger it was a reminder that, like everyone else, he had blind spots.

Taking a seat in the same booth he had years earlier, Asher recalled the two men who had shared it with him. Dunkan and

Geron. Men he had believed to be one thing but who had turned out to be something else entirely. In truth, he knew looking back that he hadn't seen them for what they really were because he hadn't wanted to. At the time, he had been desperately seeking out something in the world to cling to, something that was as far away from Nightfall as possible. Forcing such a rigid perspective on himself had, ultimately, blinded him. He had vowed since to always see the truth before him, no matter how ugly it was.

So why was Russell Maybury still breathing?

What did he think he was achieving by saving him?

These questions circled his mind while he sipped the forgettable drink and consumed the tasteless meal. So absorbed was he by his own thoughts that, at some point in the evening, he had stopped scanning every face that entered and departed Sable's Tavern. It was this slip that prevented him from noting the man before he was seated in the booth opposite him.

Every muscle in the ranger's body stilled. His left hand, hidden beneath the table, enveloped the hilt of a small knife strapped to his thigh while his right hand simply touched the knife resting on his empty plate. His broadsword stood against the booth, just behind his shoulder—an awkward reach—while his silvyr blade stood on the bench beside him. It was easier to grab but was sheathed.

Appearing far more relaxed, the pale man tucked one lock of blond hair behind his ear and offered an easy smile. "If it would make you feel better," he said, voice as smooth as silk, "you may take one in hand. But I warn you, Ranger, if you must make a scene others will die before you do."

Asher followed the gaze of those cobalt eyes to the many patrons that had packed out Sable's Tavern in recent hours. Among them, however, he discovered faces equally pale to the one who shared his booth. Male and female, they all looked back at him, angular faces of unquestionable beauty.

"This is yours, I believe."

The ranger was drawn back to the table, where the stranger had laid down a familiar curved dagger and pushed it towards him. Asher hadn't seen it since burying the weapon in the fiend that had attacked him in Russell's house.

Asher didn't reclaim it immediately, unsure if it was a trick.

"I would ask who you are," the ranger said, his voice all the more gruff by comparison, "but why don't we start with *what* you are."

A tight but knowing smile cut through the chiselled marble of that pale face. "We're complicated," he replied cryptically.

"I kill monsters for coin," Asher stated evenly. "I like to keep things simple."

The stranger twisted his lips in amusement. "Hmm," he mused. "Well I'm a *monster* and you're *food*. Too simple?" he asked, naught but amused by Asher's hard stare.

The ranger nodded along pleasantly enough. "That's one way of looking at it. Another way would be: I'm the *hunter*, you're the *prey*."

A melodic laugh escaped dark lips. "Trust me, dear Ranger, after eight hundred years of sinking my fangs into your kind, I know *prey* when I see it."

The stranger's eyes appeared dark now, and fixed on Asher as if he was the only thing in the world, though it did little to unnerve the ranger, even if he had a clue as to what he was dealing with. Turning to his right, he scrutinised a handful of those pale faces again, seeing them anew. How could he have been so foolish? Had he hunted so many vile creatures that he had forgotten that not all of them wore hideous guises. Talk of fangs, their insipid complexion, a distinct beauty about them, and only at night had he encountered them.

"Vorska," he uttered with disdain, eliciting another smile from the stranger.

"Gorgers, Vampires, Blood Fiends. Now... *Vorska*. Give it a century or two and we'll be known by another name I'm sure. Personally, I prefer to go by *Merith*."

Asher's mind had already returned to the bestiary, having tuned Merith out. Naturally, he recalled weaknesses and means of execution first.

Merith chortled, returning the ranger's attention to him. "Humans! Your thoughts are so predictable. Right now, for example, you're trying to remember all the ways you can kill me. Hmm?" Asher said nothing, the promise of death there to see in his eyes alone. "Yes," the stranger purred. "Well let's move things along, shall we? You *can't* kill me. Or any of us for that matter."

"You wouldn't be the first to make such a claim," the ranger declared.

A dead smile settled on the creature's human face, never quite reaching his extraordinary eyes. Clasping his fingers on the table top, he said, "Don't think that killing a filthy Werewolf—and a *baby* wolf at that—qualifies you for the job of facing *my* kind."

It was Asher's turn to offer a tight but knowing grin. "You come in here and sit at my table like you know me, as if this is some show of power—a predator stalking its oblivious prey. But you don't know me at all, do you?" Still smiling, the ranger confidently retrieved his dagger. "When we're done here, you and yours will be just another name on a very long list."

Merith's eyes gave an almost imperceptible twitch. "Don't be so sure, *Asher*. I've already learnt so much in the time we've shared this quaint little booth." The creature's nose crinkled. "Like me I'd say you're something of a *complication*."

"I thought I was just prey."

"What you are is just a *man*. Yet..." Those predatory eyes narrowed on the ranger. "It takes something ancient to recognise that same trait in another, and you smell..." The creature paused, inhaling Asher's scent again. "You smell older than *me*. There aren't even Vorska older than me."

Despite understanding every word the creature used, Asher didn't understand anything he said. "It sounds like your mind is beginning to slip in its old age—"

"And your blood," Merith went on, speaking over him. "It's different." Licking his lips he added, "Impure even. Yes," he said, encouraging his own investigation. "I can feel it beneath that parchment you call skin. You have a touch of magic about you. Something in your blood that shouldn't be there. You're human, of that I have no doubt. But you're also... something *else*. How intriguing."

"I didn't realise your kind killed their prey with words," Asher told him dryly.

A tired smile overcame the creature. "Forgive me. After so long, it's rare to come across a sheep that stands out from the rest. Perhaps I will make you one of us," Merith pondered aloud. "Then your secrets will be mine."

"Why are we even talking?" Asher questioned bluntly, itching to get to the fight.

The creature sat back against the booth. "I suppose it is rude to play with one's food. We can probably chalk it up to curiosity. What man, nay *ranger*, takes in a Werewolf instead of slaying them? I was astonished to discover your scents outside of Kelp Town, moving *together*. I just *had* to meet the man," he said, arms outstretched. "And you haven't disappointed me. You are a conundrum. Had I the time I would unravel the mystery that surrounds you but..." Merith glanced out of the window, its corners packed with fresh snow. "It's a first in my long life but I *am* running out of *time*. Which is why I felt it expedient, if not prudent, to remove you from the equation. I really must have that *orb*."

Asher's lips slowly parted, the truth of the matter dawning on him as he too looked to the window. "Russell," he whispered to himself, though it didn't escape the Vorska's ears, a wicked grin stretching the monster's pearly cheeks.

"He has likely been flayed by now with all the time my kin have had."

In one motion, the ranger collected his silvyr blade and broadsword and bolted for the tavern door. He was given pause as he reached the threshold by the very same Vorska he had left for dead in Russell's house, a dagger lodged in his skull. The Blood Fiend gave Asher a short bow, a promise of sorts that they would conclude what they had started in Kelp Town.

Only seconds later and Asher had left Sable's Tavern and its monsters behind, his feet racing through the snow that had recently settled over the city. He skidded round every corner and shoved any and all aside who found themselves in his way. But, all the while, Merith's words lingered in his mind like a poison.

"You can't kill me. Or any of us for that matter."

Having seen that last Vorska on his way out, Asher was inclined, if reluctantly so, to agree with the beast. He would have given it more thought had The Ranch not come into view, a dark and uninviting block between the warm glow of the houses around it. Having clipped his weapons to his person mid-run, the ranger freed the silvyr short-sword from over his right shoulder, the rare metal creating a high-pitched scraping sound as it tasted the winter chill.

He ran for the short steps, preparing to leap up to the porch in a single bound, when he heard a short sharp hiss from the adjacent alley, beside the stable. Halted in the road, Asher looked back and discovered the cumbersome frame of Russell Maybury peering out from behind a stack of crates. With a glance back at The Ranch, the ranger made for that same alley and sank into the shadows.

"They're inside," Russell breathed, his gaze fixed on the building.

Asher did his best to steady his breathing before responding. "Why aren't you inside?" he whispered.

"Needed to clear my head. Went for a walk."

The answer didn't best please the ranger, especially since the man had gone for a walk without his cloak in the freezing dead of night. "You were supposed to stay inside," he rasped.

"If I had would I still be alive?" came Maybury's reply. "I arrived back as they entered," he explained. "Saw them drop from the rooftops. They aren't human."

Asher let some of the tension ease in his jaw. "You're not wrong," he said, reassessing their next move. "We can't stay here tonight." The ranger felt the coin purse hanging from his belt, fingers deducing his current wealth. "We'll find an inn. Return in the morning."

Russell frowned in the dark. "What difference will that make? It's abandoned—they could just wait in there until we return."

Asher was shaking his head. "Trust me, they won't be

anywhere near here by sunrise. Come on." The ranger hesitated, turning back to his companion. "Do you still have it? The orb?"

Maybury touched the largest pouch on his belt. "I do."

Asher nodded his satisfaction and made for the other end of the alley, putting The Ranch behind him.

CHAPTER 13

DIGGING IN

Crownling - *No larger than a dog, these beasts might seem hardly a challenge, but beware ranger for, with jaws like a warthog, their bite can break bone and sever limbs. With that in mind, it will only take a single bite to take you out of the fight. If you can't defend yourself, the rest of the pack will descend and tear you to pieces.*
Since their back is lined with jagged rock, you will have to target their sides but don't rely on arrows for they tend to annoy them more than anything.
See below for known poisons and traps.

A Chronicle of Monsters: A Ranger's Bestiary, 12th Edition,
Page 159.

Baigan Ruun, Ranger.

aving had no sleep, Asher's sense of anticipation dimmed as he watched the dawn brighten the world. It was not chance that he observed such a thing through the window of The Jolly Rotten, for the ranger had chosen the inn above all those they had passed.

Strategically, it was well placed being near the southern road, a path that would take any traveller away from the city. It was also the tallest building on the block, giving him a good view from any room of the surrounding area and preventing anyone from invading the inn via the rooftop—a method of infiltration he and every Arakesh was well versed in. It helped too that the owner possessed a dog that barked at everyone who entered.

There was one last reason he had made directly for The Jolly Rotten, though it was yet to prove useful.

Leaving his room, partly guided by the smell of hot food, Asher walked along the hall that overlooked the tavern floor. There he spotted Russell Maybury, seated on a stool by the bar. He appeared to be in deep conversation with the owner, who was serving the miner a plate of something steaming. Only one of the tables was occupied, though Asher quickly sized them up as being no more than another patron, and not a threat.

Making his way down the stairs, the ranger overheard some of what Russell and the owner were conversing about. "That's a lot of kegs," Maybury was saying.

"Time of year," the owner replied casually enough. "Different seasons bring different customers."

"And your supplies," Russell probed, "they're all sourced locally?"

"More or less," the owner said happily.

Despite their conversation being quite light, it seemed to Asher that Russell's interest was more than piqued. Their talk came to an end, however, when the owner nodded at the ranger over Maybury's shoulder. He busied himself further down the bar as Asher took the stool beside his companion, offering no more than a friendly nod at the ranger's order of Velian tea.

"You haven't slept," Russell commented. He frowned at his own assessment. "I'm not sure how I know that. Something about the way you smell."

Asher naturally looked to the owner, who was trying his best to appear disinterested. "Always take a booth," he said gruffly, getting up from his stool. After Russell had joined him, he tapped the wall at the end of the booth. "Always assume there's someone coming for your back. You need to learn to narrow your vulnerabilities."

"You know," Maybury began, stabbing a piece of bacon with his fork, "sometimes you sound nothing like a ranger."

"I didn't realise you'd met so many of us to know," Asher quipped.

Russell chewed his bacon, eyeing the ranger all the while. "You said you've been doing this for six years. So you've spent a lot more time doing something else," he concluded, leaving his statement to sit between them.

Asher didn't take the bait. "There's a very good chance," he said instead, "that the Vorska detected our scent outside The Ranch and now know we're here. Why they didn't attack I cannot say, but we should assume they will try again come nightfall."

Maybury had stopped eating. "*Vorska*? What in the hells is a Vorska?"

Asher had spent some of the night reading and re-reading the bestiary to confidently answer such a question. "They're monsters," he put it simply, laying the foundation of all else he might say. "They've been preying on humanity for..." The ranger considered Merith's boast of eight hundred years. "Well, for as long as human history stretches."

"You have dealt with them before?"

"No," Asher admitted. "I met my first in your house in Kelp Town, then again last night, in Sable's Tavern."

"They attacked you in a tavern?"

The ranger wished they had. "No," he said. "They were trying to keep me away from The Ranch, from you."

Russell sat back, his attention set adrift for the moment. "The orb," he voiced.

"They want it," Asher reported, going on to inform his companion of the Vorska, Merith.

Maybury had let his food go cold, one hand cupping his bristled jaw. "He's out of time... What do you think he meant by that?"

Asher had given the Vorska's words more thought than he cared to admit, but he was yet to understand most of it—including the remarks concerning himself, specifically his age. And it had been most disturbing that the fiend could detect the presence of the Nightseye elixir in his blood without even tasting it.

"I have no idea," the ranger told him honestly. "Can I see it?" he asked, deciding a question to be the better approach.

Russell swallowed, the veins on his neck making themselves known. "Yes." The word broke away from his mouth, though it seemed he would have preferred to dwell longer before releasing his answer. The moment that stretched between them felt an eternity before he placed the bronze sphere on the table. It caught the morning sun that filtered through the windows, the light accentuating the three bands of ridged metal that circled the orb.

With deliberate caution, Asher slowly pushed his hand across the table until his fingers could clasp around the artefact. With equal caution he drew it towards him, never once breaking eye contact with Russell. He waited a further ten heartbeats before tearing his gaze from the man and pivoting his attention to the sphere in his hands. Examining it in the light now, he could see the intricate patterns etched into the surfaces on either side of the bands.

As he had upon first discovering the artefact, the ranger fiddled with the bands, twisting them one way then the other. Nothing happened of course. And, as much as he turned the whole thing over and over, he found nothing to suggest what purpose the orb served.

"This was hidden in the wall of your house," Asher stated, his tone more delicate than usual. "Put there by you," he added as a fact. "You said it's important." Here it became clear that Russell's discomfort was reaching new heights. "Important to *him*," Asher pressed all the same. "I'm going to assume you were talking about the one who bit you. Which leads me to believe he either gave it to you or you already had it. A poor miner from Snowfell doesn't strike me as the kind of person to possess whatever this is. So he gave it to you..." He let his words go, waiting to see what Russell's reaction might be. By his uncomfortable shifting, the ranger assumed the latter to be the truth.

Asher felt urged to question the man about the wolf who had made him, cursed him, but it seemed the subject was a volatile one. That didn't mean there weren't angles to exploit.

"Tell me about that night," he said. "The night you were bitten."

Russell visibly relaxed, fronted by no barrier where his human life had been concerned. "It was like any other," he began, voice dry. "I had been working the mine all day. I was damned tired but I still made it to The Gauntlet. Had a few drinks. Played a game of Galant." The larger man shrugged. "Nothing I hadn't done a hundred times before."

"And you walked home alone?" Asher asked, returning the bronze orb to the table.

Maybury watched the ranger's hand until it was firmly on his side of the table again, leaving the sphere to be collected and concealed without a word of acknowledgment. "I walked home on my usual route," he continued, one hand resting on the pouch that held the orb. "I would always cut through the alley between Hoburn and Kranik. Never had trouble in those parts before."

Russell paused, his memories reaching the point at which he was forever cursed and, apparently, placed under some kind of thrall.

"I heard someone running," he said at last. "I turned around but they were already half way down the alley. He was *fast*. I was off my feet and on the ground before I knew what was happening. I was powerless beneath him," he uttered. "I'd never known strength like it. Without a word he..." Russell unconsciously rubbed his right arm, just beneath the shoulder. "He *bit* me. It wasn't even for very long, or deep even. But it was enough."

"It's the saliva," Asher interjected, voicing what he had read in the bestiary. He immediately felt like he had spoken out of turn and informed Russell of something he didn't need to know right there and then. "Sorry," he offered meekly. "Continue."

Russell wiped a hand down his face, haunted by his own memories. "As he climbed off me," he began again, having lost some of the timbre in his voice, "he stuffed something into my pocket."

Their conversation came to a pause here, their private words interrupted by the owner who had brought Asher's Velian tea. The ranger thanked him and dragged the tea a little closer so he might pour in the small pot of honey that had come with it. He stirred it gently while he waited for the man to find his way back to the bar, beyond earshot.

"When I got home," Maybury continued, "I discovered the orb. I didn't know what it was. I put it aside for the night. Hells, I think I passed out. The next day, when I saw it... I just *knew* I had to hide it. I *knew* it was important."

"Did he say anything?" Asher enquired, going back a step.

Russell shook his head. "He just ran. I remember looking up at him though, before he vanished. He was covered in blood. I think some of it was his."

The ranger could see the pieces slotting together, even if he didn't understand why they slotted together. "The Vorska wanted it," he deduced, one finger tapping endlessly against the table top. "The wolf had it. They were chasing him when he ran into you." Asher glanced at the pouch on Russell's belt. "He needed to hide it. So he hid it in the most unlikely place."

A hard edge was creeping over Russell's features. "He *cursed* me," he said quietly, deliberately, "just so I would hide it for him?"

Asher sipped his Velian tea as he circled that same question. "He didn't say anything to you," he pointed out, "yet you appear to possess some kind of *built-in loyalty*. You struggle to talk about him, about what's *important* to him." He could see his last line of dialogue had cost him the precious angle. Russell's hands had come to grip the edge of the table, paling his hairy knuckles. "I've never seen two... *species* interact like this," he said, pivoting slightly, and careful not to use the word monster while talking to his afflicted companion.

"Like what?" Russell asked, the words expelled as no more than a rasp.

"Like they're at war," the ranger replied.

Fingers more accustomed to wielding a pick-axe pressed into the pouch, feeling the curve of the metallic sphere within. "What could it be that they would fight over it?"

Asher sipped his tea some more, though he barely noted the honey or mint, his mind working furiously beneath his calm exterior. "I don't know. But I'd bet it's nothing good."

Maybury nodded in agreement though his mind appeared elsewhere. "They went to the effort of keeping you out of the fight," he said, his thoughts cast back to the beginning of their conversation, "yet they didn't try again last night. Is it possible they haven't tracked us."

"If they can track us from Kelp Town to Lirian," Asher asserted, "then they can track us the short distance from The Ranch."

"So why not try to take the orb?"

The ranger gave something of a shrug. "Could be they felt they were too exposed here. Vorska are secretive creatures. It's in their nature to go by unnoticed. Or," he added, and ominously so, "something scared them off."

"Like what?"

Asher eyed the man over the rim of his cup. "Nothing good," he echoed.

Within the hour, both men were returned to The Ranch. With weapons in hand they searched every corner of the building, a scouring that eventually brought them to the largest room in the basement. Like everywhere else, it bore the marks of death, and a bloody one at that.

Asher could still envision Hanaghan, his small body sprawled across the sharp antlers of a Skalagat's decapitated head. The stench was especially foul in that long chamber, the odour of death mixed with the plethora of potions and elixirs Hanaghan had once brewed and stored in there. There remained not a trace of his work now, save the vast table that occupied most of the space.

The ranger moved his torch out to the wall, stretching the shadows of the alcove that had been carved out of the stone. Russell's eyes flared their exotic amber as the flames passed over his face, an abrupt reminder that he shared the room with a monster, even if it was hiding beneath his skin.

"I just can't believe the size of this place," Maybury announced, all thought of their ongoing predicament forgotten for the moment. "You could do so much with it."

"Hmm." The guttural response was all Asher had to offer on the subject. "Let's put that strength of yours to good use," he finally said, tapping the hard wood of the table with the tip of his silvyr blade. "Break it down into usable boards."

"Boards?"

"We only have until nightfall," the ranger reminded. "Before then we need to fortify this place. All the doors need boarding, and the windows you exposed."

"We're digging in?"

The ranger didn't answer right away, fighting his own instincts that commanded he stay on the move. "When the moon comes you're going to need containing. This is still the best place to do that. We just need to kill a few Vorska first."

Russell chuckled. "Is that all?"

What followed was a long and arduous day, for Asher at least, who was working without sleep. Maybury broke down the table and hammered boards until dusk with not so much as a drop of sweat to show for it. The ranger had helped with the labour, including making the trip for the relevant supplies to see the job done. Besides that, he had spread small shards of glass from a broken bottle on each side of The Ranch's front door. They would do nothing to prevent a Vorska from entering the premises, but it would alert them to the intrusion.

While Russell never complained about the dark, his supernatural eyes now sharp enough to pierce the abyss, Asher decided it better to ignite all the torches on both floors of The Ranch, lest the demons sneak through the shadows. More than once he considered the blindfold on his belt. Though it was no more than a strip of fabric, it was more akin to a reaching hand that clawed at him from his past. In the end, he had decided to leave it knotted around his belt. One less monster inside those walls could only be a good thing.

Then they waited.

Winter's early veil blanketed the realm in darkness, hiding even the stars and the moon with rolling clouds that would deliver yet more snow. Sticking to Asher's strategy, the companions had sealed themselves downstairs, where the fire could keep them warm and, more importantly, where the stairwell would funnel their enemies.

The hours rolled on in much the same manner as the clouds; slowly, endlessly. Asher had paced, checked his weapons individually, meditated, paced some more, and, finally, checked his weapons again. At last he gave in to the day's fatigue and allowed himself to lie on his roll, eyes fixed on the ceiling. He imagined the floorboards creaking above, alerting him to an intrusion. There was nothing. Even Russell's keener senses detected nothing.

"Why are they not coming?" the miner asked, his words the first to pass between them in hours. "They hunted us across the country. For the love of Atilan, they even hunted the *wolf*!"

Asher heard every word despite his mind dwelling in the memory of meeting Merith in Sable's Tavern. Russell was right— the Vorska were fervent in their hunt of the mysterious orb. That *need* had been clear to see in the ancient Blood Fiend.

"Are they hoping we will lower our defences if they wait?" Maybury questioned as he tried to peer between the edge of a board that covered the high and narrow windows.

"They don't need us to lower our defences. They have the numbers."

"Then where *are* they?"

The ranger didn't have an answer to that, though he did lift his head enough to spy the man. "Do you sleep?" he asked abruptly.

Russell hesitated with his reply. "Yes," he said, if unconvincingly so. "But not every night. I don't get as tired as I used to, when I was... *human.*"

Asher could see that he was on the very edge of some existential crisis where his identity was concerned, but damned if he wasn't exhausted. "You can keep watch then," he told him. "I'm getting some sleep. Wake me if you see a monster," he added casually, before his eyes closed and rest finally claimed him.

CHAPTER 14
SECOND OPINION

Xigerat - A reptilian beast to be sure. They stalk rivers, preferring fresh water, though some claim to have seen them in The Adean.
From head to tail you're looking at a monster of ten feet. They aren't a common threat, living mostly on a diet of river life, but they have been known to wander beyond the banks and attack humans.
They can do so on four limbs but be warned, when it comes to challenging them, they rear up like a bear on their back legs. That's a wall of muscle, claws, and razored teeth in your face.
There are no known poisons or even traps that lure them in. I'm afraid this is a good old fight with an equally good length of steel.

A Chronicle of Monsters: A Ranger's Bestiary, 12th Edition, Page 329.

Sham-Vet, Ranger.

The next morning was spent undoing some of the previous day's work, if only so they could leave The Ranch. Asher walked down the short steps and onto the road, where his gaze turned skyward, to the clear blue that had replaced the dark clouds. His hot breath spoiled the frigid air about him and he welcomed the cold as it filled his chest. At least it was fresh.

He looked back at the dreary building, glad to be walking away from its lingering malodour, for now at least. Hungry as they were —and somewhat fatigued by the anticipation of the uneventful night—their plan went no further than returning to The Jolly Rotten for breakfast. The ranger took solace in the fact that the Vorska posed no threat while the sun reigned, a small yet crucial reprieve when dealing with their kind.

"What's all that about?" Russell asked, unnecessarily directing Asher's attention to the mob that had gathered about the street ahead.

Skirting around the edges until they found a good viewing point, the companions looked upon the wreckage of what had once been a bookmaker's shop. The city watch were urging people to stay back but Asher could still see the damage between them. It seemed the wooden pillar that had supported the corner of the first-floor building had been snapped—and by something powerful at that—causing a portion of the first floor to break away and crash into the street, taking with it much of the shop front.

"A storm," the aged man beside the ranger was muttering. "Got to be a storm."

"What storm?" another scoffed. "Weren't naught but a drizzle of snow last night."

The ranger returned his attention to the wreckage. He decided that both men were correct—there had been no storm and yet the damage could only have been wrought by such. A storm of what then? he pondered. It was too much of a coincidence that a whole nest of Vorska had infiltrated the city. Asher sighed, the pieces failing to go together.

Nudging Russell's arm, the pair moved on and continued

across the city. Only two streets away from The Jolly Rotten, however, and the duo had cause to halt their journey once more. Another mob had crowded the head of an alley, each person vying to see over the one in front. The billowing cloaks of the city watch could be seen amidst the people, their clipped orders commanding space be made.

"Now what?" Maybury voiced.

Asher had a bad feeling, as if a cold hand had reached into his gut and clenched. "Wait here," he instructed.

Walking away from the mob, the ranger rounded the block, where the other end of the alleyway had been bricked up years earlier. He naturally garnered a look or two as he sprang from crate to ledge, his right leg rolling up to find purchase before his hands continued the short climb. Here the lowest of the roofs slanted, allowing Asher to crawl up the rest of the way and surreptitiously peer down on the alley floor.

The city watch crowded the other end, preventing the onlookers from getting a good view, though two of them stood over the body that had caused all the fuss to begin with. Asher tilted his head to see the dead woman face to face. She was partially covered in snow, her body frozen by both the cold and death. Still, she was paler than perhaps she should have been, as if the life had been drawn from her, leaving a figure of marble behind.

Not drawn, the ranger corrected himself. *Drained*. It was hard to see with the distance between them and his awkward angle atop the low roof, but he was sure he could see a dark purple mark on the woman's neck.

"Vorska," he muttered to himself, before sliding down the roof and jumping back onto the street.

He soon reunited with Russell and informed the man of his findings, all the while ushering him to move on. He also opined that the creatures were being sloppy, as the bestiary described them as meticulous killers in both provocation and discretion. Again, the pieces weren't slotting together, adding to the ranger's mounting irritation.

Rounding the last corner, The Jolly Rotten came into view, its white face and black beams standing out against the forest behind it. Only feet away from the front door, Asher and Russell paused to the sound of some ardent disagreement. A second later, that disagreement turned violent. Glass was smashed. Wood shattered. A blow landed true, underscored by a pained grunt. It seemed Russell had a better understanding of what was taking place inside the inn, sweeping one hand across the ranger's chest to move him aside.

The door exploded open, preceding the man that staggered and fell into the street.

"Say it again!" came the angry growl from inside.

And there it was, that familiar voice and the last reason why the ranger had made directly for The Jolly Rotten.

Asher didn't even realise he was smirking as he entered the establishment. The gloom felt oppressive compared to the clear winter's day, but the ranger's eyes quickly adjusted and discovered two other men, one of whom was crawling on all fours, blood oozing from his mouth while one hand cupped his crotch.

The other was firmly in the grip of a dwarf.

"Say it again!" Doran Heavybelly commanded, pulling the man closer by his collar so that he might feel the son of Dorain's hot breath on his face.

Asher quietly moved around the dwarf's field of vision and covertly removed a handful of coins from the son of Dorain's saddle bags, left draped over one of the chairs before their argument had turned physical. He placed two of the coins flat on the counter and pushed them towards the owner, who had shrunk in demeanour, his back pressed to the wall behind the bar.

"For the door," Asher said, his voice no more than a hush.

"Say it again!" Doran bellowed.

The man in his grasp swallowed, eyes pleading. "Bearded... *Bearded gnome*," he managed.

Heavybelly's teeth clamped together in a tight and seething hiss. "Ye've caught me at the back end o' a long journey, laddy! On a good day I'd normally jus' throw ye a spankin' an be on me way, but me belly's empty an' me tongue is awfully dry, so I'm to be enjoyin' this..."

Asher shuffled the dwarf's coins in his hand and placed another two on the counter. "For the table," he assured.

Right on cue, the son of Dorain dragged the man by his collar and forced the side of his head upon the nearest table, breaking two of its legs in the process and toppling it under his opponent's weight. Three teeth were also sent skittering across the inn floor.

One table over, the man who had been crawling away had found his reserves and managed to stand. He noted his friend on the floor and took more offence, his face screwing up into a mask of rage—as if such an emotion would see him overthrow Doran Heavybelly, or any dwarf for that matter.

The son of Dorain spat on the floor and snorted. "Slow learner, eh? I've got somethin' for that," he added, and grinned.

The foolish man advanced and threw a punch from so far away he might as well have verbally declared his intentions. Doran bowed his head at the last moment, providing his opponent with a skull that had often been compared to stone. Keen ears would have heard not one, but two knuckles crack upon impact. The sharp yelp that followed seemed unavoidable, that mask of rage replaced by sheer pain. What might have been avoidable, however, was Doran's choice to use the chair beside him.

Asher sighed as he slid another coin across the bar, his finger releasing it as the chair came down and broke into pieces around the man's head. He dropped to the floor, there to join his friend and a handful of teeth. Flattened as he was, the ranger could now see beyond him, where a notorious Warhog lay on its side, a bottle of ale hanging out of its mouth.

"Here," the ranger offered, placing the rest of the coins on the counter. "For your troubles."

"Are ye next?" Doran barked, squaring up to Russell's superior frame in the doorway.

"He's with me," Asher announced.

The son of Dorain whipped his head around to lay eyes on the ranger. "Asher! Is that ye, lad?" The dwarf glanced up at Maybury.

"He's with ye?" Doran chuckled. "Are ye handin' him in for a reward or somethin'?"

Asher briefly met Russell's eyes. The dwarf had no idea how close to the truth he was. Before he could give any kind of answer, the third man, previously thrown through the door, stumbled back inside. Maybury moved so the man might see what had become of his friends, a sight that put a touch of fear in him.

"Unless ye want to join 'em," Heavybelly stated, "I suggest ye drag 'em into the cold an' make yerselves scarce."

The man wiped blood from his bottom lip and wasted no time, pulling one after the other outside. After the last, the door was closed and the gloom returned, trapping them in torch and candle light and a few shafts of pale sun.

"Apologies, Jeri!" Doran called over the bar. "I'll take that breakfast now!"

Asher waited until Jeri, the owner, had peeled himself away from the wall before ordering a Velian tea. With Russell in tow, they joined the dwarf in his booth, where Pig still lay in a stupor.

"What animal is that?" Maybury enquired with some derision.

"That ain' no animal," Doran corrected, reaching for his tankard of beer. "*That* is a Warhog, a beast o' Dhenaheim, the scourge o' Grimwhal, an' a monster bred for naught but war."

Pig chose this moment to let loose a throaty burp and unleash a hellish gas from its other end.

"I see," Russell muttered.

"So," Heavybelly began, drawing the word out as he turned his attention on Asher. "Where in the hells have ye been? I came last year—second week o' Dunfold—an' ye never showed up! I waited a damned week! I almost didn' come this time."

"I got held up in Longdale," Asher told him.

"What were it?" Doran asked, his beard dripping with alcohol.

"Wraith."

The dwarf made a face. "Nasty buggers," he remarked. "Ye seen Salim?"

The pivoting question turned Asher towards the rest of the

tavern area, where Jeri was sweeping up debris. "No," he answered simply. "You?"

"He was 'ere last year," Doran reported. "Jus' come off a job in Wood Vale. Somethin' about a Dredlin'."

"Dredling?" Asher echoed, a hint of concern about him.

Doran waved a hand. "Nothin' Salim couldn' handle. I partnered with 'im for a job in Namdhor. Ye should o' seen 'im—cut through 'em blasted Triffids like a pro."

Asher didn't doubt the southerner's skills, though he would have liked to have seen him, if only to know that he was thriving as a ranger. In fact, he would have liked Salim to be present for their current predicament. Rarely did the ex-assassin seek allies—or help of any kind—but there was something more going on here, something more than Werewolves and Vorska. He could feel it.

A seeming empire of quiet tension then settled over the trio, Doran's eyes shifting repeatedly between Asher and Russell. "So are we goin' to talk abou' the Lumber Dug in the room or what?"

Mention of a Lumber Dug pulled at the ranger's memory, casting him momentarily back to Dragorn, where such a monster had escaped the dungeons of Viktor Varga. It had taken him and Salim near on a week to slay the creature amidst the chaos and destruction it created. Such was the damage it caused that the ruling families of that wretched island had put a price on the beast's head. Even splitting the reward in half, Asher and Salim had come away from that particular hunt very rich men, if nearly having been split in half themselves.

"The name's Russell," the largest of the three voiced, and confidently so. "Russell Maybury."

The dwarf eyed him a moment longer. "Well met, *Russell Russell* Maybury. Ye're talkin' to Doran, son o' Dorain, o' clan Heavybelly."

"You never said your friend was a dwarf," Maybury commented Asher's way. "And a funny one at that," he added dryly.

"Friend?" Doran repeated, a broad grin spreading his blond beard. "Did he say that?"

Quite coolly, Asher replied, "I think I said ally, which might be stretching the truth, depending on the day."

"Bah! Come on now! I only sold ye into slavery the once. That second time was yer own damned fault!"

Russell's interest raised one of his eyebrows but Asher waved the tale away. "You just arrived?" he asked the dwarf.

"Aye, not that long before ye got 'ere. Lirian's finest were in 'ere celebratin' some hunt or such. As if bringin' down a *deer* is worth celebratin'!" he mocked with a laugh. "Try bringin' down a fully grown Praitora!"

Given the timing of Doran's arrival and The Jolly Rotten sitting on the edge of the city, Asher reasoned that the dwarf hadn't heard of the woman murdered in the alley. Which meant he had no idea he had entered a city preyed upon by the Vorska.

"Perhaps we should order you another drink," the ranger said, considering the tale he had to tell.

By the time Asher's recounting was concluded, bringing the son of Dorain up to date, the ranger had finished his pot of Velian tea though, quite surprisingly, Doran had consumed but half of his tankard. His focus had sharpened when informed that there was a Werewolf sharing his booth, just as his lips had parted and failed to meet again.

With nothing more to hear, the dwarf sat back against the dark green leather, his gaze routinely drifting towards the axe and sword fastened to Pig's saddle. Asher recognised the look on his face for he had wrestled with the same thoughts.

Doran eventually cleared his throat and leant forward. "I understood everythin' ye said—an' I've got questions for, well, *all* o' it! But I 'ave to know: why's he still breathin'?"

Russell shifted uncomfortably in his seat but, credit to him, he kept his jaw clamped shut and allowed the hunters their exchange.

"He's one of us," Asher stated, aware that he had been vague when detailing their first meeting in the woods and, specifically, his feelings at the time.

"One o' us?" Heavybelly spat incredulously. "I'm aware we've all got our own monsters," he said knowingly, "but there's a difference between *havin'* 'em an' actually *bein'* one."

"He's a *ranger*," Asher maintained.

"What he *is* is exactly what ye're supposed to put *down*. He should be on the sharp end o' yer sword."

"He's a ranger because I *say* he is." Asher's tone was dangerously close to threatening, a tone never taken lightly by a dwarf.

Doran sat back, chewing over his own response. "As yer *ally*," he emphasised, "heed me words when I say yer judgment is clouded 'ere. Jus' because he's sittin' there lookin' like ye an' me, doesn' mean he *is* like ye an' me. We've had our own trouble with *Lycans* beyond Illian an' I can tell ye, the beast inside o' 'im is always closer than ye think. An' as yer *friend*," he added, "I know yer conscience doesn' need any more deaths on its hands, an' that's exactly what ye're goin' to get if ye let 'im live."

Asher held back his biting response and took a calming breath, deciding he would take the shortest route to the end of the conversation. "You can either help, or move on."

"Help? Ye're askin' if I fancy gettin' in the middle o' some monster feud over a trinket?" The dwarf blew hard through his lips, blurring them beneath his beard. "O' course I do!" he exclaimed, reversing direction as only Doran could. "I ain' ever put me blade to a Werewolf, or a Vorska for that matter! An' ye know I like me a good fight. Though I'm bettin' there ain' no coin to be gained."

"Probably not," the ranger confirmed, his voice returned to its familiar even tone.

Doran mumbled something under his breath, eyes darting to Russell. "An' *ye*. This is truly the life ye seek? A ranger's life? Ye see yerself roamin' the land in search o' monsters an' the like?"

The questions appeared to cut through some of Maybury's rising ire. He swallowed once, a nervous glance cast Asher's way. "I'm not for much else. I already have... blood on my hands. If I can put the wolf in me to good use, then I would see it done. Though, I confess," he added, "I know little beyond swinging a pick-axe."

The son of Dorain maintained his hard gaze. "Yer intentions are in the right place, I'll give ye that. But they don' change what ye *are*, lad. All the will in the world won' keep the wolf at bay. An' all this *fuss* will only make what's to come all the harder," he pointed out, looking to Asher now.

"Changes nothing," the ranger stated. "He gets a second chance, just like the rest of us."

The dwarf offered him a scowl. "That chip on yer shoulder's goin' to get ye killed, laddy."

Asher didn't acknowledge the comment. Instead, he took another breath, determined not to remind the son of Dorain that he owed him for everything that had transpired on Dragorn. At the time, he had told Doran he expected nothing from him but the promise that he would keep the Stormshields safe. Still, it was awfully tempting given the rock and the hard place they found themselves between.

"So, you will help?" he asked again, though his thoughts were already wandering back to the Stormshields, the spark of an idea at his fingertips.

"I said I would didn' I?" the dwarf replied with a shrug. "I'll even help ye when the time comes to... ye know..."

"Chop my head off?" Russell queried dryly.

"Aye!" Heavybelly said jovially. "Until then," he continued, "let us see where this strange an' twisted road may take us, eh?"

Russell shifted where he sat, fingers clasping together on the table top as if he was about to offer up a prayer to the gods. "I'm not so foolish as to believe this *will* work. But, for your sakes, if it doesn't, make sure you kill me before the full moon returns. I would not take your deaths to my grave with all the others." Maybury laid his eyes on Doran. "Yours perhaps," he added with a wry grin.

Asher imparted a grin of his own. "It seems you're quickly getting a measure of Master Heavybelly," he quipped.

"He's got a point," Doran said bluntly. "In a couple o' weeks ye're goin' to come face to face with the very monster I've been sittin' 'ere tryin' to warn ye abou'. What are ye goin' to do? Offer it some Velian mint tea an' put a sword in its hand? *Ye're a ranger now, wolfie!*" he cried mockingly.

"That's why we're here, in Lirian. That abandoned building I told you about: it has ample space in the basement for... *containment.*"

Doran blinked, then again, one hand running through the beard about his chin. "Ye mean to lock it up in a basement? In the heart o' Lirian?" The dwarf licked his lips. "Jus' how many blows to the head 'ave ye taken since last we met?"

"A long-term solution is required if Russell is to make a real life of this," Asher insisted, talking about the man as if he wasn't there. "Having somewhere safe he can return to every month will provide that. If the moon enthrals him out there somewhere, there's no telling what might happen."

"It'll reduce the distance he can travel for jobs," Doran commented, finally returning his attention to the tankard still gripped in one hand.

"A small price to pay," the ranger reasoned on Maybury's behalf.

Russell cleared his throat, reminding the hunters he sat among them. "Though I hate to say it, I agree with the dwarf—"

"The *dwarf,*" Doran cut in, "has a name, *wolf.*"

Asher remained silent for the exchange, allowing the pair to navigate each other in their own way.

Maybury tilted his head, an affectation of an apologetic bow perhaps. "It is folly to allow the transformation to take place in a densely populated city. And I am not convinced that room will be anywhere near ready when the full moon returns."

The ranger fixed his sight on the son of Dorain, his idea from earlier fully in his grasp now. "With all the time in the world, that room will never contain a Werewolf," he finally accepted aloud. "Not if it's prepared by *human* hands," came his final and all the more leading comment.

Doran's eyebrows—hedgerows of blond tuft—rose into his

forehead. "I don' know the first thing abou' buildin' a bloody dungeon!"

"That and so much more," Asher replied rather quickly. "But," he went on before the dwarf could argue, "we both know someone who could."

Revelation crossed Doran's face. "Danagarr? He's in Darkwell!"

"You could send a raven this very day," the ranger put to him. "Impress upon him the need for haste."

"Who's Danagarr?" Russell asked.

"A mutual acquaintance," Asher explained.

"A *friend*," Heavybelly specified. "An' a dwarven one at that."

"He will come if he knows it's for me," the ranger told them confidently.

"Aye, he will," Doran agreed. "But even if he comes right away, it's goin' to be damned tight, lad."

Asher kept his gaze on the son of Dorain, pressing upon him an almost real weight.

"A'right," the dwarf conceded, "I'll send a raven today." He swigged another mouthful of warm beer. "Oh, an' what exactly *is* a Vorska anyway?"

Asher watched Doran move further into the main room of The Ranch and waited for his predictable assessment.

"I've slept in worse," the dwarf announced. "Though not by much," he added quietly.

The ranger simply nodded along, sure that the son of Dorain—like him—was thinking about the dungeons beneath Blood and Coin. "Come on," he bade, making for the door on the far left. Asher paused when he noticed Russell on the other side of the room, apparently lost to some daydream, hands on hips. "Maybury," he cajoled.

In the basement, where the largest room almost mirrored that above, Doran whistled into the gloom. "Ye humans 'ave no idea how to build anythin', but this is a damned good bit o' space. How does somethin' this big jus' get abandoned?"

Asher had no intention of getting into the specifics of the building's history or that the deeds belonged to him. "Humans are good at losing track of things," he said, playing on the dwarf's view of Illian's inhabitants.

Doran chuckled to himself. "Ain' that the truth?"

A moment later and Russell descended the stairs to join them, his considerable frame reducing the size of the room. "I can still smell them," he reported. "Their stench lingers as if commanded to."

"Best be keepin' comments like that to yerself," Doran warned. "It jus' reminds me what ye are."

Maybury tensed, his chest rising and jaw firming. "If you think you have the stones, *Master Heavybelly*, I'll let you have the first swing."

Asher was impressed by the menacing tone, though not nearly as much as Doran. "Maybe we'll make a ranger out o' ye yet, laddy! An' don' worry, big fella, when it comes time, I won' need any more than the first swing to get the job done."

Russell didn't move, his gaze transfixed on the dwarf. Asher could see that the man's knuckles had whitened, the blood forced away by his knotted fists. "They're just *words*, Maybury," the ranger reminded him. "You're going to have to get thicker skin."

"Wait until the full moon," Doran remarked offhandedly, turning to the rest of the room, "then his skin will be plenty thick."

Russell started forward until six foot of Asher was standing in his way, a single hand pressed into his chest. "Stop," he commanded. "And you too!" he added, whipping his head around to the son of Dorain. "*Stop!*" he decreed, that one word enough to convey his meaning.

"Bah!" the dwarf grumbled, waving a hand at the whole situation. "It's damned cold down 'ere. Asher, do yer thing an' get the fire goin' would ye?"

The ranger waited a moment, specifically waiting to feel some of the tension drain from Russell's body. Only then did he move away from the man and address Doran's request. "*Any* of us can get a fire going, Heavybelly," he said, and deliberately so, for the son of Dorain was referring to the black gem and its unusual abilities—neither of which were known to Maybury.

"Oh," Doran replied flatly, perhaps remembering that he had sworn to keep the gem's existence a secret. "Aye, right."

"*I* will see to the fire," Russell offered gruffly, marching past Doran.

Before the dwarf could make any kind of comment, Asher retrieved A Chronicle of Monsters: A Ranger's Bestiary from beside his bed roll. "Here." He handed the book to Heavybelly, the pages open to the Vorska.

One bushy eyebrow arched into Doran's forehead. "If ye brought me 'ere jus' to read a book, Asher, ye might need to rethink what ye know abou' me."

The ranger sighed and took the book back. "Dwarves," he muttered, finding rest in one of the dusty armchairs. "These are the words of Dobrin Vansorg," he began. "Vorska: *These monsters have gone by many names over the centuries. Your great grandparents likely called them Vampeer or Vampire. Before that, they were Gorgers and Blood Fiends. Whatever you wish to call them, know this: they are the real hunters. They have been preying on humanity since the dawn of time—*"

"What does that even mean?" Doran interjected. "*The dawn o' time!*" he mocked. "Me kin 'ave walked Grarfath's hard earth far longer than yer own people, an' I've *never* heard o' any o' those things ye jus' named."

Asher gave no response but to maintain his level gaze with the dwarf. "*Should you cross them in the light of day,*" he continued, "*you will see their true appearance and what a monstrosity they are, their nightmarish features forged in the pits of the lowest hell. But, by night, they will appear as the most beautiful person you could imagine. They will charm their victims into seclusion before their beastly tongue drains them of blood.*"

"Wait," Heavybelly pleaded, settling into one of the other chairs. "They look like monsters durin' the day an' people at night?

I've never known any beast capable o' such a feat. I suppose the closest would be..." Doran trailed off as his eyes drifted towards Russell and the small flames he had started.

"Indeed," Asher breathed. "*Silver, my friends,*" he read. "*They abhor its touch. Use this to reveal them, then take their head with a good piece of steel.*"

"It's as simple as that then?" Doran asked, genuinely surprised.

"If only it was," Asher replied, letting the book rest on his lap. "I've read this multiple times and found it lacking where my own experiences lie."

"Ye said ye faced one in Kelp Town."

"I did, and I put *a good piece of steel* right through its head. Yet I saw the same creature in Sable's Tavern only days ago."

Doran licked his lips and glanced at Asher. "Ye ran its head through an' it didn' die? What manner o' demon are we dealin' with 'ere?"

"That's just it," the ranger explained, "I thought it *was* dead. I buried my knife in its skull and the fight ended. I've seen more than my fair share of death. I was *convinced.*"

Heavybelly gave an overly dramatic shrug. "Well, if rammin' a blade through their brain don' kill 'em then what will? Silver? Who carries silver on 'em?"

Asher gestured at the book. "There's mention of fire, but not much else."

"It could be," Russell pointed out, "Dobrin Vansorg meant to write that a good piece of steel is needed to cut off their head. There's not much that can survive that. Is there?" His question reminded Asher of how much training the man required.

"Decapitation an' fire will kill most things," Doran informed cheerily.

Russell seemed happy to hear it. "You said it appeared dead, in my home. Doesn't that suggest it needs its brain, even if your blow wasn't enough to kill it?"

"Aye, he's got a point," Heavybelly agreed. "Maybe decapitation is the answer."

"It's a sound theory," Asher muttered, his attention circling the bestiary. "There's no description of pain either."

"Should there be?" Maybury asked.

"The Vorska I fought in Kelp Town..." Asher trailed off, recalling the violent encounter. "I maimed it again and again yet it felt no pain. It just kept coming."

"Maybe the answers can' be found in yer fancy book," Doran told him, retrieving a pipe from his pocket.

Asher eyed the dwarf. "Perhaps."

"An' ye say they've jus'..." Doran paused while he lit his pipe. "Disappeared?"

The ranger was shaking his head. "That woman's body the watch found would suggest otherwise. They're still hunting in Lirian. They've just abandoned their hunt of *us*."

The dwarf exhaled a cloud of smoke into the room. "I thought they were after some ball, the one ye mentioned."

"After meeting Merith I would say their desire for it is great. I don't understand why they would cease their attempts to claim it."

"Maybe they got wind o' me an' thought better o' it," Doran grinned.

Asher's amusement was cut short when Doran went on to make a demand of Russell. "Let's see it then—this *orb*."

Seated by the fire, Russell became unnervingly still, his hard gaze locked on the son of Dorain.

Doran frowned. "Why's he lookin' at me like that?" he asked Asher, his own gaze never straying from Maybury.

The ranger closed the bestiary and moved to the edge of his chair. "It seems to be some kind of constraint left by the one who bit him. They never exchanged any words, but the wolf who gave him the orb was apparently very attached to it. It seems Were-wolves can transfer their desires into the ones they sire."

"Handy," Doran opined, his pipe clasped between his teeth. "Well ye can stop lookin' at me like that now," he told Russell bluntly. "I want to *see* this thing, not *take* it from ye."

"Russell," Asher said quietly, but firmly. Maybury didn't

change a thing about his rigid posture. Worse still, his gaze became all the more predatory.

"Asher," Doran voiced. "If he tries somethin' foolish I'm goin' to put 'im down for good."

The ranger did the only thing he could—again—and stood up to put himself physically between them. "Perhaps now," he suggested, "would be a good time to send that raven."

The son of Dorain looked up at him, unable to see his potential foe. "Aye," he grumbled, rising to his feet. "I think ye're right. The sooner we get this done the sooner ye can see that *I'm* right. Ye don' put Lycans in cages, Asher." The dwarf paused at the bottom step and looked back over one shoulder. "Ye kill 'em, like everythin' else."

CHAPTER 15
A FOOL'S HOPE

Moss Fiends - *Irritating buggers, though irritating is perhaps too harmless a word. Do not get me wrong, for a single Moss Fiend is capable of killing a man. It's just that such a man would have to be uninitiated in the ways of the sword.*

These creatures prefer to hide in forests, though some have been found in fields and across the plains of Alborn. You won't even know you're looking at one, and especially from afar. The bulk of their body is covered in some kind of false moss that lends them the appearance of a small and natural mound.

When close enough, they will explode from their apparent hiding place on six pale legs and spit venom from their spider-like head. The venom isn't deadly to humans but it will still irritate your eyes and even blind you for a time.

Personally, I have found it quite satisfying to use flaming arrows from afar while they remain in 'hiding'.

**A Chronicle of Monsters: A Ranger's Bestiary, 12th Edition,
Page 216.**

Old Carduune, Ranger.

. . .

Though winter's days were short, the days that followed felt an eternity before word returned from Darkwell, the parchment lined with dwarven glyphs and signed with Danagarr Stormshield's name. More importantly, it had returned with his promise to meet them in Lirian.

Asher hated the waiting, which he found ironic considering how much waiting had been required of him during his years as an Arakesh. Days, weeks, even months could be spent tracking down a target or monitoring them for the perfect window of execution.

Of course, with every day that passed, they grew closer to the wolf's return. Russell's mood became noticeably worse, though whether that could be attributed to his curse or Doran's presence was debatable. More often than not, the two butted heads, and over trivial words no less, forcing Asher to intervene.

And, all the while, the bodies were mounting up. Asher had secretly investigated them all, some even in the guise of a watchman, and discovered that every man and woman who had fallen victim across the city bore the tell-tale markings of the Vorska's fangs and tongue.

Yet they never once assaulted The Ranch. It had become a fact that disturbed Asher all the more.

"He needs somethin' to take his mind off it," Doran said early the next morning. "He's only a few days from the moon. There's only so much he can sweep an' dust an' fix in 'ere."

"What did you have in mind?" Asher asked.

"Well," the dwarf began dryly, "we've sampled what feels like every tavern in the city an' spoken to everyone an' anyone who might be able to source the materials we need." He shrugged his rounded shoulders, currently absent the usual black and gold pauldrons. "He wants to be a ranger, aye? Let's see what he's got."

Asher knew that mischievous grin. "You wish to fight him," he reasoned.

"He's a miner," Doran pointed out. "It ain' goin' to be a fight. He needs trainin'. Besides, it will give 'im somethin' to think abou'.

He can' move past the next few days, but he could do with lookin' to the future a bit."

The ranger observed the dwarf a moment longer. "Are you actually trying to help him?"

"O' course not," Doran argued. "I'm mostly jus' itchin' for a fight an' the sight o' 'im sets me off."

That made more sense to Asher. "You'll have to take him out and buy a sword first." Aware that Doran would never part with his coin for Russell, the ranger tossed him a small purse. "I want some of that back," he added.

"I make no promises, ranger man!"

Now, a little over an hour later, Asher was seated atop an old barrel in the private courtyard behind The Ranch. He didn't like what he was seeing.

"What's that?" he questioned, pointing at the pick-axe in Russell's hand.

"I tried to tell 'im," Doran said with a hopeless shrug. "Took 'im to Smithy's on Kyvern—had the pick o' the lot. Nothin'. Then," he added, shaking his head, "he saw *that* outside the supply shop round the corner."

"That's not a weapon," Asher remarked. "It's a *tool.*"

Maybury took on a defensive posture, his large hand tightening around the haft. "I know what I'm doing with it," he protested. "I've been handling them since I was a boy. And trust me, I've got into plenty of scraps with a pick-axe in hand. They're perfectly good weapons."

Asher wasn't convinced, his eyes shifting across to the dwarf as if to lay the blame on him.

"Don' look at me! I once saw ye kill a Royal Gobber with a blasted ladle! Compared to that, this is a battle-axe o' pure silvyr!"

"You said you would train me," Russell stated, his gaze unwavering. "Are you saying you can't if I wield a pick-axe?"

Doran began to laugh, turning back to move into the open space of the courtyard. "He's got ye there, laddy! Why don' ye look at this the way I do? When the time comes to put him in the dirt, gettin' past a pick-axe'll be easy!"

A disgruntled sound rumbled from deep in Russell's throat. He pivoted on his heel and marched into the open space to oppose the son of Dorain, his boots crunching through the snow. With no more than trousers and a loose-fitting shirt, he was a stark contrast to the dwarf, who had donned a tightly-fitted jacket to keep out the cold and retained his armoured cuisses around his thighs. Then there were his weapons—a sword and axe of Danagarr's making—vastly superior to any pick-axe.

"Two weapons?" Maybury voiced, seeing inequity.

"Aye," Doran replied. "If ye're to face monsters then ye're to face their *claws*."

"Technique," Asher called out before the fight began. "It is the cornerstone of combat. It will always overcome brute strength. If you truly wish to learn, Russell, then hold back. Look for the openings and strike. Keep your feet moving."

"A'right! Enough talk. Let's get to the trainin'." The grin that followed Heavybelly's interruption spoke of his eagerness.

Asher sighed and reached for his pipe, deciding that the pair just needed to hit each other for a while if they were to survive each other.

Man and dwarf charged, kicking up snow in their wake. Maybury was the quicker of the two, closing the gap in powerful strides. It seemed a foolish thing to the ranger, who knew Doran had only to swing his axe and end the fight in bloodshed. Displaying some of the skill he boasted, Russell turned his charge into an unpredictable manoeuvre, sliding the last few feet on his hip, the pick-axe extended to take out the dwarf's legs.

The son of Dorain swore upon realising what was happening. Rather than be tripped, he opted to dive over the weapon and roll across the courtyard. Likely out of anger, if not embarrassment, Doran emerged from his roll and launched his axe at his opponent.

"Doran!" Asher chastised, pausing in igniting his pipe.

The axe would have split Maybury's head down the middle, Doran's aim dangerously true, but Russell's advantage in fighting any monster would be his reflexes, which were far more excitable than that of an ordinary man. Or dwarf. Displaying as much, he shifted his shoulders, twisting at the hip, and merely watched the axe fly past his face and lodge itself in one of the stone pillars that surrounded the courtyard.

"Control!" Asher yelled, hoping to break through the red mist that had overcome the fighters. "Combat requires control. Holding back is harder than letting go, but you'll learn nothing with savagery."

Doran rose from his crouch, sword scraping deliberately across the stone floor. "Ye've nothin' to teach me, Asher. I was bred for war," he remarked darkly.

"You're *not* to kill each other," the ranger reminded sternly, though mostly it was said for the dwarf's ears.

"A'right, a'right." Doran waved Asher away. "Ye heard 'im wolf! Technique. Control." A short sharp bark of laughter escaped the son of Dorain's lips. "I don' think they go well with a bloody pick-axe!"

Asher refrained from intervening, wishing to see how Russell would react to the jibe. Impressing the ranger somewhat, the miner adjusted his grip to hold the pick-axe upright at chest level, two hands grasping the haft as if he wielded a longsword. There seemed a measure of control about his expression, a hardening to words that would have fuelled his rage a few days ago.

Then Doran howled at the sky as if he were a wolf.

The armour of discipline was shattered and Maybury leapt at his enemy. The pick-axe arced high and hammered down again and again, each swing missing its target by inches as Doran's foot-work saw to his survival. By the third swing, the dwarf had formu-lated his counterattack. As the tip of the pick impacted the stone, Heavybelly pivoted and rounded his sword under the haft, catching the inside corner of the pick with enough force to tug it forward; bringing Russell with it.

The big man fell flat on his front, one hand still clasped to the haft of his weapon. To the sound of dwarven laughter, Doran shoved the sole of his boot into the side of Maybury's head and sent him rolling away. With a feral look in his eyes, the wolf rose from the floor with a scuff across his cheek and a cut marring his chin.

"First blood to clan Heavybelly!" Doran cheered.

Having finally lit his pipe, Asher observed from atop his barrel with the jolt of arakan spices on his tongue. Now was the moment of Russell's true test. The taste and smell of his own blood on the air would set his veins on fire, igniting that instinctual imperative to survive, a feeling the ranger knew all too well.

"This is *your* fight, Russell," he cried from the edges. "Not the wolf's. Only you can tell it who's in control."

Doran sneered. "He can' do a damned thing, Asher. Look at 'im! It takes nothin' to strip 'im back an' reveal the beast!"

Asher wanted desperately to silence the dwarf, if only to give Russell a moment to think, but he could see what Doran was really doing. He was trying to prove to the ranger that they had naught but a monster on their hands and that, even in human form, Maybury was a danger to everyone around him. And so Asher held back, wishing to see the truth of that for himself.

Whether Russell had heard a word of Asher's advice remained to be seen, though it seemed he had heard everything Doran had to say. Again he charged the dwarf and leapt high to close the gap via the air. His pick-axe came down in two hands, forcing Heavybelly back a step.

In came the son of Dorain, a veteran of numerous wars, and struck the miner across the nose with the pommel of his sword. Russell didn't so much as grunt at the blow.

Instead, he bolted forwards into his opponent and flattened the haft of his pick-axe to Doran's chest. The assault knocked him back all the more until Maybury thrust the horizontal haft up into the dwarf's throat, lifting him from his feet and pinning him to the pillar at his back.

The son of Dorain immediately dropped his sword in favour of holding down Russell's wrists, lest the wood crush his windpipe. Still, it was pressed deep into him, turning his face a contrasting red to the mane of blond. A sharp hiss pushed through his bared teeth before he began to ram one foot after another into Maybury's chest. The wolf didn't budge.

Doran resorted to hammering the arms that held the pick-axe in place. By the look of him he needed air soon.

"Control, Russell!" Asher called, on his feet now, hand reaching for the safida spices on his belt. "Doran is not your enemy! Find your control!"

At last, dwarven strength proved its legendary worth. Doran dislodged Russell's arms and fell back to his feet. His inevitable gulp for air was that of a drowning man breaking the water's surface. Still, he launched a club-like fist into Maybury's gut, then a second to the inside of his knee—dropping him down—and, finally, a third to his jaw. The wolf fell back and rolled lazily through the snow, a pained groan his close companion.

The dwarf's arm shot out, a single finger pointed like an arrow at Russell. "He can' be trained!" he rasped, his other hand soothing his throat. "There's nothin' in 'im but the beast!"

Russell was already rising, shaking off the assault, and looking a little sheepish. "Apologies," he offered gruffly.

"Damn yer apologies! The full moon is days out, *days*, Asher. There ain' time to build no cage, Danagarr or not. An' as for trainin' him..."

"You must be hungry," the ranger assumed, cutting through the tirade and grabbing Doran's attention by the stomach. "Let's find some lunch. And a drink," he added, sweetening the deal. "On me."

The son of Dorain took a few breaths and straightened up, his normal colour returning. "Aye," he said, with no more than a glance at Russell.

"Stay here," Asher instructed the man. "I'll bring you some food back."

Sullen, Maybury recovered his pick-axe and nodded his under-standing.

∾

Asher hadn't caught the name of the tavern they entered, satisfied to have walked out of The Ranch and followed his nose to the nearest source of food—Doran wasn't fussy. The dwarf was soon tearing through a chicken leg with ale and debris mottling his beard. His cutlery remained untouched while his stubby fingers grabbed at buttery new potatoes and shovelled down mushrooms, all of which were soothing his wounded pride.

Taking his time with his leek and potato soup, the ranger watched and waited for the son of Dorain to reach a level of civility that would allow for reasonable conversation.

"Ye must see now?" Doran eventually said. "Ye must see 'im for what he is?"

"I see the need for *training*," Asher countered. "You, me, Salim, we have all received training, whether we wanted to or not. We're fighters before all else. Russell just needs to... adjust his perspective."

"That may be so," Heavybelly replied, bits of chicken falling out of his mouth, "but there ain' time for that before these Vorska come for 'im. He's goin' to 'ave to rely on his strength an' brutality to survive 'em. An' then what? Ye saw 'im. The wolf takes over an' he don' see friend from foe."

Asher agreed with the dwarf, preventing him from forming a counterargument. Instead, he continued to eat his soup, the weight of his decisions upon him.

"Ye know," Doran went on, "ye can train 'im all ye like, with or without that damned pick-axe. He's good to no one until he can keep that temper in check."

Asher couldn't help his groan. "I've already tried. I can't count how many times he's failed at meditation."

Doran tutted and shook his head. "Ye an' meditation," he chastened. "Elf talk if ever I heard it."

"You could do with mastering it yourself," Asher commented. "You wear your anger on your sleeve."

"I wear what?"

The ranger thought better of explaining the human idiom and

shrugged his shoulders. "You're not exactly a monk yourself," he rephrased.

"Bah! I'm exactly the way the Mother an' Father made me!" The dwarf picked the chicken bone clean and let it clatter onto his plate. "So why hasn' he taken to this meditation babble then?"

Asher considered the question carefully before answering. "The point of it is to separate himself mind and body, to find a way to make an island of his emotions from where he cannot rise to... well, what you saw today. In truth, achieving that kind of isolation from oneself is a painful method that takes years. I had hoped he would pick up at least enough to keep the wolf's influence at bay." The ranger returned his spoon to the bowl before it could reach his lips. "All it did was make him angry."

Doran harrumphed. "Don' blame 'im. Sounds like it'd make me angry too."

"You're right though," Asher said. "If he can't control himself he can't..." The ranger was ever the pragmatist, yet he struggled to voice the rest of that sentence.

Heavybelly sat back in his chair, quite satiated by the look of him. There was no better way to calm the dwarf and reset his emotional state than with food. "Maybe ye're lookin' at it all wrong," he suggested.

The ranger narrowed his eyes. "How so?"

"Ye're lookin' at it—at 'im—like one o' 'em assassins."

Asher leant forward, eyes shifting round to take in the other patrons before finally landing on the dwarf. "If you think you're whispering, you're not."

Doran held up his hands in apology. "Ye're lookin' at Russell like he's an assassin o' Nightfall," he began again, achieving something closer to a whisper this time. "But he ain'. He ain' even a soldier. He's an amateur brawler at best."

The ranger took a breath and folded his arms. "So how *should* I be looking at him?"

"Like a man," Doran declared simply.

Asher chewed over that for a moment. "What does that mean?"

Sitting forward again, the son of Dorain idly picked through the bones on his plate, searching for scraps. "In me experience—which is more than yer own," Doran felt the need to point out, "all men 'ave one thing in common."

Asher rolled his eyes. "Here we go."

"They all dream o' bein' somethin' else," the dwarf stated quite profoundly. "Or they want somethin' else. Or they jus' want *more*," he added with his usual tone of derision. "Either way, they're all dreamers who aren' happy with their lot."

"I won't disagree," the ranger replied, aware that he himself strived to be more than what he was, a hope, he knew, that would see the *Ranger* overcome the *Assassin* some day. "But how does that help me train him?"

Finding a green bean hiding beneath a pile of bones, slathered in gravy, Doran scooped it up—gravy and all—and stuffed it into his mouth. "Men cling to their dreams do they not? It's what keeps 'em... well, *them*, I suppose. Maybe it's folly to break his mind into pieces an' hope he can forget who an' what he is for a while. Maybe he needs to know *exactly* who he is. An' who he is, I reckon, is whatever he dreams o' bein'. In that moment, when the wolf's risin' an' his blood's alight with fire, he needs to hold on to that dream." The dwarf shrugged. "It's got to be better than some cold dark place in his mind, eh?"

Asher's gaze fell adrift among the patrons, barmaids, and hanging decorations, just as his focus moved seemingly without purpose. It felt inherently wrong that Doran Heavybelly could speak so much sense while simultaneously pointing out the flaws in the methods used thus far; as well as the fact that they were undoubtedly dark. Asher knew of no other techniques besides those Nasta Nal-Aket had taught him. It had never occurred to him that there would be other ways and means to accomplish that same goal, or that he could change the goal itself.

"Regardless," the ranger said, pivoting while his subconscious quietly reassessed his approach, "you have to stop antagonising him. He's wanted to rip your head off a dozen times in the last two weeks. He needs a clear head."

"I've nothin' against the man," Doran admitted. "It's the wolf that's not to me likin'. As far as I'm concerned, Russell Maybury died the moment he was bitten. He's so cursed, Asher, he's jus' a walkin' dead man. It would be a mercy to kill 'im."

Asher shot him a warning look.

"I know," the dwarf quickly replied, hands in the air, "he's one o' us. Speakin' o' which, when's he goin' to get his first beastie under his belt? He ain' one o' us until he's *received payment for services rendered!*"

"In time," the ranger asserted. "He has his own monster to deal with first. Once we've got past the next full moons we'll have a month to continue his training, and find a contract somewhere."

"*If*, Asher," Doran emphasised gravely. "*If* we get past the next full moons."

❦

The clear day had prevailed and a twilight of pink and orange hues stretched across the sky by the time Doran and Asher found their way back to The Ranch. Both rangers came to a stop when they caught sight of a familiar donkey and cart outside.

Asher felt a warm sensation stir in his gut and move up to his chest and knew it to be hope, even if it was a fool's hope.

"Danagarr!" the dwarf declared, clapping his hands together.

The dwarven smith was soon found inside, sitting on a crate beside Russell, who had apparently made them both a cup of tea. Danagarr's wild eyebrows rose up so his dark eyes might take in the rangers as they entered, a broad smile stretching his dense and neglected beard.

"Asher! Doran!" He stood to greet them.

"Danagarr!" Doran cheered.

Asher maintained his calm composure but allowed himself that warm and genuine smile he could feel bursting to break free. "It is good to see you, old friend."

Upon parting from their embraces, the smith peered up at the hilt poking over Asher's right shoulder. "Let me see it then!" he urged with child-like giddiness.

How could the ranger refuse? The silvyr blade slipped free of its sheath, ringing in the cold gloom of the large room. Danagarr licked his lips and accepted it with delicate fingers. He turned it one way then the next, his blacksmith's eyes examining its shape and edge.

"So fine a thing I will never make again," he said to himself, lost in his old works. "The forests will grow an' retreat an' the mountains will rise ever higher an' fall into ruin... but this will never change." The dwarf chuckled. "It looks good on ye, fella," he complimented, handing it back.

Asher slid the weapon away, happy to have its familiar weight strapped to his back once more. "We are in need of your fine works again, good smith. And there is no time to waste."

Danagarr nodded along. "Doran's note spoke of haste, though ye friend 'ere," he added, gesturing at Russell with a friendly smile, "has been fillin' me in a bit more. Ye need to trap a monster? In 'ere? Before the first full moon?" His incredulity was elevated with each question. "What are ye tryin' to trap?" he asked with a short laugh. "A Lycan?" His laugh increased until he noted the expressions of all three companions. "Ye can' be serious?"

Only minutes later, they were showing the smith the room that required so much alteration. As was natural to him, Danagarr entered the space and immediately began rapping his knuckles against the walls, pinching the bolt heads and stamping his feet into various boards. He muttered to himself as he walked around, all in his native tongue and beyond Asher's understanding.

Instead, the ranger looked to Russell. He didn't like the idea of lying to Danagarr but he was impressed the miner had retained his secret while imparting the necessary information to get the job done. The less people who know the truth the better, he told himself.

"So," Doran began. "What do ye think, Danagarr? Can it be done?"

The smith contorted his mouth in consideration. "It can be done, aye. But it's goin' to take some work, fellas. This room wasn't designed with what ye've got in mind. I'm goin' to need to tear most o' it down and rebuild it from scratch if it's to contain a Lycan. The reinforcements..." he agonised. "An' I haven' brought nearly enough o' what I'm goin' to need."

"Lirian's a big city," Asher told him. "It should have everything you need. And we have some coin to pay for it." They would have nothing left, he knew, but he had never found coin hard to come by or even live without.

Danagarr nodded along, one hand repeatedly stroking his knotted beard. "Even if I had everythin' I need," he replied, "these hands alone can' get it done before the first full moon. Hells, even with a team o' smiths an' carpenters it couldn' be done before then. I'm sorry, fellas."

A fool's hope indeed, Asher thought.

"If you could," the ranger said, "I would have you begin at once, full moon or not."

"Asher," Doran began, a frown forming. "Ye heard 'im. It can' be done. Maybe we need to—"

Asher cut him off with a raised hand. "We will need it ready for all the moons that follow," he said, his tone so confident his words might as well have been etched in stone.

Danagarr put up two rough hands. "I'm not followin'. I thought ye were jus' trappin' a Lycan in 'ere. Why do ye need it for all the other full moons?"

There was a pregnant pause before Russell just came out with the truth.

The next pause filled the room with considerably more tension. Danagarr swallowed, eyes wide. Then he hurried from the room, shoving his way past.

"Danagarr!" Doran yelled.

"No, no, no, no. I'm not standin' next to a damned Lycan!" the smith shouted over his shoulder. "Me great uncle, Grarfath rest his soul, was killed by such a creature. His only mercy was that it ripped 'im into so many pieces there were nothin' left to be cursed!"

Doran sighed. "I'll speak to 'im."

Asher watched the son of Dorain take off after his kin, taking what little hope he had left with him. The truth, it seemed, always found its way into the light. "He'll come around," he said to Russell, who stood tall, even with his shoulders stooped in dismay.

"I suppose I should get used to that reaction," he concluded miserably.

"What you should do is keep your mouth shut," Asher corrected, perhaps a little too firmly.

"Is it not my secret to tell?" Maybury snapped, his emotions always quick to get the better of him.

"I'm trying to find a way for you live *with* the secret," the ranger argued. "The more people you tell, the harder that becomes. If this doesn't work," he went on, pointing at the barren room, "I don't see any way forwards. We *need* Danagarr. And we might need others. So keep the truth to yourself," he commanded, turning to leave.

"You don't own me," Maybury retorted.

"I never said I did," Asher spat back, quick to turn on the man. "I'm the only one trying to find a way for you to live."

"Aye," Russell agreed, "so you keep saying. Yet you treat me more as the monster than the man. I might be a Werewolf and a poor miner before that, but I know a man ain't supposed to live like you do. Don't get me wrong. I'm grateful for all you've done— for what you're *doing*—but you cannot expect me to live as you do. I can't move about, and I'm isolated from everyone and everything. I need more than that. Otherwise," he added hopelessly, "I might as well let the wolf out. Better yet, I might as well let you put me down."

Asher stood in the torchlight a moment longer, his gaze unable to keep with Russell's. Then he turned to leave.

"Where are you going?" Maybury called.

Asher didn't falter in his departure. "To find the strongest chains in Lirian."

CHAPTER 16

CREATURES OF THE NIGHT

Smilers - *Disturbing are these monsters of shadow. In truth, they are creatures of the Shadow Realm, a land of darkness that should never have been tapped by foolish mages.*

Standing like a man, they mirror many of our features—if you can imagine a man who wears his skin inside out. Worst of all our similarities, these beasts wear a permanent expression; the very same that has lent them their name.

They are simple monsters, seeking flesh for sustenance. It would seem, however, that they seek to induce fear in their prey first. Some have theorised that it makes us taste better.

A Chronicle of Monsters: A Ranger's Bestiary, 12th Edition,
Page 86.

Callum Forgson, Ranger.

Though few words passed between The Ranch's four occupants, its walls were filled with the thunderous sound of Danagarr's work. For three days the dwarven smith had taken to the room in the basement as an angry Broxon might take to the markets in Lirian's busy central square. Demolition was apparently step one.

After his first whole day scouring the city and making deals with numerous vendors, The Ranch saw delivery after delivery of raw materials and various tools. On the rare occasions he emerged from his work, the dwarf was coated in a sheen of sweat, his belt always laden with tools and rags.

He was always sure to give Russell a wide berth. Asher didn't know what Doran had said to the smith to turn him around, but it had done little to change his mind about the danger Maybury posed. The ranger was just glad he had chosen to stay and help them. Besides his considerable skill, Asher wasn't sure there were any he could trust to see the job done right.

Having briefly spoken with the Stormshield on his most recent sojourn into the light, Asher now stood alone in the private courtyard behind The Ranch, and under gathering clouds that promised fresh snow. He looked into the cart Danagarr had said they could borrow and scrutinised the heavy chains, hooks, and bolts that he had acquired. His doubts were creeping in, just as the end of the afternoon was and, with it, the first full moon to signal the approaching end of Dunfold.

"Is it goin' to be enough?" the son of Dorain asked, appearing in the doorway.

"It'll have to be," the ranger said, before turning to the dwarf. "You don't have to come."

"I know," Doran replied. "But I told ye I would help."

"I know what you told me," Asher intoned, recalling the dwarf's promise to slay Russell should it come to that.

Doran tilted his head to spy from under the canopy. "We'd best be off soon, eh? We'll want 'im secure long before the moon shows its face."

Asher nodded absently, unable to picture the night to come. "Any word from Salim?" he asked, wondering if they might have another ally to call upon.

Doran shook his head. "I've been back to The Jolly every day. There's every chance he's too far away. Or he's in the middle o' a hunt. Or he jus' doesn' want to see yer ugly mug."

Asher agreed with all the possibilities and even found an amused smile for the lattermost. "Let's go then."

Russell was found seated on the top step of The Ranch's porch. Asher had believed he was simply watching the world go by, perhaps wistfully so as he observed the people going about their ordinary lives. But he was wrong. On Maybury's lap rested a board and a single sheet of parchment atop that. Damned if the miner from Snowfell wasn't sketching, and sketching well at that.

"Is that a tavern?" the ranger asked, recognising a bar and the placement of stools in the background of the picture.

Russell quickly scrunched the image up. "It's nothing."

"For a man who claims his only skill comes with a pick-axe in hand, that wasn't half bad." It wasn't the best compliment he could have given, but it was the best he could manage given the lack of communication since their argument.

"Is it time?" the big man enquired, yet to look up at him.

"It is," Asher confirmed. "Have you hidden it?"

Russell nodded his head. "No one will find the orb," he confirmed.

Doran pushed through the faded green door and joined them in the brisk air. "I've told Danagarr we're goin' to be gone for a while. He's happy to get on with it."

"I'll fetch the cart," Russell offered, standing from the creaking steps. "Meet you round the back."

Considering the transformation Maybury was to undergo, both Asher and Doran decided it was best to leave Hector and Pig where they were and make the short journey on foot. And so they met Russell outside the gates to the courtyard and began to weave their way through the streets, searching for that familiar gap in the eastern tree line.

"You've been here before?" Russell asked, and not for the first time.

"Yes," the ranger answered, wondering if the man simply needed something to occupy his mind. "From here," he said, indicating the pointed boulder that sat in the middle of a small clearing, "we head south for about two miles. There we'll find the ruins."

"Now here's a question," Doran announced from the back of the group. "What would happen if we were to get ye drunk—good an' proper like? Ye know, that kind o' blindin' drunk where ye can' even recall ye own name. Would the wolf also be drunk? 'Cos that would make things a lot easier."

Leading the way, Asher was shaking his head—smiling, but shaking his head all the same. "Only you, Heavybelly, could conjure such a question."

"I'm more than happy to find out," Russell chirped, his tone surprisingly cheerful.

Doran laughed. "Attaboy! If only we'd brought more than a ton o' iron, eh?"

Asher glanced back. "I half expected you to bury the chains beneath a keg or two."

"Had I any coin left I might," the dwarf called out. "Soon, lads, we're to find a monster that needs slayin'. It ain' me wit that wets me lips with sweet ale an' salted pork, ye know!"

Their light-hearted merriment continued for the remainder of their journey, ending only when they arrived at the ruins. The hewn slabs of stone sat upon the earth as ancient bones long forgotten, some of which were now leaning as the weight of time bore upon them. There were archways that led to nowhere and walls that no longer defined chambers, and all dotted around a hollow structure that rose three storeys.

Russell set down the cart he had so effortlessly pulled and moved to the nearest archway, one hand running over the weathered stone. "It's ancient alright," he surmised. "From the time of Gal Tion?"

"Earlier still," Asher reported.

Maybury turned to see him, a sense of wonder in his voice. "The elves?" The ranger nodded, kindling that wonder into amazement. "I don't believe it!" Maybury went on, looking at the site with new eyes. "I've never seen anything of their world. There's nothing in The Ice Vales, nor Lirian for that matter. You could almost believe they were naught but myth."

Asher thought back to Nightfall's best kept secret: Alidyr Yalathanil. An elf of unknown years, though unmistakably ancient, his own dark talents were responsible for the Nightseye elixir that coursed through the ranger's veins. He was no myth.

"They had their time," Doran grumbled, ploughing through the snow to find the right spot. "An' what did they leave o' their great deeds? This," he declared flatly, gesturing to the ruins.

Russell eyed the dwarf. "Have you ever met one?"

The son of Dorain stopped and turned to the man with a hint of offence, though Asher could see the mockery behind it. "How old do ye think I am, lad? O' course I ain' ever met an elf. They buggered off a thousand years ago. Me *father* weren' even a pup."

Cutting through it all, Asher pointed at the largest column to have survived the ages. "There," he stated. "That will do."

Doran made his way over to it, looking the stone up and down. "Ye never can tell with the elves, Asher. They hadn' long got into stonework before they upped an' left these shores." The dwarf gave the stone a kick and rapped his knuckles against its freezing surface. "Hmm. Should do," he reasoned, as if he, a prince among his kind, was any authority on masonry.

"I'm glad you approve," the ranger said dryly. "Let's get to work."

Using what time they had, the three companions implemented the plan they had devised the previous day. Step one included the gathering of strong sticks or branches that could be whittled to sharp points and driven into the ground, creating a circle of makeshift spears around the stone column.

While the latter was being done, Russell put step two into motion, digging a shallow moat around the column and filling it with oil. The fire that would burn around him would be far enough away to see him unharmed but close enough to deter the wolf or, in the worst-case scenario, at least slow it down for a moment.

Step three required the chains and iron bolts. Stripped to his trousers, the miner from Snowfell pressed his back to the stone, seemingly immune to the temperature. Taking into account the size of the Werewolf that would emerge, they deliberately fastened the chains with some slack, lest the transformation simply snap the chains or disturb the bolts. Using one of Danagarr's spare hammers, Doran secured the bolts to the column and the chains with them. By the time they were finished, there wasn't much of Maybury's body left to see.

"How does that feel?" Asher asked, wiping the sheen of sweat from his brow.

"Loose," Russell replied gravely.

"It won't be when the time comes," the ranger reassured, the only one among them to have seen Russell's wolf.

Looking up at the night's sky, framed by the edging of tall trees, Maybury remarked. "It won't be long now. I can feel it."

Turning his own gaze skyward, Asher searched for any flash of the moon through the clouds, though they refused to reveal so much as a glimpse. "We will stay with you until..."

Russell shook his head. "Don't. Just leave me."

The ranger nodded. "We'll remain close by."

"Good luck," Maybury offered gravely, tarrying their departure.

"An' to ye, lad." Doran's response relayed a notch of sympathy Asher hadn't expected from him.

Together, the rangers ascended the large and uneven slab of wall that had fallen centuries past, creating a ramp up to the first floor of the hollowed ruins. Sheltered from the snow and the wind, Asher started a small fire while Doran plated up some food for them both. Not two bites into their meal, Russell's screams filled the night and gave them pause.

Man and dwarf shared a look before getting on with it, finishing off their food and drinking from their skins, though the son of Dorain had decanted his into a tankard that had been hanging from his belt.

It didn't take long for those screams to morph and devolve into something terrifying and bestial. The rattle of the chains diminished as they became taut around Russell's enlarged body. Asher was specifically listening for the sound of them snapping, though such a thing never occurred. Had he anything resembling a faith he might have offered up a prayer of thanks to Atilan. He smoked his pipe instead.

Doran made to speak for the first time since walking away from Maybury when a piercing howl cut through the night as well as his words. The wolf was fully realised. Russell was gone.

"We're both agreed, aye?" he eventually managed. "Should the chains fail to hold 'im..." The dwarf adjusted the axe he had laid to rest across his lap.

"If the wolf breaks free," Asher explained, "we will never see Russell again." His response might not have been as definitive as Doran would have liked, but they were the only words the ranger felt like giving on the matter.

There would have been several minutes of silence between them had the imprisoned Werewolf not dominated the quiet with its inhuman roars and furious growls.

Doran's lips failed to find purchase on his pipe, his hand hesitating while he sighed instead. Asher responded with a slow and deliberate blink, aware that his dwarven companion was about to say something he didn't want to hear.

"Don' think, laddy, that I don' see right through ye. I know what's really goin' on 'ere." He emphasised his last statement by pointing the tip of his pipe at the ranger.

"That doesn't surprise me," Asher replied with dry wit, "given how *insightful* you usually are."

Now it was Doran's turn to offer a slow blink. "I see the draw in all this for ye. It would be easy to think ye've a death wish given what ye've put yerself in the middle o', but I know better. I know *ye* better."

Asher didn't particularly want to hear it, but their ongoing conversation was helping the wolf's cries to withdraw in his mind.

"But of course you do," the ranger said, his words still barbed with sarcasm. "You're Doran Heavybelly, *sage* to the common man."

Doran let him say it all and gave no sign that the words had punctured his thick skin. Instead he eyed the ranger all the while, the flames flickering in the reflection of those dark orbs. "Ye're not the same," he began earnestly. "Yer monsters that is. They aren' the same."

"What are you talking about?" Asher asked him, his level of discomfort quickly rising. "I'm not convinced that's water."

"Ye think that if ye can save 'im from his monsters, *ye* can be saved from yer *own*." Doran paused there, perhaps waiting for an argument that never came. "An' I might only 'ave glimpsed the creature that hides behind that blindfold o' yers, but we both know it's there. Always there. Waitin'."

Glimpsed indeed, Asher thought. Those who had come face to face with his monster, with the *Assassin*, never lived to talk of it.

"Yer own road to... *redemption,* or whatever it is ye strive for, is yer *own*. I don' know what it's goin' to take for ye to feel that yer debt has been paid. But I know it has nothin' to do with Russell Maybury an' the curse that has befallen 'im. He can' be saved, Asher. It's not his fault. It's jus' his lot. Don' throw yers in with his, lad. Keep puttin' monsters down. Keep savin' lives. Ye'll get there."

The dwarf had hit the nail so accurately on the head that the ringing truth of it pushed all thought from Asher's mind. "I think I preferred you when you were drunk all the time," he quipped in place of a serious reply.

"Aye, me too," Doran replied with a light chuckle. "An' I would be too if ye hadn' got me involved in a hot bed o' Vorska an' Werewolves."

For a time thereafter there was only the sound of an angry Werewolf, its howls and roars carried through the ruins as if on the currents of a ghost.

"Perhaps," Asher said tentatively, "I have tied something of my fate to his own. His monster is... It feels a reflection of my own. He wants to be rid of it, but it's inside of him. The two can never be parted. It's naive, I suppose, to believe that one can find victory over the other."

"Havin' hope ain' the same as bein' naive," Doran told him quietly. "It's a fine thing what ye're tryin' to do for 'im. A second chance. Hells, a life even. Ye're a good man, Asher. That's how I know ye're goin' to beat yer demons some day. I'm afraid the same doesn' apply to Russell. It don' matter how good he is or how many good deeds he accomplishes. Every month that monster will devour 'im an' all else besides. If ye tie yerself to 'im ye'll never believe ye can defeat that which haunts ye."

"I have to try," Asher affirmed. "Russell's life deserves that just as much as the next..." The ranger had more to say on the matter but his attention was pulled away, sharpening to a point.

The wolf had gone silent.

"Please don't stop on our account," came a familiar and melodic voice, the pitch cutting through the dark. "And here I was," Merith continued, slinking out of the shadows, "thinking there were no good men left in the world. What *honour*! Even in the face of certain death..." Four pearly fangs caught the firelight as the Vorska offered the rangers his most menacing smile.

Like nightmares emerging from the subconscious abyss, Merith was soon accompanied by half a dozen of his wretched kin, each dropping from the floor above or crawling over the lip of stone. They stood as frozen shadows, silhouettes of men and women.

"So noble," Merith commended, "believing you can help the little cub. He belongs to *Creed* now, even if he doesn't know it yet."

Asher logged the name and immediately put it to one side. "If you came for the orb it isn't here," he told the pale creature.

"I'll tell ye what ye *can* 'ave though," Doran threatened, hefting his axe in one hand and his sword in the other.

Merith's dead eyes snapped to the son of Dorain. "A dwarf," he drawled. "I haven't seen one of your kind since..." The Vorska let out a short sharp bark of a laugh. "Since I was human!" he exclaimed. "I have to say, Ranger, you were intriguing *before* I knew of the company you kept."

Asher twisted his sword around, bringing it up into a two-handed hold. "It isn't here," he reiterated.

"So you said," Merith replied, hands clasped behind his back. "You wouldn't happen to know where it is, would you?"

"If we did, laddy, ye can bet we'd be takin' it to our graves."

The Blood Fiend's immaculate eyebrows rose up into his marble-like forehead, though there was a hint of mockery behind his expression. "Is that so? Hmm. Well that does make things simpler." Merith glanced over his shoulder, taking in the monsters at his back. "We can question Mr Hobbs in the morning. Let's spend the rest of the night having some fun." Again, that minacious smile brought forth his fangs.

Stepping into the light, the other six were revealed in all their pale glory. So beautiful were they that it was hard to be threatened by them, yet any one of them could take a sword to the heart and still tear out a man's throat in seconds.

"Come on then," Doran grumbled, his legs braced and feet wide apart.

The Vorska that had taken Asher's dagger to the skull advanced directly towards him, his tongue running across his top lip. "Take their heads," the ranger breathed, though Merith grinned wildly when he caught the words.

A seizing howl penetrated the mounting tension, holding the Vorska fast. They shared a look between their group only a moment before another howl racked the night. Then another, and another. Then came the growls and deafening roars.

The Vorska retreated a step, as if being closer to Merith would save them.

Asher took his own step back and peered over the side of the ruins. He could just see the top of Russell's wolfish head thrashing against the stone column, his chains groaning. Then he glimpsed a moving shadow beyond the tree line, dashing from sight. Looking elsewhere, the ranger observed reflective eyes observing him from the darkness.

"We're surrounded," he surmised.

"A'right," Doran replied, a touch of concern about him. "So which do we kill first then?"

The answer was taken by chaos and blood.

Unbridled speed and strength saw one of the Werewolves burst through the ruins and ram into one of the Vorska. Two more charged in, scattering the Blood Fiends, though claws still found their immortal bodies and dragged them from the building. Merith was the only one to pivot in time to greet a leaping wolf. Where an ordinary man would have been barrelled over and ripped to pieces, the Vorska gripped the beast around the waist and twisted it over the edge of the ruins, taking them both from sight.

Asher instinctively reached out and grabbed Doran by the collar, pulling him from his feet before the entwined force of a wolf and Vorska could slam into him. Dragging the dwarf to his feet again, the ranger compelled him to jump over the edge. They impacted the snow and rolled away from the ruins, and all to the sound of passing roars and breaking bones.

"Just kill anything that moves!" Asher instructed, throwing back his green cloak.

A dark blur moved in the corner of his eye, dropping him into a crouch and roll. The Werewolf's attacking leap took it over Asher mid-manoeuvre to strike the misshapen wall on his right, knocking several ancient stones loose. The beast growled and recovered quickly, its snouted head swivelling on the ranger with thick saliva oozing between its teeth. Asher twisted as he came out of his roll and rose to meet the monster head on, broadsword pointed in both hands.

The wolf cared little for the threat Asher posed and advanced a step, claws splayed. One swipe would turn the ranger inside out, potentially killing him faster than the black gem could heal him. Indeed, those claws went high, ready to descend on him with fury, but they never came down. A sharp whistle preceded Doran's axe, its journey coming to an end in the creature's face. It stumbled and groaned, one hand streaking bloody marks down the stone wall as it grasped at the wooden haft protruding from its head.

Asher was never one to waste an opportunity.

His broadsword swung true, separating all but a few strands of the monster's neck. Blood and gore splattered over the claw marks, drenching the wall in a red so dark it was almost black.

Doran jogged over and dislodged his axe with one strong tug. "Together," he suggested.

Asher nodded once. "Together," he agreed.

Moving away from the body, they first laid eyes on Russell, the light of his fiery moat surely dying now. He appeared incensed by the presence of his own kind, large clawed hands pushing out from between the chains and scratching at the iron. His rage increased all the more on seeing a man and a dwarf at the base of the pillar, just outside the circle of spears.

Another wolf materialised atop the nearest wall, its attention slipping from Russell to the rangers, a snarl curling its lips. The beast slid down the wall with one hand scraping over the stone. Its hind legs had barely taken its weight before the monster pounced at them. Asher dived to the side, his reactions just quick enough to see him evade the impact. Doran could not say the same.

Four of the wolf's five claws raked the dwarf's left pauldron, barrelling him over a low wall. The creature skidded to a stop in a flurry of snow and mud, turning on the son of Dorain as it did so. Asher was already on his feet again and closing the gap with sword raised. One of Merith's Vorska beat him to it, emerging from behind the ruins and colliding with the wolf at speed.

"Get up!" Asher barked, covering his companion while the two creatures tumbled over each other.

"I'm up, I'm up!"

Only feet away, the Werewolf clamped its jaws around the Vorska's arm, filling its mouth with blood. The pale creature seemed not to notice. Using its free arm, the Blood Fiend hooked its thumb into the wolf's right eye and squeezed its fist. The beast howled, releasing the arm. With brutal efficiency, the Vorska wasted no time grasping its foe's top and bottom jaws, paying no heed to the teeth piercing its flesh. In one smooth motion, it pulled the jaws beyond their natural limits, breaking bones and tearing tendons. The wolf's cry of pain was instantly garbled before being snuffed out completely when the fiend snapped its neck.

Grinning wickedly at its kill, the Vorska took too long admiring its work to realise a silvyr short-sword was flying towards its head. The creature fell flat in the snow with a piece of the most expensive and rarest minerals in the realm protruding from its skull. Finishing the job where he had not before, Asher stepped in and chopped his broadsword across its throat, severing head from body.

"I'd say it's no theory," Doran said cheerily, removing the short-sword and kicking the head away.

Asher accepted the blade back and returned it over his shoulder. "Let's see if it *stays* dead."

Moving away from the bodies but staying close to Russell, the duo ducked and weaved between the ruins to better see the monstrous warfare. Werewolves stalked the perimeter of the clearing before dashing in left and right, always targeting the Vorska. To see one monster next to the other it seemed no contest at all, yet the wolves were brought down just as often as the Vorska. That is to say, they were ripping each other limb from bloody limb.

Merith stood defiant at the base of the hollowed building, a wolf on its knees and at his mercy. He had none. Proving their methods tried and tested, the lead Vorska pulled the beast's jaws apart. It sounded to Asher like someone was breaking a tree branch in half.

Leaving the Werewolf to flop at his feet, Merith drew a sword from within the shadows of his long coat. It looked an antique, its design from another era, with a cross guard that curled up into points not unlike the creature's bottom fangs. The Vorska strode out from the ruins and met an oncoming Werewolf with the self-assurance not likely seen in the hearts of men.

Like a wraith, Merith accurately predicted the wolf's movements and evaded its initial strikes while simultaneously whipping his blade from side to side and over his head in a graceful arc. The fight, if it could have been called such a thing, was over in seconds and ended with the Werewolf strewn in the snow, its major arteries exposed.

Asher looked from the dead wolf to Merith and discovered the Vorska was already watching him from afar. A devilish grin pulled at his dark lips, pushing together the gash in his left cheek. When his smile faded, the gash was healed, leaving his marble-like skin intact once more.

"Let's take his head!" Doran urged, stepping out from behind the wall.

Since that had been the ranger's plan from the beginning, he joined the dwarf, his broadsword still dripping with Vorska blood. Merith welcomed the challenge and began walking towards them, his weapon held out to one side, catching flakes of snow as they drifted down.

Another Werewolf tried to interfere, hurtling towards Merith on all fours, but was intercepted by two Vorska that pulled it down by its hind legs. The beast scrambled to be free of them but the nimble fiends navigated its thrashing body like ants swarming an insect. Together they dismantled the wolf until it was naught but a torso and a head.

As thunder might tear through a silent sky, so too did a savage roar cut through the surrounding forest and spill into the ruins. Everything stopped. The Vorska paused as no more than gargoyles amid the stonework while the wolves hesitated to pursue battle, with some even retreating a step.

Most telling of all was Merith's reaction.

The lead Vorska turned to the tree line, the rangers forgotten. Mimicking his Lycan foes, the fiend's lips curled into a snarl of derision.

What silence and mounting tension followed was disturbed by movement slightly behind Asher. The ranger pivoted on his heel, blade rising to meet the new threat. In truth, he didn't know what to make of the man who leapt from the first floor of the ruin, nor did he have much time to make an assessment. Hooded and draped in blue and grey robes, the stranger landed between the rangers and Merith, a wooden staff held high in one hand. The moment that staff impacted the ground, pushing through the snow, the other end exploded with light. Vorska and Werewolf alike were bathed in the radiance, their heightened senses momentarily overwhelmed.

When Asher peeled his arm away from his eyes, the figure was already rushing past him. "Run!" he cried. "You cannot hope to fight what is coming!" When the rangers hesitated to follow, he called back, "You should be running!"

That terrible roar split The Evermoore again, heralding the arrival of something new. "Go!" Asher encouraged, shoving Doran after the fleeing stranger. Together, they followed in his wake, leaving the Vorska and the Werewolves to renew their war.

They were also leaving Russell to his fate.

CHAPTER 17
A NEW ALLY IN AN OLD WAR

Thindle - These scrawny monsters might not look like much, being skin and bone and with a head of thick hair that conceals their everything from the neck up, but they're vicious little blighters. They lurk around swamps mostly but that don't mean they're confined to such.
Now, if you consider yourself a strong but slow hunter, these aren't the contracts for you. Speed is required to tackle a Thindle's agility. And never let them get a single swipe in. Their nails carry disease that will spoil your blood and put you in the ground within days.

A Chronicle of Monsters: A Ranger's Bestiary, 12th Edition, Page 50.

Authen Madwell, Ranger.

Doran damn-near fell over when they eventually reached the edge of Lirian. He was sweating like the others but his breath was far more laboured. "I'm out o' shape," he rasped, doubled over with his hands on his knees.

Asher ignored the dwarf and put himself between the son of Dorain and the stranger they had followed from the ruins. He had his back to them, facing the city of candlelight. From his attire, the ranger might have assumed he was simply a vagrant, with naught but a tired satchel over one shoulder and a wooden staff in hand.

His recent display of magic, however, informed Asher that he was standing behind a mage.

"Who are you?" he demanded, fighting the urge to retrace his steps and return to Russell.

"We're still not safe here," the stranger replied, the movement of his hood suggesting he was taking in the city. "We must seek shelter."

"I'm not going anywhere with you," Asher stated. "Not until I know who you are."

The figure sighed. "You have only survived this long because the wolves arrived in Lirian the same night the Vorska came for the orb. Their constant fighting and hunting each other has kept them out of the city for the most part. After tonight, who can say if that will last?"

"Wait," Asher interjected. "Have you been watching us?"

"Of course I have. You have no idea what has been in your possession. And you bring it here of all places," he barked, waving a hand at The Tower of Gadavance, its crooked structure looming over the city. "We must seek shelter immediately," he pressed again. "Somewhere we can put a wall to our backs."

The ranger couldn't agree more, but he was nothing if not stubborn. "I'm not going anywhere with you until I at least know your name."

The stranger was shaking his head. "I can tell you my name, Ranger, but names rarely have anything to do with who we really are. Should it move things along, however, you may call me... *Hadavad.*"

The dark of night yet reigned when the trio descended to The Ranch's basement. They heard Danagarr long before they saw him, his work continuing seemingly without a break. When he did appear, it was only to retrieve more supplies from the courtyard. He offered Hadavad no more than a nod, being either too exhausted or too ingrained in his work to care who he was.

"He gets like that," Doran assured, dipping a cloth into a bowl of water. "Best to leave 'im to it for now." The dwarf went on to dab the cut above his eyebrow, likely gained after leaping from the ruins, if not in the attack he suffered.

Asher absorbed the information with little effort, his attention fixed on the mage. Hadavad made immediately for the fireplace, leaving his staff to stand perfectly on end in the middle of the room. Doran raised an eyebrow at the trick and couldn't help but poke the staff to see if it would fall over. It didn't. The dwarf's fingertip bent and his face flushed with blood, but the staff refused to budge.

He tutted. "Mages..."

The ranger ignored the staff's placement and moved to come up on Hadavad's side. He was yet to even see the man's face without the shadows of his hood. "Remove the hood," Asher commanded.

Hadavad didn't move, his palms held out to the flames. "I see you trust people about as well as I do."

"I want to see your eyes," the ranger told him firmly. "And your skin."

"Prudent," Hadavad remarked, pulling back his hood. "Though I could not be a wolf, and I am certainly not a Vorska."

"There are many things you could be," Asher replied. "I would make that judgement for myself." Indeed he did, scrutinising the man before him. He was older, perhaps in his late sixties, though his display at the ruins suggested his body was in excellent condition. Long white hair fell over his shoulders in waves and blended into an equally long beard of the same colour. His skin was creased with time and paled by winter's lack of light, but his dark eyes were full of so much life that they might have belonged to a younger man.

"Well?" the mage enquired. "Do you see man or monster?"

In truth, Asher found the two hard to distinguish most days. "What part do you have in all this?" he asked instead. "Why would you help us?"

Hadavad chuckled lightly to himself. "I have oft found that questions such as those are like the seeds of a great tree: small and easy to handle, until they grow wildly beyond your ability to manage what comes next."

Doran rolled his eyes and slumped into one of the armchairs. "I'm already lovin' where this is goin'."

"Speak plainly," Asher instructed. "I still haven't decided whether you are friend or foe."

"Trust me, pal," the dwarf commented with some amusement, "ye don' want to be the latter when it comes to this fella."

"Friends are like leaves," the mage said dolefully, his gaze drifting back to the flames. "They all have their time until they wither and fall from the branch."

"It's to be *foe* then?" Doran looked almost eager at the possibility, the thrill of the fight still lingering in his veins.

"If only the world were so black and white," Hadavad mused, taking the seat opposite Doran's. "If my centuries of life have taught me anything, it is that the world is infinite shades of grey. In that regard, perhaps you should consider me more *ally* than friend."

Asher tried to absorb the mage's words just as he had Doran's but, like the dwarf, he was stumbling over the timescale Hadavad referred to. "Centuries?" The ranger's voice had dropped an octave, adopting a threatening tone.

The mage smiled knowingly. "Like I said: shades of grey."

"Ye're not human then," Doran concluded, shuffling to the edge of his seat, eyes darting to the axe and sword he had discarded.

"You needn't fear me," the mage replied, hands flicking up from the armrests. "I assure you, I am human. Painfully so," he added, clenching one fist and frowning at the pain he felt there. "I must admit, it's been some time since I inhabited a body of this age."

Asher looked Hadavad up and down again before sharing a quizzical look with Doran. He was also discreetly gripping the dagger hidden at the base of his back. "If you're pretending to be human, you're doing a terrible job."

Hadavad responded with a hearty laugh, one hand pressed to his chest. "It's also been a long time since I have held a conversation with anyone. Forgive me. I only mean to speak plainly, *truthfully* that is. If we are to be allies—and given what we're up against we really should be—then we ought to lay our cards on the table as quickly as possible."

"We're rangers," Asher said succinctly. "What the hell are you?"

"Aye," Doran directed, thumbing at Asher. "Let's start there. Then tell us how ye're connected to the monsters."

Hadavad took a breath, considering where to start. "There are many beginnings. My own goes back five hundred years, when I was truly an old man. Perhaps that is too far to begin," he pondered. "I could start my tale when first we met, Asher. Back then you saw only foes—I certainly considered you one. Then again, who wouldn't consider an Arakesh to be a foe?"

Quite confounded, the ranger could only blink, his grip relenting somewhat on the dagger.

"Ye two know each other?" Doran glanced at Asher and saw the same level of confusion his own tone had conveyed.

"I rarely forget a face," Asher said. "Nor a name. I have no memory of you, mage."

"I didn't know your name then," Hadavad clarified. "But like you, I rarely forget a face. Even a blindfolded one."

Where he might have initially been disarmed by the unfolding revelation, Asher was beginning to feel *seen*, a sensation that pressed upon him a degree of threat. His grip tightening once again around the hilt of his dagger, the ranger asked, "Where did we meet?"

"In Kelp Town of all places," the mage answered cheerily. "I'm aware that you have recently come from there. Even after five hundred years I cannot say whether I believe in coincidences or fate."

"When?" Asher probed.

"Fifteen, twenty years ago," Hadavad estimated. "I had never seen such proficient butchery," he went on, no hint of judgement in his tone. "I am glad to see you have chosen a different path."

"Yorvun Geld," Asher stated, recalling his target's name with ease.

"That was the fellow," Hadavad confirmed. "A talented mage. Destined for greatness. Well, he had been until..."

"Until I killed him," Asher confessed, his sight lost to memory now.

"I had befriended him in his earlier years," the mage continued. "I would come by from time to time and check on his progress. He had a natural talent for magic. Barely needed an ounce of Demetrium to control his spells. Alas, such talent does not go unnoticed."

"Belik Nyson," Asher recalled, the name peeled from the depths of his mind. He had last read that name on a length of knotted red string. "He ordered the death."

"Belik, yes..." Hadavad ran a hand down his beard. "I turned his blood to ice a little over a decade ago. He was but one man. One of many who submit to the ways of The Black Hand."

"What's that?" Doran asked.

"Death," Hadavad stated grimly. "And the reason for my crusade. Though," he added lightly, "for once, they have little to do with the events you and your friend, Russell, find yourselves in."

"Wait," Asher commanded. "*You* weren't in Kelp Town—when I killed... Yorvun."

"Not as you see me now," the mage admitted. "Back then I inhabited the body of Hosun Vord. A good man," Hadavad mused with a wistful smile. "From Ameeraska. He was *young* and *strong*."

Asher blinked again, recalling the image of a young man, his skin a shade darker than the sands on which his people lived. He had prevented the assassin's first attempt, forcing him to change his plan and, unfortunately, kill several others before his target again presented himself.

"I know of the man you speak," he breathed, gripped by disbelief.

"A good man," Hadavad repeated fondly. "I lost his body eight years ago. Thankfully, by then, I had a new apprentice." He rolled his hands down and over his lap to indicate his current form.

"You can possess bodies," the ranger surmised.

"I can. And I will continue to until my mission is complete."

Doran leant forward. "And that is?"

"The demise of The Black Hand," the mage replied coolly.

Asher absorbed every word but continued to focus on the mechanics of how the man before him had cheated death for five centuries. "How are you possessing people?"

Hadavad didn't answer him, but looked him dead in the eyes, as if he was exploring every crevice of the ranger's mind. "You seem a man of secrets, Asher. You must be, given what you used to be—who you used to serve. The order of Arakesh is nearly as wicked as The Black Hand. Such organisations breed secrets. To that end they breed secret-keepers. Am I to take it that you will hold my secrets as your own? That you would feign ignorance in place of knowledge?"

The ranger wasn't so foolish as to answer right away, giving the appearance that he was actually considering his response. "I will," he said truthfully.

"And you, master dwarf?"

"I'll probably 'ave forgotten most o' this by next week anyway," he replied with a shrug.

"You'll both probably be dead by next week," the mage corrected.

"Probably," Asher echoed severely.

Hadavad took a slow breath before adjusting the folds of his marred tunic. There shone a chain looped around his neck, concealed mostly by his beard. Hooking it with one finger, the mage presented them with a ruby half the length of a man's thumb and almost twice as wide.

Doran's eyes widened. "Ye could buy a kingdom with a gem that size."

"'Tis the Viridian Ruby," the mage declared.

The dwarf's look of awe fell into ruin. "Viridian? Ain' that a colour?"

Hadavad smiled knowingly and raised the ruby into the torchlight, revealing the bluish-green pigment at the gem's heart. "It is no ordinary ruby," he explained. "The blue heart is the real source of its magic but..." The mage shrugged. "I would have to break it open to know for sure. To even try would likely be the end of me."

"How does it work?" Asher enquired, his fingers still fastened around the hilt of his dagger.

"In truth, I have no idea *how*. I know how to *use* it, how to transfer my consciousness into a willing host. But the magic that fuels it or the spells that direct it... It is from a time before... Well, *before*!" Hadavad laughed. "I fear I will one day perish before learning all of its secrets. Or learning where the other four lie hidden."

"Other four?" Doran burst. "There's five o' those things out there?"

"So the legend goes," the mage confirmed. "Though, if the legends are true, each gem is capable of its own miracle."

"What happens to the hosts?" Asher asked pointedly, darkening Hadavad's demeanour.

"Cheating death comes at a price," he told them gravely. "My apprentices do not survive the transfer."

"They die?" the dwarf spat.

"They each volunteer knowingly," the mage was quick to explain.

Asher wasn't convinced. "Why would anyone do that?"

"My apprentices—all of them—have in some way been touched by The Black Hand. That touch is ruinous. Be it their loved ones or livelihoods, they have each lost something dear. They wish to see The Black Hand destroyed. They sacrifice their lives to that end."

An uneasy silence fell over the room, save for Danagarr's distant sawing.

"I do not employ such methods lightly," Hadavad eventually said, speaking over the crackling fire. "But make no mistake, you and I are fighting different battles. Yours is merely to survive in the world, to kill hungry beasts who poke at the edges of civilisation— and for coin no less. I fight for *good*. I fight to rid our fair realm of *evil*. And believe me, evil is ever at work. True evil is not mindless such as the monsters you hunt in the dark. It is thinking. It is determined. Worse... It is *winning*. There are too few who know that evil even exists and fewer still willing to hold the line. So do not stand there, Ranger, and judge me."

Asher slowly let go of the dagger at his back and adopted a more relaxed stance, leaning against the wall beside the fire. "What exactly is this Black Hand?" he asked, his tone softer now.

"In a word: *necromancers*. 'Tis but a word, but I hope it conveys something of their character. The depths of their nature and the means they employ to meet their wretched ends are fouler still but, as I said, their part in this is a step removed. My personal history with The Black Hand is my own. I have told you as much because it is entwined with current events."

"How so?" the ranger pressed.

Hadavad hesitated, his jaw contorted beneath his beard. "Is it here? The orb?"

Now Asher hesitated, more than aware that the bronze sphere was already desired by two other parties. "It's hidden," he said. "Only Russell knows where."

The mage sighed. "That's a shame. We won't know his fate until morning."

The ranger stepped away from the wall. "What is it? Why would the Vorska be after it? And the Werewolves besides? Monsters never seek anything but their next meal."

Hadavad tapped his finger against the armrest. "It is all entwined," he said again. "Though I feel compelled to point out that Vorska and Werewolves are not your typical monsters. I can see why they would be clumped together with the rest of them, but they possess key distinctions."

"Such as?" Doran asked, doubt in his voice.

"Chiefly, their origins."

Here Hadavad took a short break and retrieved an elegant and intricately detailed pipe from inside his right sleeve. He packed the bowl with herbs of his choice and clicked his fingers to light it. Asher had never seen a mage use magic without their staff or wand in hand—at least not without disastrous ramifications—and assumed this particular mage had most at a disadvantage given his lifespan. Still, he made no comment and allowed Hadavad the time he needed to inhale and exhale.

"You see," he finally began again, "most monsters, the ones you commonly come across, are just as natural to this world as the animals we hunt for food. Their nature places them above the common animal, but animals they remain, despite being called *monsters*. Vorska and Werewolves, however, are supernatural in nature. Think about it. A Vorska's true appearance is revealed while the sun is up. Not *in* sunlight," he specified. "But simply while the sun is *up*. It doesn't matter if they hide in shadow, they are still revealed for what they are. That isn't *nature*. That's *magic*. If their skin reacted to sunlight, you could argue that they're natural. But it doesn't. The spell that governs them is that of day and night.

"The same logic can be applied to Werewolves. Why should their bodies react to a full moon but no other variation? If they turned into wolves by the touch of the moon it could be reasoned that they are part of the natural world in some way. But they don't. 'Tis magic. Like the Vorska, they are governed by spells. By a *curse*."

Asher looked away before focusing on the mage again. "You're saying that they were both... *made*."

"And so the roots begin to twist," the mage said with a tight smile.

"They were made by The Black Hand," the ranger assumed.

"Not exactly," Hadavad replied, his frown pinching his thick white eyebrows together. "I do not have all the pieces, I confess. No one does. Save Merith perhaps. The origin of both species goes back even further than myself."

"Eight hundred years," Asher uttered, momentarily cast back to his conversation with the blond Vorska.

The mage's eyes narrowed on the ranger. "You have spoken with Merith then."

"Briefly."

"I have long suspected he was the first of his kind, but…" Hadavad raised his hands in the manner of a shrug. "Merith has lived long enough to master most things, especially lies. Whether he was the first or not, I do not doubt that he was there for the birth of the Vorska. Perhaps even the Werewolf." The mage puckered his cheeks and lips to draw on his pipe. "He claims to have been his assistant."

Asher glanced at Doran, his curiosity deepening with every word. "Whose assistant?"

There came no immediate response from Hadavad, the mage content to smoke his pipe for the moment. When, at last, he turned his gaze up at the ranger, there was a shadow gathered about his eyes. "Kargon Iskander," he spoke, and precisely so.

Doran sat back and sighed. "Are we supposed to know who that is?"

"He was a mage," Hadavad told them. "Well," he added, correcting himself, "he was a *necromancer*—Black Hand through and through. Then… he wasn't anymore. They keep little in the way of archives, especially regarding members who walk away. Traditionally they have them killed, lest their secrets get out."

Asher didn't miss the glance Doran gave him, the dwarf likely making the same comparisons that he was between Nightfall and The Black Hand.

"If I had to guess," Hadavad went on, "I would say Kargon had ideas that went beyond even the dark parameters of the order. Only Merith could say, but I am loath to converse with that monster for any longer than it takes to utter a destructive spell." The mage inhaled and exhaled a cloud of sweet-smelling smoke.

"After breaking away," he shared, "Kargon apparently experimented with the dark and forbidden magic his masters had imparted, twisting it further, and pushing the boundaries of nature. I cannot speak of all the fiends he created, but Merith would have you believe his master fathered the Vorska and later the Werewolves."

"So you *have* spoken with Merith?" Asher reasoned.

"Many times over the centuries," Hadavad admitted. "It always ends in violence, mind you. Three centuries past he succeeded in killing me—my host at least. I was saved by my apprentice. He likes to talk," the mage detailed. "I would say he enjoys the sound of his voice more than the taste of blood."

Doran looked left and right. "I can' help but notice ye've no apprentice right now."

"Indeed. I am... between apprentices." Hadavad smiled. "Perhaps *you* would be interested, master dwarf?"

"I'm nobody's replacement, laddy," the son of Dorain replied friendly enough.

"A pity. Your strength. Your long life. You would be a formidable weapon against The Black Hand."

"Why is the orb of any importance?" Asher interjected, cutting through any adjacent conversations. "Even you have asked after it."

Hadavad pointed his pipe at the ranger and poked the air. "It is here the roots twist again, bringing everything together. That orb is said to have belonged to Iskander himself, an artefact of his making."

Asher could only imagine what horrors a necromancer might conjure. "What does it do?"

The mage opened his mouth to speak but his lips slipped into a lazy smile instead. "That's the question," he eventually said. "Merith, Creed, myself even—we all have our theories."

"What do *you* believe?" Asher asked.

Hadavad let his head roll against the back of the armchair, his eyes briefly roaming over the flames. "I believe... I believe it houses the Obsidian Ruby."

"Oh 'ere we go," Doran complained, shaking his head. "Why is it every time ye open yer mouth, the rabbit hole gets a little deeper?"

Hadavad's response was in his eyes alone; severe things they were. They beheld the dwarf until some unseen weight pulled them down and away. Indeed, his entire demeanour sagged beneath that same weight.

"Do not take my words so lightly, master dwarf," he beseeched, his tone so serious as to match his expression. "*The Skaramangian Stones* make short work of *fools*."

Doran bristled, as he would, but Asher spoke first. "The Skaramangian Stones?" he questioned, the name foreign to him.

The bowl of the mage's pipe blossomed with heat and light, illuminating his eyes for but a moment. "Who can say when they were forged," he began, "for none still live who can tell of it. They are ancient. Older, perhaps, if there is such a thing. Like my words, they are not to be taken lightly. Each has the power to undo men and whatever world they might hold to."

"I've never heard of them," Asher said, his curiosity rolling over itself to new heights.

"Mage business," Doran grunted, arms folded.

"The Skaramangian Stones were once the focus of my life," Hadavad said, ignoring the dwarf. "I spent a life's work just researching this one," he added with a short laugh, partially lifting the Viridian Ruby. "In five hundred years I haven't come close to finding another of its ilk. But I believe The Black Hand did," he went on gravely, his gaze piercing the far wall. "I have scoured numerous Black Hand archives over the years. There were never more than snippets here and there, a note perhaps, or an old account. I believe Kargon Iskander took it with him when he fled the order. I also believe it was the Obsidian Ruby that aided his dark magic and helped him to realise the nightmares he brought forth. And I believe he locked it away inside that orb before he died."

Again, the trio were reigned over by silence, as if history itself was pouring out of the past and into the present.

"Skaramangian Stones..." Asher muttered, the name new to his tongue. There were many pitfalls in life—a lesson the ranger had learnt time and again—but none so deep nor so labyrinthian as the machinations of mages. He couldn't help but wonder if he was in over his head.

"They are each a powerful relic of an ancient era." Hadavad indicated the gem about his neck. "They will not remain lost forever—they *must* be discovered by those who would not use them for evil. They certainly cannot be allowed to lend their magic to the likes of Merith or Creed."

"Who is this Creed ye keep mentionin'?"

A hint of disdain crossed Hadavad's features. "Creed is a once in a generation Werewolf—to put it simply. I had heard of others like him, in times past, but I have never seen one before Creed. Who can say why he is different, but different he is. He is bigger than any Werewolf you have encountered. More ferocious. More... *everything*." The mage took a short break to draw on his pipe. "Brutal though he is, it is the power he holds over other wolves that truly stands him apart."

"Power?" Asher repeated, sure that he wasn't going to like what he heard next.

"You might have noticed that Werewolves are solitary creatures, unlike their smaller, natural counterparts that roam the wilds." Hadavad was shaking his head. "Creed is a pack leader. Other Werewolves are drawn to him. Those he sires personally are under his thrall while the full moon reigns."

Doran was wagging his finger in the air. "Was he one o' the first then, like this Merith fella?"

"No," Hadavad replied emphatically. "Those cursed by the wolf's bite do not suffer immortality as the Vorska do. In fact, Creed is the oldest I have ever met. He is nearing on two hundred years by my count."

"He bit Russell," Asher disclosed.

The mage's lips twisted while he considered his response. "He is your friend," he stated. "I have observed you both from afar these past weeks. I have never seen anything like it—and that's coming from a man who's seen a *lot* of life. A ranger and a Werewolf," he pondered with a warm smile. "How unusual."

Uncomfortable with the direction their conversation was taking, Asher took charge again. "You said they have their own theories," he stated, his tone uncompromising. "Merith and Creed. They don't believe the orb holds this... Obsidian Ruby?"

"Creed has likely never even heard of the Skaramangian Stones," Hadavad opined. "If Merith truly was Kargon's assistant, he may well have heard of them, though he has never voiced such knowledge."

"Then what do they think it holds?" the ranger asked.

"Both Merith and Creed believe the orb contains a spell, though they each believe it to be a *different* spell," the mage added with some amusement. "Merith has convinced his followers that Kargon's original spell is inside the orb, and that with it they can remould the details—remove the *imperfections*."

The conclusion was obvious to Asher. "They want to remain in their human form during the day."

"Precisely," Hadavad confirmed.

"And Creed?" Doran probed.

"To be unshackled from the moon of course," the mage answered. "He desires the ability to shift forms at will."

"Either outcome would be bad," Asher reasoned.

Doran held up a hand before one stubby finger pointed at Hadavad. "What would *ye* do with it, wizard?"

"If anything I have learnt of the Obsidian Ruby is true, I would not dare wield it, nor even carry it on my person. I would bury it somewhere so deep and dark not even the combined power of every mage in Korkanath could find it."

"Ye can' jus' destroy it?" Doran asked in a very dwarven manner.

"Were it so easy," Hadavad said ominously. "Our focus should be opening the orb before Merith or Creed. Staying ahead of them long enough to conceal the stone is our only chance."

"*Our?*" Asher echoed.

"Of course," the mage replied, his pipe almost falling out of his mouth.

The ranger stood a little taller, cutting an imposing figure. "If you wish to ally yourself with us you will have to shift your focus, mage. *Our* plan is to help Russell. Ancient necromancers and magical stones come second."

Hadavad removed the pipe from his mouth entirely. "You can't be serious?"

"Oh, he is," Doran chipped in unhelpfully.

"Did you not hear a word I said, *Ranger*? The spells they seek might not be inside that orb, but they could do far worse if they got their hands on a Skaramangian Stone!"

Asher folded his arms and said nothing.

Hadavad sat back after his heated response had pushed him forwards in his seat. It was impossible to say what his centuries-old consciousness was mulling over, though his features did soften. "'Tis foolish to put the one life before so many. But it is undoubtedly virtuous. A quality I have not practiced in some time," he added quietly, and more to himself. "You said that Russell is the only one who knows where the orb is. Hmm. Then perhaps saving the one will save us all."

Satisfied, Asher nodded just the once. "You're welcome to rest here if you can. But we return to the ruins at dawn."

CHAPTER 18
A SHORT REPRIEVE

Oligort - Sticky buggers—literally. I fought one only ten days ago in Whistle Town. It decided one of the outlying barns was its territory and it guarded it so.

In their natural position, they're no taller than your waist. This is due to their six legs always being bent. When they spring for you, their length is considerably more.

These are the first monsters I've ever crossed that possess a mouth on both the upper and lower part of their bodies. Truth be told, I'm not sure they have a right way round. What they do have is an awful amount of sticky fluid across their entire body. They secrete all their life and this can often be used to track them.

Interestingly, and most fortunately, this same fluid is rather flammable.

A Chronicle of Monsters: A Ranger's Bestiary, 12th Edition, Page 391.

Caleb Moore, Ranger.

The smell of the ruins found Asher long before he laid eyes on the carnage that littered them. Where there had been Lycan bodies, butchered and bloody, there now lay naked men and women. Here and there, the stone of faded grey was splattered with blood and raked with claw marks.

Looking down from his saddle, the ranger could see the hind paw print that Hector's front hoof was standing in. It was enormous—easily twice that of an ordinary Werewolf.

"No Vorska," Doran announced from atop Pig. "I saw more than one get their head ripped off though."

"I told you," Asher said, "they're secretive in nature. They take the bodies with them."

The muted hooves of Hadavad's white mare pushed through to pass them. "We cannot linger," the mage warned. "Somewhere out there, the wolves will be waking up in their human forms. Should they return they will still prove difficult to put down."

Asher agreed and even thought of the Vorska, who could still attack them in their nightmarish forms in such seclusion. "Russell?" he called, edging Hector further into the ruins.

The ranger was already climbing down before the horse came to a stop. He rounded a broken wall and navigated the standing archways until he could see the lone pillar that had defied time. The makeshift spears that had surrounded it were broken and strewn across the ground, along with the chains.

He was gone.

Marching through the snow, Asher crouched to inspect the chains, noting how so many of the links were warped and snapped. After feeling the edges of the severed links he let them fall back into the snow, his hopes dashed and heart gripped with unease.

"Asher!" Doran cried.

Hopping over the low wall to his left, the ranger hurried through the ruins, homing in on the dwarf. Hadavad too had dismounted and was now striding through the snow, with his staff keeping in step. Being closer, the mage arrived at Doran's side a second before Asher, his ragged blue robe almost blocking the ranger's view of the naked body that rested in the snow.

"He's alive," the son of Dorain reported, rolling the body over.

There was Russell Maybury, unconscious in the snow, his bare chest and every limb covered in smears of blood and patches of dirt. Indeed, his chest was rising and falling with steady breaths. Asher crouched to join Doran, his gaze captured by the grubby gash that tore through Russell's hip. Before his very eyes, the wound was creeping closed, as if time itself was reversing.

"For all of Kargon's failings," Hadavad commented, "there are some advantages to the curse he created."

"We need to get him back to The Ranch," Asher instructed, moving to lift the man.

The sound of lightly crunching snow and a barely perceptible moan reached the trio, turning them east. Hadavad moved first, looking over what remained of a low wall. "'Tis a wolf," he reported.

Asher rose to join him, quickly sighting the woman slowly crawling through the snow, her matted hair concealing much of her face. Like Russell's, her naked body was smeared with blood and dirt. Her human mind was steadily rising from the depths of the Lycan slumber.

Without a word, Hadavad navigated the low wall and confidently approached the woman. Sharp as her senses were, her waking mind appeared too burdened by the transition to register his steps. Nor did she register the mage's staff as its bulbous top was angled down over the back of her head.

Asher instinctively moved back a step at the low-level *boom*. The spell, invisible to the eyes, had ripped the air and caved in the wolf's skull, dispersing blood, bone, and gore across the snow. The ranger looked from the dead woman to Doran, who had come to his side a moment before the spell had been enacted.

The dwarf glanced at the black gem on Asher's finger. "If I were ye, lad," he whispered, "I'd make sure that never comes off."

Yet to be convinced of Hadavad, Asher certainly agreed. The power of mages was not to be trifled with.

221

"That's one less for Creed to call upon," Hadavad said upon his return. "He has nothing more than a band now, but I recall the days he commanded near on an army of wolves." The mage turned his attention on Russell. "Allow me," he offered, taking his staff in two hands.

Maybury was soon lifted effortlessly from the ground, his body tethered to the end of the mage's staff by unseen magic. Quite carefully, he was placed over Asher's saddle and then covered by the blanket the ranger kept strapped to it.

"Let us be gone from this place," Hadavad declared, mounting his mare and leading the way back.

~

Asher looked from Doran to the bucket of icy cold water he held. "What's that for?" he asked dubiously.

"To wake 'im up!" the dwarf replied honestly. "If he sleeps any longer he'll be turnin' back into a damned wolf!"

A scolding look in his eyes, the ranger firmly gripped the rim of the bucket and took it from Doran's hands.

Hadavad walked into view, his attention cast down at Russell's sleeping form beside the fire. "He is just a pup in their world," he remarked. "The earliest transformations are quite taxing." The mage sighed. "But I am inclined to agree with Master Heavybelly. We need him to retrieve the orb."

"Russell is the priority," Asher reminded, putting the bucket to one side.

"The branches of life are ever entwined," the mage replied.

"Relatin' everythin' to a damned tree ain' helpin' yer cause," Doran quipped.

"I only mean to say that retrieving the orb is integral to helping Russell. We must leave Lirian at once. There are other forces who would seek the orb if they knew of its existence, and those forces are right here in this very city."

"The Black Hand," Asher concluded.

"Exactly. I have long suspected that they have assumed control over The Tower of Gadavance. It is not safe here so long as the orb remains with us. So we must flee and take it with us. We can use the light to put some distance between us and the Vorska. We cannot stop the wolves from tracking us but leaving swiftly might give us the edge we need."

Asher was shaking his head. "We can't leave. There are still two more full moons to come. We need somewhere secure to hold him."

"It is folly to stay, Asher," the mage insisted. "We must leave at once. Only after we are free of the orb can we return."

The ranger raised a hand to halt the conversation. "We stay. For now."

With that, he turned away from his companions and made for the sound of vigorous work. Danagarr was stripped down to his breaches, his bare chest protected by no more than a leather apron. His back glistened in the torchlight, his powerful muscles rising and falling with every hammer blow.

"How goes it?" Asher enquired. He then waited patiently for the smith to complete his stage of work.

"Has he woken up yet?" the Stormshield asked.

"Not yet," the ranger told him, leaning against the doorframe that no longer had an actual door.

Danagarr wiped his brow with a near black cloth. "I still don' think any o' this is right," he voiced. "I'm doin' this for ye, I'd 'ave it known."

"Your efforts are appreciated," Asher assured, examining the iron lattice that covered most of the walls. "Your speed and precision puts every human smith to shame," he complimented.

The dwarf eyed him suspiciously. "Ye're not tellin' me anythin' I didn' already know. Is there somethin' ye need?"

"I need it tonight," Asher announced evenly, as if he wasn't asking for the impossible.

Danagarr guffawed, his grin spreading as one finger came up to wag at the ranger. That grin slowly faded when he realised the man before him was being serious. "Tonight?" he spat. The dwarf gestured at the room and tools and debris that crowded it. "Look around, Asher. It can' be done. I've not even started on the ceiling and the door isn' nearly finished!"

"We don't have a choice," Asher began before Danagarr spoke over him.

"The hells ye don'! Buy more chains an' take 'im back to 'em ruins!"

The ranger moved to stand firmly on both feet, filling the doorway. "We cannot return to the ruins. The Vorska and the Werewolves surround the city. We wouldn't survive another night out there. And there isn't time to get Russell away from the city before the wolf in him returns. He needs to be secured."

Danagarr groaned into his wild beard. "I hear ye, fella, I really do, but it doesn' change the fact that it ain' ready. I've got the chains, sure, but the bolts I need don' arrive until tomorrow. An' the door hasn' got nearly enough layers added to it, not to mention the locks! Puttin' 'im in 'ere right now is as good as takin' 'im out into the woods an' hopin' for the best!"

Asher remained where he stood, intransigent as always.

Equally inflexible, Danagarr held his ground and folded his arms.

The tension rose for naught but seconds before the old smith gave in with a sigh. "Ye'll be the death o' me," he said. "I'll do all that I can. I'll likely 'ave to cut a few corners," he muttered to himself. "I can' guarantee it'll hold a wolf. Hells, I can' guarantee that even after I'm done. I'll remind ye this has never been done before, an' for good reason."

Asher was nodding his head sympathetically. "Do what you can."

The morning soon slipped into the afternoon, a pale and grey affair that brought more snow to Lirian. Doran spent most of that time snoozing in the armchair, not far from Russell, while Hadavad used a piece of white chalk to scribe runes and glyphs into the floors—warning wards he called them. Asher didn't understand them but he was glad of the mage's spells. The ranger had, instead, spent his time retrieving more supplies and, where he could, encouraging vendors to expedite their deliveries. The latter had proven less fruitful.

When Maybury finally awoke, he did so with uncanny swiftness, as if he had never been asleep at all. He sat up, surprised it seemed, to be attired in a loose-fitting shirt and his breeches. He quickly put it all together, including his surroundings, and turned to spy Asher watching him from the corner.

"What happened?" he asked, throat dry.

"It seems we're caught in a war," the ranger told him, stepping into the shaft of dusty light that filtered through the high and narrow windows. "And it's a war far older than either of us."

Asher poured them both a cup of water and brought the miner from Snowfell up to speed on recent events, divulging all that Hadavad had imparted as well as the mage's identity and extraordinary origins.

"We can trust him?" Russell asked.

"For now," Asher replied. "Given what we're up against he is an ally we can't afford to ignore." The ranger then went on to inform Maybury of his plan for the evening and their eventual plan to leave Lirian altogether while they made sense of the bronze orb and its secret.

Upon his last word, Russell sat back in the same chair Hadavad had occupied the previous night. Considering his humble beginnings and honest life as a miner, he absorbed the unimaginable information with astonishing speed and understanding—even if he did look somewhat bewildered.

"Ancient mages, necromancers, magical gems." Maybury shook his head. "What are we in the middle of?"

"It ain' ranger business, that's for sure," Doran chipped in.

Asher refrained from rolling his eyes. He should have known the dwarf was awake since he had stopped snoring several minutes ago. "He's not wrong," he reluctantly agreed. "But we are in the middle of it, of a *war*. The Vorska and the Werewolves won't stop hunting for the orb and they know we have it."

"So we're to what?" Maybury began. "Stay here until the full moons pass? And then what? If we survive the wolf in here we're to just run, get away from the city?"

"It would help," Hadavad announced from the bottom of the stairs, "if we could get inside that orb. Perhaps then we could more accurately determine our next move."

Russell stood up. "You must be the mage."

"And you are Creed's latest recruit," Hadavad replied, watching the man closely.

Maybury shifted on the spot, uncomfortable perhaps, having only recently heard his maker's name from Asher.

"Forgive me," Hadavad began again, his tone softened to that of an old man. "I was merely testing the limits of your bond. I wanted to see your reaction at the sound of his name. You show some resilience," he complimented. "That's good."

"Do you recall where you hid it?" Asher asked him.

"I do," Russell answered quietly.

"Well we're to be needin' it, laddy," Doran told him, rising from his chair. "The sooner we crack it open the sooner we can be rid o' it. Then the Vorska, the wolves, an' the necromancers, or whatever, will leave us well alone." The dwarf rubbed his hands together. "Then we can get back to earnin' some real coin!"

Russell's hesitation was easy to read, his bond with Creed making a mockery of his will power.

Hadavad walked a little further into the room. "Asher told you what's inside the orb?" Russell nodded. "Then you know how dangerous it is. If the Obsidian Stone could be used to create fiends such as, well..." The mage swallowed his words before starting again. "It could be used for terrible things, *evil* things, that only creatures such as Merith and Creed might dream up. It *must* be dealt with."

With slow but deliberate steps, Russell made his way past the mage and dropped into a crouch half way up the stairs. There he tackled one of the flat and creaky boards until it came free in his hands. Reaching into the step, he retrieved the orb, the sphere held steady by the tension in his fingers and thumb. Its bronze surface gleamed as it was moved into the shaft of light.

"It might be best," Russell managed, his gaze tethered to the orb, "if you take it after I'm chained up. I'm not sure I can part with it."

Asher agreed, seeing the man's rage bubbling ever closer to the surface. That was still an aspect of his character that they would need to deal with, he knew, but one problem at a time was ample given that their immediate concern was only hours away from emerging.

"Keep it," the ranger said, making no move to take it. "Get some food and drink."

"Now ye're talkin'," Doran chimed in.

"Not you," Asher said, halting the dwarf mid stand. "The three of us," he continued, encompassing Hadavad with a gesture, "are going to aid Danagarr with all that we can before the moon rises."

Doran groaned, completing his stand. "This should be fun."

CHAPTER 19
SURVIVE THE NIGHT

Wyvern - Said to be extinct, the rangers of old have continued to include Wyverns in every edition of the bestiary.
If you were to compare these creatures to anything it would be dragons. They looked exactly the same save for their number of legs. Wyverns have but two hind legs, using their wings in the manner of front legs, much like a bat.
It was also said that they were smaller than dragons though far more agile. And instead of breathing fire they were capable of spitting some kind of acid. If it is to be believed, they were made extinct by the dragons themselves.

A Chronicle of Monsters: A Ranger's Bestiary, 12th Edition, Page 347.

Norm Bronson, Ranger.

S till glistening with sweat from the afternoon's labour, Asher secured the second manacle around Russell's left forearm, positioning it slightly higher than the wrist to accommodate for growth. On Maybury's right side, Danagarr was yanking hard on the iron fastenings, trying his damnedest to rip them from the wall. They didn't budge but the dwarf still didn't look convinced, his brow furrowed in concern.

"It'll hold," Asher told the smith, even if he didn't quite believe it himself.

"The ankles," Russell cut in, his jaw so tight it seemed impossible he could speak at all.

Again, the iron was locked into a loose loop about him, securing the powerful legs he was soon to conjure from his own bones. The ranger himself pulled hard on those chains—a band of iron links so thick he couldn't wrap his hands around them—and found it hard to believe that any but a Giant could break free.

"When I'm finished," Danagarr said, wagging his finger from one side of the room to the other, "there'll be a harness for yer waist—chained at the back. Could probably do with one for yer neck too, but without measurements it could choke an' kill the wolf an' er... I ain' comin' back in 'ere after I leave."

Russell might have thanked him were he not so focused, his eyes piercing the open door and wall beyond. They were amber now, his natural colour swallowed whole by the emerging wolf.

"You've done good work, Danagarr," Asher praised on his behalf.

"This ain' the work o' Danagarr Stormshield," the smith protested. "Not *yet* anyway. I'll not have ye thinkin' this is the extent o' me skills." The dwarf gestured at the door they had recently reattached. "That needs some serious reinforcement. I've barely touched it."

"You can work on it tomorrow," Asher told him. "This will do for tonight."

"You need to leave," Russell blurted, those predatory eyes fixed firmly on the ranger now.

Danagarr didn't need telling twice, departing with naught but a whispered prayer to Grarfath on his lips. Asher stalled for another moment, aware of what he needed to do before he could leave. The ranger closed the gap between them and pressed his closed fist to Maybury's bare chest, both a gesture and a way of concealing his free hand.

"I'll see you at dawn," he promised.

There wasn't enough of Russell left to acknowledge the words. When Asher stepped back he did so with the orb. Maybury realised all too late that it had been taken from his pocket and he advanced on the ranger with bared teeth. Loose as his manacles were, there was every chance he might have slipped free of them and reclaimed the relic by force.

But the power of his curse could not be denied.

Racked by a spasm, Russell doubled over as much as his chains would allow. He cried out in agony as his muscles and bones were reconfigured and his skin torn and shed for that which rose from beneath. So too did his voice change, dropping so low that it quickly became the roar of a beast.

"Asher!" Doran warned, his heavy steps approaching from the hall.

With the orb in hand, the ranger departed the room and locked the door before the transformation completed. Only seconds later and the chains ceased their rattling, each pulled taut by the monster. Asher closed his eyes at the dreadful howl that would freeze any man to the spot.

Quite naturally, the wolf began to thrash wildly. The walls creaked and the floor shuddered. Dust rained down on them as they watched the door with new intensity.

"It'll hold," Asher breathed into that silence, breaking the tension.

Leading the way, he returned to the seating area, where the fire had been neglected, its flames reduced to embers. Hadavad casually tapped his staff twice into the floor and the fire was given new life, though its crackling did nothing to drown out the wolf.

"You have it?" the mage asked.

Asher presented the orb, its reflection burning in Hadavad's eyes where it caught the light of the flames. The mage didn't hesitate in taking it from the ranger, leaving his staff to stand perfectly still beside him.

"Get some sleep," Doran was saying to Danagarr, one hand gesturing to the hammock the smith had set up in the corner of the room. "I'm settin' meself up over 'ere, lads," he said to Asher and Hadavad, indicating an area that would give him a view of Russell's door.

The ranger merely nodded his understanding, his attention quick to return to the mage and the orb he held. Having claimed the same armchair in front of the fire, Hadavad sat with his hood already pulled back. Unlike the others, he wasn't sweating from their laborious hours under Danagarr's instruction—his magic having replaced the need for his muscles.

"What do you make of it?" Asher asked, the heat of the fire insufficient to keep his breath from the air.

The mage's eyebrows fluffed up into his brow. "I am just as baffled as I was the first time I possessed it."

Asher's head twitched. "You've seen this before?"

"Oh yes," Hadavad replied, his eyes yet to leave the orb. "How do you think Creed got hold of it in the first place?" The mage caught the look of revelation mixed with curiosity that crossed the ranger's face. "I told you: you're in an old war. The pieces have been moving on the board since before you were born."

"How did you come by it the first time?"

A coy smile illuminated Hadavad's creased features. "Merith and that mouth of his," he informed. "Thanks to him, I knew roughly where Kargon Iskander had established his infamous laboratory, though Merith himself didn't know its exact location." Another grin cut through his beard. "He may have wielded some degree of magic once, but he was ever the assistant and no more, hardly an apprentice even. He was never a true mage. Merith should have been looking for the orb, if not the lab, as if he were looking through his master's eyes. Where would a *mage* hide it?" Hadavad spun the orb around in one hand. "I found it in a pocket

231

dimension. You've heard of such things?" he asked, eyes snapping to the ranger.

"I have."

"Very good," the mage replied evenly. "Chests, satchels, even drawers, I have seen, but never have I known a mage to use the hollow of a tree. Quite ingenious," he commended, before his tone dipped to that of lamentation. "No sooner was it in my hands, however, than Creed and his band of beasts were upon me. Unlike Merith, he had had the good sense to track me, believing *I* was the more likely to discover the orb. I survived, of course, but he still claimed the orb. It was not long after that our paths began to entwine. From the pieces I've put together, Creed was soon in the sights of Merith and his Vorska."

"Kelp Town," Asher voiced, putting the timeline together. "This was recent."

Hadavad's mouth opened to respond but the mage paused, waiting for the wolf's deafening roar to pass. "Indeed," he eventually said. "He fled the Vorska and bit Russell and... Well, here we are."

The ranger eyed the orb. "Can you open it?"

Taking the relic delicately between all of his fingers, the mage began to twist the rings one way then the next. Nothing happened. He continued to twist them, his speed and, perhaps, his irritation increasing. His efforts were to no avail. The orb remained intact, its secrets still its own.

"No," he finally answered, and curtly so.

"A spell perhaps?" Asher cajoled.

If Hadavad heard him he made no acknowledgment. Instead, he raised the orb to his right ear and shook it vigorously. There came not a sound from inside.

"It's spell-bound," he reported. "I tried all manner of magic when first I held it. It seems Kargon placed a very specific locking spell over the orb. When I tried to unlock it with the *wrong* spell it changed the nature of Kargon's original spell. Now it can never be opened by magic. You see these rings? You have to know the physical combination to open it."

Asher frowned. "But there are no numbers."

Hadavad nodded his agreement. "Nor letters or any markings to make sense of it."

"Then how would anyone open it?" the ranger posed.

"I have had time to consider that. Two theories come to mind. The first is simple: Kargon Iskander didn't want anyone but himself to open it—a theory that lends to the likelihood of a Skaramangian Stone being inside."

"And the second?"

Hadavad's lips twisted as he scrutinised the relic. "Kargon didn't mean for it to be opened by a human."

The ranger narrowed his vision on the mage until the answer clicked into place. "Merith," he said simply.

"It's a possibility," Hadavad admitted. "By night, the Vorska have very sensitive... well, *everything*. There's a chance that—in his hands—he could detect the subtleties within the shell and discern the combination by touch alone. But if that were true," the mage posed, doubt in his voice, "what purpose would Kargon have in ensuring Merith came to possess the Obsidian Ruby?"

"To alter the curse he had put upon him," Asher theorised.

Hadavad didn't look convinced. "From the few accounts that still exist of the man I would say it seems unlikely. In the end, he used Merith as he would an animal—a *thing* to be experimented on."

"To continue his work then," Asher suggested.

"That is more likely," the mage agreed. "Still, it doesn't help us. And I hate to think what *work* Kargon would see finished in the hands of a Vorska." Hadavad clenched the orb in one fist and looked at the ranger. "I would take some time, while we have it."

Asher required another second to understand the mage's meaning. "I will leave you to it."

~

The night stretched on, and all to the sound of Russell's torment. The wolf howled and roared and thrashed, fighting its restraints and protesting its imprisonment.

Inevitably, Doran fell asleep with his feet propped up on one of the wooden chairs, his snores added to Danagarr's and the overall cacophony of noise. Hadavad alternated between sitting with the orb and pacing with the orb, though it continued to defy his efforts.

Asher passed the time by checking the doors and peering through the frosted windows, ensuring The Ranch's security. He spent one of the hours laying out every weapon he had, inspecting them, cleaning them, even sharpening a knife or two. More often than not, he found himself drawn back to the basement, back to Russell's door.

The irony hadn't escaped him. How long had it been since he was the one who had been chained up in that room? After reminding himself that he wasn't one of *those* rangers, he made to walk away. Perhaps, he thought, he would check on Hadavad's progress.

But the distinct sound of metal snapping and bolts clattering against the floor gave him pause.

Slowly, he turned back to face the door.

The ranger took a sudden step back when a handful of claws raked down the other side, stressing the lock on the door. Then came another and another. He imagined one arm set free and reaching for the door. The remaining chains would be under more duress, testing the limits of the bolts and fastenings.

Asher swivelled on the spot, his mouth opening to yell Doran's name, when a shadow passed over the light of the moon and ran across the high-set window. It was soon followed by another shadow. Then, a distant *thud* reverberated down from the roof.

The ranger couldn't help but wince as a high-pitched wail tore through The Ranch. Darting into the larger room, he saw that Hadavad was already reaching for his staff, his touch enough to silence the alarm it emitted. On the other side of the room, Dana-garr had twisted round in his hammock and fallen onto the floor.

Doran's chairs scraped across the boards as he jumped to his feet, hands gripping his axe and sword, teeth clenched and bared.

"We have visitors," Hadavad reported gravely. "That was the back door—the courtyard."

Asher turned his head back to Russell's door. "One of the chains has snapped," he informed, his hand going high for the silvyr blade on his back.

"Is it free?" the smith called out, a two-handed hammer in his grip now.

"Not yet," Asher replied. "But I fear it is only time."

"I told ye it weren' ready!" Danagarr blasted.

"We can't fight Russell down here and whatever's up there," the mage pointed out.

"He's not getting out of that room," the ranger stated, his words more command than anything else.

Doran groaned. "Come on, Asher! We tried! It jus' ain' natural to keep 'em locked up. We should take its head while it's still chained up."

"Watch the stairs!" Asher ordered, striding for the hallway once more. "Danagarr, with me!"

The smith soon caught him up, though he was sure to give the rattling door a wide berth. The dwarf entered what had once been the office, where Asher was hurling everything off the shelves of the large cabinet on the left-hand wall. Together, they manoeuvred it through the doorway and down the short corridor until it could be placed in front of Russell's door.

"Watch out!" the smith called, seeing the cabinet pushed away from the door.

Asher caught the edges and pressed it flat again, but Lycan claws had penetrated the wood, preventing the cabinet from sitting flush. With a burst of strength, the ranger tipped the cabinet onto its side, bringing it lower than the piercing claws.

"Get more!" he barked at the dwarf, wedging himself between the cabinet and the adjacent wall.

Russell hammered the door from the inside, the fastenings having clearly strained enough to see him advance. Again and again his clawed hand beat the door, sending splinters of wood into the corridor.

"Danagarr!" he bellowed.

The dwarf came out of the office backwards, his thick arms dragging something heavy. Asher would have continued to watch his approach had the high window in the large room not shattered.

Standing only feet away was the same Vorska the ranger had fought in Russell's home.

On the creature's other side, Doran pivoted away from the stairs with a growl rumbling out of his chest. The dwarven warrior exploded with violent intent, his axe and sword swinging for the kill. The Vorska evaded the axe with a dashing sidestep, but the sword cut a neat line down its thigh, momentarily dropping the monster to one knee. Proving it was force and not pain that had brought it down, the Vorska immediately rose to its full height and launched that same leg into Doran. His cuirass took the brunt of the impact but he was still thrown back to the bottom of the stairs.

"Doran!" Asher yelled out of concern, seeing the Vorska advancing on the dwarf.

A blinding flash that would shame lightning filled the basement for half a second, almost concealing the spell that burst across the room and thrust the Vorska into the wall, cracking the brick. The creature was crumpled into a pile, its limbs at unnatural angles with bloody bones protruding through ripped clothing. Yet still it rose, those broken limbs snapping back into place.

Another of its wretched ilk curled and flipped its body through the narrow window, its fangs bared. So too did its thick tongue whip through the air and lick its top lip. What a hideous tongue it was, its surface dotted with suckers designed to draw out its victim's blood.

By then, of course, Doran had recovered and leapt forward with his axe curving deftly round in a low arc. The new Vorska lost everything below the knee, its leg no match against dwarven strength, and fell flat on its face. Trained to give no quarter, it lay there for no more than a heartbeat before the dwarf came down with his sword, the blade chopping easily through its neck and biting into the boards beneath.

"Go!" Danagarr stressed in Asher's ear, having reached the ranger with another cabinet in tow.

Asher scrambled to his feet as the smith replaced him and manoeuvred the new cabinet into place behind the other. The wolf had applied enough strain to the door now that the hinges were already loose. It wouldn't be long before the top half of the door was gone entirely.

The ranger barrelled into the remaining Vorska, determined to end the creature this time. The two became entwined in a tangle of punching limbs, each taken off their feet, as they toppled over a table and impacted the floor.

"They're on the stairs!" Doran yelled, pausing Hadavad from intervening on Asher's behalf.

"Don't let them down!" the ranger managed between the constant wrestling.

The mage took his magic to the stairs, from where a moment later the room was filled by flashes of colour and thunderous *booms*.

"The window!" Doran cried.

Asher saw none of it—he was pinned beneath the Vorska. As well as being free from pain, the ranger had deduced that they were a degree stronger than humans, though he knew it could be the illusion that accompanied their lack of pain, being able to push themselves beyond the limits of an ordinary person. Whether that was the case or not, he would have to rely on his key advantage.

Hard-earned skill.

There was an artistry and finesse to the teachings of Nightfall, a prowess that informed their technique. It was this training that made each Arakesh a professional killer; that is to say, Asher approached every opponent with cunning, deftness and, ulti-mately, an uncompromising command of his craft.

The Vorska, on the other hand, had come to rely too heavily on its ability to instil paralysing fear in its victims and its inability to feel pain. It possessed no training in the ways of combat, suggesting it was far younger than Merith, who had displayed quite the degree of experience.

To that end, Asher twisted his body into an unorthodox position, using his hands, hips, and legs to coil around the Vorska. In no more than a second, the ranger had flipped the creature onto its back and come down on it with the blade he had freed mid-roll. The tip sank without protest through his opponent's chest, piercing flesh, muscle, and heart before reaching boards.

The Vorska smiled up at him. "You *are* a slow learner," it mocked.

Indeed, Asher was a slave to his instincts, instincts that always drove him into a killing move. But he wasn't done yet. Nor was he using any blade of mere steel. With a smile of his own, the ranger adjusted his position and ran the silvyr up the Vorska's chest, pushing the edge of the exquisite blade through bone until it was slicing the monster's neck and head right up the middle.

With laboured breath, Asher rose from his crouch and beheld his work, a nightmare in the eyes of any man. To the ranger, however, the real nightmare was watching strands of the Vorska reconnecting the two halves back together, starting in its chest cavity. Soon, its cursed form would be whole again and the fight renewed.

At least it would have been, but a flash of silvyr brought an end to the creature's twisted immortality. Asher kicked the head away from the body, just for good measure. "Grow that back," he muttered.

Turning back to his companions, Doran was keeping two Vorska from reaching Danagarr and Russell, his axe and sword swinging wildly, while Hadavad was nowhere to be seen.

Asher wasted no time closing the gap and throwing himself into Doran's fight. His last step was a short leap that gave him some height over one of the Blood Fiends, his short-sword pulled back like a snake's head. When the distance was just right, his arm sprang out, sending the length of silvyr through the monster's chest.

His own momentum thrust the blade on and pinned the

Vorska to the wall, but damned if the creature wasn't fast. It shoved his sword hand aside and backhanded the ranger away, leaving the silvyr blade lodged in its chest. Similarly, the son of Dorain lost his own sword in a miscalculated attack, the steel clattering not far from Danagarr, who had added his weight to the cabinets.

Asher left the dwarves to it, confident that both could handle their individual situations. The advancing Vorska was all confidence, a creature that had killed again and again, believing that its dominance over the meek prey it hunted in taverns and alleyways made it an apex predator.

The ranger would teach it a lesson.

What followed was a brief altercation of fists, elbows, and feet, a test of sorts to see what the monster knew of combat. Little to nothing was the answer. Of course, it still threw itself at him, hurling punches with abandon, no care given to any injuries it might gain. Asher let it come at him, seeing clearly its intentions. Positioning his hands and feet as he had been trained to do, the ranger straightened his left arm and swung it round into the Vorska's chest, just above the short-sword.

Down went the creature, flung onto the back of its neck. Asher thrust his hand forward, chasing its descent, and gripped the hilt of his lodged blade. While sliding it out, the Vorska foolishly wrapped its hands around the silvyr, believing its strength and immunity to pain enough to halt the weapon. It was wrong. By the time the short-sword was returned wholly to its master, the fiend had lost almost all of its fingers and both thumbs.

The ranger dropped into a crouch and plunged his weapon down through the fiend's pale face, pinning it to the floor. With silvyr running through its brain, the Vorska mimicked death perfectly, but Asher would see it finished. In one smooth and satisfying motion, his two-handed broadsword was freed of its scabbard and given a taste of the acrid air. It soon tasted blood, and another monster was parted in two at the neck.

Above, the ceiling rattled and the boards threatened to cave in. Flashes of light illuminated the stairs and destructive spells tore the air asunder. More than one body was being thrown about up there.

A savage war cry exploded from Doran's lips, turning Asher's attention to the remaining Vorska. It only remained among them for as long as it took the son of Dorain to swing Russell's pick-axe into the side of its head. The Blood Fiend was pinned to the wall with a slight bend in its knees.

"Ye know what?" Doran voiced, wiping the sweat from his brow as he picked up his fallen axe. "That ain' half bad!" he declared, gesturing to the miner's weapon of choice. The axe chopped hard into the wood, the rounded blade sitting between the monster's vertebrae. The dwarf was sure to leave his axe in the wall as the body fell to the floor, leaving the Vorska's head wedged between his weapon and the pick-axe.

The moment of levity was broken in time with Russell's door.

Another chain had snapped, allowing a whole arm and head to breach the timber. Jaws of merciless teeth gnashed at the air only a hair's breadth from Danagarr's face, sending the dwarf tumbling back into the wall. Out whipped the wolf's arm, a hand of pointed claws flexed to reach the smith.

Doran might have roared but it paled next to the Werewolf. Still, the son of Dorain mounted the nearest cabinet and fearlessly wrestled an arm as long as himself.

"Don' let it bite ye!" Danagarr yelled, before losing his place on the smaller cabinet and falling to the floor.

Doran was swung wildly about, his body shoved into the walls and down onto the cabinets. The wolf tried to bite him several times but the dwarf was saved by his armour. That didn't stop him crying out every time, fearful that those teeth would still find his flesh.

At last, the dwarf had taken all the beating he could and let go of Russell's arm. He landed at Asher's feet, bloody and bruised, but his eyes were alight with searing wrath. The ranger stepped over him, having swapped his broadsword for the silvyr blade, and swiped at that deadly arm. The wolf yelped, retracting the limb, before returning a roar of defiance. Asher stepped back just enough to avoid the claws and lashed out himself, scoring another blow with his short-sword.

"That ain' goin' to do it!" Doran growled, turning Asher's attention back.

"We're not killing him!" the ranger protested, seeing the axe freed of the wall and firmly in its master's vengeful hands.

"It ain' a *him*!" Doran argued. "That's a damned monster, Asher! Look at it! Russell wouldn' want this fiend usin' his body!"

Another handful of claws came dangerously close to Asher's face, pushing him back another step. How long did they have before the other fastenings and bolts gave way? "We're *not* killing him," he repeated, slowly and deliberately.

"Get out o' me way," the son of Dorain ordered. "It'll be quick an' clean—he won' feel a thing."

Asher moved again, this time placing himself directly between the wolf and Doran. There were few in all the realm who could withstand the look in Asher's eyes and advance to challenge him, but the son of Dorain was easily counted among them.

The tension between was shattered by Danagarr's fearsome cry. They turned to see the smith swing his hammer and land a heavy blow across Russell's snout, splattering the wall with blood. The wolf yelped again and momentarily fell back into its cage.

"I didn' come all this way to build a prison for a *dead* wolf!" the smith exclaimed. "Let's jus' survive the night, eh?"

The Werewolf made itself known again, its ire directed at Danagarr. Doran hefted his axe and moved in for a killing blow, shouldering Asher as he did. The ranger dropped a heavy hand on the dwarf's black pauldron but it was quickly shrugged off.

"Doran," he snarled, hand tightening around the silvyr hilt.

The ranger failed to follow through with his threat of violence. Instead, he listened to that sixth sense that he had honed over years of fighting and stalking his prey, a sense that told him he was being flanked.

Pivoting on his heel, Asher came face to face with four Vorska, their fangs catching in the torchlight. "The wolf will be coming with us," Merith announced, emerging from the back of the group.

His voice was enough to turn Doran around and their collective presence was enough to enrage Russell's wolf. It seemed to fight its restraints all the more, though whether it wished to flee or fight remained to be seen.

Staying beyond its impressive reach, Asher adopted a fighting stance, his knees bent and weapon raised in a reverse grip. He was already envisioning the six moves it would take to decapitate Merith.

"You fought the good fight," the ancient Vorska continued, his expressive grin exposing more fangs. "But as I'm sure the mage has already informed you; you're in the middle of a war, and there's no room for a third party."

"The *mage*," came a hearty interruption, "has a name."

The Vorska turned to see Hadavad at the base of the stairs, his staff in one hand and a leathery pouch held out in the other. Quite casually, the mage tossed the pouch into the midst of the Blood Fiends. While it was still flying towards them, the creatures reacted as one, dropping themselves into a crouch, a snake-like hiss pushing through their cold lips.

Then Hadavad tapped his staff against the floor.

Mid-air, the pouch exploded, filling the basement with glittering dust. Asher shielded his eyes before realising it was harmless, though the Vorska could not say the same. The creatures shrieked and wailed, their pale bodies thrashing against each other in the confined space. Their skin was burning black, adding smoke and a rank odour to the glittering dust.

Trained to use every opportunity, Asher reacted first, using the chaos to his advantage. Merith had already fallen back behind two of his underlings, the only one to have retained some measure of control. Determined to reach him, the ranger reduced the level of chaos by two bodies, dropping one Vorska after the other in a flash of silvyr.

Beyond his reach, Merith found a strength his cursed kin could not. The ancient Vorska grabbed and violently shoved one of the remaining two fiends directly into Hadavad. The mage was thrown off balance, allowing Merith the opportunity he needed to dash up the stairs, and be taken by shadow.

Hadavad hit the floor and was quickly encumbered beneath the screaming Vorska. Despite its new-found pain, the monster tried desperately to sink its fangs into the mage's throat. Its slimy tongue, singed by the floating dust, slithered over Hadavad's neck, its puckering suckers eager to taste blood.

Having thrown the other Vorska back, towards Doran and his waiting axe, Asher had advanced into the room and flanked the flailing fiend. With one hand, the ranger dragged it off the mage and even backhanded his silvyr blade across the creature's swiping attack, relieving it of everything from the knuckles down. A swift slash of his short-sword, bringing the weapon back the other way, sliced through all but the Vorska's spinal cord. Though it did not grant death, it was enough to bring an end to the monster's thrashing.

Positioning his feet either side of its still shoulders, Asher plunged the tip of his sword down through the back of the Blood Fiend's neck, finishing the job. Hadavad offered his thanks and accepted the ranger's hand to regain his footing, though the two paused to watch another decapitated head fly out of the corridor and roll across the floor.

"What in the hells is this stuff?" Doran's voice boomed over the wolf's continued growls.

Rounding the corner, the dwarf was wafting the air in front of his face in a bid to escape the dust. Asher ignored him, his attention captured by the Werewolf clawing at the outside wall, its surviving chains barely keeping it contained.

"Move!" Hadavad barked, pushing past Asher. "Get back!" he instructed, gesturing for the dwarves to get behind him.

After Danagarr had timed his climb and jump over the cabinets, the mage stepped in, his staff angled high. Asher could see his lips muttering something but he discerned no individual words.

Then—as was the way with magic—the spell he enacted came as if from nowhere. Within seconds, smoke was pouring out of the staff and concealing the wolf. The beast coughed and spluttered before being pushed back into its cage. Hadavad, however, did not relent. The mage inserted his staff into the room and continued to bring forth more smoke, filling the cage until the wolf was taken from sight.

"What are ye doin'?" the dwarven smith asked, his hand now working to keep back smoke as well as dust.

"A monster it may be," Hadavad replied, finally removing his staff, "but even monsters need to breath." The mage stepped back from the broken door, one hand raised as if to cup the moats of dust. "As for this..."

"Silver," Asher stated, finally having a moment to examine the glittering cloud.

"Indeed," Hadavad confirmed. "It is the only thing I have ever known to inflict pain upon a Vorska. Damn expensive though," he added dourly. "I have no more."

Doran waved the conversation away. "What about the wolf?" he asked pointedly.

The mage looked back before directing his staff at the room. A slow but forceful pulse was emitted from the balled end and cleared just enough of the smoke to reveal the wolf on the floor.

"I doubt it is so easy to kill such a beast," Hadavad opined. "But, for now, we might just see the night through." The mage sighed. "I for one am ready for the dawn."

CHAPTER 20
MOVING ON

Berserker - *Another foul abomination from the depths of the Shadow Realm. I hate to imagine what that hellish plane of existence truly looks like. Going by the monsters brought forth, it would make a man go mad. The Berserker is no exception. We have to assume some devil beyond understanding gave this beast life. 'Tis a man made flesh with a scorpion. They possess three scorpion tails and arms that end in hideous claws. Their head can only be described as a man's split in half and peeled over the shoulders.*
At ten to twelve feet in height, these behemoths aren't easy to kill. See below for known traps and baits.

A Chronicle of Monsters: A Ranger's Bestiary, 12th Edition, Page 405.

Benjamin Cawl, Ranger.

After a long day of clearing up debris, replacing boards to windows and doors, and piling up Vorska bodies in the courtyard, Russell was faced by that same room for a second time. By the look of him, Asher could see that the previous transformations had taken their toll. His appearance was haggard, his demeanour one of exhaustion, despite having slept away most of the day.

"I've made the repairs," Danagarr announced from inside the room, one hand coming up to wipe a filthy kerchief across his sweating brow. "And I've attached the harness I told ye abou'. Oh," he added, one finger raised. "I've also fitted an extra pair o' restraints. We're goin' to fit these abou' yer legs, jus' above the knee I think."

Russell didn't look convinced, even if his expression remained as untouched as the mountains. "This isn't going to work," he said hopelessly.

"It will," Asher reassured, backhanding a collection of sweat from his right eyebrow. "Hadavad's going to fill the room with smoke as you turn. We'll see you again, just like we did today."

"What if they come back?" Maybury posed. "What if the Vorska return? What if this *Creed* attacks?"

The ranger half turned to regard the mage, for it had been Hadavad who earlier that day had answered the very same question, though it had been Doran who had asked it then.

"I am fortunate enough," the mage began, "to have friends in high places in this city."

Doran snorted. "High places? It don' get much higher than the king an' queen o' Lirian, Mage."

"The king and queen?" Russell questioned, a portion of himself rising from the slump of depression.

"I made a point," Hadavad explained for the second time that day, "a long time ago, to ingratiate myself with the ruling family. I have served the kings and queens of Lirian in a number of ways, often to the ire of their court mages," he added with some amusement. "But my continued aid has granted me certain... privileges in these parts."

"Such as?" the dwarven smith demanded, absent from their earlier conversation.

"As we speak, the city's perimeter guard has been doubled and the king has requested patrols by the local Graycoats. The knights of West Fellion dare not refuse the king who contributes so much coin to their order. There aren't many of them, mind you, but their skill and reputation will be of much use. Fear not," the mage said finally, resting against his staff. "We can take care of ourselves, Mr Maybury."

"An' that," Doran pointed out, his thick arms folded across his chest, "would be all the easier, if ye would..." The dwarf nodded at the open door, urging Russell to take his place inside the cage.

Preceded by a great sigh, Maybury entered the room where he allowed Danagarr and Asher to secure the manacles and chains about him. Lastly, the harness was attached, a thick strap of leather laced with chains that fastened to the wall behind him.

"What did you do to the door?" Russell asked from within his bonds.

Danagarr glanced back at his handiwork. "It's not the door I had in mind—nor is it the one I'll fit when time is on me side—but it might just be enough to dissuade the wolf from giving it a pounding."

Asher had to agree, seeing the numerous rows of large nails that had been hammered through an iron sheet and welded to the back of the door, a door the smith had taken from the hinges of another room. The wolf would mutilate its hands if it managed to break free and attack the door again. Asher could only hope it wouldn't come to that this time.

"Are we all set?" Hadavad asked from the threshold.

Russell immediately tested the strength of his chains, his whole body surging forwards. Danagarr jumped back, one hand reaching for the small hammer on his belt, while the ranger stepped forwards, one arm pressed into Maybury's chest.

"What were that?" Doran demanded, forcing himself into the doorway.

Asher looked back, his attention caught by the torchlight reflecting off the bronze orb in the mage's hand. He had spent every spare moment investigating it. "Easy," he bade the miner from Snowfell.

"Curious," Hadavad uttered, revealing the orb all the more. "Earlier today you saw me with this and said nothing. You had no reaction at all..." The mage's eyes drifted with his words.

"Put it away," Asher ordered, his arm still across Russell's chest.

Hadavad slipped the relic into one of the many pouches that weighted his belt. "It would appear that Creed's thrall over you has its boundaries. The closer you are to the time of the wolf, the more you heed his will."

Doran cocked an eye up at him. "Fascinatin'," he said with all the intonation of a rock. "But the moon's risin'. Best we get on with it, eh?"

Feeling some of the threat reduce in Russell's posture, Asher removed his arm and stepped back to cast one last inspection over the restraints. It was Russell's eyes, however, that drew him in. The unnatural amber had returned and was visible without the need of torchlight. The curse was upon him.

Indeed, after filing out, leaving Hadavad and his staff to the final task, Maybury was on his knees with a feral growl in his throat. They heard his bones cracking and reforming and his skin tearing. The mage kept the door open just enough to insert his staff and exact his spell. Soon, the smoke was pushing beyond the room and exploring the hallway. The wolf's hacking and stuttering now drowned out the last of the transformation.

"Shut it!" Danagarr urged.

The moment Hadavad was clear, the smith stepped in and slid the newly-fitted lock across the doorframe. Next came the various pieces of heavy furniture that, together, they positioned between the door and the adjacent wall.

"Right," Doran announced, wiping his hands together. "'Ere we go again."

～

How the night stretched, as if the dawn was reluctant to return. Neither dwarf nor man found a moment's rest, each alert and always with a weapon in hand. They patrolled the two floors in silence, pausing frequently to peer out between the boards at the sleeping world. The curfew, enacted in light of the number of bodies showing up, kept the streets bare but for the snow, which fell upon the city without a sound.

More than once, Asher spotted a group of Lirian soldiers, attired in their iron plate and draped in the green and gold of their country. But only once did the ranger sight the legendary Graycoats as they rounded the corner and walked past The Ranch. There were two of them, as there so often were, each a warrior capable of challenging an Arakesh, though that wasn't the same thing as beating an Arakesh.

Asher had instinctively backed away from the window, despite the deep shadows and boards that concealed him. He didn't fear the Graycoats, but they were undoubtedly a complication he wanted to avoid.

Turning away from the window, he was faced by Doran Heavybelly, his hands resting atop the flat of his axe as it stood between his feet. Asher had heard him coming—how could he not?—and been content to let the dwarf stand idle for a moment. It never hurt to give a dwarf some time to collect their thoughts.

"Are we really doin' this?" the son of Dorain asked.

"Doing what?" Asher replied, his voice low.

"Leavin' the city," the dwarf specified. "If we survive the night, that is."

"Hadavad is right," the ranger insisted. "We need to get ahead of Creed and Merith for a while. Besides, Russell isn't going to learn our craft stuck in the city. He needs to get out there."

Doran's expression pinched upon hearing the latter. "Ye're stickin' to that course then?"

Asher gave a slight shrug. "I see no other."

"The hells ye don'," Doran countered. "It's one thing to let 'im live at all—if he could 'ave such a life—but it's quite another to send 'im out into the realm to do what we do."

"You already agreed to this course. I'm not having this conversation again," the ranger warned him.

"Ye'll not brush me off," the dwarf told him firmly. "An' it's easy to have yer mind changed after seein' the beast under his skin." Doran was shaking his head. "Ye're blinded by yer own need to prove somethin' abou' yerself. That's what this is. If ye don' see sense it's goin' to get us all killed. Hells, if ye take 'im away from that cage ye're goin' to get others killed! What if somethin' happens out there? Hmm? What if he can' get back in time? I'll tell ye what will happen: the wolf'll 'ave 'im an' then he'll kill anythin' that moves! That'll be on *ye*."

Asher was rubbing his eyes, his mind and body all too aware of the many hours he had been awake. "He will require more discipline than you or I," he conceded.

Doran scoffed. "Ye think it's jus' discipline? Ye think discipline can defeat a Werewolf? 'Ave ye heard yerself? Ye're a ranger damn it! Hells, ye're supposed to be the damned scourge o' the monster world! Ye should o'—"

"I know what I should have done!" Asher retorted, cutting the dwarf off. "But I didn't. He deserves a chance."

Doran puffed out his chest, rising to the occasion. "He's cursed, Asher. Curses don' give chances, they take 'em!"

"We're not killing him," Asher seethed, voicing the topic they were circling.

"I'm not sayin' that!"

"You are!" the ranger told him.

"I'm not!" the son of Dorain fired back. "I'm sayin' he can' be allowed to stray from Danagarr's cage. Takin' 'im away from 'ere is dangerous for everyone. Himself included!" the dwarf added, thumbing at the door over his shoulder. "If he spills innocent blood he's goin' to bring vengeance down upon 'imself. He'll be hunted by everyone."

He'll be hunted by me, Asher thought, but he decided it was a thought that didn't need sharing.

"We're training him," the ranger said flatly. "*I'm* training him. If you want no part in it, you're welcome to take your leave, master dwarf."

"Bah!" Doran spat, hammering the haft of his axe once into the floor. "Ye'll not cast me aside with words, *boy*! An' ye'd be foolish to rid yerself o' the only true ally ye've got! I'm 'ere because..." The dwarf hesitated, his brash tone dampened by emotion. "Hells, ye can' even see why I'm 'ere."

Because we're friends, Asher desperately wanted to say. But the words would not form.

"Come the dawn," the dwarf continued sombrely, "I'll still be 'ere. An I'll go with ye too, if only so I can be there when the truth hits ye. I'll be there to save yer sorry self."

Asher turned away from him. "I don't need saving," he uttered.

"Do ye really know that?" the son of Dorain asked him.

The unexpected question locked the ranger's jaw in place. From his tone, it was clear the dwarf hadn't been referring to his literal life, but his soul, his conscience, those scales that had long been tipped against him thanks to his past deeds.

Asher swallowed, freeing up his jaw. "You don't owe me anything, Doran," he said, his anger having passed. "Dragorn is behind us."

"I know, lad," the dwarf replied, turning to the stairs. "But is it behind *ye*?"

The ranger remained where he stood, quiet and still, while he listened to Doran's steps descend into the basement. When had the dwarf learnt so many words, he wondered? But even that thought could not prevent his mind from conjuring images of death and blood; specifically, the blood he had spilled on that island and the trail of death he had created while hunting Viktor Varga for ten long months. For a time, the *Assassin* had reigned.

He had welcomed it.

Since then it had felt closer than ever. A dark presence that seeped into his thoughts and taunted him in his sleep. Asher couldn't help but think of Russell, who now lived with a similar demon. The comparison lent him some conviction, pushing down Doran's warnings and complaints.

"Master Heavybelly seems in high spirits," Hadavad remarked, appearing at the top of the stairs, his gaze still cast down to the basement where he had passed the surly dwarf.

"As ever," Asher replied, returning his sight to the gap in the window boards.

"He disagrees with departing Lirian," the mage reasoned.

"He disagrees with everything," the ranger told him, exhaustion in his voice.

Hadavad slowly made his way across the room, staff in hand. "Is there any part of you that *agrees* with his disagreement?"

Asher sighed. "You certainly talk like a mage."

The response made no impact on Hadavad, who continued to close the gap between them. "He has a good heart," he said. "It might be plated in armour and drowning in ale but it is a *good* one. He voices concern for Russell as much as the people he might hurt. Can you not find common ground?"

The ranger shut his eyes and clamped his jaw. He missed his days alone on the road with naught but Hector for company. People spoke too much and the mage was no exception.

"Like all things," he eventually replied, "Doran needs action to prove the truth of it. There are no words—in his language or ours —that will convince him otherwise."

"Then you truly believe it," Hadavad concluded.

"Believe what?"

"That Russell Maybury can overcome the curse of Iskander, that he can be *more* than what he has been *made* to be."

Gripping the window ledge, Asher's knuckles paled beneath his fingerless gloves. "Yes," he breathed, though he was not thinking of Russell when he did.

The mage folded his arms, staff stood upright beside him, while his hot breath clouded the air about him. "I have lived long

252

enough to know that it cannot be done," he uttered, turning Asher's frown on him. "At least," he intoned, "it cannot be done *alone*. It is the belief and hope of others that give one a strength unlike any other."

"That... That doesn't sound like me."

"Yet—for Russell—it *is* you. Sometimes who we *think* we are and who we *truly* are can be two separate things. Whatever you believe of yourself, Ranger, I would say you are something else entirely."

Asher was quiet for a time, the mage's words sinking in through hard layers of doubt and self-loathing.

"And," Hadavad continued, "you are not alone in your support of Russell. If reluctantly, Master Heavybelly remains at his side. Even Master Stormshield works tirelessly to aid him. And," he said, drawing out the word, "though my belief might not match your own, Russell certainly has my hope that he can find something of a life to salvage. I will help him wherever I can."

The ranger maintained his stoical nature, giving nothing away of his thoughts and feelings, both of which were brewing like a storm. Instead, he nodded his head and asked a question that would pivot their conversation. "Have you had any luck with the orb?"

The mage wiped his mouth and ran that same hand through his beard. "If only I had some luck to use," he said. "The intricacies of Iskander's little lockbox continue to confound me. It will not open."

"We leave at dawn," Asher informed him, and not for the first time. "You will have more time while we're on the road."

"I feel," Hadavad began, "I should stress the point that we will not be rid of Merith and Creed by leaving the city. We might outrun them for a time but they each possess enough ability to track us beyond Lirian. They will know we have left and they *will* pursue us."

Again, the ranger nodded his head in silent agreement. "Time is against us. It will *always* be against Russell," he lamented. "If the orb remains a mystery by the time we are forced to return to Lirian, you *must* assume it contains the Skaramangian Stone and hide it."

"Hmm. Living without the truth of it will haunt me for centuries to come. But yes. You are right. Let's hope it doesn't come to that, eh?"

"I think I'm all out of hope," Asher muttered, catching the distant howl of the wolf below.

"One step at a time," Hadavad bade. "Speaking of which; where will we go?"

Asher ceased his leaning against the windowsill and straightened his back, arms folded. "Wherever the monsters are."

It was only in the light of the dawn that Asher realised how much sleep he had lost. But it was a crisp and clear dawn that brought relief to them all, and much needed after the last *three nights of fright*. The ranger had stood on The Ranch's porch and watched the sky brighten, free of the recent snow clouds. He breathed in the cold air, its biting edge enough to stave off some of his fatigue.

He didn't believe in the gods but damned if it didn't feel like a miracle to have survived the third night—in fact, any of them. Seeing one of the patrols in the distance, Asher wondered whether the increased security had been enough to keep their foes at bay. Having seen the Vorska and the Werewolves clash, of course, it was also just as likely the fiends of Iskander were too busy fighting each other in the shadows.

The Ranch's green door opened behind the ranger, turning his attention to Hadavad. "The wolf has had its time," he reported.

The mage's words brought a new thought to mind. "Why have Creed and his lot not attacked us? There aren't enough soldiers in Lirian to keep that many Werewolves back."

"Had they a mind to they would have," the mage offered. "But under the full moon they do not boast the minds of men. They are but beasts. They follow their instincts more than anything. I imagine it's part of the reason why Creed seeks to control his transformations. He could use the wolf as you would a bow and arrow."

"Aim and release," Asher finished, the metaphor clear in his mind.

"Aim and *unleash*," Hadavad corrected. "Though..." he added, drawing Asher in. "I find myself more concerned with their human counterparts. They could track us as easily as the Vorska. So why haven't they made their move while the sun is up?"

The thought of it put the ranger to action. Regardless of his need to rest, Russell was forced awake and urged to dress himself as quickly as possible. Doran collected anything and everything that could be strapped to their saddles, though he grumbled incessantly as he did so. Danagarr was left to his work after assurances that both Creed and Merith would waste no time in tracking them beyond Lirian. To be safe, however, they pooled what coin they could and insisted that the smith find somewhere else to sleep for a night or two, leaving The Ranch to any possible investigation.

Without enough coin to purchase a horse, Russell had to walk while the others rode out of the city on their mounts. Asher was astounded by Maybury's recovery time. They hadn't put more than a mile between them and Lirian before he appeared his usual self, tall and strong with an unrelenting step.

Despite his vigorous demeanour, he maintained an air of depression about him.

The ranger felt tempted to slow Hector down and speak to the man but he didn't know what to say. Indeed, none of them did. For their own reasons each of the companions kept mostly to themselves for the short journey. After a day and half the night of travelling in relative silence, they found themselves entering the city of Vangarth, its borders nestled inside the southern trees of The Evermoore. Though not as big as the region's capital, it still boasted a healthy population and a sprawling selection of taverns and inns.

Much of Vangarth was cut through by numerous streams that fed towards The Unmar River in the east, making it a city of small bridges and with entire streets of buildings propped up on thick stilts. Lanterns and torches brought a gloomy illumination to those

PHILIP C. QUAINTRELL

streets. It was true warmth and rest that they needed, however, and so the ranger guided them to an inn he had earmarked some time ago but never stayed in. He never slept in the same place twice.

"Get some sleep," Asher insisted. "We move on again at first light."

"We're moving on again?" Russell enquired incredulously.

"We only have a month," Asher told him while dismounting, "and we're not nearly far enough from Lirian to continue your training. Tomorrow we forsake the road and take our leave to the east. We'll cut through the forest and cross The Unmar."

Maybury's eyes shifted to the right. "Where will that take us?"

Asher handed the man his pack of belongings and supplies. "To the city of Palios."

CHAPTER 21
PALIOS

Kraken - *You likely don't need to be reading this to know that The Hox is the domain of a beast so terrible no kingdom dare set sail across it. That monster has gone by many names, I don't doubt, but folk in these parts refer to it as the Kraken or sometimes Leviathan.*
We have decided to include it in this edition of the bestiary due to its undeniable nature, but don't be thinking you can fight it. The last time a sighting was reported—by my grandfather's generation—it was seen taking down a whole vessel in minutes, dragging it down to the depths. There were reports of tentacles and a mighty tail but little else. Besides that, we know nothing of the monster. Well, that's not strictly true, I suppose. We know it won't let any ships cross that sea.

A Chronicle of Monsters: A Ranger's Bestiary, 12th Edition,
Page 481.

Varys Nad, Ranger.

After spending the very last of their coin on a bed and a hot meal, the four companions reunited with their mounts and weaved through Vangarth's various districts until they were able to breach the tree wall in the east. As before, Russell seemed content to walk at the back of the group, never to complain about the miles he covered on foot.

Looking back at the man, between the trees, he remained that pillar of sheer will. It only assured Asher all the more that he had the necessary strength to beat his demons.

"You were up before the dawn today," the ranger casually remarked after several hours, walking beside the man with Hector's reins in one hand.

Russell adjusted the strap of his pack across his chest, shifting the position of the pick-axe he carried. "I didn't get much sleep. Too many new... smells," he admitted, if shamefully so.

Asher accepted the answer without judgment, instead recalling the snippet of conversation he had heard that morning between Russell and the owner of the inn. Maybury had enquired about the menu of food on offer though, curiously, he had no interest in the food itself but the rotation of food being served.

"Why Palios?" he asked, cutting through the ranger's thoughts.

"It's a big city. Big cities have big problems. Even if we find nothing to hunt, just being there will prove a training ground for you."

"You've been there before?"

Asher nodded, though Russell could not see his face for the hood that concealed it. "It'll take a little over a week to reach, but it's a damn sight shorter than taking The Selk Road through Whistle Town."

"You know your way about the wilds of the world," Russell complimented. "I'll give you that."

"And so must you," the ranger instructed. "You especially," he felt compelled to add. "You will be tethered to Lirian, so you will have to learn the shortest routes to everywhere. If it takes you two weeks to reach your destination then it will take as much time to return. Find that boundary and never stray beyond it."

There came no reply from the bigger man, forcing Asher to turn his head to lay eyes on him. He appeared to be absorbing the information, though it did nothing to remove his sullen expression.

"I know it sounds confining," the ranger began again, before Russell interrupted.

"Confining?" he echoed with half a laugh. "I hadn't left The Ice Vales until recently. Two weeks out from Lirian—in any direction —is more world than I know what to do with."

"Then what is it that's keeping your eyes on your feet?" Asher asked, aware that he was heading into a realm he didn't know how to navigate.

Russell thought on the question for a moment but, just as he made to speak, Doran spoke up from the front of their modest caravan. "Tracks up ahead!"

"What kind?" Hadavad questioned from atop his white mare.

The dwarf moved on from Pig and crouched to better investigate. "Rabbits maybe," he guessed. "Whatever it is, I'm o' a mind to put it on a spit. Me belly ain' used to skippin' breakfast an' it's informin' me we're past lunch now too." The son of Dorain stood up and looked back at Asher, his eyes finding the ranger's arrows protruding over his right shoulder. "Ye still any good with that thing?"

Asher retrieved the folded bow from his back and snapped it to life, deciding he would answer the question with skill. He also decided it would be a good training exercise for Russell, who needed to learn the vital skills of hunting and foraging. It soon became clear, however, that the man needed no help in the art of tracking, his nose and ears more than enough to find all the creatures of the forest.

The week that followed was pleasant enough, the four companions slowly but surely becoming more comfortable in each other's company. Though Asher and Doran possessed a common history, they spoke the least, each lingering on an unsure footing where the other was concerned. They had disagreed one too many times. By the fourth day, the ranger decided that this was actually a good thing, as it forced the dwarf to make more conversation with Russell. It turned out they had an extensive knowledge of the ales, ciders, and beers of the world, and a common love and dislike for the same potations.

By the sixth day, it became quite clear that they had a lot in common; more, in fact, than the dwarf had with him. Their discussions remained light but they always flowed easily and often incorporated Hadavad who, as always, had an opinion on everything. Every now and then Asher would hear Doran imparting some wisdom when it came to hunting monsters. The ranger always made a mental note to speak to Russell afterwards and straighten out some of that *wisdom*.

By night they would set up a small shelter around a fire. The mage had lived so many lives and in so many places throughout history that he was never short of a tale. Asher welcomed them all, happy to have his own thoughts drowned out for a time. Of course, whenever Hadavad wasn't recounting he was consumed by Iskander's relic. He tinkered with the orb almost constantly, turning his curiosity into frustration as the days went on.

On the seventh day they put The Evermoore behind them, leaving those tall trees—if only for a time. They travelled north for three miles, where the waters of The Unmar were shallow enough to be crossed. It was on the eighth day that they saw it, The All-Tower of Palios gleaming in the low midday sun.

Russell stood atop the rise and looked on in wonder, his jaw slack. "I've never seen anything like it," he beamed. "I didn't even know man could build anything so big."

Asher regarded the tower, a structure he had viewed many times before but had never really *seen*. There was a beauty to the monolithic sculpture of white stone. Its square base—large enough to swallow villages whole—rose up to a flat top, as if an arrow head had been blunted. Windows, arches, and balconies of greenery decorated the tower. At its base, inside strong walls, was the sprawling city of squat domes and twisting spires that stood dwarfed in the shadow of The All-Tower.

"Our ancestors had nothing to do with this," Hadavad revealed, his old mind a font of knowledge. "You look upon the work of elves," he explained, eliciting more wonderment from the humble miner.

"This is not like the ruins," Russell commented.

"No," the mage agreed, drawing out the word with a smile beneath his beard. "Though it might have suffered a similar fate had we not adopted it as our own." Hadavad gestured loosely at the city. "Most of what you see has been built by human hands, including the wall. But, as you can see, for all the centuries that have passed, we still cannot equal the works of our inheritance."

"Bah!" Doran spat. "Grimwhal's most junior mason could knock that out before breakfast!"

"What's inside it?" Russell asked, ignoring the dwarf's comment.

"Scholars," Hadavad answered, a note of derision in his voice. "A stuffy breed in my opinion. Too many believe all the answers can be found in scrolls and books. They'd learn the truth if they ever left their precious tower."

"We aren't here for the scholars," Asher spoke up as he directed Hector towards the main gates, in the south.

Following his lead, they trailed the ranger down the slope and round to The Selk Road, where throngs of merchants and the like were selling their wares from carts and makeshift stalls. The exterior market was considerable, though not nearly as large as the lower town that had formed outside of Velia's gates or at the base of Namdhor. Still, it took some time to move through it and pass under the arch of the great doors.

It was then that Palios engulfed them.

The buildings were taller than anything in Lirian, save for The Tower of Gadavance which would have been taller still were it not so crooked. The stonework of every street appeared stronger, though Asher considered the surrounding trees of The Evermoore likely offered Lirian a softer look. It wasn't all stone and paving, however, with trees lining almost every block and walls of ivy adding green to the palette of white. So too did the hanging banners and waving flags add colour, displaying the black wolf against a cross pattern of red and blue.

Beside the ranger, Russell was forced to move constantly, pivoting and shifting to get out of the way. "It looked bigger from the outside."

Asher suppressed his smile. "The streets are narrow here, the buildings closer together."

"It's so they can fit more inside the walls," Hadavad remarked, guiding his horse. "They couldn't have guessed the population would swell when they built the wall. This is all they have."

"It reminds me too much o' Dragorn," Doran chipped in, elevated atop his Warhog. "Even if it does smell better."

As the city naturally turned one's head skyward, Asher's attention was brought to the tops of the buildings lining the main road that ran through the centre of Palios and ended at the steps of The All-Tower. His assassin's eye immediately picked out the soldiers that occupied those flat rooftops, attired in the red and blue of Alborn and all armed with bows.

Moving steadily further into the city, Asher looked left and right down the streets and avenues and discovered more soldiers on rooftops. Looking about, he didn't see a single one amongst the people, nor even a watchman.

"What is it?" the son of Dorain asked him, recognising the expression on his face.

"There's an unusual number of guards on the rooftops," the ranger reported.

"Aye, I suppose there is," Doran agreed. "Probably too crowded down 'ere," he said, shoving his way past a donkey.

"Watch it, you big lug!"

Asher turned to see the man who had barked at Russell, a large sack of goods slung over one shoulder. He appeared to have already moved on from the abrasive encounter by the time the ranger spotted him moving away. Maybury, however, looked to be on the verge of a violent outburst, his teeth clenched and bared.

"Russell." The name snapped out of Asher's mouth. "That might as well be a greeting here. Get used to it."

Maybury swallowed his anger down and tried to make himself a little smaller—no easy feat. The ranger continued up the road, one hand probing the pouch on his belt for the safida spices. It would certainly be a strange sight—placing the vial under the man's nose—but if it stopped him from putting someone through a wall he wouldn't hesitate. It was better than the methods Doran would employ at least.

The son of Dorain climbed down from Pig and made his way to Asher's side. "That temper's goin' to get us *all* in trouble."

The ranger made eye contact with the dwarf but said nothing. He was right though. Russell had a lot to learn and it was a necessity that he learn it fast.

"So," Hadavad began, inserting himself. "What's to be our next move? What does a ranger do in these circumstances?"

"We'll start with the notice boards," Asher told him, gesturing to one in the distance. "Every district has one."

The mage was nodding along. "And how many districts are there in Palios?"

The ranger spared him a glance. "A lot."

The first three notice boards, spread over two miles of walking and navigating the busy streets, proved fruitless. Though over-crowded with notices, not one pertained to a monster.

"Do people really leave notices about monsters?" Russell had asked after walking away from the second board.

"More often than not," Asher had replied, "you're looking for notices about missing people. Warnings about areas where dead bodies have been found."

Maybury had seen some sense in that. "Start with the victim," he had concluded.

"There's always a victim," the ranger had intoned.

In the north-east district—standing in front of the seventh board—Asher tore free a single notice that stood out to him.

"Ye found somethin'?" Doran's voice bore all the hallmarks of a frustrated dwarf, if not a thirsty one.

"Grave robbers," the ranger said.

Hadavad twitched. "Hmm. Grim business. I've dealt with such robbers myself in the past."

"It says," Asher continued, "six bodies have been dug up in the last ten months. They were never recovered."

"What's that to us?" Doran demanded. "Let the watch deal with it. Hells, they've got enough o' the local garrison here to catch 'em. Besides," the dwarf went on, "ain' no one payin' our rates to deal with a couple o' grave robbers."

Russell stepped a little closer to Asher. "You see a monster in this?"

"He sees monsters everywhere," the dwarf muttered.

"Trakians," Asher stated while looking down at Doran. "It could be Trakians," he said again, turning to Russell.

"What are they?" he asked, his expression suggesting he didn't really want to know.

"Monsters with a taste for dead flesh," the ranger shared. "They're attracted to graveyards. They typically nest nearby."

"Perhaps we should investigate the site," Hadavad suggested.

"No, no, no," the son of Dorain protested. "Ye don' hunt the beasties before gettin' a contract! *First*, ye find the one with the coin. *Then* ye find the monster."

Asher was shaking his head. "It's just a note of warning. No seal from the watch. I have no idea who posted this."

The dwarf sighed, though the sound of it was drowned out by the thunder, brought by the dark clouds that had rolled in with the late afternoon. "Brilliant," he said, the word as dry as old bark.

"There are other things to be learnt," Asher pointed out, before turning to Russell. "Tracking monsters. Knowing the signs they leave."

Doran's face dropped. "So we're goin' out there then? With no promise o' coin?"

The ranger held up the notice between two fingers. "I have a good feeling about this."

"Ye know, Asher, the next time ye get a good feelin', why don' ye go ahead an' bury it deep down, where it can' bother people?"

Asher wiped some of the rain dripping from one of his eyebrows, not even bothering to look down at the dwarf. "I didn't *push* you in the hole—you *fell*."

Doran, whose appearance was well hidden beneath the wet mud, looked up at the ranger with cold fury in his eyes. "A hole ye say! It was a grave! An' ye shoved me, ye dolt!"

"I walked past you," Asher corrected, "and you lost your footing."

"I know *exactly* where I'm goin' to lose me foot!" the dwarf threatened.

"Gentlemen!" The barkeeper's voice cut through their mounting argument, reminding both that they were standing in a crowded tavern. "Can I help you?" he asked, his inquisitive gaze drifting over the four strange companions.

"Aye," Doran was quick to respond. "I'll take a room, a bath, an' all the Hobgobbers Ale ye've got. An' I mean *all*."

The burly man leant over the bar to better see the dwarf. "And erm... You've got the coin for all that then?"

Before the son of Dorain could respond with some biting retort, Asher placed a hand on his pauldron and spoke first, though he quickly came to regret touching the mud-coated armour. "We are rangers by trade," he told the man as he dripped rainwater all over his floor. "We have been investigating the fiends that have been disturbing graves in the west field."

"Fiends?" The barkeeper scratched his head. "In the west field?"

"The grave robbers," Asher cajoled. "We saw the notice—"

"Monsters you mean?" The barkeeper's eyes widened, the beginnings of a great smile on his ruddy face. "You've been hunting monsters in the west field?" He began to laugh hard. "Did you hear that?" he called out, gaining the attention of the other patrons. "These fellas have been hunting monsters in the west field!" Now the entire tavern was laughing with him.

Russell leant in to speak in Asher's ear. "Is the laughing normal?"

The ranger could but give the man a look, his own ire rising to unsteady heights.

"We believe," Hadavad said, attempting to speak over the ruckus, "your graveyard is plagued by Trakians!"

"By what?" the barkeeper managed through his amusement. "Them robbers were caught," he told them. "About three months back. That notice you found was old, I'm afraid."

"Caught?" Doran nearly choked on the word. "It were jus' a couple o' men!"

"Having trouble finding monsters are you?" one of the patrons yelled above the din, instigating another wave of laughter from every corner.

"Am I missin' somethin'?" Doran grumbled, looking about.

The question set the barkeeper off again, his cheeks flushing red with laughter. "Just arrived have you, eh?"

Asher stepped forwards and leant ever so slightly over the bar, drawing the man in with a cold gaze. In the flickering gloom of the various flames, the ranger's eyes lost their colour, and so he looked upon the barkeeper as a shark might look upon its prey. The amusement drained out of the man and he was filled up with the kind of dread that only instinct could breed, an instinct that told him he faced a predator.

"Speak plainly." Asher's words thickened the atmosphere between them.

"Well you see, it's just..." The barkeeper required an extra moment to collect himself, perhaps to remind himself he was a man and not a lamb. "You're having trouble hunting a monster down and... well, everyone knows about the monster—the whole kingdom's talking about it."

"We have crossed Felgarn's borders to be here," Asher told him, maintaining the ice in his voice. "We have not heard such things."

"Aye," the man said hesitantly, "but, did you not see it?"

The ranger could feel his patience slipping. "See what?"

"The *dragon*."

266

CHAPTER 22

THIS IS WHAT WE DO

Trappers - Experience you'll need, Ranger, if you're thinking of taking on a contract concerning these beasts. They've been known to dwell in both deserts and muddy plains—wherever their prey believes they walk on solid ground.
While underground, these monsters have a unique way of vibrating their bodies and liquifying the hard earth. The next thing you know, you're sinking into the world and the hungry maw of a Trapper.

A Chronicle of Monsters: A Ranger's Bestiary, 12th Edition,
Page 228.

Balen Stone, Ranger.

Asher craned his neck and narrowed his eyes, but the rain fell in relentless sheets and the night had robbed the world of its details. The All-Tower was all but invisible, seen only in the sporadic flashes of lightning that danced across the sky.

"Can ye see it?" Doran called over the rain and the great clatter it made upon meeting his armour.

"I can't see anything," Russell yelled, one hand sheltering his face.

Hadavad twisted his hands around his staff as he leant in to it, the only dry one among them thanks to the spell that arched and shimmered over his head. "It hardly seems a dragon would find room to even perch up there, though I should imagine that flat roof is half a block end to end."

"Aye," Doran agreed, an air of doubt about him. "But come on! There's no *dragon* nesting up there."

"He wasn't lying," Asher spoke up for the first time since walking out of the tavern.

"Doesn' mean he wasn' wrong," Doran pointed out.

The ranger, at last, averted his gaze from the top of the tower and found the dwarf. "Finally, we agree on something."

The son of Dorain met his eyes, though his stature still put him at the mercy of the rain. "What is it then?" he asked, his face all the cleaner thanks to the natural wash.

"I don't know," the ranger admitted. "But it can fly. And it can fool an entire kingdom into believing it's a dragon."

"That has to narrow it down," the mage remarked.

Asher took one last look at The All-Tower, its walls a pillar of white in the staccato of lightning. "Considerably," he uttered.

The day that replaced the night carried no memory of the storm. White clouds floated across the vast blue like reaching fingers and Palios shone in the morning sun. Asher was oblivious to the spectacle of it. Instead, he watched the distant All-Tower from the western rise, well beyond the city's wall, and waited for any sign of movement.

The dizzying heights of that white stone were hard to make out, but he was certain to see anything if it moved. Especially if that something was close in kind to a dragon. The moment the rain had passed and the dawn had crested the eastern horizon, the ranger had moved away from their small camp and needlessly pored over the bestiary, as if he didn't know it cover to cover.

He had since closed it, of course, confident that he had found the only creature capable of being mistaken for a dragon.

"What is that?" Russell asked on his approach, his eyes downcast to the book beside Asher.

"A companion of sorts," the ranger replied.

Maybury sat down and handled the book, one thumb flicking through the pages.

Asher regarded the book for a moment. "A Chronicle of Monsters: A Ranger's Bestiary," he read. "We'll have a copy made for you." The ranger paused, a thought coming to mind. "Can you read?"

Russell opened the book at a random page. "Stravakin," he began. "So wicked and foul a creature could only have been born of nightmares."

"Good," Asher stated. "That's one less job to do. You need to become at least familiar with every monster between those covers. Investigate first. Use whatever clues you might find to narrow the possibilities. Then consult the bestiary. Sometimes a sword is all you need but, more often than not, there's a better way to bring your quarry down. Poisons, baits, traps... It's all in there."

Maybury continued to flick through a few pages. "You've written in this," he observed, pointing out the scribbles in the margins and the lines here and there that had been crossed out and replaced.

"A few notes," the ranger told him. "Additions, corrections. You can learn a lot from it, but not everything. Use it as a guide. Don't *rely* on it."

Russell nodded his understanding and closed the book. "So... Are we to fight a dragon then?"

"There are no dragons, laddy." The answer came from Doran as he made his way over, his armour and clothes still partially coated in crusted mud. "Their kind hasn' cast a shadow over these lands in a thousand years. I'd bet me beard another thousand will go by before they do."

"That," Hadavad interjected, "is not strictly true, my dear dwarf."

"Oh aye? An' what 'ave ye been puttin' in yer pipe?"

The mage rose to his feet and stretched his back. Subtle were his fingers as they flexed by his side, extending the flames of Asher's small fire so he too might feel its warmth. "Have you not heard of the dragon that guards Korkanath?"

"Pff! Tall tales spun by wizards I say."

"Not so," Hadavad rebuked. "I have seen it. *Glimpsed* it," he corrected himself. "It is said the beast was enthralled centuries ago by Korkanath's earliest mages."

"It's not a dragon," Asher said definitively, his eyes still on that distant tower. "My best guess... We're dealing with a Dathrak."

"Dathrak," Maybury repeated, testing the name on his tongue. "It doesn't sound good."

"An' ye'd be right," the son of Dorain replied.

"They're Basilisks with wings," the ranger informed, quoting the bestiary. "A distant cousin of the dragon perhaps, but *not* a dragon," he repeated.

"Does it breathe fire?" Russell asked, doing well to keep any trepidation out of his voice.

"No," the ranger answered, wondering if he had just seen a flicker of movement atop the tower.

"Have you faced one before?" Maybury continued.

"Yes. There was a Dathrak on Dragorn," he added with a glance thrown at Doran.

"How did you kill it?" the mage enquired.

Asher took a breath. "I didn't."

"Ye didn' kill it?" Doran blurted. "*Ye?* I thought ye were supposed to be the ultimate monster slayer," he goaded.

The ranger didn't rise to it. "It flew away," he explained briefly.

A short sharp laugh escaped the dwarf. "It *flew away?*"

"Do you have wings, Heavybelly?" Asher snapped. "Because I

don't. Salim and I cornered the beast and it just... flew away. Left the damned island in fact."

"Oh," Hadavad sounded. "So... This could well be the same creature you faced on Dragorn?"

Doran patted him roughly on the back. "Fancy a rematch?"

Asher pointedly turned to look at Russell. "This isn't my kill."

The man never looked more the miner than in that moment, his eyes wide. "My first monster is to be a... Dathrak?"

"Think o' it as a small dragon," Doran suggested with great amusement. "A baby really!"

"It's *not* a dragon," Asher repeated. "They look more like giant vultures."

"Oh aye, with hard scales and talons the size o' yer arm. Then there's the beak—"

"Enough," Asher cut in, his voice low but even. "It's like you said," he went on, meeting the dwarf's gaze. "First, we find someone willing to pay for our services. We'll worry about the monster once it's ours to kill."

"I should also point out," the mage announced, "that a Dathrak is not the only monster that casts a shadow over us. We might be ahead of Merith and Creed but for how long I cannot say. With time against us," he continued, "I shall bow out of this *training exercise*. I will, instead, endeavour to open Iskander's orb."

"As you will," Asher replied, seeing the importance of both tasks.

The four companions soon abandoned their camp and returned to the city, where Hadavad peeled away in search of those he called *trusted mages*. Whenever he could, Asher would turn his attention to The All-Tower in the hope of glimpsing the suspected Dathrak. Having yet to actually spot the creature, he would have entertained the idea that the barkeeper had been joking, if not outright lying. The presence of so many soldiers, however, all posted atop such lofty vantages, spoke truth to the matter.

"Where are we going?" Russell asked, doing his best to weave through the crowded streets.

"Under normal circumstances," Asher replied, "you would seek out the relevant watch house and speak with the captain, to nego-tiate the terms. Since this has become a city-wide issue," he continued, "and the local barracks have been emptied, we need to speak to someone higher than the watch. Someone who commands the king's men."

Doran chuckled on his other side. "That ain' goin' to be a nego-tiation," he reckoned. "These are soldiers we're talkin' abou'. They're bred to believe they're the best o' the best an' all that. They won' see any sense in payin' folk like us to do the job. Jus' makes 'em look bad."

"Where will we find this... commander?" Russell queried, making no comment on Doran's warning.

"They've more than likely taken over the largest watch house in the city, which would be the one on Lindon Street."

Russell glanced at the ranger, his greying eyebrows arching beneath his grubby hood. "You know all of the watch houses in Palios?" he asked the question with a hint of amusement if not scepticism. "Does this knowledge extend to all the realms?"

The answer was yes, of course, but Asher never said as much. Of his companions, however, Doran did not require an answer to know the truth. The pair shared a knowing look, a secret unsaid and one of the tethers that bound them in friendship, even if that friendship was hard to see at the moment.

"Didn' ye once tell me yer father built the watch houses in Palios?" the dwarf offered as a way through the lie of it.

"Galosha too," Asher replied smoothly. "At least, he was one of the bricklayers."

With the added detail, the subject was swiftly dropped and the ranger thanked the son of Dorain with a slight nod. It was a small bridge to close the recent gap between them, but it was a bridge all the same. It wasn't long, however, before Doran opened his mouth again and Asher felt like closing it permanently.

Rounding the corner onto Lindon Street, the son of Dorain gestured at the armoured guards stationed outside. "I'm tellin' ye, this is a waste o' time. If ye want to train 'im then get on with it an' train 'im. He's got the basic principle o' findin' a contract. Goin' in there is jus' goin' to be humiliatin'. I'm tellin' ye from experience, fellas, bad things get escalated to soldiers and they don' come back down again. An' as far as they're concerned, we're the bottom rung. Hells, we ain' even on the ladder!"

Asher stopped in the street and turned to the dwarf. "This isn't some village or town. We're not going to be permitted to hunt the beast, let alone ascend to the rooftops, without their consent."

"This is a bad idea," Doran argued, as he always would. "Coin or no coin, pittin' 'im against a bloody Dathrak is a death sentence. Ye might as well 'ave let me sink me axe into the wolf's head when I had the chance."

"Why don't you stay outside," Asher recommended, and firmly so. "Keep an eye on them," he added, referring to Hector and Pig.

Doran's jaw dropped. "Keep an... If I thought it wouldn' make ye look prettier, I'd introduce ye to me boot!"

The street between them was filled with foot traffic, leaving Asher to barely hear the barbed words. He turned his head only to check that Russell was still accompanying him. The big man was a step behind, his expression set hard upon his face. It was clear to see that Doran's continued doubt in him was taking its toll.

"Pay him no mind," Asher advised, drawing Russell into step beside him.

"I have no quarrel with Doran," Maybury replied, surprising the ranger enough to raise one of his eyebrows. "He has given up time and coin on my behalf. Not to mention the threat of death he has faced. *Twice*. And his concerns for me and those around me are valid. And he's not wrong; I am untested in this profession and fighting a creature easily mistaken for a dragon would seem folly. I would say his real problem lies with you."

Asher slowed his pace and refrained at the last moment from making eye contact with the man. "Me?" he echoed.

"Aye," the miner confirmed. "I can't say what it is for the two of you share a history. But I reckon I'm just the thing in the middle."

The ranger picked up his pace again. "Let's not concern ourselves with what passes for a thought between dwarven ears, eh?"

Russell nodded along, whether he agreed or not. "What am I to say? In there, I mean."

"Nothing," Asher instructed. "I want you to observe for now. Watch, listen, learn." Even as he said the words he could hear Nasta Nal-Aket's voice speaking them to him from his youth.

They had arrived at the watch house.

"State your business," one of the guards demanded, his spear crossing his comrade's to bar them entry.

Asher raised his chin a notch—confidence was half of the pitch. "Ranger business," he answered, his tone suggesting he was already having his time wasted.

The guard who had spoken simply blinked. "And what business is that then?"

Asher wasn't accustomed to embarrassment, yet there it was, forcing him to glance at Russell. "We're monster hunters," he said plainly.

"What's that to me?" the soldier retorted.

The ranger narrowed his eyes as he half turned to regard The All-Tower. "You have a monster problem," he pointed out.

"What's that got to do with *you*?" came the obnoxious retort.

Asher refrained from resting a hand on his broadsword. "That isn't just any monster you've got up there," he said.

"Oh, fancy yourself a dragon slayer do you?" the soldier replied with a mocking chortle.

"It's *not* a dragon," Asher told him, already exhausted with the repetition. "It's likely a Dathrak—"

"It *is* a Dathrak." The declaration was made by a new voice, turning every head to the newcomer.

Both guards stood a little taller and planted their spears into the ground beside them. "Lord Constable!" they addressed, each slamming a fist into their chestplate.

Asher got the measure of the man in mere moments. His armour was decorative—or, at least, it was now, in his older years. Even then, the lord constable only wore pauldrons and vambraces, his heavier cuirass absent due, no doubt, to his rotund shape. The chestplate had been replaced by hardy leather robes that stopped just above his standard military boots. Of course, the emblem of the wolf was imprinted black over the brown leather and emblazoned on every piece of armour. His white goatee was well-trimmed and his moustache fashioned to a pair of fine points that stood out against his round face. His impressive height, however, lent him an air of authority that offset his lack of physical prowess. Indeed, Asher could see echoes of what had likely been an outstanding soldier once upon a time.

He was also highborn. The ranger couldn't say exactly what informed him of that fact—his elocution perhaps—but highborn he was. It was also an indication that the man had seen little in the way of real action and had likely been promoted through nepotism. Asher had met others of his ilk, who held similar stations of power, and knew their level of apathy determined their demeanour.

The lord constable nodded at Asher. "It has taken us some weeks to identify the creature. Who are you, man, to know such a beast?"

"We are rangers, sir," he explained, his head dipping into a slight bow that Russell was slow to adopt.

"Not seen your lot in a while," the constable remarked, his personal guard of four soldiers and a decorated knight granting him a wide berth from the ever-moving population. The old soldier craned his neck to peer up at The All-Tower. "You are familiar with this breed of monster then?"

"We are, sir," Asher confirmed.

"Familiar enough to have killed one?"

"I have bloodied my sword with their kind," he replied, his words carefully, if quickly, chosen.

"Sounds like a *no* to me," the lord constable replied just as quickly, informing Asher that this particular highborn had learnt to see past his own nose. "Good day to you, gentlemen," he offered by way of a farewell, his confident stride taking him towards the watch house.

"We *can* kill it," Russell blurted, before retreating a notch to hand back control to Asher.

"Oh can you now?" the lord constable questioned incredulously, pausing his step. "You believe you can do what we have not?"

"With respect, Lord Constable," Asher began again, daring not to look back and see Doran's *I told you so smile*, "this is what we do. Yours is the way of war—and the kingdom of Alborn stands tallest in all the realm atop your shoulders. *Monsters*, sir, are *our* business. And I did not lie," the ranger added, speaking now to uphold some virtue, "I have fought a Dathrak and I have drawn blood. More importantly, I have fought one and lived. How many have you sent up that tower who can say the same?"

"Do not speak of the dead as if they are lesser men than you," the old soldier spat. "It is I, not you, who must write to their loved ones and inform them of their courageous efforts."

Asher bowed his head. "I meant no disrespect, sir. We only wish to offer our services, our *experience*," he specified, adding a strong word to his pitch.

"I have brought half a battalion of the king's men to arms, Ranger. You believe your experience trumps that?"

Asher knew well the impact the individual could make where even an army could not, but the highborn soldier would have no understanding of it, and so he said nothing of the sort. "I believe, sir, you have nothing to lose by engaging us."

"Except the coin, eh?" the lord constable countered. "I would bet my left arm your services aren't cheap."

"You need not pay us if we're dead," Asher pointed out. "Sir," he added at the last moment.

A diminutive figure stepped into view, previously hidden behind the soldiers and their cloaks. "My Lord," he began in his nasal voice, his face upturned. "The missive *must* be sent today." The small man gestured to the bundle of parchments he held under one arm.

Whatever the missive in question, the lord constable did not appear too pleased to be reminded of it. "Yes," he said, drawing out the word. The old soldier took a breath and licked his lips, his eyes shifting between Asher and Russell, calculating. "Let's take this inside," he bade, pausing just long enough to speak with the previously vocal spearman. "You do your job well," he complimented. "Now try doing it with less words spilling out of your mouth."

The guard swallowed, eyes forward. "Sir," he acknowledged.

Asher shared a look with Russell and wondered if the man knew how close they had been to rejection. If he did—recognising the luck they had just enjoyed—he made no note of it. The ranger did, however, make the effort to look back and spot Doran on the other side of the street. His sour expression was satisfying enough.

On entering, there was no trace of the watchmen inside their own house, all cleared out to make space for the king's men. Asher had expected to be reminded of the watch house in Kelp Town, but, in keeping with Palios, the interior was one of clean lines and strong stone, the windows arched and decorated with stained glass. Where the men of the watch might have once sat together for briefings, or even shared a meal, there was now a long table covered in overlapping maps of the city and various reports from across the region.

One by one, the constable's personal guard peeled away, taking up different positions inside the building, until only the knight and his lordship's assistant remained by his side. Asher didn't miss the knight's scrutinising gaze as it lingered upon Russell. The soldier was likely sizing him up, convincing himself that Maybury's superior size would prove no contest in a fight. He was wrong, of course, but not for the reasons he believed.

The lord constable assumed the high-backed chair at the head of the table. "So tell me, do rangers still have names these days?"

"My name is Asher. This is Russell Maybury."

"Well met, I suppose. I am Lord Constable Thwaite."

"We are but half of our band, Lord Constable. We boast a mage and a dwarf among our company."

"A dwarf?" Thwaite echoed. "Strange days indeed that the mountain folk would walk amongst us. Are they as strong as the stories say?"

"Stronger," Asher assured. "And more stubborn," he added honestly.

Thwaite sat back, one hand resting on the table while a single digit tapped incessantly. "I am to a write a report today, a report of our efforts here. Do you know who lord constables report to?"

Asher could guess but he got the sense he wasn't meant to answer the man.

"The *king*," Thwaite went on, voicing the status that had granted the rangers entry in the first place. "King Rengar is not a man who likes to hear of one's *efforts*. He enjoys *results*. As it stands, my report can do naught but detail the deaths of thirteen citizens, sixteen fine soldiers, and two overly-confident mages."

Asher looked away for a moment, realising now why he hadn't seen the Dathrak yet—it was satiated.

"So," Thwaite continued, "the question is: will I add two rangers to that bleak list, or will I report the victory my king expects?"

"Do you have a strategy in place to ensure the beast's demise today?" Asher asked brazenly, all in now.

The lord constable leant forwards. "My strategies are not for the likes of your ears."

"Sounds like a *no* to me," the ranger said, echoing Thwaite's own words.

The knight stepped forwards, his hand already gripped to the hilt of his sword.

"Easy, Sir Olin," Thwaite commanded, one hand raised to halt the armoured soldier. Indeed, the lord constable wore something of an amused smile now as he looked up at Asher. "I'm sure the good ranger here is just trying to get the point across that they can slay the creature this *very day*."

Asher employed his most stoical expression to conceal his unease. "We are to kill the Dathrak *today*?"

"Yes," Thwaite replied, his smile widening. "Did you not hear me? I cannot send out a rider any later than dusk. So you have until sunset to kill it. If you haven't succeeded by then, you had better be monster food, eh?"

The ranger managed to crack his expression with an easy smile. "As I said: this is what we do."

CHAPTER 23
FIRST BLOOD

Dathrak - *In the cities, I have oft heard the pigeons be referred to as 'rats with wings'. If such a phrase was to be coined for Dathraks, it would be something akin to 'a Basilisk with wings'. In truth, one of the strongest theories I've come across actually suggests the Dathraks are distant cousins of dragons.*

If the true size of dragons is to be believed, then Dathraks are considerably smaller. That's not to say they aren't large monsters in their own right. The largest recorded possessed a body close in size to a shire horse. Believe me when I tell you, a Dathrak will have no trouble snatching you in its claws and returning you to its high nest (see A Charter of Monsters, Page 112, for known locations).

On two legs, their stance is not dissimilar to that of a vulture's. Their snout is even beak-like, with a razored hook on the end. 'Tis their hide that sparks the debates regarding their relation to dragons. Dathraks are scaled from head to tail and hard it is too, harder than any scales a Basilisk might boast. See below for list of viable poisons and proven traps.

A Chronicle of Monsters: A Ranger's Bestiary, 12th Edition, Page 266.

Arn Grawly, Ranger.

S at at a table outside, under the shelter of the tavern's porch roof, Doran's booming laugh might have drowned out the street were it not so busy. Asher couldn't look at the dwarf and, instead, tried to see through the frosted window of the tavern. Closed as it was, there was no distraction from inside, leaving him to face the son of Dorain and his irritating amusement.

"Today?" he echoed for the second time. "We're to kill it today!" His laugh began anew.

Asher glanced at Russell, who was seated beside him. The big man was diligently reading and rereading the bestiary, the covers stretched open to the pages that concerned Dathraks.

"A'right, a'right," Doran eventually said, clearing his throat to overcome the laughter. "An' how much did he say we'd get?"

Asher hesitated. "Four thousand," he uttered.

The dwarf was laughing again. "Four thousand! It should be double that for a..." He couldn't finish his words for all the laughter.

"He said something about making it stretch," Asher added, his gaze dancing over the many faces that passed them by.

Doran tried to repeat the words though he never made a sound, trapped within his choking amusement. "I thought," he finally managed. "I thought ye were supposed to be trainin' 'im! What's he learnt from that? Roll over?"

Asher called upon his endless hours of training, hours spent finding the calm in the storm. "If the Dathrak didn't offer a training opportunity," he said evenly, "we wouldn't have taken the deal."

Doran barked a laugh. "It sounds like ye would 'ave taken anythin'!"

"Enough!" Asher snapped, one hand slapping down on the table.

Indeed, the son of Dorain's fun came to an abrupt stop and

Russell ceased his reading. Man and dwarf held the other's hard gaze for a time, each imagining their first blow.

"Go for a walk," Asher commanded of Russell.

Without a word, he swept up the book and excused himself, soon to be lost in the flowing crowd.

"Is it so wise to let 'im wander unattended?" Doran posed, his voice low and far from amusement now.

"He isn't your problem," Asher protested. "I am. So speak, and speak plainly."

Weighing up his response, Doran held his tongue for the moment.

In his silence, Asher said, "Whatever bond there might be between us, it isn't strong enough to stop you from killing Russell if you thought he was a genuine threat. I've seen the two of you—you get on. Hells, you get on better than we do. And you might disagree with my methods, but I don't think that's—"

"Yer methods are yer own!" Doran interrupted. "Folly as they might be!" the dwarf added spitefully. "It's the *why*, Asher. *Why?*" he agonised. "Ye think ye're addin' to our numbers with 'im but ye're not! He's not o' our stock—an' me choice o' words is a compliment to ye, I'd say. Grarfath's beard, Asher, he's a miner from Snowfell! He's only 'ere because ye think savin' 'im means savin' yerself!"

"What does that even mean?"

"Don'!" Doran warned with a finger in Asher's face. "Ye know *exactly* what I'm talkin' abou'. It's the same reason ye threw yer lot in with me an' Danagarr an' gave yerself up to Viktor *bloody* Varga! Ye're tryin' to atone or ye're tryin' to outrun yer own demons. Well, somethin' like that," he decided with a shrug. "I've no doubt there's blood on yer hands jus' like there is on Russell's. But ye seein' yerself in 'im will do neither o' ye any good. Ye're jus' givin' 'im hope that there's a life to be had. There ain'. He's cursed. Not that such a thing matters now ye've pitted 'im against a Dathrak. He's goin' to die fightin' that thing."

"You underestimate him," Asher barely managed, ignoring most of his words.

"Ye're not gettin' it!" Doran fumed, slamming one fist onto the table top. "I wouldn' mind ye trainin' 'im if it were because ye knew, ye jus' *knew*, that he would make a damn fine ranger. But ye don'. I know ye don't, because how could ye? Instead, ye're trainin' 'im because ye think a second chance will wash away the blood on his hands, an' if *he* can, maybe *ye* can." With that, the dwarf sat back and settled his gaze on the ranger as firmly as the horizon settled on the edge of the world.

"Maybe I am," Asher admitted after the uncomfortable pause. "Or maybe this world just needs a few more monster hunters in it. All that should matter to you is that I've made it my business, whatever my reasons. And Russell *will* prove his worth."

Deflated more than angry now, the son of Dorain let his bearded head hang low. "When he dies, be it in the talons o' a Dathrak or beneath me axe, ye're goin' to *feel* it. Ye're goin' to add 'im to the tally an' I'm tellin' ye, ye needn' put yerself through it. There's no need to drag this out for 'im either. Russell's a good man. Cut 'im loose. Let 'im 'ave what days he's got left. When next he turns we'll hunt the wolf an' put an end to it."

Asher stood up. "I'm putting an end to this conversation."

"Ye're doin' this for all the wrong reasons, lad!" Doran blurted, doubling down. "As yer friend I'm tryin' to warn ye! Yer past is already behind ye. Ye've done good things. Ye don' need to prove anythin' by savin' Russell. He's cursed. Ye're not. But if ye carry on down this road ye might as well be cursed! Ye're chasin' misery, Asher. Maybe even death…"

The dwarf's words trailed off, lost to the hubbub as the ranger strode away. Doran didn't know what he was talking about, aware of but a fraction of the dark deeds that lay behind him, that came back to him in his dreams every night. He could atone for the next century and it still wouldn't matter.

He was already cursed.

~

Finding Russell again proved all too easy.

The ranger broke into a run; no easy thing in the streets of Palios. He darted and weaved between the static carts and moving horses until the crowd thickened like mud around a swamp. Pushing his way through was made all the easier when Palosians caught sight of the swords he carried.

The scene he discovered matched the brawling he had heard half a street away. A merchant's stall selling a variety of fruits had been brought down and the produce scattered across the muddy ground. The owner was on the other side of the crowd, shouting profanities. Two men lay amidst the fruit. One was groaning and attempting to crawl away while the other remained still, oblivious to the world around him. Between the two walls of a wide alley, Russell held his own against three others. Like the men on the ground, they all wore plum-coloured hoods. A gang, Asher decided, though which gang they belonged to was beyond him.

Most curious of all was the red-headed woman on the other side of Russell. She was cowering by a crate, her glassy eyes fixed on the miner who was tossing men around like rag dolls. Two details immediately jumped out at the ranger, giving the scene more context. First was the dark bruise that surrounded her left eye. She still cradled it in one hand, suggesting it was very recent. The second was her attire. Her cloak had been discarded on the ground and her dress had been torn around the right shoulder.

Whether Russell had stepped in to defend the young woman or not, there was no sign of that good man in his eyes now. His anger had taken over and his supernatural strength was there to see as he lifted one man bodily by the throat and squeezed, apparently oblivious to the others of the trio, who pummelled his side with fist after fist.

Asher stepped in.

The ranger crossed the gap in a few meaningful steps. He roughly grabbed one by the shoulder and neck and spun him about before casting him aside. The other thug punching Russell was quick to turn on him, his swing wild and clumsy. Asher blocked it with a forearm and landed a knotted fist in the man's face, taking him clean off his feet.

"He's got a knife!"

Asher heard the shriek from someone in the crowd and pivoted to see the thug he had previously thrown aside. Risen to his feet, the man had indeed produced a knife, a butcher's by the look of it.

"Oi!"

The thug hardly had time to register the short sharp call before he was swiftly brought down by dwarven strength. Doran was quick to stand over his fallen foe and bat the knife away with a backhand. Grabbing the man by the collar, the son of Dorain hauled him just enough to lift his head from the ground, where he delivered a solid blow—a headbutt that could crack bone.

"Russell!" Asher bellowed from only a couple of feet away, yet it was not enough to break the spell of rage.

Maybury continued to stare into the eyes of the man in his grip, watching them flutter and drift as the lack of air forced the life from him.

"Bring 'im down!" Doran shouted, calling for Asher to assault the crazed miner.

The ranger gripped Russell's wrist and shoulder, hoping the physicality of it would be enough to shift his attention. It wasn't. He was determined to kill the man in his grasp, his mind set alight by the wolf's fury. Taking his hands back, Asher untied the rough pouch on his belt and extracted the safida spices, one thumb popping the cork as he shoved it under Maybury's nose. As it had the last time, the pungent spices cut through the fog and returned him to his senses with watery eyes.

The thug fell from his grip and crumpled like parchment at his feet. Russell staggered back until he was pushed back all the more by Asher, who sought to put some distance between them and the many onlookers. "What happened?" he growled.

Russell stumbled over his response until he saw the young woman, who had pressed herself back against the stone. "They were... They were hurting her," he explained.

While Asher was glad of the reason for Russell's interference, he was greatly disappointed by his loss of control. He slapped a

284

heavy hand into the man's chest. "You nearly killed him!" he chastised.

"He would 'ave if ye weren' 'ere," Doran chipped in as he entered the alley behind them. "An' ye won' always be here to—"

"Not now!" the ranger snapped, throwing a pointed finger at the dwarf.

"Where's the watch?" came a call from the crowd.

"Get the watch!" another yelled.

"You'll need soldiers for that one!" a woman added over the din.

"We need to get out of here," Asher concluded, his eyes wandering to the other end of the alley.

"What about her?" Russell asked.

The ranger looked over the assaulted woman, his critical mind at work. "She's alive—that'll have to do." He began ushering the big man down the alley, away from the crowd.

"Here they are!" a man cried, his words preceding the sound of clattering armour.

They were out of time it seemed, the mob splitting apart as three soldiers in their cloaks of red and blue arrived on the scene. "You!" one of them barked.

Asher's hand desperately wanted to draw his broadsword, to fight his way out of capture and the irons they would seek to bind him in. But what a mess that would cause. It would end their time in Palios and see them flee as fugitives. It was not the training he had had in mind.

The soldiers' advance was halted and the city's disquiet drowned out by a monstrous screech. The nightmarish sound increased until a shadow swept over the alley. In its wake came the twang of bow strings, dozens of them let loose from the rooftops in pursuit of the fiend.

"Everyone inside!" one of the soldiers exclaimed.

Chaos reigned and the brawl was forgotten in an instant. The crowd was already dispersing in every direction as people sought shelter anywhere. The Dathrak swooped low having retraced its flight. Asher but glimpsed the monster as it glided overhead, a dark blur between the buildings. Then came the stray arrows, taken by the wind without a care. Four struck the alley floor, forcing the companions towards the other end. Asher reached out to offer the woman a hand only to find she had already fled in the pandemonium.

"Come on!" Doran shouted, running for the street.

Free of the alley walls, the trio turned their eyes to the sky. There was no missing the Dathrak, its dark leathery wings flexed like a bat's. It sailed across the sky, its long and spiked tail trailing in its wake, while its bird-like legs remained tucked up to aid its flight. The creature banked to the left and dipped. It was flying down towards them.

"It's comin' this way!" Doran warned, his sword in hand.

Asher narrowed his eyes, focusing on the fiend's foul head as it arrowed towards them. Indeed, it was an amalgamation of lizard and eagle, its mouth a razored beak that contrasted with the scales of its body. Those same scales repelled the numerous arrows that cut through the air and found their mark.

Amidst the tumult and confusion that had overtaken the streets, the ranger spotted a young boy standing still in the middle of it all. He was red in the face and crying, too distressed in the shadow of the beast to even call for his mother.

"It's not coming for us!" Asher reasoned, breaking into a sprint.

As he was closing the gap between him and the child, so too was the Dathrak. Its talons came forward, each splayed and ready to ensnare the boy. Asher pushed himself, running as fast as he could while leaping over abandoned debris. It was no use, for a bleak calculation of speed and distance spoke of his failure and the child's ultimate demise.

He wasn't going to make it.

The Dathrak had descended below the lip of the rooftops.

Asher pulled free his silvyr blade, determined to attack if he couldn't reach the boy.

The beast's wings fanned out, slowing it just enough to snatch the child.

But there was no such prey to snatch.

Russell had sprinted past Asher with inhuman speed, over-taking him with ease, before diving headlong at the boy. As those talons searched for flesh, Maybury engulfed the child and rolled under their reach by mere inches. So low now, its tail whipped the ground, missing them by no more than a foot.

Asher's relief was short-lived. The Dathrak's flight path was still bringing it directly towards him, even if its wings had begun to beat the air to take it up. Faced by those same talons, the ranger had no choice but to thrust his blade.

The silvyr sliced through its scales without issue, sinking deep into its underside before lodging against bone. The monster roared and beat its wings all the harder, clearing the street in seconds. Unfortunately, Asher was still holding on to his weapon. Worse still, one of three talons that extended from each leg had pierced his shoulder and back. By the time he was finished yelling in pain, the rooftops were laid bare beneath him.

Let go, his instincts insisted.

Never one to ignore such things, the ranger promptly released his grip on the short-sword. His body quickly slid away from the piercing talon until he was just falling, the Dathrak shrinking into the sky above. Carried forward and down, Asher struck a wall and skidded down the face of it. Before meeting the ground again, he crashed through a stack of crates and careered off the edge of a cart.

Finally returned to the flat of earth, he was a broken man.

His breathing was laboured and the sound of it was wet in his ears. There was likely a rib or two poking into his lungs. He couldn't feel anything in his right leg and his hip felt like someone had run him through with a searing poker. Both hands were bleeding and throbbing, though they were numb to the patch of ground they rested on. The shoulder that had been pierced by the Dathrak was also dislocated, now situated further down his torso. The taste of blood was increasing and he could feel more pooling beneath him.

Cold and alone, he was to die on that street. He could feel it. Death was approaching, its feet treading softly but without obstacle. How many times had it stretched out its hand for him? How many times had Death risen to collect him? And how many times had he nearly succumbed to the rest that it offered him?

No more pain. It was tempting.

But while the ranger still had thought, he also had will, and his will could be weaponised. Asher looked at his right hand, at the lump beneath his fingerless gloves where his ring could remain unseen. He poured that unyielding will into the black gem, calling on its inexplicable power. Bone by broken bone his body began to remember its form. The pain flared and, as always, died away, leaving him whole in its wake. Death could only retreat, left to watch from the ether as the man waged war with himself as well as monster kind.

Asher knew that, one day, it would catch up with him, that one day he would have to face the end. But it was not this day.

As he slowly rose to his feet, spitting blood as he did, Doran rounded the corner at a run. The dwarf was brought to a gradual halt as he sighted Asher and the blood smeared across his leathers. His eyes naturally found the pool of blood beneath the ranger before snapping to his right hand, where he knew to find the ring.

"Are ye alright?" he asked, grave concern about him.

Asher regarded the concealed ring and clenched his fist. "I am now."

Doran sighed, his chest heaving. "I thought ye were..." He gestured up at the sky and then to the top of the building. "Ye should be dead. Very dead, in fact."

Asher could only nod. Doran knew of the ring and its power, swearing to take the knowledge to his grave, yet it still created a sense of unease in the ranger, as if he was exposed, vulnerable to attack. "The boy?" he queried, moving things along and away from himself.

Doran thumbed over one shoulder. "Russell's got 'im," he said. "He erm... he saved the lad."

Asher could see that it wasn't enough to wholly change the dwarf's mind about the man, but it seemed to have made an impression. The ranger gladly walked away from the blood on the ground, his gaze scanning every window and doorway for potential witnesses. Thankfully, the Dathrak's presence had forced everyone into shelter and his recovery had taken place behind the ruin of crates and a loaded cart.

Rounding the corner together, the pair discovered Maybury in the process of handing over the boy to what appeared to be his older sister. He barely received a word of thanks from them before they darted away. Russell watched them go, a look of epiphany about him. Asher knew that look, recognising it in himself. It was the profound feeling earned from saving a life. It was just as lasting as the feeling earned from taking a life.

From then on, Russell Maybury would chase that feeling. The *Ranger* was in him now.

The big man's expression fell into distress upon seeing Asher. "You're hurt!"

The ranger held up a hand to calm him. "It's the Dathrak's," he lied. "The fiend has my blade in its side."

Russell looked beyond him, to the buildings that lined the street. "But... the fall."

"It wasn't that high," Asher replied casually, avoiding eye contact with Doran. "Caught a ledge on my way down."

Russell accepted the explanation, his eyes wandering skyward to spot the monster. Its flight had taken it back to the dizzying heights of The All-Tower, absent its next meal and with a wound to endure. One by one, the buildings began to empty of their occupants, filling the streets with cautious Palosians. A few who had witnessed Maybury's heroics from nearby windows came over and patted him on the back, completely unaware that he had nearly killed a man only minutes before.

"He did well," Doran remarked to Asher alone, a note of reservation in his voice.

"But..." Asher said for him.

"Ye know the but," the dwarf replied.

The ranger stood still, his head giving the subtlest of nods as he regarded the miner from Snowfell. It was that understanding that turned Asher to the alley from which they had come. "We should leave this area," he urged.

"Agreed."

With Russell dragged from his praises, the trio made west across the city, putting some distance between themselves and the site of the brawl. Glancing over his shoulder, Asher could see the new lease of life that had settled over Maybury, easing him of the burdens that had been weighing him down. Though the ranger was pleased to see such elevation in his mood, he didn't like that the man had so quickly forgotten the near murder he might have committed.

"So," Russell eventually said, slowing their pace. "What next? How do we bring it down for good?"

Asher stopped on a street corner that formed one of the spokes of a grand courtyard. "How would you bring it down?" he returned. "You've read the book."

Maybury adjusted the pack strapped to his back, where his pick-axe rested. "I would bait it," he began. "We can't hope to beat it up there," he pointed out, craning his neck to The All-Tower. "I'd wager that's how they lost so many soldiers. I saw the plans on the lord constable's table. On the top floor, there's a single ladder built into the stone, so they could only send up one man at a time. Easy pickings for a beast like that."

The man had damn good eyes to have picked that detail out of the mess of parchments on Thwaite's table, but Asher kept the compliment to himself. "And how would you bait it?"

Russell licked his lips, his eyes shifted to one side while he recalled the bestiary. "Fish guts," he declared.

"Fish guts?" Doran echoed in disbelief.

"Craw fish preferably," Maybury responded. "The bestiary says they typically make their nests by the shore, in the cliffs in the mouth of The Unmar. Arn Grawly made a reference to craw fish in that area."

The dwarf blinked. "Am I supposed to know who that is?"

"The ranger who made the Dathrak entry," Asher swiftly explained, gesturing to Russell to continue.

"I can't say why the Dathrak is here of all places," Maybury continued, "but its craw fish pickings are slim I'd bet. Maybe we could tempt it out with something more familiar to it."

Asher maintained his stony expression. "Let's say you manage to lure it out with this bait, what then? How will you slay it?"

Again, Russell took the moment to consider what he had read. "Grawly made mention of a poison, something he made himself. Skell weed," he said with a click of his fingers. "Skell weed and..."

"Skell weed and the liver of a Red Daliad," Asher finished.

Russell gave a single, if satisfied, nod. "That's it," he replied.

"Skell weed only grows on The Shining Coast and has no medicinal purpose, so you won't find any in Palios. The nearest Red Daliad is in The Evermoore, though where exactly I couldn't say and, if you did find one, you'd find a hundred. Then you'd have a real fight on your hands."

Doran was chuckling to himself. "That's the end o' that then."

Somewhat deflated, Russell asked, "Then how else am I to kill it? I can swing with the strength of two men but I have no experience in traps and the like."

"That's why we're here to train you," Asher reassured, turning a mischievous grin on the dwarf.

Doran eyed the ranger, his curiosity tinged with concern. "What did ye 'ave in mind?"

"Do you remember how we lured that Rakenbak?"

The son of Dorain looked away in thought. "Oh no!" he protested. "That's not happenin'! Forget it!"

Russell was torn between the two. "What happened? What did you do?"

"I'll tell ye what he did," Doran replied, one finger wagging up at Asher. "He used me pig to bait a very *angry* Rakenbak! He barely got away with his life!"

Asher landed a weighty hand on the dwarf's pauldron. "And I would never wish to put that poor creature through such an ordeal again."

Doran's head naturally retreated from the ranger's wicked smile.

CHAPTER 24

RANGERS AREN'T BORN, THEY'RE FORGED

Gilgamorg - *You've likely heard of the demon, no more than a myth to most; a bedtime story. But more than one ranger has sighted the creature and lived to tell of it, so we will continue to pass on what we know.*

It is said the Gilgamorg came into being during the first civil war, when Gal Tion's kingdom fractured into six. His court mage enacted a terrible spell in the middle of a heated battle. The nature of that spell remains unknown, but the devastating consequences were felt by all that day, to be sure.

One by one, the dead littering the field were brought together into one nightmarish fiend. So massive was it that all could see the terrifying creature wrought from dead limbs and severed heads. Imagine a beast with a thousand hands and a sword in each.

It's enough to keep me away from The Vrost Mountains.

A Chronicle of Monsters: A Ranger's Bestiary, 12th Edition, Page 158.

Craegor the Long-lived, Ranger.

One foot raised on the edge of the roof, Asher held out an arm and rested his thumb on the horizon, where the setting sun was almost touching it. They didn't have long before their contract was null and void.

The ranger sighed. This had not been the training experience he had intended. Besides Doran dogging his every decision, much of their progress could have been chalked up to no more than chance. Even the contract they had secured had come down to the king's ire looming over the lord constable.

Asher had hoped to display a sense of control over the path Russell had chosen, to give him something he could command in his life. Instead, chaos had ensued since arriving in Palios. And now, with a monster for their foe, the bestiary offered little help, forcing them to rely on an element of cunning and a heap of brute force. The inelegance of it irritated the ranger.

Still, Doran's discomfort was a real boon.

"THIS. IS. RIDICULOUS!" the dwarf bellowed.

Asher tore his gaze from the orange sky and looked upon the son of Dorain. By his side was the bucket of fish guts. It was empty. The contents had been poured over Doran by the ranger himself, and damned if he hadn't enjoyed it.

They had purchased the bucket from a fishmonger's on the north side of the city, where fishermen would come after sailing down The Unmar with their catch. Though they couldn't say for sure, there was every chance the guts of a craw fish were mixed in with the rest. Either way, Doran stank, his foul odour running wild in the breeze and assaulting Asher's senses from the other side of the roof.

He only hoped the Dathrak caught wind of it too.

"You need to move around more!" the ranger called, moving back to his hiding position behind a large chimney.

"I'll move *ye* around in a minute, laddy!"

Russell shifted his position, allowing Asher more space to crouch beside him. "Is this really going to work?"

The ranger tried to appear confident despite the shrug that manifested. "Dathrak's have—"

"A powerful sense of smell," Maybury finished. "I don't doubt the bait," he continued, his nose crinkled in distaste. "It's what comes after."

"He'll be fine," Asher assured, flicking his head back to where Doran stood beyond the chimney.

Russell responded with a light chuckle that didn't mirror up with his serious demeanour. "I am sure Doran can take care of himself. And between us, I am confident the Dathrak will die this day. I was talking about what comes after this for *me*. Those men... in the alley. I just..." His head dropped in shame.

Asher rested his arms across his knees and took a breath while his thoughts shifted from the hunt to matters of the mind. In truth, he was grateful Russell had brought it up himself for, if nothing else, it proved that his good nature disagreed with his actions.

"Those men deserved a beating," the ranger began. "Some might argue they deserved more," he added, thinking of the woman they had assaulted. "Hells, had I come across the same situation *outside* the city I might have..." Asher stopped himself from voicing the potential outcome. "Whether they deserved it or not, their actions aren't my concern—*yours* are. Your reaction was all rage. *Again*. So much so that you abandoned sense and nearly killed a man in *broad daylight*."

"I know," Russell admitted quietly, his eyes on his boots. "But I don't know how to control it. I can't find that... *island*. There is no solitude. The wolf is in here *all* the time. When I get mad I just... forget who I am. It's like the wolf reminds me I'm an animal and I always give in to it."

Asher said nothing for a time, his memory cast back to Doran's advice. Rarely did the ranger pay the dwarf's words such heed—especially when it came to matters of the mind—but he couldn't deny that they had been circling his thoughts of late.

"All men dream of being something else," the ranger told him, recalling Doran's words. "We cling to those dreams, to what we *could* be. The world might fall apart around us but if we hold on to those dreams it can keep the hope alive." Even as he said it, Asher could feel nothing but the embers of his own hope, the feeling buried beneath too much pain. "Perhaps you shouldn't search for that solitude."

"Then what?"

"When the wolf makes itself known," the ranger replied, "maybe you need to focus on that dream. On whatever it is you want to be. Hold on to who you are. Only then will you know who you are *not*."

Russell was looking at him now, though Asher couldn't guess for how long he had been doing so, his own gaze having wandered to the cityscape laid out like a carpet before them.

"How do I know what I want to be?" he asked.

"Only you can say," Asher stated, treading well beyond his experience.

"This is beneath me!" Doran yelled, cursing through their moment. "I'm the son o' Dorain! A descendant o' Thorgen the Unbroken! I shouldn' be flappin' around like some fish on the deck!"

Russell remained in deep contemplation while Asher laughed silently to himself. The moment of levity was short-lived when Maybury rested his head back against the stone and declared his dream with wistful intonation.

"I've always wanted my own tavern."

It was all-too easy for Asher to bury his amusement, returning his attention to the miner from Snowfell. "That's why you keep asking all the questions," he said with revelation. "Everywhere we go you ask the owner about their business."

"Aye," Russell agreed with a refreshing smile upon his face. "It's been interesting to see how they're run outside o' The Vales. My uncle ran one in Snowfell—The White Orchard. I practically grew up in there."

Asher tilted his head and assessed the man with new eyes. "I can see you doing that," he agreed. "Breaking up petty brawls. Serving beef stew. Wiping down tankards."

"Sounds great," Maybury affirmed. "It also sounds expensive.

Even with the savings I made in Kelp Town I couldn't afford a place of my own."

"With this and this," Asher replied, gesturing to the bestiary poking out of Russell's pack and the pick-axe resting at his feet, "you can earn good coin. Complete enough contracts and you can turn that dream into your future. *But*," the ranger intoned, "you have to hold on to that. If you give in to the wolf, if you let it convince you you're nothing but an animal, that dream goes away."

Russell met his eyes, perhaps hearing the threat woven between Asher's words, a threat that would always hang over him. "You really believe I could achieve something like that? Hells, I'm not even a ranger yet and I'm dreaming of another life."

That wasn't how Asher saw it. "You encountered a once in a generation Werewolf and lived," he said. "You then met a ranger who should have cleaved your head there and then. You've since survived Vorska, three bone-breaking transformations, and a Dathrak. Not to mention Doran," he added dryly. "I'd say you're very good at defying the odds. Keep at it and that tavern might be in your future."

Russell was nodding absently, his thoughts lost to possibility. Asher could only hope he was turning a page. It wouldn't matter if he turned out to be the best ranger who ever lived if the problem couldn't be resolved. If he couldn't be around people without hurting them or worse, then he couldn't be allowed to carry on. And that would come down to Asher.

"Oi!" Doran cried. "It's left the tower!"

Asher's mind reconfigured just as Russell's body did under the full moon. Gone was the man who might relate to another. Now he was the hunter. Peering round the chimney, he caught sight of the beast gliding away from the white stone and hanging gardens. The distance between them gave the Dathrak the appearance of a vulture with the wings of a bat.

"Get ready," he instructed, cajoling Russell to heft his pick-axe. "Get its attention, Heavybelly!"

"What do ye think I've been bloody doin'? I'm not slathered in fish guts for the fun o' it, laddy!"

"Move your arms about!" Asher urged. "You have to look in distress!"

"I *am* in distress!" the dwarf pronounced. "I'll be smellin' fish for the rest o' me days!"

Asher pulled hard on the rope he had lashed around the chimney, checking one last time that the knot was strong enough to take the dwarf's weight, for once he leapt over the edge there would be nothing to save him if the rope tied around his waist failed.

The ranger turned to Maybury. "As soon as he's past us—"

"I jump out," Russell finished, confirming his part in the plan.

"Swing hard and aim for its head," Asher told him for the second or third time. "Our presence might spook it and we can't risk it flying away again."

"It's comin'!" Doran warned.

Asher peered out again. The Dathrak was spearing down, its wings folded in. The ranger glanced about the surrounding rooftops, making certain Lord Constable Thwaite upheld his part in the plan and kept his archers at bay, lest the three companions end up in the crossfire.

"Get ready, fellas!" Doran shouted, his voice suggesting he was running towards them.

Asher returned his attention to the son of Dorain. He maintained an impressive speed considering the armour he wore. Faster still was the Dathrak, which had caught the vile scent of fish guts and was now gliding at speed over the rooftops.

"Not yet," Asher uttered, his broadsword coming free of its scabbard. "Not yet..."

Doran ran past them and jumped over the edge of the building, the rope between him and the chimney pulling taut in an instant. The dwarf grunted and yelled out as his fall was cut short and he was brought back into the wall at force—the rope had done its job.

Now Russell had to do his.

The big man dashed out from cover and swung his pick-axe

with enough strength to dent stone. It was impossible to say what such a blow might have looked like against the scales of a Dathrak, for the weapon never landed. Instead, Maybury was swept away in a dark blur and a gust of wind. Taken clean from his feet, both he and the monster crashed into the roof of the adjacent building.

Asher swore.

He quickly sheathed his sword and put some distance between him and the lip of the roof. Then he bolted. His toes felt the edge as he leapt with all his strength, arms extended, and hands ready to grip the other side.

"Where are *ye* goin'?" Doran called from below, his body hanging limply.

The ranger's chest hit the wall, robbing him of precious breath. As his hands scraped over the lip, his fingers found purchase and held him fast. Beyond his sight, he could hear Russell clashing with the Dathrak. The man grunted and yelled at the beast as his pick-axe chopped through the air. The monster's wings could be heard to beat the air, its claws scratching at the rooftop and its razored beak snapping at its defiant prey.

"What's goin' on?" Doran hollered.

Asher ignored the dwarf and ascended with all the upper-body strength he could muster. At last, he could see the battle playing out across the roof. The Dathrak's long neck extended as its rounded head shot towards Russell. Its beak, more than capable of fitting Maybury's head inside, opened wide only to be forced shut when the tip of his pick-axe was buried into the side of that wicked mouth.

The creature shrieked and swiped its wing, forcing Russell into a roll that nearly saw him pitched from the roof altogether. Disori-entated by his own manoeuvre, he was at the mercy of a taloned foot. He cried out in pain as one stabbed him in the thigh, preventing him from fully rising from his roll. Again, that beak came in for the kill only to find a pick-axe in its way, the iron head keeping the top and bottom of the beak apart. It thrashed until the weapon was shaken loose and Maybury with it, his body cast sideways.

That might have spelled his end had Asher not found his feet and drawn his broadsword. As the Dathrak moved in to tower over the man, the ranger entered the fray with steel swinging in both hands. The edge of the sword caught the monster above the eye and turned its head away. The blade was left with a single streak of blood where it had hacked between the scales, but that single streak was urging him to press the attack, to draw more blood.

The ranger's second swing was aimed at the creature's throat, where the tip scraped across the scales and achieved naught but a nick. It was enough, however, to send the Dathrak back a step and grant Asher more room to manoeuvre his weapon. His intended thrust was batted away when the beast brought forth its left wing, shoving Asher away with the bony ridge.

As he fell, Russell was rising to renew his charge. The pick-axe tore cleanly through the membrane of that same wing, eliciting a sharp roar from the Dathrak. Be it pain or simple reaction, the beast swept the injured wing out and put Maybury on his back again.

Bulging black eyes shifted between the two men as its beak stretched wide and let loose an ear-piercing wail. Both Asher and Russell attempted to get up at the same time but the Dathrak was quicker, its advance predetermined. Its wings flapped just the once, giving it some height, before each taloned claw reached out and ensnared the companions mid-rise. Its grip was crushing, forcing both the wind from Asher's lungs and the sword from his grip.

Within seconds they were above Palios, the fall guaranteed to kill them on impact. It seemed, however, that such a notion hadn't reached Russell, who was twisting his pick-axe round in one hand and preparing a devastating swing.

"Don't!" Asher managed, forcing the word out. It was enough to delay the big man and turn his attention on the ranger. "The fall will kill us both!" he warned.

Maybury looked down for the first time since leaving the rooftop. The people of Palios were no more than dots scattering in the streets, their cries of distress never to reach such dizzying heights. The pick-axe was stayed.

"What do we do now?" he shouted over the buffeting winds.

"There's nothing we can do!" Asher called back. "We have to wait until it puts us down!"

"Puts us down?"

The ranger turned his head, guiding Russell's attention to The All-Tower. Maybury's jaw remained ajar as he took it in, for there were none who had seen the tower from the sky. The Dathrak cleared the lip of the flat top by mere feet, where it unceremoniously deposited its prey. By the time they had stopped rolling and tumbling across the roof, the creature had stretched its wings and come to a halt.

Picking himself up, Asher kept his focus on the Dathrak while Russell's attention had been spell-bound by the vista. It seemed all of Verda lay before them, the lines on its map wiped clean as the sun blanketed the realm in burnt orange and hues of pink. The edges of the world were fogged by pure distance, but it was a scale of land the man from Snowfell had never seen nor, perhaps, even imagined. Indeed, Asher might have been mesmerised by the view had his instinct to survive not been so overwhelming.

"Russell!" he snapped, one hand following his waist round to the dagger at the base of his back.

Maybury's head flicked back to the rooftop, an area of stone that might have housed half a street. On the other side, the Dathrak had made its nest of branches, bones, and even a broken cart. Carcasses and partial skeletons lay strewn about it, picked clean of meat, between piles of the creature's filth.

Quite deftly, Russell twisted his pick-axe round between his fingers and brought it up into a two-handed hold. "Is that all you have?" he asked, spotting Asher's dagger.

"No," the ranger replied, his eyes locked to the hilt of his silvyr blade, now visible protruding from the Dathrak's side.

"Oh," Russell replied, the sound laced with disbelief. "How do you plan on getting *that* back before it's dead?"

Asher slowly stepped sideways, his movement forming a circle with the Dathrak's. Maybury's question reminded him of the red cloth knotted around his belt. The urge to blind himself with it began to mount. In darkness he might find a solution, see a path that led to victory. But what could Russell learn from that? He couldn't replicate the Nightseye elixir in his veins just as the ranger couldn't replicate the wolf's strength or stamina. Then there was the explanation he would demand.

"You're going to get it back for me," Asher asserted, leaving the blindfold where it was.

The Dathrak squawked threateningly, the setting sun at its back. It advanced cautiously using its wings like front legs. That rounded head and razored beak shifted from man to man on its snaking neck. It knew it had them at a disadvantage, but it also knew this particular prey could hurt it.

"What does that mean?" Russell was keeping step with him, his shoulders hunched.

Asher came to a stop when the sun was at his back and in the monster's eyes. "Tell me how you're going to kill it."

Maybury dared to peel his eyes from the monster and look at the ranger. "Are you serious, man? Now?"

"We're here for you to train," Asher reminded him. "Well here's your test. You've got no poisons, no traps, and your only companion is without an appropriate weapon. How are you going to bring it down?" This was not the position he had hoped for Russell to be in, but the pressure was a test in itself.

"I don't know!" Maybury spat, his attention fully returned to the approaching beast.

"Think," the ranger bade.

"Damn it, man, I'm not a ranger! I was born a miner's son!" Russell sighed, though the high winds stole the sound of it.

"Rangers aren't born," Asher told him, the dagger turning endlessly in his grip. "They're forged." In a bold move, the ranger turned his back on the Dathrak to face Maybury. "What are you going to do?"

Russell regarded him for a moment before the creature demanded his focus once again. "Its eyes," he breathed. "Its eyes!"

he exclaimed with confidence now. "There's no certainty we can pierce its hide before it kills us," the man explained. "So we blind it. The damned thing has massive eyes—should be easy enough."

"Never underestimate your enemy," Asher advised, pivoting on his heel. At the same time, his hand came up with the dagger in his grip. From somewhere between skill and muscle memory, he aimed and released the weapon. The blade made short work of the gap between them and plunged into the corner of the Dathrak's left eye.

The shriek that followed could have drowned out thunder.

"That's the only help I'm giving you," Asher reported. "Use its blind side to your advantage." He stepped aside, clearing the path for Russell, though the man was still staring at the staggering monster in amazement.

"How did you do that?" he shouted over the wind.

"Your window is closing," the ranger informed, his green cloak billowing to the west.

Russell clenched his jaw, his knuckles white against the haft of his pick-axe. There was no trace of the miner from Snowfell. His expression had hardened to iron and his eyes... His eyes were amber now. The Dathrak had met its match.

Explosive was his movement, taking him from Asher's side to the winged beast in seconds. While the monster fretted over its wounded eye, Russell was leaping through the air, his pick-axe wielded in one hand as he swung it round in a wide arc. The tip dug through the creature's scales and flesh, just behind the beak on its blind side. The infliction of more pain sent the Dathrak's body into an unpredictable spasm, bowling Maybury over. He was nearly squashed by its sheer bulk, but the man had the sense and the reflexes to roll aside and save himself.

Displaying his impressive stamina all the more, he skidded and skipped across the ground, crossing under the Dathrak's shaking head, where he reached up and yanked his pick-axe free. Again, the creature shrieked and thrashed, its talons searching for the man beneath it. Catching sight of him, it arched its neck and brought its head down to snap at him. A deflection with his weapon saved his life but he failed to move and suffered a knock from the monster's thick skull.

"Keep moving!" Asher yelled. "Stick to your plan!"

Too slow in his recovery, one of those talons finally discovered him and scored a line across his chest, dragging a sharp yelp from the man. The beast pressed its attack, beak snapping until one of its wings clipped the ranger-in-training, sending him flipping through the air.

"Blind it!" Asher shouted.

Maybury rose from the floor as if he had never been put down. Keeping his movements balletic, he darted in and out. While openings presented themselves, he never struck. Asher was on the verge of directing him again when he realised Russell was waiting for a very specific opening.

When at last he took it, he was inside the Dathrak's personal space, between its shoulder joint and head, where its neck couldn't coil enough to reach him and its wing couldn't touch him. His jump appeared effortless, bringing him up and level with the beast's head. One bash using the bottom of the haft caved in the remaining eye.

This time, Russell had the sense to dive and roll when he touched down, avoiding the monster's violent reaction. Its wings stretched in spasms and its talons scarred the roof while its long tail of spikes whipped about with wild abandon. Its squawks and shrieks came in short bursts as it staggered in all directions, blood oozing from both sides of its head.

Having fully turned away from Maybury, that deadly tail was his new foe. It lashed at him, though whether the creature had intended to or not remained to be seen. Either way, the fight wasn't over yet. Russell ducked and weaved to evade the spikes, any one of them capable of spearing his heart or brain. Again, Asher had advice on the end of his tongue but Russell's actions kept his mouth shut.

As the tail came arcing in at speed, Maybury angled his pickaxe down and rolled under the sweeping attack. Coming out of the manoeuvre, his free hand snatched at one of the longer spikes and yanked the end of the tail, positioning it to take his hammering blow. The pick-axe ran through the scales and meat and pinned the Dathrak to the stone.

Asher barely noted the creature's roar for his attention was entirely captured by Russell who, in a single bound, was upon the Dathrak's scaly back. For all its thrashing it could not shake the man as he made his way to its neck. One last jump had his arms and legs wrapped around the beast's throat. The ranger thought the move folly, for even Russell did not possess the strength to snap the monster's neck with his bare hands.

It was not strength he employed, however. It was a feat of pure aggression.

Maybury pulled free the dagger lodged in the creature's left eye and pushed it deliberately between the scales of his enemy's throat, burying it to the hilt. The Dathrak's shriek was quickly garbled, its tongue bathed in blood. Ensuring death, Russell began to saw from one side to the other, spilling a copious amount of blood on the white stone. The creature's legs soon faltered and it succumbed to its own weight with its killer still atop.

Asher remained where he stood, giving the man his moment of victory.

He eventually walked over, his stony expression concealing his deep satisfaction. "Good job," he said gruffly. "You could have ended it a lot sooner though if you had stayed on the move and kept your attacks to its blind side."

Russell didn't seem to notice the ranger or his words. He stayed seated astride the dead beast a while longer, somewhat bewildered by the look of him. "I did it," he finally said, looking up at Asher.

Deciding his previous remark had been a touch harsh, the ranger simply echoed his companion's words. "You did it." Leaving Maybury to stare at the monster he had brought down, Asher retrieved his silvyr blade from its side. "Here," he announced, interrupting the man's thoughts as he offered him the weapon.

"What's this for?"

"You need proof of the kill," Asher informed him, gesturing at the beast's ravaged head. "You'll be here all night with a pick-axe."

Russell accepted the blade and sighed. "This wasn't the end I imagined," he admitted.

"Did you think there would be a parade?" Asher quipped. "There's a ladder over here that'll get us inside the tower," he reported, "but there's still thousands of steps ahead of us and I can't imagine we're going to be a welcome sight; so take the head and be quick about it."

~

The moon had reached its apex by the time they saw the sky again, its crescent glow haloed by clouds sweeping in from the east. In the biting chill, Palios had become a city of candlelight and flaming braziers. It had even been peaceful until the doors of The All-Tower opened.

The sound of outraged scholars and their live-in servants hounded Asher and Russell as they descended the exterior steps, a trail of blood in their wake.

They had suffered such verbal abuse after progressing down through the first four floors and had been pursued all the way to the doors. Tall as the tower was, however, the irate scholars had been forced to create a relay to keep up and continue their tirade, and so those who passed through the exterior doors of The All-Tower had only been with them for the last three levels.

They might have harangued them further had they not seen the lord constable and his procession of soldiers approaching the steps. They nearly filled the path with six men abreast. Asher knew a show of force when he saw one.

"This isn't going to go our way," he warned Russell as they closed the gap. "Follow my lead," he instructed, trying to combat his exhaustion.

The pair were soon halted by the wall of armour and the imposing lord constable. "My oh my..." Thwaite was scrutinising the Dathrak's head that Russell had carried down untold levels without complaint. "I have seen a great deal in my time," he began, which Asher was already doubting, "but your display was some-

305

thing else." The old soldier was waving one finger through the air. "I thought for sure you would both be dead."

Asher's suspicious gaze roamed over the hardened men behind the lord constable. "It was all part of the plan, good sir."

Thwaite offered a knowing smile. "I'm sure it was."

An uncomfortable silence befell them, giving Asher a moment to look back over his shoulder and spy the mob of scholars overseeing their meeting. "We'll just take our coin and be on our way," the ranger suggested, gesturing for Russell to toss the head at Thwaite's feet.

"Late is the hour of your success," the old soldier said. "I have already sent a rider to Velia."

"We slew the beast before dusk, sir," Asher insisted. "We lost time navigating The All-Tower."

"Indeed." The lord constable turned the creature's head with the tip of his boot, where he might see one of its ruined eyes. "Tell me, Ranger: *how* did you kill it?"

Asher straightened his back. "I told you, sir: experience."

"Hmm. It's a pity you didn't inform me of your whole plan."

The ranger did his utmost to hold in his sigh. "Lord Constable?" he questioned.

"Well, you see, in Palios it is against the law to enter The All-Tower without permission from the Prime Scholiast. Further still, that crime carries the punishment of *death* should the accused have, in any way, damaged the tower and its most precious contents." Thwaite looked down at the severed head. "I'm willing to bet this has left a bit of a mess, eh?"

Now the ranger sighed. "It was not our intention to break any laws, sir. We only wished to free the city and its people of a monster."

"For a *fee*," Thwaite pointed out, one finger coming triumphantly into the air. "Let's not overstate your virtue. This was transactional, nothing more. And, regardless of the hour, your services have breached our contract."

Again, Asher looked over the gathered soldiers, wondering now how many it would take to bring him down. He would kill them to survive, he knew that much. There was no use pretending otherwise, though he hated to think of the impression that would leave on Russell.

"Lord Constable, there was no other way of getting down—"

"I'm afraid," Thwaite cut in, his thumbs hooking into his belt, "the details don't change the crime."

Asher's jaw locked up and his breathing slowed as his body endured the calm before the storm. His mind was a quiet place before bloodshed. It was in that quietude that his unthinking mind brought one hand to rest on the dagger at the base of his back.

As one, the soldiers of Alborn drew their swords in a scraping of steel.

Thwaite raised a hand to halt any attack. "I am not unreasonable," he declared. "A crime you have both committed, but a good deed you have fulfilled. Perhaps death is a punishment too far. Instead, I would have you pay a fee and be gone from Palios forthwith."

Asher swallowed, though he might as well have been swallowing his righteousness. "That is... gracious of you, sir. But the only coin we could pay you with is the very same we were expecting for the contract."

"How fortuitous for you!" the lord constable announced with open arms. "That is the exact price for your freedom this night." He turned to the secretary standing behind him and took the bag of coins he had been holding. "Very good," Thwaite beamed.

That smile was wiped away the moment he turned to one of his soldiers. "Find me an outrider *now*. Tell him he can have this," he continued, thrusting the coin purse into the soldier's chest, "if he can beat our man to Velia. Have word sent that we have destroyed the monster."

Asher's head dropped down to his chest. Doran had been right.

"Assemble a team, Commander," Thwaite went on, turning now to another of his men. "I want that carcass brought down here before sunrise. We'll show the people they have nothing to fear anymore." The lord constable made a deliberate move towards Asher and Russell, his step inevitably prevented by their continued presence. "Forthwith, I said. That means *now*. If you are still here come sun-up you will find yourselves in irons and destined for the block."

The old soldier remained rooted to the spot, forcing the rangers to go around him and navigate the chaos caused by recent orders. Putting The All-Tower behind them, they exited the gardened courtyard and departed the grounds via the open gates.

Across the street, leaning against a horse trough, was the son of Dorain, and soaking wet by the look of him. The dwarf, now absent the coating of fish guts, straightened upon sighting them and entered the street.

"Ye've certainly got the favour o' Grarfath, I'll give ye that! Ye've quite the tale to tell, I'm sure." Doran looked from one man to the other, his excitable expression steadily falling away. "Oh," he said with revelation. "They stiffed ye then."

"We have not *one* coin to our name," Asher reported wearily. He was tired at just the thought of Doran's smug reaction.

"I were hangin' off that roof for an age!" the dwarf snapped. "Ye're tellin' me we get *nothin*?" Doran set a hard gaze upon the iron gates. "Right." The word was a declaration of war.

"No." Asher moved to intercept the son of Dorain, bringing his march to an end. "You were right," he said, hoping his words might act as a balm. "We should never have trusted them."

Doran huffed, his fists still knotted at his sides. "We're *owed*," he stressed.

"If it makes you feel any better," Russell voiced, "they were never going to pay us."

"Bah! Let's jus' be done with this foul city! They've seen the last o' me services!" he yelled at The All-Tower. "Ye can deal with yer own monster next time!"

"Is that my sword?" Asher queried, spotting the two-handed blade propped up against the wall where Doran had been waiting.

"Aye," the dwarf replied, his voice clipped. "Ye left it up there. With me, I'll add." Doran was shaking his head. "Not only do I lack the feel o' coin in me pocket, but me blades remain clean!"

Asher looked back at the iron gates, where a pair of soldiers now stood watching them. "We need to leave."

Doran heard the ranger's serious tone and raised an eyebrow. "Eh?"

"On pain of death," he elaborated.

The dwarf's rage swelled all the more. "As if takin' our coin weren' enough! I've a good mind to bloody me blades after all."

"I thought the ruckus might lead me to you," came Hadavad's voice, turning the trio around. "I half expected to find you surrounded by soldiers."

"We need to leave now if we're to avoid that fate," Asher told him.

The mage looked over them, spotting the blood and grime, and expressed a modicum of understanding. "I get the feeling it's been quite the day. But the fiend is dead?"

"We'll tell you about it back at the camp," Asher assured, fatigued as he was. "Let's just get the mounts and leave."

Still itching for a fight, Doran said, "Well, Russell, I hope ye take this for the lesson it was: an exercise in what *not* to do!"

Asher didn't have the energy to fight back. Though even he couldn't fight the truth.

CHAPTER 25

SHORT DAYS AND LONG NIGHTS

Razor Hog - *The history of this beast has been passed down from our very first edition and those most earnest of rangers who had dealings with the dwarves of Dhenaheim.*

According to them, the dwarves ride on mounts called Warhogs, brutish animals that make the children of the mountain all the more formidable. The Warhog, however, is not the monster in question. It is the monster from which they are bred.

The Razor Hog is said to be equal in size to a shire horse and roughly the same in appearance as an average hog. The exception is its numerous tusks and trio of horns that line its head.

Should you cross one of these behemoths, I would simply recommend running in the opposite direction.

A Chronicle of Monsters: A Ranger's Bestiary, 12th Edition, Page 478.

Liam Kelin, Ranger.

It was late morning when Asher awoke, his body recouped enough to face the world. The ranger's mind was always quick to assess his surroundings, shaking off sleep with practised ease.

He immediately noted Hadavad's absence. Doran was further out from camp, seated upon a boulder that protruded above one of the rises, his gaze distant to the eastern horizon.

The dwarf's ire had continued well beyond the borders of Palios, his temper only to be dampened by Russell's tale. Doran had asked for every detail of the battle and Maybury had happily told him, excited, it seemed, by his own great feat atop The All-Tower. Lacking Russell's supernatural stamina, Asher had fallen asleep by the fire before the story had found its end.

"Hadavad left at dawn." Russell's voice turned the ranger to the south, where the big man was walking towards him. "He returned to the city," Maybury explained. "Said something about unfinished business."

Asher had no comment on the matter, already accustomed to the mysterious ways of mages. "And Doran?" he enquired.

Russell glanced at the dwarf. "He's spent most of the morning cursing the city. And the ground upon which it sits. And the sky above. Oh, and everyone under it."

"His usual self then," Asher reasoned, though he suspected the son of Dorain was still seething after their heated discussion the previous day, the true root of his disquiet.

"How do *you* fair?" Maybury asked, coming to sit opposite the ranger.

"I would face a Dathrak every day for the rest of my life if it meant I never had to face that many steps again."

Russell laughed, the sound of it refreshing after so much hardship. "True enough," he agreed.

As the moment stretched out between them, Asher decided to acknowledge Doran's criticism from the previous night. "He was right," he began, nodding at the dwarf. "Since leaving Lirian, almost everything I've tried to show you has been an exercise in what not to do."

311

"I have learnt a lot," Russell countered.

"I bet you have," Asher replied, thinking of the mistakes the man now knew to avoid. "This wasn't the kind of contract I had in mind when we set off from Lirian. Still, the Dathrak was slain by your hands. For all my failings, you still succeeded."

Russell offered a warm smile. "For someone who lives without bond or tether in life, you surely pile the world upon your shoulders. I thought *I* was the cursed one," he added with an encouraging grin.

Some of the weight Russell spoke of cracked in that moment, bringing forth a quiet laugh from the ranger. "I only meant to..." The word *apologise* never quite made it to his lips. "I dragged you into this life when it seems even I cannot navigate it."

"If we could all navigate life so easily it would be a bore," Russell reassured, a casualness about him that Asher hadn't seen previously. "Besides," Maybury went on, "if we hadn't been there that little boy would have perished and who knows how many more after him. Coin or no coin, that felt damned good."

The ranger was nodding along, having shared that very same sentiment many times. "You did well to stay calm," he complimented. "You would have been well within your rights to argue with the lord constable."

Russell tilted his head in acknowledgment. "Don't think I wasn't standing there thinking about ripping his head off."

"But you didn't," Asher pointed out, his pride returning.

"Don't think me good so soon. Even I could see there was only one way we were walking away from that situation. But," he added wistfully, "I did conjure that image. My own tavern. A life I thought only a dream. That felt worth fighting for. Or *not* fighting for, I should say. It won't always be that easy, I know."

Asher couldn't help but envy the cursed man. How simple he made their life seem. Know the man you want to be and fight for it, even if that meant fighting yourself. The ranger wondered if he had been fighting himself too hard and lost sight of the path he walked. The lives they saved was the cleansing water that washed away the blood on their hands. Asher desperately wanted to believe that.

He just didn't.

It was something, however, to know that it was a possibility for Russell. The man hadn't asked for the life that had been thrust upon him and the lives he had taken could never be truly laid at his feet. Maybe something similar could be said of him one day. Maybe.

"Oi!" Doran cried down from his perch. "Hadavad's on the return!"

Indeed, the white mare crested the rise in time and brought the mage into view, the low sun at his back. He patted his mount affectionately before climbing down and taking his staff in hand. Asher didn't miss the full saddle bags and extra sack, bulging with items, that sat upon the horse.

"It seems you have faired better than any of us," the ranger remarked.

"Hardly," Hadavad protested. "You have saved lives. I have merely performed a task or two for old friends."

"Ye got some supplies then?" Doran called out as he descended the jutting slab.

"Enough to see us returned to Lirian I think," the mage estimated. "We may need to hunt here and there depending on appetites," he added, eyeing the dwarf.

"Have you had any luck with the orb?" Asher asked, Iskander's relic a brewing storm that shadowed their every move.

"None," Hadavad reported, his tone dropping. "For all the skills I was able to call upon here, there were none who could fathom the blasted thing. It remains closed to me."

"Then you are to conceal it?" Asher posed.

The mage appeared hesitant. "I would keep it a few more days."

The ranger maintained his level gaze, arms folded.

"I will die before I see it in the hands of Merith or Creed," Hadavad stated.

"Are ye mad?" Doran put to him bluntly. "That's the only reason we're pursued. Be rid o' it!"

"The Obsidian Stone poses a threat to us all, master dwarf. I would sleep easier knowing I was burying it rather than *hoping* so."

"With or without it," Russell said, "we will still be hunted. Merith and Creed would know we were the last to have it. They will demand answers from us."

"Are ye sure that's really *ye* talkin', lad, an' not yer *master*?"

Asher was slow to blink, already exhausted by the argument that was about to unfold.

"I have no master!" Russell fumed, his right foot taking a threatening step forward.

"I've seen otherwise," Doran countered.

"Enough!" Asher snapped. "Enough," he repeated in a calmer tone, his eyes falling on the dwarf. "Mage business belongs with mages. The orb is Hadavad's responsibility. Let that be the end of it."

"I don't think that's up to us," Doran remarked grimly.

The dwarf marched off, leaving Asher with a touch of ice in his veins. After all, the son of Dorain wasn't wrong: only their enemies could determine the end.

Putting Palios behind them the following morning, the companions retraced their steps—crossing The Unmar, and the remaining land—to reach The Evermore. For every mile they had journeyed, Asher had carried an uneasy feeling in his bones, a feeling that had grown, swelling until he looked upon that wall of trees.

Their foe had yet to track them down, suggesting that they were likely to be somewhere inside the forest. Added to that, the afternoon was quickly passing. Soon, the Vorska would be on the move again, tracing their scent. And who could say what Creed and his band of wolves were doing? They hadn't met a single one in their human form, a fact that only disturbed the ranger more.

"We should reach the border before nightfall," Hadavad called out, slightly ahead of the group. "I would suggest a good night's rest before we trek the forest for the next week."

"Agreed," Asher replied, his legs more than a little fatigued after descending The All-Tower.

They travelled on for, perhaps, another mile before Doran's voice reached Asher, though the dwarf wasn't speaking to him. "I'm erm... I'm sorry abou' earlier, lad. What I said... Maybe I shouldn' 'ave. After the monster business an' bein' stiffed by them lot... I've no head for mages an' magic an' all that. It were jus' one more thing that got me all turned around. An' besides, ye've proved yerself a ranger now."

"Even though I didn't get paid?" Russell checked.

Asher wanted to turn back and spy the dwarf's expression, guessing him to be squirming. "Coin or not, ye earned it with *that* kill. It weren' yer fault ye didn' get paid. Ye'll come to learn that half the job is knowin' who ye're dealin' with. An' if we're all bein' honest," he proclaimed at volume, "I'm guessin' some o' us knew ye'd be damned lucky to get that coin."

It didn't take much introspection on Asher's part to know the truth. He had walked out of that watch house well aware they wouldn't see a coin from the lord constable. He had—at the time—agreed with Doran's opinion on the matter, but the dwarf had been so obnoxious as to blind Asher to sense. And, perhaps foolishly, he had just wanted to pit Russell against a monster, any monster, to prove his worth as a ranger. While he knew that was either right or wrong, his feelings on the matter were ambiguous for, ultimately, they had set out from Lirian to give Russell his first taste of the life and provide Hadavad with more time. They had achieved both, even if neither had the most favourable outcome.

But a small voice from his subconscious told him he was wrong, that he had been selfish, and that he shouldn't have forced Russell onto *his* path in the first place. Putting him on the road to being a ranger should have been enough, leaving Russell to find his own way of doing things, just as Doran and Salim had. But the curse had complicated things, and muddied the waters. Asher had seen himself in the man. It was too late, however, to undo his failings as a mentor. His focus now, as it should always have been, was on separating Russell from the machinations of Creed and Merith —so the man might stay on the ranger's path; so he might save more lives.

And damn if Doran hadn't been right. Worse still, the dwarf had been right not once nor even twice, but three times now.

Asher then contemplated but one thought: he and Russell were not the same.

The ranger wasn't sure what to do with that revelation yet, and it certainly wasn't what he had expected to glean from their time in Palios. Nor could he see if such an understanding about himself would help with his own demons. He only knew that adopting Russell into his way of life had been for the wrong reasons. To admit such a thing would put a smile on Doran's face that might never go away. That alone might be enough to keep the ranger's mouth shut on the matter.

Since the dwarf was in the middle of patching things up with Maybury, Asher decided to keep not only his thoughts to himself but also his remark where the dwarf's loud comment was concerned. Instead, he kept Hector on a westerly heading and left the two unusual rangers to their conversation. After all, it seemed the son of Dorain actually knew a thing or two worth passing on. Again, Asher decided to keep that particular thought to himself.

And so they camped that night like they had many others, each taking it in turn to keep watch. More than once, Asher thought to steal a moment and speak to Russell. He didn't know what he would say, though he foresaw some kind of apology for guiding him with selfish reasons. Apologising, however, did not come naturally to the ex-assassin. An Arakesh was never wrong—could *not* be wrong. They were trained to get it right the first time.

That reasoning, in and of itself, was some form of proof that he wasn't the man he used to be. Proof then that the *Ranger* was winning. Asher contemplated that over and over as he lost himself in the flames of their fire hoping, as he fell asleep, that he might awaken having wholly absorbed the belief. Only then, whenever that day that might be, would the *Assassin* be truly dead.

Another night of restless sleep and nightmares breathed life into the Arakesh that lingered just below the surface, never letting him forget what he had done. Sure that those around him could see the blood on his hands, Asher started the day in a foul mood and quickly pushed the group on before breakfast. His dire mood persisted, preventing him from speaking much and avoiding any and all moments with his individual companions.

For five days they journeyed through The Evermoore, experiencing stretches of quietude and laughter between Doran and Russell, and all to the background noise of Hadavad's stories.

On the fifth night, Asher's tumultuous dreams saw him roll away from the light of their campfire and bury his head beneath his blanket, plunging his eyes into true darkness. The Nightseye elixir could but obey the conditions of its magical structure, flooding the ranger's senses with its potent spell.

Tick, tick...

Tick.

The metallic sound pierced his slumber, cutting through his nightmare.

Tick, tick, tick...

Click.

Asher's eyes snapped open as he fought free of his enveloping bedroll. The glow of the fire banished the effects of the elixir and the noise of the world was instantly reduced, quieting the insects until they were drowned out by the crackling flames.

Even those flames were dampened by the cacophony created by Doran's and Pig's regular snoring. The ranger rolled back towards the fire and sat up, spying Russell asleep on the other side, his pick-axe resting between his arms.

Hadavad was on watch, the mage seated beside his sleeping mare. He seemed oblivious to Asher, his hood blocking most of his peripheral vision. Absent the hood, even, there was every chance he still would have missed the ranger awakening, for his focus was intent upon the relic in his hands. Hadavad twisted both halves of the bronze orb to no avail.

"Can't sleep?" the mage uttered, reminding Asher that magic users were not to be underestimated.

"What are you doing?" the ranger asked in place of an answer.

"You don't like questions very much," Hadavad observed, though his visual observations remained solely on the orb. "I suppose that's an echo from your... *previous career.*"

Asher sighed and looked away, one hand going up to rub his face. His dreams lingered close to the surface. He could still see the brothers he had murdered in Longdale so many years ago, their deaths paid for by their uncle. He could smell the barn in which he had set his trap and feel the weight of the dagger he had plunged into their bodies. Seeing the fire before him reminded him of the flames he had then taken to that barn, concealing the truth of their bloody demise.

If he could, Asher would have clawed through his face to destroy the memory.

"It's nearly dawn," Hadavad told him.

"We should get moving," Asher commented, rising to his feet.

"You are eager to reach Lirian," the mage remarked. "The full moon is over a week away."

"Danagarr might need assistance," Asher said without much thought to tone. "Besides," he added, giving in to his dark mood, "We should not linger. This expedition was already a waste of time."

"On the contrary," the mage replied. "I have seen quite the difference in Mr Maybury since our departure. He holds his head a little higher. Surely you did the same the first time?"

The ranger looked down at the mage, who was now gripping a pipe between his teeth. "First time?" he echoed.

"The first time you saved a life," Hadavad answered, as if it was obvious. "More so, he brought down a monster. Can you honestly say you're not addicted to this life?" The mage shrugged. "Why else would you do such a perilous job? A man of your skills could find rich employment in every kingdom from Namdhor to Karath."

"The same could be said of you," Asher deflected.

"Oh yes," Hadavad agreed with a broad smile. "But I *am* addicted. Fighting monsters is one thing, and saving a life never gets old. But rooting out evil, *true* evil... Now that's like sucking on air. I *need* it."

Drawn in by the first piece of conversation in several days, Asher ended up sitting on a log not far from the mage. "Is that what you see there?" he asked, nodding at the orb in Hadavad's hands. "True evil?"

After exhaling a cloud of scented smoke, the mage held up the relic, so one side bathed in firelight. "The Skaramangian Stones aren't evil, just as magic isn't evil. Like most things they can be used to achieve great good. I seek those who would impress their will upon others to trample them into submission. Unfortunately, they do so by using tools such as these," he lamented, one thumb moving across the surface of the orb.

Hadavad's eyes shifted from the relic to the ranger. "If there's one thing I've developed over my centuries of life, it is my intuition. Do you know what my intuition tells me about you?"

Asher's unwavering gaze settled on the face of the old man. "What?"

"That you believe *yourself* to be evil," the mage said, twisting the orb in the air, "when, in fact, you were the *tool* of evil. Unlike most tools, however, you have taken command of your own destiny. Now you can use those skills to do good. Making that choice is proof alone that you are not as evil as you believe."

Asher said nothing.

"I do not seek to judge," Hadavad reassured. "Nor do I wish to talk about your time in Nightfall. Your business is your own. But you should know, you carry the weight of your past on your shoulders. I can see it in you. Perhaps you mean to alleviate some of that burden by helping Russell. Perhaps you don't," he went on, his tone lightening. "I have only intuition, not knowledge. Though, I do know you have a friend in Master Heavybelly, as unlikely as that bond might seem."

"That depends on the day," Asher interjected, taking a swig from his waterskin.

Hadavad chuckled. "Only friends could tolerate each other as you two do. Though," he continued, serious again, "sometimes, it can be hard to speak our truths, even to friends—*especially* to friends. Sometimes, it can be easier to speak to another, a stranger even."

Asher eyed the mage, aware of what he was insinuating. "It's a shame you're not a stranger then," he said bluntly.

Hadavad offered a warm smile. "I would be honoured were you to count me as a friend. I get the feeling you don't make them very often."

Asher stewed. He could feel his two halves warring inside, each battling with no clear path to victory. "Emotional bonds make you... vulnerable." It had been a long time since he had heard those words come out of Nasta Nal-Aket's mouth but he was still able to recite them to Hadavad without thought.

The mage chewed the end of his pipe before removing it. "That is exactly the belief I would instil in a person were I to wield them like a weapon. Weapons need to be cold, sharp, unthinking. What better way to forge such a thing than to isolate it, to keep it away from the influences of others."

Asher knew it to be a crisp truth, but that didn't help him to find the response.

"I have experienced my share of isolation," Hadavad continued. "Decades wandering the world alone. You don't just forget who you are, but *what* you are. I have come to find that friends bring out the best in me—my humanity. I think those finer qualities only come out in us when we're together."

The ranger swallowed, his gaze struggling to find the mage. "You would... You would befriend me despite knowing what I've done? Knowing I killed your friend."

Hadavad drew on his pipe for what felt like an eternity. "We were all something else once," he said wistfully. "Be it good or bad. I have so *much* history now that were I to dwell there I might never take another step forwards. I would say it is a waste of time to live in the past. Better, I think, to see what's right in front of you. I see no assassin here, no *Arakesh*. I see only the *ranger*. And yes, I would befriend that man."

The emotions brewing within Asher were becoming hard to chart. He had never been taught how to manage his emotions, only how to manipulate them in others. Ultimately, it robbed him of words. He could see no way of navigating the conversation without feeling vulnerable, a state that put his nerves on edge.

"We should go," he eventually stated, bringing an end to their discussion.

"As you say," Hadavad replied quietly, dissatisfied perhaps.

Standing again, the ranger made to collect the meagre supplies about him and kick Doran awake. But Asher never moved, his head cocked to one side. He wasn't sure he had heard anything between the rise and fall of snores, but that warrior's sixth sense told him he *had* heard something. A snapping twig, beyond their camp.

"What is it?" the mage enquired.

Asher offered no reply, his eyes scrutinising the dark around them. Again, he heard *something*, only it was on the other side of camp this time. Though his sight told him otherwise, the ranger could feel the shadows moving, gathering about them. The conclusion was grim.

"We're being surrounded."

CHAPTER 26
THEY THAT MUST ENDURE

Witchweavers - There has been much debate whether these fiends are of our realm or the Shadow Realm. I personally believe they hail from that dark place but there is no proof.
Witchweavers favour forests for their skill comes from their ability to weave walls from twigs and branches, creating corridors that force their prey in a particular direction.
By wailing and screeching, they terrify people, inducing such fear that they flee into these 'natural' corridors and get lost in a hellish maze. From there, any and all are easy pickings for the spider-like witches.

A Chronicle of Monsters: A Ranger's Bestiary, 12th Edition, Page 182.

Roy Clement, Ranger.

The ring of steel leaving Asher's scabbard was enough to wake Doran and Russell. It was also enough to alert the encroaching Vorska that the intended prey had become aware of their presence. From all sides they came, pale wraiths born from the shadows, deadly and beautiful.

There was no time to count their number, but the ranger guessed at least ten had surrounded them. While the Blood Fiends stalked towards them, their nails sharp and strong, Merith—a creature from centuries past—entered the firelight with his sword in hand.

How different the Vorska were to their Lycan counterparts. These monsters of the night were slow to attack, enjoying the fear they brought out in those they hunted. Had Creed and his band ambushed them, the Werewolves would have rushed them by now, relying on their animal savagery.

It was a mistake on the Vorska's part, for they were not hunting just any prey that night. Their deliberate approach from the dark had simply given the rangers enough time to rise and bring their weapons to bear. It was arrogance, Asher realised, though an arrogance born of experience where spilling blood was concerned.

The ranger held his sword high, and in both hands, ready to swing.

"Hadavad?" Merith's voice was a cold blade that cut through the night, his breath notably absent on the frigid air. "Is that you? You're looking old, my friend. Perhaps it's time to move on, eh? Find a younger body."

"Merith." Hadavad said the name as though it were mud in his mouth. "Isn't it getting a little late for you? First light will soon be upon us. Don't you have a *hole* to crawl back into?"

"This won't take long," the ancient Vorska assured, a wicked smile morphing his face of marble. "I know you have Iskander's relic," he continued, ignoring the three rangers altogether. "Give it to me now, mage, and you have my word the slaughter will be quick and painless." Merith's dead eyes flitted over Russell. "Mostly painless," he corrected.

Russell sneered at the lead Vorska and, for once, Asher hoped he *would* unleash his rage. Doran pivoted every which way, his axe and sword twisting restlessly in his grip. Asher remained a pillar of readiness, his mind moving through every intended swing as he predicted all potential attacks. For all his plans, fighting Vorska came down to one simple thing: take the head.

"You're fooling yourself," Hadavad told the fiends, his gaze briefly leaving the oldest among them to take in the others. "How many of you even met Kargon Iskander? I'd wager just you," the mage reasoned, eyeing Merith. "Recall your master, prince of fools. Did he really seem like the man to create a cure? Is that what you think this is?" he asked, holding up the orb. "Kargon Iskander was in the business of curses and monsters. He gave you nothing but the cold night."

Merith tilted his head of ashen blond hair, his sight fixed on the bronze relic. "You cannot speak of him, mage. Even you did not breathe the air of his time. My master's work was interrupted. Like you, there were others who envied his skill, who coveted his great works. We were to be his finest achievement, his protectors. He would not have forsaken us to this existence. That which you hold in your dying hand is Kargon Iskander's legacy and our destiny." The creature's black eyes shifted to his wretched kin. "Feast."

The command received, the Vorska closed in like a clenching fist.

Asher took his first step, his footing essential if his blow was to land with maximum impact. The broadsword rolled over his shoulder, ready to come back down and round with precision and force.

"Cover your eyes!" Hadavad bellowed, his instruction swift and sharp.

The ranger had no choice but to hold his stance and shut his eyes tight, despite being aware of the female Vorska hurtling towards him. Still, he had faith in the mage or, at least, in the mage's abilities. Though he didn't see it, he heard the spell explode from Hadavad's staff and the resultant yells of pain from the

Vorska. Asher had heard that same spell the night they met the mage in the forest.

Confident the spell was over, Asher looked upon his foes once more. The Vorska were staggering about the camp, blood dripping from their eyes and smearing down their pale cheeks. All but Merith that was. It was likely the elder Blood Fiend was more capable of controlling his bloodlust and seeing sense where the others saw only pulsing veins and heard beating hearts.

Like a snake, Merith lashed out with his sword, the blade arcing from high to low and perfectly in line with Hadavad's head. Asher leapt in and brought his broadsword up in both hands, blocking the steel before death could be delivered. The mage was just as swift, though he pivoted from the ancient Vorska and aimed his staff at the others. One after the other he struck with a near-invisible spell, flinging the beasts into the forest. One of them caught fire mid-flight while another began to freeze. Where one landed and writhed in fire, the other impacted a tree and shattered into pieces.

Asher caught it all in his peripheral vision, his focus ever shifting to Merith's next attack. The Vorska was a master swords-man, a fact that the ranger quickly took on board. His centuries of life were showing through with every new step, stance, and style of attack. He had clearly studied every facet of the art and enjoyed the advantages his curse granted him, chiefly his supernatural strength and inability to feel pain. Paired together, he was able to wield his blade one-handed, freeing his other hand to leave its own mark.

It was a white-hot pain that raked down Asher's face, his skin torn by four pointed nails. It was but one of two blows the Blood Fiend dealt, also slicing a neat line with his sword across the ranger's hip, just beneath his leather cuirass. Staggering back, he could feel the blood dripping down his jaw and leg. Merith licked his lips before they turned up into a cruel smile.

Moving in for the kill, the lead Vorska cocked his sword arm, ready to deliver a final thrust that would send Asher down into the dark for good. He might have seen the deed through had one of his blood-sucking kin not slammed into him at speed. The pair cleared the ground and were sent careering off an unrelenting tree. The ranger turned to see Hadavad, his staff still levelled at where Merith had been standing.

There was no time for thanks or even a nod of the head. One of the Vorska leapt clear over Doran and darted towards Asher, perhaps tasting his blood on the air. It wasn't to reach him, a fate determined by the dwarf's flying axe. The weapon took the Vorska in the back and threw it from its feet. Asher sidestepped—wincing with pain as he did—and brought his sword down across the creature's neck.

Doran cheered though he hadn't the time to linger on the monster's demise. With sword alone, the son of Dorain now defended himself against two Blood Fiends set on tasting dwarven blood.

Only feet away from him, Russell pinned one of their kind to a tree with the haft of his pick-axe and swung the weapon round to bury the spike in its skull. He might have gone on to remove its head and actually slay the creature, but another of its ilk jumped on his broad back and clawed his flesh.

Asher moved to help him but was immediately thwarted by Merith, who had dashed back into the fray with a shoulder barge for the ranger. He might have found his footing and stood his ground, but the damage done to his hip was enough to drop him to one knee. Merith showed no mercy and stepped in with a boot to Asher's face, sending him reeling across the forest floor. Hadavad was there again, the mage placing himself between the ranger and death.

"You face true death this night, old man." Merith followed his promise up with three successive swipes of his blade, each deflected by Hadavad's staff. The last attack, however, had been a deliberate manipulation, opening the mage to a swift open-palmed blow to his throat. With ease, Merith then tossed the mage aside. "Perhaps I will let you live," he taunted, watching Hadavad gasp for air at his feet. "You should be there to see us as my master intended."

"I'm not finished with you yet," Asher announced, on his feet again.

Merith turned to face him, an arrogant smirk ruling his expression. It was short-lived. The Vorska's acute senses absorbed everything there was to know about the ranger and surmised instantly that he was not the same man who had been kicked to the ground. Gone was the wound to his hip. Healed was his face, absent the claw marks that would surely have scarred any man. And there was no sign of the boot that had hammered the side of his jaw. Asher stood before him, whole.

Whole and strong.

A frown ruined the creature's marble features. "Fascinating."

The ranger pounced forwards, his body twisting as his feet left the ground, and his broadsword following in his wake. Steel clashed with steel as the Vorska defended himself and the two danced across the camp. Asher relied more on his elven techniques, confident that for all of Merith's extensive training, he would never have had the opportunity to learn the ways of the immortals. It worked for a time, pushing the creature back and even scoring numerous blows to his limbs and a severe gash down his face, but the Vorska was quick to adapt. Asher overstepped, believing he had his enemy at a disadvantage, and received a pommel to the temple.

With passive interest, Merith looked over the new injuries the ranger had inflicted, each of them in the process of healing. "Now where did you learn all that?" he asked, his words just audible between the fighting that surrounded them. "And how did you heal yourself?" The Vorska barked a laugh. "You vex me, mortal! I would learn your secrets." The monster's mouth stretched unnaturally wide, allowing all four of his fangs to catch the firelight.

Asher blinked hard to regain his level sight. It returned to him just in time to see Doran lop off a head with his reclaimed axe, though there was already another Vorska leaping towards him. Russell remained on his feet, a vision of strength despite the claw marks that raked his body and stained his clothes with blood.

Sensing Merith closing in, the ranger swung back and hard. It was subtle, but he felt the tip of the blade nick the creature's neck.

It was just enough to force Merith back a step and allow Asher another swing. The fiend, however, was coming for his blood now and used its years of experience to dominate him.

In one abrupt movement, Merith dropped his sword and nimbly stepped inside Asher's attack. With one hand he intercepted the ranger's sword arm, halting the blow, while with the other he struck Asher in the cleft of his neck and forced him down onto his back. The wind was instantly knocked out of him and his broadsword was batted from his grip.

Merith was upon him in that same moment, flattening him with his body while pinning his head to one side, exposing his throat. "Let's see if I can taste that magic in your blood."

Asher fought against his enemy but had no limbs to call upon. He could do naught but watch. Watch as Hadavad crawled across the ground, his face flushed. Watch Russell shrug off a Vorska only to be hounded by another that took a chunk out of his arm. Worst of all, he could only watch as Doran was swarmed by three of the wretches. The dwarf was disarmed in seconds and brought down under their collective weight. He thrashed and cursed to no avail for they had him, with all but one leg in their hands.

They were going to tear him apart.

"Doran!" Asher cried, almost oblivious to the tips of Merith's fangs as they pressed into his skin.

Russell barrelled in, taking two of the Vorska with him before they could kill the dwarf. Asher's relief was tainted by pain as Merith sank his fangs into his throat, spilling naught but a trickle of blood across his neck. The creature's hideous tongue bathed in the rest, the suckers inhaling every drop. Unable to fight against it, the ranger watched Doran grasp a dagger from his belt and plunge it into the head of the remaining Vorska. Beside him, Russell cracked the neck of one and backhanded the other.

With a gasp, Merith yanked his head back from Asher's throat. His was not the only sudden reaction. Simultaneously, the remaining Vorska cried out, each scrambling to get away from the rangers. Blood running from the wounds in his neck, Asher turned his head, his gaze specifically drawn to the east.

The dawn had arrived.

Turning back to Merith, he no longer looked upon the chiselled features of an angel carved from stone. Banished was the beauty, and exiled the allure of his supernatural facade. Kneeling over the ranger now was a true monster, its hideous form destitute of humanity.

The jaw was misaligned, shunted painfully to one side so that saliva continuously pooled and poured out of the corner. The cheekbones had lost their symmetry, with one cracked open and oozing blood, while the other sported a gash that cut up through Merith's eye and along his forehead.

Those eyes. Horrors of blood red that stared down at Asher.

His locks of thick hair were gone, replaced by wisps of white and knotted strands that revealed his balding head and mottled skin. The rest of his skin was lumpy, as if moles had grown upon moles and hardened or cracked. His head cocked to one side, Asher could see the ruin of some old burn that scarred the ruinous flesh and pointed ear—the only ear Merith boasted.

Staggering away from the ranger, the ancient Vorska winced with every step, its hands held up to display only seven fingers. Asher knew pain when he saw it, and Merith was in agony. He also knew the wounds he had inflicted, seeing them now upon the Vorska's body. Yet he had witnessed those same injuries heal only minutes ago.

Clenching his right fist, Asher saw to his own wounds. Calling on the power of the black gem, he reversed the puncture marks to his throat and healed the throbbing bruise to his temple. With clearer vision, he rose to his feet, collecting his broadsword on the way. Merith watched him. Was that fear in his scarlet eyes? This was not even close to the monster he had faced before the dawn.

"Where are ye goin'?" Doran growled at the Vorska who had been upon him. His sword cut through the air and cleaved through the creature's delicate neck. The dwarf proceeded to toss his axe to Russell, who caught the weapon and swung it in the same motion, decapitating the Blood Fiend that hissed in his face.

On the other side of the camp, Hadavad was rubbing his throat as he pressed one boot into the crawling back of a surviving Vorska. He executed the beast in the same manner he had the Lycan, pointing his staff to its head and unleashing a devastating pulse.

Though the four companions stood bloody and beaten, they *stood* all the same. Of the Vorska, only Merith remained and, for all his skill, he could not defy his curse. Nor, it seemed, could he defeat his own hunger, though it was not blood he so craved. Even now, he looked at Iskander's relic, hanging from the mage's belt; that which he had recklessly pursued to this end.

A monstrous shriek turned the companions to the north, where a stray Vorska, blasted aside in the battle, emerged with a limp. A wild backhand caught Hadavad by surprise and cast him to the ground. In the light of their fire its hideous form was laid bare, revealing a plethora of open wounds, bubbling sores, and misshapen bones and joints. Frenzied by pain and hunger, the creature leapt at Asher with abandon. The ranger's immediate counter robbed the monster of its left arm, slicing through the limb just above the elbow. The Vorska howled with pain, contrasting all the more its existence under a sky lanced by sunlight.

Silencing the beast, Asher chopped his broadsword down, burying almost all of the weapon within his enemy's skull, just between the eyes. As it dropped to its knees, sword and bone came apart and the ranger swung again, bringing his blade in from the side this time. The Vorska's head bounced across the ground and found its end in the camp fire.

"Asher." Doran's tone was flat, informing the ranger that something was amiss.

Merith was gone.

Asher searched the trees but the dawn was young, its dim light little help. He could see the blood trail left in the Vorska's wake and could likely track the beast, but could he find it before nightfall?

As of that moment, Asher classed Merith as one of very few in all the realm who could outmatch him. That was no easy thing to accept, but the Arakesh in him was nothing if not pragmatic when it came to survival.

"He's gone," the ranger declared.

Doran dropped his sword and practically fell onto the log beside him, his elbows propped on his knees while his head hung low. "Does that mean," he said between laboured breaths, "I can bleed out in peace for a minute?" He then slid off the edge of the damp log and rested his back against it.

"You're hurt?" Russell's concern moved him to the dwarf's side.

Doran lifted his head, revealing new bruises and cuts that still trickled blood down his face. "Nothin' I can' handle, lad." Despite the obvious pain he was in, the son of Dorain patted Maybury on the back. "Ye saved me life back there. I'd be a few limbs short if ye hadn' jumped in when ye did. Ye have me thanks, Rus."

Rus? Asher echoed in thought alone. It seemed with every passing day the dwarf's misgivings about the miner from Snowfell slipped away, there to be replaced by a friendship Asher couldn't have predicted. Knowing the son of Dorain as he did, saving his life would solidify that bond. Now the ranger could only hope that Doran accepted Maybury as a suitable candidate for their unofficial order.

Russell merely nodded in return of the thanks. He appeared to have taken his own punishment from the Vorska, his clothes ripped and red lines marring so much of his skin. How long he would have to wear them Asher couldn't say, but he guessed the man would be whole again by the time they reached Lirian.

"Are you well, mage?" the ranger enquired.

Hadavad had already recovered from the backhand he had received and stood tall again, staff in hand. "I will survive," he reported, his voice strained as he rounded the dying fire to be in their midst. "Do you understand their curse now? Do you understand why Merith would risk the dawn to have this?" he questioned, indicating the orb on his belt.

"They are tormented under the sun," Asher concluded.

"It is worse than that," the mage replied gravely. "You saw them. By night, they are whole and strong, immune to pain even. They are like gods among men. But when the dawn breaks, they must carry their wounds—*all of them.*"

"All of them?" Asher repeated, taken aback by the statement and its implications.

"You saw the burn to Merith's face? I did that to him nearly two centuries ago, yet to this day he must endure it."

"That sounds like hell," Russell opined.

"It is," Hadavad confirmed. "And it is why Merith will never stop hunting for the orb." The mage looked into the forest, where the trail of blood vanished into the foliage. "I pity him. He believes Kargon Iskander was interrupted, and that his transformation wasn't completed." Hadavad shook his head. "I would wager he and his wretched kind are exactly as Iskander intended. There is no peace for those who bear his curse."

Inevitably, all eyes fell on Russell.

"Forgive me," the mage beseeched. "I did not think."

Maybury shrugged the remark off. "I will find my own peace," he stated, rising to his impressive height. "Even if I have to carve it out of a monster's hide."

He looked at Asher before offering the ranger a slight nod. Asher could do naught but return the gesture, for his mind and heart were too occupied with the hope and pride he felt in that moment. Each of those emotions on their own was new to him, but together they confounded the ranger.

"Now that's ranger talk if ever I heard it," Doran voiced, cutting through any emotional growth Asher might have been experiencing. In truth, the ranger was eager to move on, sure that such feelings served no purpose. He was to atone, not find new life as Russell might.

"Eat, drink," he instructed. "We make no further delay."

"*I* would delay us," Hadavad interjected, turning himself to squarely face Asher. "I would also know where your wounds have gone."

Asher blinked. "I have no wounds," he informed.

"Precisely," the mage replied. "But I saw Merith wing you with his blade—twice."

"Obviously you didn't," the ranger countered, sliding his broadsword back into its scabbard.

"No? Then I didn't see Merith bite you either? That isn't your blood?" The mage was gesturing at the ranger's collar and neck, both soaked red.

"No," he said firmly.

"It is," Russell confirmed, inserting himself. "I can smell it, Asher. It was your blood in Palios too."

The ranger glanced at Doran, who could offer little aid in the face of Russell's Lycan abilities. "You don't know what you're talking about," Asher said flippantly. "There was a lot going on—in Palios too."

Hadavad took his staff in both hands, though he wasn't so careless as to point it at Asher. "I would say, between my eyes and Russell's nose, we know exactly what we're talking about. You possess an ability not unlike the Vorska and the wolves."

The mage's tone was laden with suspicion now, his feet moving subtly though not subtly enough that Asher didn't see the bracing stance he was assuming. "Hadavad," he intoned.

"You will have to forgive my mistrust," Hadavad began. "There are many, beside Merith and Creed, who long after the Obsidian Stone, or even the lesser works of Iskander. And if you do not count yourself among them, perhaps you work for those who do."

"I'm not your enemy," Asher insisted, though the step he took was threatening enough for Hadavad.

Snow, mud, and leaves were scattered in the shape of a great wave that exploded from the mage's staff. In less than a heartbeat it closed the gap between them and impacted Asher with no more than the force of a breeze. The ranger's cloak blew out behind him with a dramatic flare that his body hadn't experienced.

Hadavad's wrinkled brow pinched in a brief moment of disbelief. Then he exerted his will and cast another spell. The blue flash streaked through the air and dissipated upon the ranger's chest. Now the mage assumed something like a battle stance, his staff levelled at shoulder height in both hands. Flames erupted from the wood, hurled by his magic and sent again into Asher's chest. Not even a patch of leather was singed by the fire spell.

Asher wafted the smoke from his face. "Are you done?"

Hadavad harrumphed and jabbed his staff at the ranger. Ice this time. Like the spells before it, the magic was harmless, the ice shattering into snowflakes. Asher ignored Russell's wide eyes and advanced towards the mage at a steady, if unyielding, pace. Spell after spell struck his chest, lighting up the early dawn and nothing more. Finally, the ranger whipped out his hand and snatched the haft of the staff, forcing it away from himself.

"Enough," he growled.

A bead of sweat had developed on the mage's brow, where his wild eyebrows had intruded. "You are no monster," he breathed. "There is no beast who can withstand such magic." Hadavad took back control of his staff and retreated a step. "You are a man, of that I'm sure. Though that might only increase my suspicion of you. Speak, Ranger, if that is truly what you are."

"Like he said," Doran announced, stepping closer to Asher, "he ain' yer enemy."

"What's going on, Asher?" Russell asked, his tone more concern than suspicion.

The ranger tried to see a way through, and with as few lies as possible, but there seemed no path that didn't tear their alliance apart. "I..." His feeble beginning died on his lips and he spared the dwarf a glance.

"Ye trusted me, lad," he said quietly, though not quietly enough that the others didn't hear him. "They're certainly men o' secrets themselves, eh?"

Indeed, Asher thought, he knew things about Hadavad and Russell that, effectively, put their lives in his hands. There would be mages in Korkanath who would not tolerate Hadavad's unusual form of immortality nor his possession of a Skaramangian Stone. And Russell... Asher could ensure his end with a handful of words to the right people.

He wasn't sure if that's what trust was supposed to be, but it was all he had for now.

"I have... an artefact," he began again, choosing a word that would resonate with the mage. "A gem," he specified, pulling off the fingerless glove from his right hand.

Hadavad's attention was immediately sucked in by the black stone, just as it absorbed the light and remained dull as coal. "An artefact," he repeated absently. "May I?" he asked, one hand held out.

Asher did not offer his hand. "No one can touch it," he warned.

"I will not take it from you," the mage promised.

"That's not what he means," Doran intruded. "If anyone but Asher touches it they'll 'ave the life sucked out o' 'em—trust me."

Asher contemplated the description for a moment, having never asked the dwarf what it had felt like when he held the gem on Dragorn. Even with his natural resistance to magic, it didn't sound like a pleasant experience.

"Fascinating," Hadavad replied, drawing the word out as he cautiously closed the gap. "It is bound to you then," he concluded. "Was that spell your doing or..."

"There was no spell," Asher informed, though he couldn't say that with absolute confidence. His earlier years remained buried beneath brutal training and mental torment. "I have had the gem for as long as I can remember."

"You don't recall how you came by it?" Hadavad enquired, his intense gaze examining every facet of the gem.

"No," the ranger confirmed.

"Is it one of those stones?" Russell asked, looking between them. "A Skara... erm, Skaramangian Stone?"

"There are many artefacts of power in this world." The mage held out his hand, offering Asher somewhere to place his own. "But there are not many capable of warding off *all* magic. Nor heal you so well."

The ranger, if reluctantly, put his hand in Hadavad's, where the mage could pore over the gem without actually touching it. He manipulated Asher's hand so he might see the gem from all sides.

"It is not a Skaramangian Stone," he declared with naught but a few seconds' inspection.

The son of Dorain, confident they were past any confrontation, planted himself on a nearby log and huffed at the effort of it. "How can ye be sure?"

Hadavad tapped the Viridian Ruby that hung from his neck. "If it were, the stone would be encased as this one is."

Asher raised an eyebrow. "Encased?"

"You recall our first conversation," the mage said, his eyes yet to leave the black gem. "The Viridian Stone is the true source of the power. It is my belief that the shell—a ruby facade, I might add—is needed to contain the magic therein. That," he voiced mindlessly, "or it's to protect those who wield it from death. Perhaps yours should have one, eh?"

"If it's not a Skaramangian Stone," Asher posed, "then what is it?"

Hadavad appeared bemused by the question. "I have no idea," he admitted. "Can it do anything else? Besides heal you and protect you from magic?" he added with a short laugh of disbelief.

Asher licked his lips. "I can... start small fires."

Again, the mage's eyebrows intruded on his brow. "Would you?" he asked, gesturing to their dying fire.

Asher didn't like to perform, but he was keen to move things along. As he had many times before, the ranger waved his ringed hand over the fire and set it to flames with a mere thought.

Hadavad's jaw dropped. "You..." The mage ran a hand through his beard. "The ring, it is Demetrium?"

"Iron," Asher answered.

"Astonishing. You require no Demetrium to shape your magic."

"Is that important?" Russell asked.

"It certainly increases the value of the stone." The mage sounded as if he was losing himself to his thoughts. "I have never, in five centuries, come across anything even close to this. It is unique. And most dangerous," he intoned. "Perhaps," he continued, meeting Asher's eyes, "it is fortuitous that it remains bound to you. Fate even."

"I don't believe in fate," Asher stated.

"You don't need to believe in something in order for it to be true. And I would say that a humble ranger of the wilds possessing an artefact so powerful as this does not happen by chance. Though, whether *you* are protecting *it* or *it* is protecting *you* I could not guess." The mage looked upon him with new eyes. "Perhaps you are meant for more than this life."

"I believe in destiny about as much as I do fate," the ranger told him bluntly, returning the glove to his hand.

Out of sight, it seemed the spell was broken and the mage able to return to the present. "Whatever that is, I must stress secrecy. In the wrong hands there's no telling what devastation it might cause."

"If I were ye, fella," Doran said, "I'd be more concerned who he'd kill to *keep* his secrets."

Hadavad nodded, almost approvingly. "Where that gem is concerned, I feel such measures only prudent. And you have my word, I will not risk its safety. Not while it remains in good hands, at least."

Asher recognised a threat when he heard one, even if it was delivered pleasantly. In truth, he appreciated it. He had no idea what the gem was or, indeed, what it was capable of, but he didn't doubt it could do so much more than what he had seen.

"I owe you everything," Russell rejoined. "I would never betray you. Your secret is my own."

Asher nodded his thanks, adding two more to the short list of people who knew of the gem. "We should be going," he told them, spying the first rays of light to pierce the forest. "We need to put as much distance as we can between us and Merith before nightfall."

"Agreed," Hadavad voiced. "And... apologies," he offered, signalling his staff.

"I would have done the same," Asher assured, though where the mage had used spells he would have used steel. And he would have killed him.

Doran looked about the camp. "Where's Hector?"

Asher quickly scanned their surroundings. Hadavad's white mare was beyond the camp, still visible between the trees. Pig was still snoring on the periphery of it all, its deep sleep undisturbed by the night's ruckus. Of Hector there was no sign.

Asher sighed. "Damn coward."

CHAPTER 27
A MIRROR DARKLY

Sirens - There are plenty of sailors around Velia's port and the like who will swear blind that Sirens exist. They'll recount sightings and tell tales of men hearing the sweet and hypnotic song of these creatures.
They don't exist.
If they did, we would have killed one by now. It is unanimous amongst our order of hunters that Sirens are no more than fairy tales.

A Chronicle of Monsters: A Ranger's Bestiary, 12th Edition,
Page 66.

Neave Gladwell, Ranger.

U nder thick clouds and a storm of wind-swept snow, the companions looked upon the faded green door of The Ranch once again. Standing beneath the porch roof, Asher looked back over his shoulder and scrutinised the street. It was late morning and the grim weather had done little to deter

Lirian's populace from going about their business. It had, however, produced crowds of cloaks and hoods that concealed the faces of those around the rangers.

Asher didn't like it.

He felt eyes on him but he could not spy them among the moving throng. It had been days since their clash with the Vorska; that was several nights in which Merith could regain ground in their pursuit. Was he out there somewhere, his nightmarish features hiding within the folds of a cloak? And what of Creed and his band of wolves? He didn't even now what Creed looked like.

Doran hammered on the door. "Danagarr!" he yelled. "It's us! Let us in!"

Minutes went by before they heard the scraping of heavy objects and bolts and chains being removed. The dwarven smith opened the door with his hammer in hand. "Praise the Mother an' Father! I was beginnin' to fear ye wouldn' return at all!"

"Do ye 'ave any food?" Doran asked without preamble, pushing his way inside.

"A little," Danagarr replied, caught off guard. His attention, however, was quick to flit back to the others. "It went well then? Ye found yerselves a monster?"

The last to step over the threshold, Asher pushed back his hood and gave the street one final inspection before closing the door. "We have a tale or two, master smith," he assured.

While their cloaks and kit were drying by the fire, the four companions enjoyed the beef stew Danagarr had prepared the previous day and recounted their journey for the old smith. Asher was pleased to hear Doran speak as highly as he did about Russell, often pausing to pat the man on the back.

"Have you had any trouble here?" Asher asked.

Danagarr was shaking his head. "None. I stayed in The Grey Hound for a night or two, like ye suggested. Since then, I've been comin' an' goin' as the work requires. It sounds like ye've cut your enemies in half though. Did the Lycans give ye no bother?"

The four companions shared uneasy looks before Asher

answered the dwarf. "We have yet to see them since the first full moon."

"By the looks o' ye I'm thinkin' that's not a good thing."

"Werewolves are good hunters in their human form," Hadavad remarked. "I would have expected to see them before now."

"Let's just thank the Mother an' Father we haven', eh?" Doran suggested.

"We're only a few days away from the next full moon," Russell interjected. "I can feel it," he commented, as if the thought had got away from him.

Danagarr clicked his fingers. "Do ye want to see it?" he blurted. "Don' get me wrong, there's still a bit o' tinkerin' I'd like to see to but, on the whole, it's finished!"

"You did it?" Russell asked, a note of hope about him.

"Oh aye, lad! These hands once rebuilt the vault doors o' Hyndaern! I jus' needed a little more time, what with the lack o' proper resources. Ye know, with the right tools an' materials, humans could build to the heavens."

Asher raised a hand to halt the dwarven smith. "I'm sure we could, Danagarr, but we would settle for your ingenuity for now." The ranger gestured to the corridor with a tilt of his head.

"O' course, o' course! Follow me, fellas!"

Trailing the Stormshield round the corner, they soon arrived at the new and reinforced door. It was considerably thicker than its predecessor, clad in sheets of iron and held to the frame by large hinges. Indeed, Danagarr exerted some strength to open it. He then stepped back so they might see it unimpeded by his girth.

In just a few weeks he had transformed the room into a dungeon for one.

Russell stepped inside. "Is it... smaller?"

"Aye. There's new walls, ceiling too. I've fitted iron plates between them all, just in case the wolf breaks free, but I was also thinkin' abou' the racket it makes."

"Breaks free?" Maybury questioned, moving around the strange contraption in the middle of the room.

"It's unlikely," Danagarr asserted, entering the room himself.

"Not with this anyway," he beamed, patting the framework of steel and hard leather.

"What is it?" Doran demanded.

"I'll admit, it's unlike anythin' I've ever made before, but damn if it ain' beautiful! Come 'ere," the smith bade, drawing Russell round the back of it. "Stand on these," he instructed, pointing at the two pedals that stood a couple of feet off the floor. "They're spring loaded," he said, as Maybury stepped onto them. "When the wolf emerges, the extra weight will force the pedals down, beneath the floor. Now, insert yer hands though the manacles an' rest yer arms in the gutters. Don' worry abou' yer chest, it ain' meant to reach the harness until ye transform."

Russell hesitated when the dwarf closed the back half of the framework, bringing a panel of steel and leather to his spine. "Don' worry," the smith said. "I've designed the whole thing so ye can do this yerself. I'll jus' show ye how it's goin' to work. Now, if I weren' 'ere, ye'd just step in an' close the frame first, before insertin' yer hands. Ye'll note, even with the frame closed, there's still enough room to move abou' an' work the seals. I've kept it simple since the wolf won' 'ave the know-how to release itself."

"What's this for?" Russell enquired, looking up at the sloping section that extended from the chest piece.

"That's for the wolf's head," Danagarr explained. "The frame will ensure that ye grow in the right direction. Once the Lycan is fully formed, its head will fit in there an' be held firm. So too will yer hands be bound out to the sides an' yer ankles secured. Jus' be sure to step into the rings as you do with yer hands."

Asher stepped inside to join them, his experienced eyes roaming over the framework and the considerable chains that connected it to the floor, ceiling, and walls. It certainly appeared sturdy, if not outright terrifying. If he had been told it was a device of torture he would have had no trouble believing it.

"You've outdone yourself, Danagarr," the ranger complimented.

"There's a few additional measures I'd like to install before the first moon," the smith replied. "But, as it is, it could hold a Lycan."

341

"Russell?" Asher was yet to see any confidence from the man.

"Could this really work?" he breathed, perhaps seeing something of his dream, a future he could actually claim.

"It will," Asher said confidently.

Russell looked away as he nodded his response. "How do I get out of this thing?"

~

Despite the rain, the sun was up, and so Asher spent the rest of the day prowling the windows where he might spy the outside world. He was looking for the anomalies, the people who stood out against the usual activity.

Nothing.

He found no signs of their enemies, no disturbances in the flow of the crowds. If Merith had made it this far he was hiding somewhere. As for Creed and his band—who could say? It infuriated Asher, who felt the prey in the eyes of an unseen predator.

Infuriated or not, the day moved on and the night moved in. Soon, those same streets were sparsely populated and then emptied by the watchmen that swept through the city, enacting the king's curfew. The ranger had watched it all, waiting to see those who were slow to leave. Still there had been nothing.

Inevitably, he was forced to leave his self-imposed station and seek out food and drink with the others. They had kept to themselves for most of the day, though Russell had spent a large portion of the day assisting Danagarr with some final additions and tweaks to the wolf cage.

Doran volunteered the first watch and Hadavad the second, allowing Asher to sleep until his time, pre-dawn. Rest didn't come easy to the ranger and, when it did, he was plummeted into dreams of torment. He had seen so much death and caused so much despair that his mind struggled to let go of it, any of it. He could recall with ease the faces and names of every one of those he had destroyed.

Cutting rhythmically through it all was his time in Nightfall.

He was thrown from one bloody scene and hurled into another, where his old masters would beat him to turn him into the monster they desired. Every one of the Arakesh he passed in those dark halls wore the face of Nasta Nal-Aket.

When, at last, he met the Father, in The Cradle of Nightfall, Nasta handed him a length of knotted red string. With finger and thumb he deciphered the Arakesh language and discovered the two names hidden therein.

Russell Maybury—his target.

Asher—the one who sought his death.

Stuck in his dream, the ranger staggered back from Nasta and cast the knotted string away, where it melted from his perception. "No," he protested over and over again.

"You must obey," the Father told him, his lidless empty eye sockets boring into him.

"I will not," Asher hissed.

"You already have," Nasta replied coolly. "*You* brought him into this. You have done more than ensure his death. You have given him *hope* before the end. It will make his death all the *sweeter*." Nasta's mouth stretched beyond the ordinary and his fangs grew out around a thick tongue of suckers.

Asher stepped back from the Vorska but made no ground in the dreamscape. He wanted to defend himself, to lash out at his foe, only his arms would not move. He could not beat the Vorska. Those deadly fangs, however, never reached him. Instead, Nasta stepped back and swung closed the framework of Danagarr's design, imprisoning Asher within.

The chains rattled about his wrists and ankles, refusing to let him go. Standing before him were his three companions, a gallery of passive watchers to his misery.

"The beast will out," Hadavad announced.

"It *always* gets out," Doran added.

"It must have its pound of flesh," Russell said.

"No," Asher muttered repeatedly, fighting against the bars. "I won't let it."

343

Nasta emerged from the shadows behind the others. "There is no cage that can contain an Arakesh. Why even bother trying?"

"That's not what I am!" Asher yelled. "That's not what I..." His proclamation faded as a new figure pushed past Nasta and parted his companions to stand before him.

Asher now looked upon himself, clad in the dark leathers of an Arakesh and blindfolded in red.

A disturbingly wicked smile stretched beneath that blindfold. "You will always think like me," the Arakesh told him. "In the end, your deeds will reflect that." The fiend laughed, short and sharp. "You're already bathed in blood. This *Ranger* will not undo that. Be what you were *bred* to be."

Asher felt nothing in the dreaming world, but he perceived his body changing as the werewolf emerged, its hulking size expanding from within and stretching him into nothingness. The darker version of himself now brandished a dagger, the blade curved and shining in the torchlight. It was soon angled to come down, between the bars where it might plunge into his heart.

Tick, tick.

The Arakesh hesitated, his head cocked to one side.

Tick, tick, *click*.

The assassin was now holding Iskander's orb, the dagger replaced.

Tick, tick, tick, *click*.

The room quickly faded to black and the Arakesh with it, leaving only the orb to shine without any source of light.

Tick, tick, *click*, tick.

Click.

Asher's eyes opened to the real world, one hand grasping the hilt of his broadsword. He rolled over, towards the fire and welcomed the light. Just as he had in the forest, the ranger's restless sleep had turned him away from the flames, entangled him in his bedding and set his heightened senses off. Despite the cold, he had worked up a sweat. The dream came back to him in pieces, the fragments having lost some of their finer edges.

The ranger wiped his brow and rubbed his eyes. *Be what you were bred to be.* The words haunted him—his own words. Asher felt as if he was sinking, soon to be swallowed whole by the *Assassin.*

Doran's snoring turned him to the dwarf, a few feet away, who was sleeping back-to-back with Russell. Asher stared at Russell for a time. The man had already made strides towards conquering the monster within him. Yet he, whose monster dwelled only in the mind, could not boast the same strides.

A second and more animalistic snore interrupted the ranger's introspection. Danagarr was nestled inside his hammock in the far corner.

The ceiling creaked, turning his attention up to the dusty beams. The mage, he thought. Careful not to make a sound, Asher reattached the scabbard to his hip and made for the stairs. With no more than a single candle for company, he discovered Hadavad seated on the floor, in the middle of the large room, with his legs folded in the manner of a sage. Between his fingers he worked the two halves of the orb.

"I keep finding you like this," Asher remarked on his approach.

"Yes," Hadavad agreed. "I am reluctant to part with it. The pursuit of knowledge was a large part of my life's work. My first life, I should say."

"It must be buried somewhere deep, Hadavad," Asher insisted, taking a seat opposite the mage. "If it is the Obsidian Stone—"

"I know," the mage cut in, his frustration showing through. "But," he continued, glancing at Asher's right hand, "since learning of your own relic I have begun to wonder if there is another way. Perhaps, as you have, I can keep it safe until such time as—"

"No," Asher whispered, if firmly. "There are six people, including myself, in all the realm who know of this." The ranger held up his right hand without revealing the gem. "Of which, I trust you the least," he stated, hoping the point would hammer home just how well his secret was kept. "It *is* safe with me. But that, whatever it is, cannot be kept like a trinket. Merith and Creed alone are good reasons to hide it."

The mage sighed, the truth worming into his bones. "You are

right, of course. Here." Hadavad tossed the orb into Asher's waiting hands. "What did I say about the influences of friends?" he asked with a silent laugh. "I would think better without it for a time." Sounding weary, he picked himself up and walked away from the ranger, making it as far as the window before he felt the need to lean against the sill.

Asher remained seated, his fingers naturally turning the two halves of the orb while his thoughts ran away with themselves. He began to think of places to conceal the relic, dark places where none might ever stumble across it. The Adean seemed an obvious choice. They could take a boat out from Velia and drop it over the side. The depths would take it down into a vault where no man could venture.

His fingers stopped twisting the two halves.

Again, his dream pressed upon him, taking his mind back to the Lycan cage. The nightmare had come to an end when the Nightseye elixir had enhanced his senses. As always, his ears were the first to take in the secrets of the world. What had he heard? What had banished the dream?

Ticking.

Ticking and sharp *clicks*.

Asher looked down at the orb, revelation behind his eyes. He turned the pieces of the orb again, though he heard nothing, nor did he even feel anything—the motion was soundless and smooth.

Be what you were bred to be.

The words came back to him, only it was not the words of the *Assassin* but those of the *Ranger*. For so long he had tried to be one and not the other when, in fact, he was one who possessed the skills of the other. He could not be rid of the Arakesh that dwelled within, but that didn't mean he couldn't use it to his advantage, to the benefit of others even.

Determined to act before his thoughts might spiral, Asher removed the strip of red cloth from his belt and proceeded to blind himself with it. Once again, the Nightseye elixir came to life in his veins. He was immediately aware of Hadavad's creaking joints and the old sweat long soaked into his robes. That and so much more pressed against his periphery, desperate to flood his senses.

The ranger called on every ounce of his discipline to keep the world at bay and narrow his focus on the orb alone. Slowly, he manipulated the two halves, turning one against the other. The *ticking* returned. A combination lock, he realised, only it had been designed for those who could hear it, removing any need to imprint numbers on the surface.

He hesitated to twist it any further.

The dark mage had clearly designed the orb with Merith's acute senses in mind. Even if it wasn't the Obsidian Stone as Hadavad suspected, it couldn't be anything good. But they might be able to destroy it, he considered, the thought quickly taking root. That would be better than hiding the orb and its mysterious contents.

And so he twisted it one way, then the next, his sensitive fingers detecting the mechanisms inside. Turning the top half to the right, he listened for the telltale *click* that had disturbed his dreams.

Click.

There.

He continued to move it to the right, completing an entire circuit without another click. The ranger frowned and began to twist it the other way. Nothing. Holding the top half firm, he now manipulated the bottom dome. The ticking continued almost until he completed another circuit, but a second *click* cracked in his ears. Still, the orb would not give up its secrets.

As with the top half, the lower section offered no further clicks on a second turn. Determined, and confident he was on the right track, Asher twisted the top half again. Hearing naught but ticking, he slowed down in case the mechanisms had skipped over each other in his haste.

Click.

The ranger took a steadying breath and repeated his efforts with the lower half.

Click.

That was four successful twists, yet the orb remained intact. Resisting the urge to sigh and, potentially, garner the mage's attention, Asher repeated the process again until he had seven successful *clicks*. A metallic pop and a soft hiss cut through the quietude as the two halves parted just enough to reveal a delicate clasp.

The ranger sucked in a breath and never released it.

The orb was open.

CHAPTER 28
THE WOLF AT THE DOOR

Skulldiggers - *Imagine, if you will, a butterfly the size of your hand and
with teeth like a beaver. Oh, and an appetite for human brain.
At speed, one of these critters will fly directly into your face and
immediately begin digging through flesh and bone until it's situated
inside your skull.
If you see a swarm—hide. If you're hunting a swarm, stock up on salt;
they hate the stuff. I would also recommend smoke, to make them drowsy
first.*

***A Chronicle of Monsters: A Ranger's Bestiary, 12th Edition,
Page 236.***

Haylin Nord, Ranger.

Hadavad was slow to turn around. His gaze shifted repeatedly between Asher's blindfolded appearance and the orb. "Impossible," the mage breathed, his feet carrying him across the floor without thought. "How... How did you..."

"I can hear and... *feel* everything inside the orb," Asher informed him, fighting his conditioning.

The finer muscles in Hadavad's face twitched and danced as a range of emotions came over him. "Incredible," he uttered. "I always wondered how it was the Arakesh could fight so well without their eyes. An elixir, I assume." The mage waved away his own comments. "Another time," he insisted, his attention returning to the orb.

Asher carefully thumbed the clasp and gripped the top half. "Easy," Hadavad hissed, that same hand reaching out towards the orb. "There could be a trap."

Asher doubted it. The orb had been clearly designed with a Vorska in mind. Iskander wouldn't have expected anyone else to open it. Still, he released his grip on the small dome and allowed his companion to lift the top free, the mage better versed in traps of a magical nature.

The old man inspected the curve of the orb as he lifted the top free. As the ranger had expected, there were no such traps, though there was certainly a spell at work.

Hadavad sat back and Asher leant away, taking the lower half with him. In so doing, both men sat between a floating object that had no need of its previous shell. Removing his blindfold, the ranger remained on the floor but began to move around the object, examining it from every side. Asher was sure he recognised it for what it was.

"Fascinating," the mage muttered under his breath.

"It's an arrow head," Asher stated.

Hadavad's eyebrows flitted as he spared the ranger a glance. "Oh yes. Yes it is. How curious..."

Dissatisfied with the mage's lack of assessment, Asher tilted his head to look past the object and find Hadavad's face. "Arrow heads don't usually float," he pointed out, hoping to draw something out of the man.

"No," the mage agreed, still enthralled by the discovery.

"Why might that be, Hadavad?" the ranger asked pointedly.

"It's not the Obsidian Stone," the mage uttered, mostly speaking to himself it seemed. "I thought for sure..."

Asher adjusted his position on the floor, intending to break the mage's focus. "Hadavad, why would Kargon Iskander place a floating arrow head inside the orb?"

Hadavad chuckled to himself and tapped the edge of the arrow head, sending it into a lazy spin. "This begs so many more questions than the presence of a Skaramangian Stone." The mage waved two fingers over the candle and renewed the dwindling flame before picking it up. "How intriguing," he voiced.

"What?"

Hadavad licked his lips again and gestured at his side of the arrow head. "See here," he bade, making Asher move. "Do you see that?"

The ranger narrowed his eyes to better make out the details. Caught in the light, the shadows of a shallow engraving could be seen laid into the surface of the iron head. Were he to trace it with a finger he would have drawn a spiral with a triangle on the end.

"What is that?"

The mage ran a hand through his beard, his old eyes never straying from the glyph. "*That*," he intoned, "is one half of a lock and key spell."

"A lock and key spell?" Asher echoed when no further explanation followed.

"Yes. Somewhere, there will be a corresponding pattern that..." Hadavad trailed off and, for the first time, his gaze drifted from the arrow head. "Somewhere," he repeated mindlessly. "No," he added gravely. "Not just... *somewhere*."

"Hadavad?" Asher pressed.

His train of thought broken, the mage turned back to the

ranger. "It's a key," he said simply. "Insert it into the right lock—a lock with a matching pattern—and it will open the door."

Asher shrugged. "What door?"

Hadavad held the ranger's attention, though his lips remained sealed. He didn't need to speak for Asher to know the answer was nothing good. But any potential conversation was interrupted when the door to the basement burst open, there to reveal the wide frame of Russell Maybury.

Asher swore before rising to his feet.

"What is that?" Russell demanded, his voice ragged.

Even in the gloom, Asher could see the feral look in his eyes. They were edging closer and closer to the first full moon, a time when Creed's command intruded on Russell's mind. The ranger placed himself between the arrow head and Maybury, one hand coming up to stop the big man on his approach while the other hand slid up his scabbard, towards the hilt of his broadsword.

Russell's nose twitched, his eyes looking right through Asher. "What is that?" he demanded again, deliberate strides bringing him closer.

"Doran!" Asher called, his tone pitched to convey some urgency.

"That's mine," Russell growled.

Inevitably, the two collided, though the violence lasted no more than an instant as the ranger was flung to one side. The wall greeted him with pain before the floor welcomed him back. He regained his senses just enough to witness Russell meet Hadavad. The mage's staff swept high and so too did Maybury, as if gripped by some invisible hand.

The ceiling protested his bulk as he was slammed and subsequently pinned in place by magic. Russell writhed, fighting the spell, but managed no more than strained muscles and bulging veins. He grunted and snarled, his teeth bared and eyes flaring with Lycan amber.

"What's goin' on?" came Doran's voice from the stairs, his heavy boots pounding the old wood.

Asher picked himself up and rolled his left shoulder as he did. It was nothing the black gem couldn't fix in a heartbeat.

No more than a glance was required to make certain the arrow head remained untouched. Hadavad stood sentinel now, his staff rooted to the floor by one hand, as he barred the way. The ranger crossed the room to stand beneath Russell's face.

"Enough," the ranger ordered.

"It's mine," Russell seethed.

"You're letting it slip," Asher told him, his words enough to draw in those amber eyes. "Remember who you want to be. Hold on to it."

The son of Dorain joined them now, careful not to walk under the big man laid flat to the ceiling. "Did I miss somethin'?" he asked, to which the mage indicated the arrow head behind him.

"Ye opened it!" Doran exclaimed before frowning. "What in the hells is it?"

Asher ignored the dwarf, his attention fixed on Russell. "Remember the dream," he insisted. "It remains alive so long as you *hold on to it.*"

Maybury blinked, his eyes watering. "I... can't," he groaned. "I... *need* it." Again, his nose crinkled as he inhaled the scent.

Asher dared to look over his shoulder, though he couldn't see the arrow head past Hadavad. "What is it?" he asked Russell. "What can you smell?"

Russell's jaw quivered. "Blood," he declared.

Daring to turn away from him, Asher instead narrowed his eyes questioningly at Hadavad. The mage returned his attention to the arrow head, pausing only to pick up the candle once more. Crouching beside the floating object, he scrutinised its two sides in the light.

His head tilted within his hood. "He's right. One side is stained with blood." Again, the mage's attention fell away, his gaze taken by the shadows about them.

"Whose blood is it?" Doran asked.

Again, Hadavad met Asher's eyes with a hard expression in place of words.

Doran was looking from one to the other. "Can someone tell me what in the hells is goin' on 'ere."

Asher didn't have the answer to that exactly. Though, in looking at Doran, the ranger viewed the street beyond the window. Something tugged at his senses, something out of place. He quickly moved past the dwarf and stared through the glass, taking in the snow-covered street and rooftops, the result of the evening's plunging temperature.

"It's not snowing," he said absently.

"What are ye on abou'?"

"A patrol comes through here just past the hour," Asher explained.

"And? What o' it?"

"What's wrong, Asher?" Hadavad asked, his passive will enough to keep Russell pinned in place.

"There's no tracks in the snow," the ranger told them. "The patrol hasn't come through."

Before any more questions could be levelled at him, Asher unbolted the front door and took to the freezing air. The short steps creaked as he descended to the street, where the snow was finally imprinted. Looking left and right, the street was empty, with no more than a handful of buildings illuminated by candlelight.

"Where are ye goin'?" Doran asked after him, but the ranger was already striding down the street, away from The Ranch.

The snow crunched under his feet, the only sound but for the silvyr blade that rang free from over his right shoulder. He stopped at the branching streets, taking in each dark lane. Nothing. No torchlight from the patrolling watchmen or soldiers or even the Graycoats the king had pressed into action. With a pit forming in his stomach, Asher turned around and retraced his steps.

It was only a glance but the image struck him a moment later, halting his steps. He could see Doran in the distance, watching him from outside The Ranch. Turning his sight from the dwarf, Asher retraced a step to stand before the alley in which he had glimpsed a single boot protruding from behind a large crate. Even at a glance he knew a Graycoat standard issue boot.

Short-sword first, he entered the alley with caution, his eyes naturally checking the rooftops either side. He soon rounded the crate and discovered, as he had suspected, two dead Graycoats. Bloodied and beaten, their cause of death was manifestly a broken neck.

It was not the work of a Vorska.

The alarm in Asher's head was at full ring now, sending him into a sprint. Upon sighting his haste, Doran fell into a brace, his axe and sword coming up. The ranger had a warning for him, a barking command to get back inside, but the words never left his lips. Movement in his peripheral field turned his head to the left and up, where two men were hurtling along the rooftops, leaping the gaps with ease.

No, not men. Werewolves.

As with Russell, Creed's band of wolves did not require the full moon to possess supernatural strength and speed. Though they retained the shape of men, they took to the roof tops like Wraiths. And there were more to the ranger's right, a man and woman matching his speed.

Doran saw them too and took steps towards the porch. "Come on!" he called to Asher.

Of the four, one of the men made the jump from roof to street and landed ten feet in front of Asher. He displayed no weapon and wore no armour, relying solely on strength. It was a poor choice, however, when faced with skill and experience. Even more so when that skill and experience were wielding a silvyr blade.

Asher dropped to his knees, allowing his momentum to carry him across the snow and under the wolf's swinging arm. One strong slash was more than the silvyr edge required to slice through his foe's hip, separating enough bone and sinew to rob the man of his balance, if not his right leg. As the wolf fell in a spray of crimson, Asher leapt back to his feet and finished his run to The Ranch.

"Bolt the door!" Danagarr yelled, clearly woken from his slumber by all the activity that had taken place above his head.

No sooner had the door slammed shut behind Asher than the Lycans rammed into it. Reinforced by the combined strength of Doran and Danagarr, it held fast. They attempted to gain entry three more times before the trio backed off, retreating to the street.

Asher watched them through a slit in the boards of the nearest window. They were soon joined by more of their ilk, each dropping from the roof tops or slinking out of the shadowed alleys. The one he had wounded half limped half crawled to meet them, his blood trailing the snow behind him.

"There's more than a dozen of them," he counted.

"Lycans!" Doran cursed. "Damned be those odds. But," he bellowed into the door, "ye can bet I'm goin' to take a few o' ye with me!"

As one, the group of Werewolves parted down the middle, framing the alleyway directly opposite The Ranch. Asher gripped the hilt of his silvyr blade a little tighter as his eyes narrowed on those shadowy depths.

A single man was born of the dark.

His feet flattened the white powder as he cut through the Lycans and presented himself. His stature was that of Russell's, broad and tall, though he was made all the larger by his mane of wild hair and thick beard. Wearing loose-fitting clothes, and absent a cloak or coat, he appeared comfortable in the frigid air and visibly unarmed. Of course, the man known only as Creed was far from being truly unarmed.

"You already know who I am," Creed called out, his grizzled voice piercing the walls. He left his ominous introduction to hang in the air and sit with the rangers a while. A fear tactic, Asher knew.

The ranger turned back to observe Maybury's reaction, his master's voice sweet in his ear. The miner from Snowfell was all veins and bulging muscles as he fought against Hadavad's spell.

"Russell," Asher hissed. "Remember who you want to be. Hold on to it."

"What he wants, *Asher*," Creed responded, his incredible sense of hearing taking the ranger off guard, "is to be with his pack. That's all there is for him now. This monster business you've tried to get him into..." Creed shrugged. "It's a waste of time. Russell isn't one of *you*. He's one of *us*."

Seeing Maybury now, that was all too easy to believe. "What do you want?" Asher asked quietly, with no need to raise his voice.

Creed casually hooked his thumbs into his belt. "Oh," he drawled, "I'm just another dreamer who isn't happy with his lot." At this the old wolf grinned knowingly.

Asher and Doran locked eyes, each recognising the dwarf's words from their private conversation, prior to leaving Lirian.

"I suppose," Creed went on, "I just want *more*." Again, his words were taken directly from Doran, making Asher feel all the more the fool. "To *be* something more," he specified, before a rasping chuckle left his lips. "We've been watching and listening for some time now. Patience is easy when you don't live every hour under the sun in torment though. Those pesky Vorska just can't help themselves. Too eager. Then again, there is no better hunter than the wolf," he boasted. "Luckily for you, the pack isn't hunting for meat tonight." Again, he let that stale the air for a while so the threat might sink in.

"We've been waiting for you to return," Creed began again. "It sounds like Danagarr has done a bang up job with that cage down there." The old wolf inhaled the air. "Is that dwarven fear I can smell?"

"Don' worry, lad!" Doran shouted through the door. "Ye'll come to fear the dwarves o' Dhenaheim soon enough!"

Creed was smiling through his beard, his words having hit the intended mark. "I've never tasted dwarf," he remarked, much to the amusement of his pack.

"You've come for the orb," Asher interjected, his patience quickly ground to dust.

"*No*," Creed stated emphatically. "If I wanted the orb I would have prised it from the mage's lifeless fingers by now. I want what's inside it. I know you've opened it." The old wolf gestured to his kin. "Why else would we be here?"

Hadavad stamped his staff into the floor and harrumphed. "You can't have it, Creed!" he hollered. "I'll not see it in the hands of a beast like you!"

"It isn't yours to keep, Mage," Creed scolded. Again, he deliberately sniffed the air. "I can smell it from here," he said, licking his lips. "Extraordinary... I'm not so old as to have met him, but I would know *his* blood anywhere."

Asher looked past Hadavad to the floating arrow head. He couldn't see the blood that stained it but he knew now who it had once belonged to.

"You have the blood of our maker in there," Creed declared. "Anything of Kargon Iskander's is rightfully ours. So we'll be taking it. Russell too."

"The hells ye will!" Doran bellowed.

Hadavad started forward. "There's no spell here!" he reported forcefully. "Iskander left you nothing to undo the curse! You are bound to the moon, and you are slave to the monster he put inside you!"

Creed looked to be considering the mage's words, if with a hint of bemusement. "What was it you said? It's a lock and key spell... Something tells me the magic we require is behind the door that same key will open."

"You'll never find it!" Hadavad snapped.

"Find what?" Doran asked.

"You can either give the key to Russell and let him walk out of there with it," came the old wolf's decree, "or, we'll come in there and take both ourselves."

Doran raised his head. "Ye're not the first to dictate terms to us, laddy! An' jus' like 'em, ye'll get the sharp end o' me answer!"

"I can smell the dead Vorska on you," Creed replied. "I promise you, dwarf, we are *not* Vorska. I will *break* you before I kill you."

CHAPTER 29

THE PACK

Blatenwik - A brute of a monster, and an angry one at that. If you must hunt one of them, surprise will be your greatest weapon. If your surprise attack fails and you're face to face with it, best be having your affairs in order, because running isn't an option.

With the rounded horns of a goat and a head that could only be compared to a Gobber's, it's a creature born of nightmares. Its hideous face and tusks aside, the danger posed by a Blatenwik comes from its strength. There's no fat on these creatures, just muscle. Trust me when I tell you, they will use that muscle to tear your arms off.

A Chronicle of Monsters: A Ranger's Bestiary, 12th Edition, Page 279.

The Blacksmith, Ranger.

Asher made a gesture to Doran to stop antagonising their foe, if only so he could formulate a plan to see them survive the night. The dwarf made an obscene gesture in return, eliciting an exasperated expression from the ranger. When next he looked out of the window, the pack was short by three of their number.

The revelation was followed by three sets of rapid footsteps bounding across the roof above them. Their movement led Asher's attention to the back door that led to the supply room and court-yard beyond.

"They're flanking us!" the ranger barked.

At the same time, he was replacing his silvyr blade over his shoulder and drawing an arrow from his quiver. His left hand had already retrieved the folded bow and snapped it to life, ready to receive the arrow. With naught but the narrow slit in the boards, there would be no aiming, but Creed and his pack were advancing on the door, offering a target-rich environment.

The bowstring *twanged*, cutting through the air as it projected the arrow through the narrow gap and the glass pane. Asher put an eye to the boards to see his victim, only to find his arrow in Creed's hand, the shaft then to be snapped by his thumb. Seeing the futility in taking another shot, the ranger collapsed the limbs and abandoned the bow on the floor.

Dire as the situation had become, the silvyr always felt damned good in his hand.

As one, and from all sides, the pack assaulted The Ranch. One of the female wolves bounded over the porch railing and leapt through the window and boards, forcing Asher to duck. A moment later, Creed himself put his boot to the door, breaking the bolt with a single kick and throwing the dwarves back. At the same time, the back door burst open to three more of their rugged ilk, there to be greeted by Hadavad.

The mage's magic brought an instance of light to the gloom, though it was the telekinetic wave that impacted their environ-ment the most. Dust and debris were propelled from his staff before the spell struck the middle of the trio, casting one back into the supply room and throwing the other two aside.

"Keep Russell pinned!" Asher managed to yell before the female Lycan was upon him.

She was quick. Quicker than him. Her hands found his chest and pushed him back into the wall. It was a jarring impact that nearly saw him lose his grip on the short-sword. Despite maintaining his hold, the wolf snatched at his wrist and squeezed with supernatural strength, threatening the integrity of the bones therein. Adding to her assault, she swiped him across the face, dropping the ranger to one knee. From there he watched Creed face the dwarves.

"Now ye're goin' to get it!" Doran growled.

Creed held his ground, content to let the wolves behind him flood the room and fight in his stead. Seeing how clumsy they were, and completely reliant on their inherent abilities, Asher decided they were new to this life. Damned if Creed wasn't using this to train them.

Asher felt his breath disappear as the Lycan wrapped her free hand around his throat. He was angry now, a dangerous emotion the *Assassin* would have kept in check. Proving the *Ranger* a worthy adversary, he flicked his wrist down and released the silvyr blade. So sharp was it that the short distance between his hand and her foot didn't matter. The sword spun once on its way down and plunged through her toes before sinking into the wood.

The wolf screamed and immediately released his throat and wrist. In one motion, Asher freed the dagger from the base of his back, ran it across her exposed neck, and collected his silvyr blade on his way to intercept the next foe. The fresh blood, however, a deluge of red, turned every Lycan head towards the ranger. It was just enough to alert the nearest of his enemies and see them evade his first swing. What chaos ensued then.

A backhand and a kick, from whom exactly Asher could not guess, took him from his feet and launched him into the adjacent wall. Danagarr cried out from somewhere in the melee and was sent skidding across the floor, past the ranger. Hadavad's spells continued to blast this way and that, hurling wolves in every direction. Doran was busy doing what he did best: hacking. His axe and sword chopped and slashed at anything that moved and there were more than a couple of bodies at his feet.

The son of Dorain's success did him no favours, now garnering Creed's special attention.

Asher scrambled to his feet, barely aware of the blood that oozed from his eyebrow. All of his instincts told him Creed was no ordinary foe, just as Merith had proved far deadlier than his pale kin.

Two wolves were quick to bar his way, each partially crouched in an echo of the beast they contained within. Reversing his grip on the silvyr blade, the ranger darted in, a deliberate move to force them apart. As the short-sword curled round in one hand, scoring no more than a gash across the arm of one, the dagger in his other hand came round in his pivoting twist. The steel flew the short distance—too short even for the Lycan's reactions—and drove into the man's heart until the guard slammed into his chest. Before he hit the floor, dead, Asher was already kicking out in an arcing roundhouse. He caught the second of the wolves across the jaw, but his human strength was only enough to knock the man back a single step.

The Lycan might have retaliated had he not been rammed by another of his kind, blasted like a leaf in the wind by Hadavad. The two crashed into the far wall in a heap of broken bones, not far from where Danagarr lay terribly still.

Fighting his urge to check on the dwarven smith, Asher returned his attention to the pack. He was instantly dismayed to see Doran on the other side of the room, a scattered wall of wolves between them. Worse still, he was held aloft in Creed's hands, his axe and sword on the floor. The son of Dorain appeared dazed in the old wolf's grip, his face swollen and bruised with blood finding its way down through the creases in his weathered skin.

"Doran!" Asher roared.

Years of training collided with his emotions, which urged him to wade in and reach his friend. Silvyr flashed, taking fingers and limbs from the first two blocking his path, and a swift palm to the throat sent a third staggering away, directly into Hadavad's swinging staff. The mage had been forced into fighting as the others did by the close quarters, his staff a weapon in itself. Without his magic, however, Hadavad was only as strong as his aged body.

A sharp yelp escaped him when one of the Lycans barrelled into his waist and charged him into the supply room. It might not have been so severe a blow had the back of his head not slammed into the top of the door frame.

Again, Asher had to sharpen his focus and keep to his set path —saving Doran. Of course, with Hadavad's apparent demise, the mage's will power was no longer keeping his spells intact.

Russell fell from the ceiling.

One of his arms caught Asher across the back, pushing him forwards and off balance. His intended attack missed the mark and the Werewolf who had survived threw out a solid arm across the ranger's chest, flinging him onto his back. It took some of the fight out of him, but not enough to miss the incoming boot. Asher intercepted the foot, throwing his shoulder into the man's knee at the same time. *Crack.* The Lycan cried out as his knee bent in the wrong direction.

Asher would have come down on him and finished the job had he not received someone else's boot to the gut. The force of it rolled him the other way, where Russell's amber eyes were already waiting. There seemed nothing of the man he knew behind those wild orbs. He was one of the pack now.

The instinct to roll away saved the ranger from a hammering blow. Still on the floor though, Asher had to twist his body around to thrust a boot into Maybury's face. It wasn't enough. He crawled after him with a grace no man his size should rightly command.

"Don't make me do it," Asher pleaded, his voice ragged. "Remember who you are!" he shouted as the man pinned him down and attempted to wrap his hands about his throat. "Remember who you want... to be!"

There was no overpowering Russell, his strength vastly superior to the ranger's. Inevitably, his hands found their way to Asher's throat and squeezed. As they wrestled, Doran and Creed came back into view. The son of Dorain let out a war cry to his god and pounded his head into the old wolf's. It didn't matter in that moment how strong Creed was, a dwarven skull was as good as any hammer.

Creed staggered back, dropping Doran as he did. Taking naught but a single breath, the son of Dorain then threw himself into his enemy, taking them both down to the floor in a tangle of punches and elbows.

The view was torn away when Russell forced his head the other way. With watery and bloodshot eyes, Asher looked up at his would-be killer, the man he had vowed to save from this very fate. Within reach was the silvyr blade. What little effort it would take to retrieve it and run him through, saving his own life in the process.

He left the weapon where it was.

Just as he hadn't been able to bring himself to kill Russell in the forest that day—or let him kill himself—he couldn't do it now. There was something about the man that brought out the *Ranger* in him and dampened the *Assassin*. The humanity that rose up in him as a result instilled a hope that had long been lacking in his life. It was a hope that stayed that killing blow.

Danagarr had no such compunction.

The dwarven smith had recovered enough to not only pick himself up but throw his hammer. Asher hadn't seen such a throw since Dragorn, when Danagarr had interrupted his fight with Darya Siad-Agnasi and killed the assassin. The block of iron, however, struck Russell in the ribs instead of his head, saving him from death but still powerful enough to send him reeling.

That first breath was a cooling balm to his burning lungs. Still, there was no time to recover or call on the power of the black gem for Danagarr had gained unwanted attention. Asher whipped out his legs and entangled one of the Lycans, folding the man's knees. As he came down, Asher scooped up his short-sword and sat up. It wasn't a clean decapitation, but it was more than enough to guarantee death.

Another had already moved past them and was closing the gap to the smith. Asher didn't even think as he grasped the dwarf's hammer and launched it horizontally at the departing wolf. He simultaneously cried out, turning the man's head just enough so the hammer struck his cheek on its way past. The Lycan grunted and fell to all fours. He wasn't out of the fight but, more importantly, the hammer had flown far enough that Danagarr could reclaim it and defend himself.

Asher could offer the dwarf no more aid than that, for Russell was standing over him.

The ranger was picked bodily off the floor by Maybury's large hands and immediately thrust into the wall. Then another wall. Then a block of knuckles pummelled his face. The world went black for Asher, only to return when he was on the floor.

From his disorientated view, the ranger could see Doran and Creed again. The dwarf had been reduced to no more than a rag doll. The old wolf beat him from one side of the room to the other before delivering his own headbutt. He had been gripping Doran by the jaw at the time and sent the son of Dorain onto his back.

"Doran," Asher uttered weakly.

Stubborn as he was, the dwarf threw out a foot, perhaps hoping to hit Creed in the knee and deal him some serious damage. The Lycan leader was not so easily caught off guard. He snatched Doran's foot from the air and twisted the ankle beyond its limitations. Doran's cry of pain was sudden and sharp.

Creed knelt down beside the dwarf, his hands reaching for those pinch points where a man might snap their opponent's neck. "No," Asher protested, trying to rise.

The old wolf hesitated, his hands only inches from Doran's head. It wasn't the ranger, however, who had given him pause. Creed turned back to see Russell, whose attention had been stolen by the floating arrow head only a few feet away. He was crouched beside it, his finger and thumb pinched to claim it from the air.

"Bring it to me," Creed commanded, standing to leave Doran flat on his back.

Asher took a deep breath, calling on his iron discipline to bury the pain and push himself back into the fray. He didn't even make it onto his elbows before Russell brushed the arrow head. The miner from Snowfell managed no more than that meagre touch, for the moment his finger made contact, the iron tip shot away, passing through the leg of one Lycan and out of the open door.

The injured wolf dropped to one knee and yelled in pain, but his cry was drowned out by Creed's order. "AFTER IT!"

Again, the pack moved as one, including Russell. They fled The Ranch even faster than they had breached it, taking off after the flying arrow head. Creed was the last to leave, though even he, who had better command of his free will, gave no second thought to the wounded rangers. Iskander's blood enthralled them *all*.

Silence fell over those left behind, save for the creaking of floorboards. Danagarr was in the process of picking himself up, his hammer upended to use as a crutch. Eventually, Hadavad staggered out of the supply room, blood staining his white beard and a dark bruise closing his left eye. The mage leant against the door frame and sighed.

"They'll follow his blood to the end of Verda," he remarked hazily.

Asher pushed the comment down his priority list. First, he needed to stand. Then he needed to reach Doran. When, at last, he was by the dwarf's side he could clearly see the misaligned foot. Though his most serious injury, it was but one of a bloody tapestry Creed had inflicted.

The son of Dorain groaned and turned his head to spit blood upon his own pauldron. "Did... we win?" he managed.

Asher could see how the dwarf might come to ask such a question, for how else would they still be alive? The ranger said nothing, content to crouch by his friend and pat his cuirass. He wondered if Doran had any idea how close he had just come to death. How close any of them had come.

"I'll fetch you some water," he said instead.

The remaining companions were slow to recover, though Asher was not slowed by his wounds—each healed by his ring—but by the loss of Russell. The man from Snowfell was in his every thought as he brought aid to the others. In some ways, his leaving with the pack felt worse than if he had died in the fight. He felt truly lost now, lost to the ways of the monster. It was not a fate Asher would wish upon any.

Having learnt from his wife, Kilda, Danagarr was able to tend to Doran better than Asher or Hadavad. He even constructed a splint for his kin's ankle, though resetting the limb had been an agonising experience for the son of Dorain. He had nearly splintered the piece of wood braced between his teeth. He had also nearly punched Danagarr.

Hadavad sat on a chair to one side, sipping his water between resting on his elbows. All too clear now was the old man behind the formidable mage.

"Asher," Doran called over, his tone soft.

The ranger ceased his attempt to fix the broken door bolt and joined the injured dwarf. They had laid him out not far from where Creed had beaten him, a folded cloak for a pillow. Asher himself had washed much of the blood from his friend's face and hands, but he saw now that some of his wounds still oozed here and there.

"Ye 'ave to go after 'im," Doran bade.

Asher crouched to better hear the dwarf's hushed voice. "*You* need to rest," he told him.

Doran reached out and lightly gripped Asher's vambrace. "Rus is one o' us. He don't belong with that lot." The dwarf grew stoical for a moment, his jaw locking up. "I can' go, or I *would*. It's got to be ye, lad. Bring 'im back."

"What if I can't?" Asher posed. "What if I can't get through to him?"

Doran's grip tightened. "It were *ye* who brought 'im into this life," he stated, his words so closely mirroring Nasta's that the ranger was stunned into silence. "Ye were right to," the dwarf went on, parting ways with the dream version of his old mentor. "Russell is a ranger. Ye've jus' got to make 'im see that."

"You said it yourself," Asher replied. "I brought him into this for all the wrong reasons. I'm not the one to convince him." He tried not to look at his sword, sure that he knew exactly what he was the one to do.

"'Course ye *are*," the dwarf growled, impatient as always. An exasperated sigh punctured the air before he spoke again. "Ye're never goin' to win the war by fightin' it in 'ere," he said, tapping the side of his head. "It's out there where it counts. Deed upon deed, brick upon brick. Keep buildin' that wall, lad, an' soon ye won' be able to look back. Then it's jus' the road ahead." Again, his hand tightened around Asher's arm. "Before ye go thinkin' otherwise, ye're already on that damned road. Ye've jus' got to keep goin'. Save Russell because he needs ye to, not for nothin' else. Oh, an' kill that bastard o' a wolf while ye're at it," he grumbled.

Asher slowly nodded in return. How long had he needed to hear that? He was already on the road, a path *he* had complicated and made murky with so much self-doubt. In truth, and despite his numerous failings, he had completed good deed upon good deed where Russell was concerned. Now he just needed to see it through. He needed to keep building that wall between the then and the now, between the *Assassin* and the *Ranger*.

"I'll bring him back," he promised, moving his arm to clasp Doran's hand instead.

Doran winced in pain. "This damned foot!" he complained, drawing Danagarr over.

Asher moved away, allowing the smith some space to practice his wife's healing skills. Crossing the room, he noted the two halves of the orb were no longer on the floor but in Hadavad's hands. The ranger recovered his bow and attached it to his quiver before retrieving his dagger and replacing it on his belt.

"You look like you're preparing for a hunt," the mage commented.

"That's because I am," Asher confirmed, checking the items on his belt.

"You're to track them down then," Hadavad surmised, sounding somewhat defeated.

"I am." Asher's tone left no room for misunderstanding.

"You've never tracked anything with their speed or stamina before," the mage replied quite confidently.

"I could certainly do with a heading." The ranger looked from the orb to the mage. "You said he would never find it. What door does Creed believe that key will open?"

Hadavad looked away before naturally being drawn back to the broken orb. "The same place we're all looking for now," he answered cryptically. "The same place we've always been looking for. Iskander's laboratory," he said gravely. "Creed still desires the spells he needs to control his curse. Since it was not inside here," he concluded, indicating the orb pieces, "he will assume they are in Kargon's infamous lab, just as *I* must now assume the Obsidian Stone is located there."

Asher tilted his head in thought, his eyes finding the dawn light through the broken window. "That's where the arrow head is going—the *lock*."

"Indeed, that would seem the most likely destination. Kargon must have placed a spell over lock and key, binding them. Adding his own blood was a mark of his ingenuity. Be it wolf or Vorska, they could track the scent across the known world." Hadavad gestured to the part of the room where Russell had interacted with the arrow head. "Though I cannot say for sure, it is highly probable that the spell was activated when touched by one so cursed. That must be why my own touch did nothing."

"Where is his lab?" Asher demanded with some urgency.

"Nobody knows," Hadavad said, his defeated attitude piling on.

Asher gripped the hilt of his broadsword as if the weapon would bring him clarity. "What about Merith? He must know; he was with Iskander for years."

The mage was shaking his head. "I told you before; there was a time when Merith sought his master's lab as much as he did the orb. It seems Iskander trusted no one in life, nor in death. The location died with him." Before new depths of depression could claim him, Hadavad looked up, a spark in his eyes. "Though," he drawled, a thought emerging. "I might be able to get us close enough that we could track the wolves if not the key."

"Close?" Asher questioned before he recalled the mage's tale from weeks earlier. "Kelp Town," he declared, the very place he had planned on giving a wide berth for several years.

"Yes," the mage confirmed. "It's where we were all looking, where I found the orb inside the tree. Iskander's lab is somewhere in that wilderness." Hadavad shook his head. "I never suspected it held a key, especially a key to a lab so close. What a fool."

Asher held up a hand, his mind calculating. "If Creed and the others are travelling so far, the full moons will interrupt them. That many Werewolves will cause chaos so close to civilisation." The ranger thought of Captain Lonan and the people of Kelp Town, whose ancestors had quarrelled with the Lycans before.

"I worry more about the chaos that might be wrought if they gain entry to Iskander's lab," the mage voiced. "Regardless of the spells that govern their curse, be assured, there will be far more terrible deeds of evil inside."

The ranger nodded. "Then we hunt."

CHAPTER 30
WILD HUNT

Greyfang - I have to say that these beasties are dangerous because they've been known to kill plenty of folk, but, I also have to say, they're really not. At least, they're not that dangerous if you know anything about using a sword.

Big black eyes and big sharp claws make them look more formidable than they really are. Their bodies are more bone than anything else. With little muscle, they rely on their claws to deliver damage. They're so easy to cut down it's almost fun. If nothing else, they're good for sword practice.

A Chronicle of Monsters: A Ranger's Bestiary, 12th Edition, Page 465.

Bru Vane, Ranger.

With meagre supplies, ranger and mage put Lirian behind them before the bodies could be found. The death of Graycoats would only bring more of their order to the city. Then there were the watchmen who had likely been killed on other streets. Soon, the capital of Felgarn would be swarming with vengeful soldiers and suspicious Graycoats. It was no place for an ex-assassin.

They had left Doran resting, though a cantankerous mood had beset the dwarf. He was never one to miss out on a hunt. The son of Dorain had spent most of their preparation time cursing his own foot. Danagarr was content to remain behind, having already played more of a part than he had ever bargained for. Of course, Asher would never have let him travel with them anyway, not while the smith had Kilda and Deadora to return to. He did, however, grumble about the laborious job of piling the Lycan bodies in the courtyard and putting them to flame.

At a gallop, that first mile was put between them and the city with all haste. Taking the western road, Asher was retracing the steps that had brought him and Russell to Lirian so many weeks earlier. The road and wilderness ahead, however, would account for many more miles and six days of continuous travel, five if they halved their rest time. Regardless of the strain they put on themselves to reach Kelp Town, they would never beat Creed and his pack. Russell had displayed his supernatural stamina and strength numerous times and they would likely be running without sleep.

"You seem troubled," Hadavad observed on their second day, as they began their journey across the hard plains that would take them to The Ice Vales.

Asher was surprised by the question, given everything that had happened and, by way of an answer, glanced back at the distant trees of The Evermoore's western edge.

"Acutely so," the mage specified. "It's as if that burden you carry has taken on more weight."

"I don't like being so far behind my quarry," the ranger grunted.

"It's more than that," Hadavad reasoned, his head turned just enough that he might lay one eye past the rim of his hood and spy his companion.

Asher said nothing, his sight levelled on the murky horizon.

"As you will," the mage muttered, content, if dissatisfied, to leave it there.

"In two days," Asher finally replied, if reluctantly so, "the first full moon will reign. By then, I'd guess the wolves to have reached Kelp Town."

Hadavad's mouth shaped in revelation. "You fear for the people of Kelp Town," he concluded.

The admission was naught but virtuous, yet Asher felt the fool, if not outright vulnerable, saying as much. "Seven Werewolves left Lirian," he said instead. "Including Russell. I can't imagine what carnage they might bring to the town. And if they succeed in taking command of their curse... The Ice Vales themselves will surely suffer."

"I would counsel caution," the mage replied. "You cannot save everyone, Asher. That is a burden too far. Even kings cannot protect their realms to such an extent."

"It's not the death toll that..." Asher stopped himself, his next words sure to be callous. "Russell is a good man," he declared, starting again. "I would not have him live with the blood on his hands."

"You have given him the tools to fight his monster," the mage remarked. "But Russell alone can fight it."

"And if he can't?" Asher posed, intending to put the mage on the spot.

"As you said," Hadavad echoed, "you cannot let him live with the blood on his hands."

The ranger's familiar stoicism was so easily drawn about him again, a curtain that could not be penetrated. Sensing as much, the mage said no more and the companions returned to their journey in silence.

And so the next two days passed, from sunrise to sunset, until the plains became rolling hills and, eventually, an icy vista of grey and drifting mist. The Ice Vales welcomed them with its cold embrace, reminding them that winter could always be worse. They saw few on the road, with most merchants and travellers moving in small caravans.

Despite their urgency, the mounts' exhaustion was something they could only fight for so long. Camping for the night became all the more desirable in sight of the ancient ruins that protruded from a rocky outcropping in the north. There wasn't much left of the elven site—even its name was lost to history—but there remained two or three hollows that offered shelter. Taking in the skeleton of stone that was slowly being swallowed by the years, Asher guessed it to have been a tower in its day, an outpost perhaps.

Hadavad sat cupping his beard while staring intently at Asher as the ranger started the fire with naught but a gesture. Still, the mage made no comment and refrained from asking questions. Asher was silently relieved. He had no answers to appease the man or himself. The gem had come into his possession in his childhood, a time beyond memory now. One day, he hoped, he might know more.

Physically walking away from the unsaid topic, the ranger made his way to the edge of the makeshift shelter and looked out on the land. The beauty of a clear night turned his gaze skyward, where the first full moon shone like the sun in its kingdom of stars.

Somewhere out there, Russell was no more. In his place was a wild beast that knew only hunger.

"Three nights of fright," Hadavad voiced from behind, before he came to stand beside the ranger. "Three nights of fang and claw."

"You know this saying?" Asher asked, having heard it first from Lord Kernat in Kelp Town.

"I first heard it said in Snowfell," the mage answered. "That was nearly two centuries ago. It soon spread across The Ice Vales though."

The ranger was reminded of more Lord Kernat had imparted during their initial meeting. "I've heard of this. The lord of Kelp

Town spoke of it; a time when Werewolves plagued the vales. An army he called it."

"An army?" the mage repeated incredulously. "Perhaps too big a word, though it only takes a dozen wolves to mimic the work of an army. If memory serves, Creed had seventeen wolves under his thrall."

"Creed?"

"Oh yes. I've never known one of his kind live to such an age. From what I've observed, he even remains in his Lycan form longer than others. Back in those times, of course, he was young, though his power over those who shared his curse was soon mastered. It was also that power that corrupted him. He built his band in the span of three moons. I never learnt where he was from but, if I was to guess, I would say Snowfell. They suffered the most in those dark days."

"What did he want?" Asher asked, always keen to understand the motives of others.

The mage shrugged. "Who can say? The simple pleasure of power perhaps. Dominion, control. I doubt he came from much. His ambitions were likely high."

Asher returned his attention to the moon for a time, recalling more of Lord Kernat's words. "They abandoned the region," he stated. "No one knows why."

Hadavad chuckled quietly to himself. "Would you believe that the people of the west have the Vorska to thank for that?"

The ranger couldn't help but look back at the mage. "Merith?" he presumed.

"None other," Hadavad confirmed. "I told you this was a war far older than either of us. Merith has always believed the wolves to be a mistake of his master's, an experiment that got out of control. Back then, Merith had taken it upon himself to exterminate them all. An outbreak of that scale could not escape his notice. He arrived in The Ice Vales with an army of his own. Their battles were fought in the shadows until Merith's force tipped the scales. I suppose, to the people, it would seem the wolves simply vanished."

Asher considered the location, the very same they were all heading towards. "Creed knew nothing of Iskander back then?"

"No. It was his war with Merith that revealed so much to him. Over the years they each captured and tormented the ranks of the other. What Creed gleaned from those prisoners became his new obsession. 'Tis, ultimately, the reason we find ourselves where we are right now." The mage sighed, as if so much history leant into his fatigue.

"You seem troubled," Asher commented, garnering curiosity from the mage. "Acutely so," he added with some amusement.

Hadavad crossed his arms, each hand hooking under the elbow. While the mage hadn't missed his own words being echoed back to him, he appeared too concerned to find them amusing. "In all this madness," he voiced gravely, "there is one question we have not asked, and I scarcely dare to give it life."

"What question?" Asher demanded.

Hadavad licked his lips, his gaze distant. "Why?" he said plainly. "Why would Kargon Iskander leave a key for Merith or one of his ilk to find? And, in all likelihood," the mage continued, "it's not just any key. It had his blood on it! It's highly probable that it will reveal his most secret of labs, a place he never even permitted Merith to see. Why?"

Asher hadn't given the question much thought, the answer seemingly obvious. "Ego," he said to which the mage raised his eyebrows in return. "Present company excluded," he caveated, "it's been my experience that mages are often ruled by their egos. Surely Kargon believes his work to be the greatest any mage could hope to achieve. In death, he wishes for that work to be appreciated or, perhaps, even continued."

Hadavad nodded his head to one side in a conceding gesture. "It's not an unfounded assessment of my colleagues... nor am *I* immune to bouts of egotism," he confessed. "And from everything I've learnt of Kargon Iskander he was a mage of great ego. Perhaps you're right. I only wish my gut agreed with you." Hadavad released some of the tension in his shoulders with a soft laugh. "That might be *my* ego talking."

Asher made no comment on that. "Our problem remains the same," he opined. "We have to assume the spells Merith and Creed require are inside... *wherever* that key is leading them to. If either of them goes inside, we have to make sure they never come out."

Hadavad didn't appear completely convinced that there wasn't something worse on the horizon, but he still nodded his head in agreement. "I would rest. At this rate we will reach Kelp Town before the final moon."

Asher didn't watch him move away but remained where he stood. Merith had returned to the forefront of his mind. The wretch could be out there, watching them. It unsettled the ranger.

Knowing it was the only way he would find rest himself, Asher buried his eyes behind the red blindfold and crouched by the edge of the ruin.

A light but frigid breeze blew his cloak out and ruffled the end of his hair, bringing with it the scents of the world around him. He could hear all the small animals that came alive at night, foraging in the undergrowth or hunting prey of their own. He could feel the feathers of an owl between his fingers as his senses pinpointed the bird to a tree a hundred yards south of his location.

Within seconds, he was aware of every creature, tree, and rock in the area. Besides him and Hadavad, the largest animal was a fox. No Vorska.

Asher removed the blindfold and pinched his eyes. Damned if he wasn't tired. Since they didn't have time to sleep in shifts, the ranger took to his bed roll and faced the flames of their small fire. For all his worries, sleep snatched him as the owl out there might snatch up a mouse.

As Hadavad predicted, the companions were not only in sight of Kelp Town by the third moon but at its arching entrance. The old wind chimes and discoloured bunting hung from the wooden structure, there to blow in the icy wind as the last light of the day bid its farewell.

Unlike before, the way was barred.

Asher and Hadavad brought their mounts to a stop in the face of armoured soldiers. Emblazoned on their cuirasses was the head of a roaring bear, the sigil of house Orvish, which ruled from Grey Stone. Dark blue cloaks dragged on the ground behind them as they advanced to keep the newcomers at a distance from the town.

Asher shared a look with the mage beside him but had no time to explain that King Gregorn had sent a complement of his soldiers to oversee the Lycan outbreak. In truth, Asher was surprised to see them still there, since he had reported to Captain Lonan that the second wolf—Russell—was dead.

"Ho!" one barked, a hand coming up to display a gloved palm. "State your business, strangers!"

It wasn't unusual to hear aggression in a soldier's voice—especially when that voice was spitting a command—but there was an edge to it that spoke of recent violence, as if the man's blood was still up. Glancing at those beside him, Asher could see that they each gripped the sword on their hip. It all felt too much for no more than a couple of men on horseback.

"We come as friends to Kelp Town!" Hadavad called back.

Asher allowed the mage to speak for them while he looked beyond the wall of armoured men. Kelp Town was deserted, its usual traffic of miners being carted back and forth to the Demetrium mine notably absent. There were no markets or crowds. The shops were closed. Without children playing and making mischief, the streets seemed dead. Lord Kernat had spoken of a curfew but not as the last light of the day bid its farewell.

Then he saw them.

Claw marks.

Rooftops and walls, the arching entrance itself, scored by claws. A little further up the street, on the left, one building appeared to be missing an entire wall. The ranger was then drawn to the black smoke that rose in the north. Judging the distance, he guessed it to be slightly outside the boundaries of the town, but he also guessed it to be a large bonfire.

The conclusion was gruesome if undeniable: they were burning bodies. *Lots* of bodies.

"Kelp Town knows no friends in this time," the soldier replied, suspicion behind his every word. "And I see no wares of a merchant about you. What I do see are *weapons*." By this point, the other soldiers had moved from their line and begun to encircle the companions.

Hadavad raised one hand, a gesture of peace. "You have nothing to fear from us. We only mean to resupply before—"

"We're here for the wolves," Asher announced, taking the only advantage they had left. "That's why we have arrived before you so armed."

"The wolves?" The lead soldier narrowed his eyes a notch, an inch of steel revealed from his scabbard.

"We are hunters," Asher specified. "*Rangers*. We come from Lirian, where word has reached of your plight. If we might treat with Captain Lonan, I'm sure he will—"

"No Captain Lonan here," the soldier interjected. "Nor has a single word of our *plight* left this town. Get down from your horse." The command came with the drawing of swords.

"Are you bereft of sense, man?" Hadavad snapped. "Can you not see friend from foe?"

The soldier pointed his sword at the mage, unaware of the power he wielded. "I won't ask you again."

Asher made to turn Hector away from the entrance. "Perhaps we should just take our leave," he suggested.

Another of the king's men stepped forward and grabbed the ranger's horse by the reins, while another came up on his side, the tip of his blade angled up into Asher's hip. It took every ounce of his discipline not to shove his boot into the soldier's face and knock his helm clean from his head. What followed would be far worse.

"You're to disarm," the ranked soldier informed. Asher was quickly relieved of his numerous blades and folded bow. "You can explain yourselves to General Crem."

Asher made no expression to reveal his surprise at so lofty a title. It seemed The Ice Vales took their Werewolves seriously. Still, the ranger put his hands up and allowed the nearest to unclip his broadsword and take it away. Following his lead, Hadavad climbed down from his mare and allowed one of the soldiers to search him for concealed weapons. "If you take that," the mage said, eyeing the soldier's hand on his staff, "you're going to have to carry me." A look from the lead soldier was enough to see that hand removed and a curt nod from the mage.

So as to maintain a constant presence at the town's entrance, the companions were forced to wait in the cold until a new group of soldiers arrived to escort them.

In the absence of activity, the streets were thick with undisturbed snow. Only the footprints of patrolling soldiers gave away signs of life, though Asher caught sight of eyes peering from various windows. Where once there might have been curiosity upon those faces, there was now only fear. Again, the ranger was naturally drawn to the rising smoke in the north.

With empty streets, they were soon walking up the steps of Stormwood Manor, where yet more soldiers wearing the bear upon their chest stood to attention. Asher hardly noticed them, his attention captured by the grim head that had been set upon a pike and driven into the ground beside the steps. The man's dying expression was contorted and smeared with filth and blood, yet the ranger was still able to recognise him as one of Creed's band. At least their number had been taken down to six, he thought.

It was with quiet disbelief that Asher craned his head and took in the sight of the old building. Upon his last departure, he had been sure of the years that would pass before he saw the manor again. It was the man beside him who had spoken of fate and coincidence, the latter of which was far more preferable to the ranger. Yet here he was, back where this whole saga had begun, and where Kargon Iskander's saga had ended.

As if his destination hadn't been echo enough, he entered Stormwood Manor in exactly the same fashion as he had the first time—under escort. The same faces looked back at him as he waited in the grand entrance, the walls lined with portraits. There was no tantalising scent of cooked chicken, however, the manor now filled with the musk of soldiers.

After a few minutes under guard, a familiar face emerged. "The ranger returns," Secretary Royce announced, unable to keep the surprise from his expression. "Archer, was it?"

The ranger took a breath. "Asher," he corrected.

"Ah, yes, *Asher.*"

"Where is Captain Lonan?" the ranger enquired, giving no care to the high born's station.

The hint of smugness that motivated so many of the secretary's facial muscles slipped away, replaced by a tinge of... regret? "I'm afraid he no longer holds the rank of captain. Nor any rank for that matter. Lord Kernat stripped him of title and power. You would have seen as much had you stayed and collected your reward." If that had been regret upon his face it was now entirely supplanted by suspicion.

"Why was he punished?" Asher demanded, seeing the injustice of it. "There were two Werewolves and both were dealt with. He did his job."

"That was very hard to prove in the absence of a body—the wolf's at least. We certainly had more than enough bodies piled up in the beast's wake, under Lonan's watch. Of course, it might have been cleared up had you stuck around and explained exactly how you killed that second wolf."

Asher leant down, putting his face into Royce's. "There were no more wolves at your door. He did his job."

"I agree," he said quietly, eyes averted. "But too many met their end under his watch. He was never going to keep it. Not that it really matters in our current climate," he added, gaze shifting to the closed doors on his right. "As you can see, Kelp Town is now under the jurisdiction of the king's men, specifically General Crem."

The ranger spared a brief glance at the soldiers behind him. "Why are they still here? There were no Werewolves to hunt by the time they arrived."

"Indeed," Royce intoned, stepping closer to the ranger. "It is my suspicion that, wolf or no wolf, General Crem was never going to leave."

"I do love a good suspicion," Hadavad interjected, bowing his head into their conversation.

The secretary was slightly taken aback, the mage's appearance that of a true vagabond and worlds apart from Royce. "And you are?"

"Hadavad," the mage answered happily enough.

"He's with me," Asher stated when the secretary looked back at him.

Royce took too long considering the mage, his suspicions never to be voiced before those double doors opened and a squire beckoned them.

The two companions, with Royce in the lead, were shown to the same room where Asher had met Lord Kernat. Where it had appeared cosy and grand at the same time, it now appeared somewhat fortified and smaller. It didn't help that some of the tapestries had been taken down and replaced by maps of the surrounding region. Adding to that, the table acted as the foundation of a miniature Kelp Town and a portion of the mountains at its rear.

Of course, it was the soldiers therein that reduced the room's grandeur. Most were around the table, pointing out areas of the town and discussing defences. One among them stood out, his hands resting firmly against the head of the table. Though visibly older than the rest, his age did not diminish him but granted the man an air of experience. He was a warrior, Asher knew. He was also General Crem.

Pale blue eyes flashed from the table and over the companions, taking them in at a glance, before his attention returned to the report in front of him. "You're here for the *wolves*, they tell me." His voice was a deep husk, commanding even. To one side, Secretary Royce had already shrunk away, his presence muted in the absence of his lordship.

"That we are, sir," Asher answered, keeping himself tall.

"Hunters then," the general concluded, handing that particular report to his squire.

"Rangers." Asher felt compelled to make the distinction.

At last, Crem looked up from the table and met Asher's eyes. "*More* rangers? Where do you keep coming from?"

Asher couldn't keep the confusion from his face. "More? There are other rangers in Kelp Town?"

"There you are!" The declaration was exclaimed across the room, turning every head to the newcomer who had entered via a side door. "Your timing couldn't be better!"

Asher instinctively pressed one hand to his hip, where it should have found his broadsword resting in its scabbard. As it turned out, he was weaponless in the face of the eight-hundred-year-old Vorska.

CHAPTER 31
ANOTHER MONSTER IN A RANGER SUIT

Unicorn - I understand that we live in a world of monsters, in a world of things. But Unicorns are just for children.
Move on.

A Chronicle of Monsters: A Ranger's Bestiary, 12th Edition,
Page 464.

Ankar Tor, Ranger.

"Merith," General Crem acknowledged. "You know these men?"

"Of course," the Blood Fiend replied with a grin. "I sent for them myself."

The general's expression dropped and hardened. "There were to be no communications," he reiterated.

"Apologies, General," Merith replied with theatricality, his every step bringing him closer to Asher and Hadavad. "But, if we are to not only survive this night but vanquish our monstrous foes, I will need my fellow rangers by my side."

Asher quickly reassessed the Vorska, seeing now that he had changed his appearance. Where he had acquired the battle-worn leathers and chainmail was a mystery, but it seemed likely he had gone out of his way to possess a green cloak, and only a shade darker than Asher's. The wretch had used him to attain the look of a ranger. Even his hair had been styled in the same fashion, the fringe pulled back into a ponytail to sit atop the rest that fell just past his shoulders.

"Asher, Hadavad." Merith greeted them with a nod an old friend might give. "A skilled fighter and a skilled mage!" The Vorska's hands gestured to them as if he were putting them on display for a cheering crowd.

Crem took a breath, holding the room in that quiet moment while he re-evaluated. "Very well," he decreed. The general peered out of the window, where the night had entirely replaced the day. "Time is against us. Get your men up to speed."

"Thank you, General Crem," Merith replied with a respectful bow of the head. "Come, friends," he bade to the companions.

Doing his best to keep up appearances, Asher fell in behind the Vorska and with Hadavad beside him. They followed the creature across the manor, where he showed them to an empty room dedicated to sitting and staring at old paintings. The aesthetics, however, were peripheral to the ex-assassin. He saw only weapons. To his immediate right were a pair of empty silver candleholders, each capable of burning the Vorska's skin. In the corner was a wooden chair that he could stamp into usable shards to stab his opponent. Sitting on one of the small tables was a used goblet, a meagre weapon but a weapon all the same in Asher's hands.

Perhaps sensing this or merely predicting the ranger's reaction, Merith swivelled on his heel and raised his hands. "Before it comes to violence," he hissed, "I would have words."

Hadavad hefted his staff. "I have a few words for you," he threatened.

"Hold your spells, mage," Merith insisted, giving them a wide berth until he was able to close the doors behind them. "There is no need for us to be enemies this night; not while we share a common one."

"There is no cliché that will stop you from being my enemy," Hadavad countered. "The day I call you *friend* will be well beyond the end of this world."

Merith sighed and dropped into one of the armchairs, the very seat where his sword rested. "Then perhaps we can agree to kill each other at a more appropriate time," he suggested.

"You mean after we kill Creed," Asher presumed.

Merith's cold gaze fell on the ranger for the first time since entering the room, those dark orbs completely separate from his broad grin. "Ah, the man who *can't* be killed."

The statement put Asher on edge, sending his muscles coiling into tension.

"Tell me, Asher, how is it a simple ranger can heal so fast?" Merith's head tilted. "Even my fangs have failed to leave an impression, but I can still taste your blood so I know I pierced flesh."

Asher's jaw was clenched so tightly he couldn't have spoken if he had wanted to.

"I knew there was something different about you," Merith went on, almost seductively, "and your blood confirmed as much. Still, I cannot put my finger on it. What an enigma. You taste like one thing and look and smell like another." The Vorska laughed. "Human on the outside and something akin to a monster on the inside."

The fiend had no idea how close to the truth he was, yet the ranger kept his mouth shut, content to let the creature believe the answer lay in his blood and not the black gem.

Merith looked him up and down. "I am aware of everything you possess—everything that carries your *stink*. There is nothing about you that should grant such power. Your weapons are simple, though I am aware that short-sword of yours is on the rare side," he commented with a knowing smirk. "You own a single trinket, a *ring*."

Asher glanced at Hadavad and knew immediately he had made a grave mistake.

"Interesting," Merith purred, his eyes flicking to the mage and back. "There is magic attached to the ring. And *powerful* magic by the way it has healed you." The Vorska's nose twitched. "I can taste the iron and... something else. What is that? A stone?"

"Enough," Hadavad declared, stamping his staff once onto the floor. "We don't have to answer to the likes of *you*, monster. Just be glad we haven't cut your ugly head off already."

"You want us to be allies," Asher finally spoke, forcing them back on track. "Until we kill Creed," he repeated.

There came a pause from Merith, his supernatural mind calculating at speed.

"And his merry band of wild cretins," he eventually replied, with no more than a glance at the ranger's right hand. "Of which I believe your friend, Russell, is now an avid member." The Vorska offered a wicked smile. "You can't come between a dog and its master."

"How is it you've ended up here?" Asher demanded, aware that the previous line of dialogue would steer him to violence.

"Creed and his pack weren't the only ones keeping an eye on you in Lirian. I had hoped they would kill you and you would kill some of them and I would kill whoever survived and take the orb for myself but... Things went a little sideways didn't they? So, like you, I tracked the wolves. Well," Merith corrected himself, "I tracked Iskander's blood. I couldn't beat them here but I certainly covered more ground than you. I arrived last night, during their attack on the town."

Asher quickly put the picture together. "The head."

The Vorska appeared most pleased with himself. "The head," he repeated. "All I had to do was kill one of the wretches and declare myself a ranger, and..." His hands gestured to their surroundings and the freedom with which he was able to move about.

Asher shot the creature a look of pure scorn before turning away and making for the nearest window. The moon was visible but not nearly as high as it was going to be. Soon, the wolves would replace the men. "What exactly happened here?" he asked, searching for the column of black smoke.

"They've had two nights of hell," Merith told them. "Seven Werewolves and three moons are more than enough to slaughter this entire town. They had no meaningful defences on the first night. They lost a *lot* of soldiers and a handful of townsfolk. More soldiers died last night, though fewer thanks to me," he added smugly. "More will surely die this night. Unless..."

With little patience for the blood-sucking creature, Hadavad stamped his staff into the floor. "Unless what, *fiend?*"

Merith didn't so much as flinch. "Unless we give the wolves reason to leave the poor people of Kelp Town alone."

"Speak plainly," the mage commanded.

"Creed and his ilk might be mindless animals under the full moon," Merith explained, "but Iskander's blood holds its own thrall over his children. That key must have found its rest somewhere out there. Though they might not be conscious of it, the wolves will be protective over the site. If they feel it is threatened or another predator has encroached on their territory, they will abandon their attack and return."

Asher turned back from the window. "You propose luring them back to the site and facing them ourselves, *alone.*"

"Exactly. And General Crem will agree now that *you* are here. His forces have dwindled, narrowing his options. Now that he has a band of experienced monster hunters at his disposal, old Crem will happily allow us to bait the wolves away if it gives them another month to reinforce the town."

"I don't trust a word that spills out of your wretched mouth," Hadavad spat. "Why would you need us?"

"I wouldn't if I had the time," Merith assured, his expression turning sour. "In time, even one so dim as Creed will discover how such a key might open the door. I *need* to get in there before he does and stop him from interfering with things he does not understand. Besides that, the town is too fortified and suspicious to allow me to start building a force of my own kind. Luckily for me," he added, that wicked grin returning with ease, "I knew two Werewolf-slaying hunters were on their way."

"We're not helping *you* get in there," Hadavad fumed.

"You can't hope to beat six Werewolves under the full moon," Merith pointed out. "You need me as much as I need you."

"*We*," the mage stated, "can wait them out and locate the site tomorrow."

"And how many will die while you wait? *My* plan saves lives *and* rids the world of six Werewolves."

"He's right," Asher cut in, turning both towards him.

Hadavad understood his meaning immediately. "You can't be seriously siding with this monster?"

"Merith can find the site by smell. That means we can reach the lab with haste and prevent the wolves from attacking the town."

"And you believe we three alone can defeat so many wolves in their true form?" the mage countered.

"We would need more swords," Asher admitted.

"That won't be possible," Merith said, one finger in the air. "As I said, the general has lost many men. He will not jeopardise the town's safety by sending any with us. In fact, he will more likely be hoping we die baiting the wolves away."

"Leave it to me," the ranger replied cryptically. "We reach the site," he continued, attention returned to Hadavad, "and soon. There, *with* Merith, we bring down the wolves and burn Iskander's lab to the ground."

"I might take umbrage with that last part," the Vorska chimed in casually.

"You'll be dead by then," Asher assured.

"Ah," Merith replied with quiet amusement, crossing his legs. "That makes more sense."

The mage was shaking his head. "I cannot fight side by side with this *wretch*, Asher. He is treacherous."

"*He*," Merith emphasised, "has killed more Werewolves than both of you combined."

"Silence, worm!" the mage hissed, bringing his staff to bear. "I could turn your blood to ice with no more than a thought."

"You don't think as quickly as I move, old man," the Vorska breathed. "Though," he announced with dramatics, "if you truly believe I am so easy to put down, why not agree to the plan? Use my skills to slay some wolves and then turn your magic on me. Hmm?" Merith looked from one to the other.

Asher levelled a hard gaze on the mage. "The moon is rising," he reminded gravely.

Jaw clenched, Hadavad moved to tower over Merith, a pillar of fortitude that sucked some of the light out of the room, dimming the reach of the candles and torches. "You will not set one foot inside that lab, monster."

Merith slowly stood to meet the mage eye to eye. "Every time the sun rises I feel your mark upon me. The burns. The cuts. The searing pain of your righteousness haunts my every daylight hour. You plan to kill me tonight, yes? Know that I do not plan the same for you. No," the Vorska purred. "You will live for years to come, good mage. You will know something of my torment before the end."

"Enough!" Asher snapped. "We'll settle this when the *appropriate* time comes. Until then, we need only agree not to kill each other. Creed first."

Mage and Vorska stood their ground a moment longer, their rage for the other held in silence. "Creed first," Merith agreed, stepping back and breaking eye contact.

Hadavad tapped his staff twice. "Creed first."

Returning to the general with their uneasy alliance, Merith laid out their plan to bait the wolves while omitting the details surrounding Kargon Iskander. By expression alone it was clear General Crem doubted the strength of their plan. He voiced his preference they stay within the town and add their swords and magic to the defences, but Merith was able to play on the general's lack of knowledge where monsters were concerned.

"Werewolves," the Vorska asserted, "in packs this size, always keep to a nest of sorts, a den really. If we compromise it they *will* return. From there, we can keep them occupied long enough to see the sun rise again."

"You *three*?" Crem asked in disbelief.

"We will require a larger force to join us," Asher stressed, inserting himself.

"Out of the question," the general replied quickly enough. "It already sounds like suicide. For all I know they will slaughter the three of you in minutes and then spend the rest of the night invading the town. No. I need my men here."

"Agreed," the ranger said, raising the general's eyebrows. "But there are other men in Kelp Town who have faced Werewolves before and lived. One in particular I trust to fight by my side is Captain Lonan."

The general's memory narrowed his eyes. "The man Lord Kernat dismissed?"

"The very same," Secretary Royce answered, stepping into their conversation. "You conscripted him only yesterday, General, along with the rest of the watch."

Crem shrugged inside his armour. "I can spare a former watchman, and I won't stop a man from defending his home and countrymen. But I won't order them into such a desperate situation. Should *Mr* Lonan and any others agree to aid you they have my blessing. Good luck convincing them," he added knowingly.

"Thank you, General." Merith bowed his head and began backing away. "We should leave at once—it won't be long before the wolves return."

"Oh!" Crem called after them. "Should you keep them at bay *and* survive the night I will triple your reward. And for every head you bring back I will grant a bonus."

Asher refrained from laughing at the preposterous offer. The general might as well have said, *you're all going to be dead by dawn.*

With some direction from Secretary Royce, and their weapons returned, they were soon standing in the large doorway of an empty stable, where the former captain and a handful of others had been gathered by one of the soldiers. The king's man was in the middle of doling out instructions, informing the group where they were to be stationed for the night. At a glance, Asher recognised most of them from his previous visit, all watchmen in their hard leathers and dark cloaks, a simple but sturdy sword on their belt.

Only Lonan was without the armoured uniform. His appeared older, an heirloom perhaps, draped in a wine-red cloak. He had, however, been granted one of their swords, possibly the very same he had used while the captain.

Secretary Royce cleared his throat, halting the soldier mid-command. A subtle head tilt from the secretary dismissed him, sending him from the stable altogether. "I can do no more," Royce said to Asher. "May the gods be with you," he added before departing himself. Despite walking away from the stable, the secretary was soon running back to Stormwood Manor.

Facing the group, the ranger locked eyes with Lonan. If the man was surprised to see him he didn't show it, a stoical mask hardening his features. He didn't appear the same man Asher had bid farewell to. His hair had grown seemingly beyond the man's ability to tame it and he now sported a beard streaked with grey and age. There remained a strength about him though, a characteristic that Asher seldom saw in those who had been knocked back in life. He hadn't deserved Lord Kernat's punishment.

"You're the last person I expected to see, if ever again." His voice still possessed the tenor of command, as did his bearing with so many at his back, waiting on him. "What are you doing in Kelp Town?" Lonan demanded, his low opinion of the ranger informing his impatience.

Asher hesitated, his attention flitting between the former captain and the watchmen behind him. How many of them had family? How many were husbands and fathers? These were questions the ranger wasn't used to asking himself and he didn't like to think of the answers.

"We're running out of time, Asher," Hadavad intervened.

Lonan frowned. "And who are they?" he asked of the ranger.

"They're with me," Asher finally managed. "Rangers," he added absently.

"Rangers," Lonan repeated, a hint of mistrust in his voice.

"We're hunting the wolves," Asher told him. "We need—"

"*You're* hunting the wolves?" Lonan nearly laughed. "Look around, Asher. It's the wolves that do the hunting."

"We know where their den is. We're taking the fight to them, to keep them away from the town." Asher glanced purposefully at the men, who likely had family to protect, and immediately regretted his subtle act of manipulation. "We need—"

"It's him, isn't it?" Lonan interrupted. "*Russell Hobbs.* You never did kill him, did you? Now he's bitten and cursed who knows how many."

"Russell Hobbs is dead," Asher insisted, holding on to the tenuous truth of that statement. "The wolves that plague your town have come from Lirian—where we've come from. Our hope is to keep them away from the town until dawn but we need more swords on our side. General Crem won't spare any of his men."

"Of course he won't," Lonan replied, as if that should be obvious. "And you won't find anyone else to join you either. Everyone saw what they did." Though it could not be seen from their location, Lonan's head nodded in the direction of the rising smoke.

"Not even you?" Asher posed.

"We have orders to patrol the western border."

It should have been left there, the answer clear, but the ranger could feel the moon upon them as if it were the sun. The wolves might already be fully formed and, even now, racing to Kelp Town with insatiable hunger. How many would die then?

"General Crem has given you permission to accompany us, should you choose." Seeing no volunteers among them, Asher pressed his argument. "Fight them here if you wish, but remember: it will take only one to break through your line and it will be free to slaughter entire families."

Something broke in the former captain at that, his inner armour cracked. It was there to see in the softening of his features. It was his honour, Asher knew. The man truly cared about the people of Kelp Town, more so than his own aspirations.

393

Adding pressure, the ranger turned to depart, leaving them with that horrendous image.

"How do you know where the den is?" Lonan asked.

Asher turned back, thinking on his toes as always. "Merith here scouted it earlier today." The Vorska flashed them a disturbing smile that lacked all warmth.

Lonan levelled a hard stare at Asher. "Do you swear to the gods that you killed Russell Hobbs? That he is not responsible for all this?"

"I swear." Asher didn't even hesitate now.

"I cannot speak for anyone else," the former captain replied, "but *I* will join you. If there's even a chance we can keep those monsters from the people..."

The group of watchmen didn't follow his example, not at first. It took only one more, however, to step forward and the rest soon added their swords to the campaign, making them a fellowship of ten. It was meagre when compared to six Werewolves, but Hadavad and Merith counted for more than one.

"Follow me, gentlemen," the Vorska bade, reminding Asher that seven were their enemy, not six.

Trailing the Vorska's nose, the nine companions moved in relative silence given their number. Of course, there was so much more to them that gave away their presence to the likes of Werewolves. One was their scent, carried in the breeze to sensitive noses. And how quickly the Lycans could move, a fact that kept them all under constant threat.

Asher looked past Hadavad, spotting Merith further up the rise. The Blood Fiend would be the first to detect them and, at present, he appeared at ease leading their trek. It meant nothing, the ranger knew. It was just as likely that Merith was content for the wolves to thin their number somewhat.

A snapping twig jolted Asher's alertness, turning him back to the rest of the group. Unaccustomed to the wilds, and at night,

Lonan had tripped over a root. The ranger moved to offer a hand but the former captain had already picked himself up.

"I'm fine," he breathed, ego bruised more than anything else.

Asher gave him no more than a nod and returned to the path Merith was forging. He might have stuck to it had his humanity not gnawed at him for the next few steps. The ranger sighed inwardly, irritated by emotions he had repressed for so much of his life. It complicated everything.

"I'm sorry," he whispered, catching Lonan's attention. If only the man knew how hard it had been to utter those two simple words. "Lord Kernat should never have dismissed you. You did your job well. The people of Kelp Town were better off with you on the watch."

Lonan said nothing for a time, his focus held by one step following another. "It wouldn't have mattered whether you returned with Russell's body or not," he eventually replied. "Lord Kernat needed to be seen to be making changes. There aren't many who can hold on to the title of captain of the watch, whatever town or city you're in." A pregnant pause filled the space between them. "But you should not have left the way you did," he added. "It left too much room for doubt. Suspicion set in after that, putting the whole town on edge. Things only got worse when the soldiers arrived and refused to leave."

Unable to comment on much else, Asher asked, "Why haven't they left? Surely you suffered no attacks until two nights ago."

"Lord Kernat oversees the Demetrium mines, a source of great coin for The Ice Vales. He does so with no heirs to assume his seat and with growing apathy since his grief set in. It became clear from the moment they arrived that King Gregorn intends to replace Lord Kernat with General Crem, a reward for his years of service no doubt."

Asher absorbed it all with little interest—he cared nothing for the politics of the civilised world. "Would he not make a better lord?" he posed, if only to steer the topic away from his previous departure.

"In truth?" Lonan answered. "Yes, he would. But the timing...

First there was the monster in the swamp, swiftly followed by not one but two Werewolves. Bodies started mounting up, including a watchman. You recall Elias." It was a statement, not a question. Asher kept his eyes on the ground and the gnarled roots, aware that young Elias had been bitten by Russell, his fate sealed and, his family bereft of husband and father. "Then soldiers turn up," Lonan went on, "and the captain of the watch was dismissed without replacement. It was too much, creating too much unease. And the longer the mines are closed the worse things will get," he guaranteed.

"It will be a different world tomorrow," Asher reassured.

Lonan paused, one foot resting on a jagged rock. "But how many will live to see it?"

It was a question Asher couldn't answer, and so he put one foot in front of the other, encouraging Lonan to do the same.

"We're here," Hadavad soon announced, passing down the message from Merith.

Asher pressed on, making his way to the Vorska's side. On his way, he spared a glance at the night's sky, where the moon now shone from on high.

"Of course," the mage muttered, joining them by the tree line. "Where *would* a mage hide their lab?" His tone suggested he was chastising himself.

Asher returned his attention to their surroundings and looked upon a familiar sight. He was, once again, standing before the entrance to the Demetrium mine, a black void set into the base of the mountain.

"In there," Merith confirmed.

"It would be," Hadavad said. "The presence of so much Demetrium must have enhanced his spells."

Noting Lonan's proximity, Asher stepped onto the road, bringing an end to the mage's revelation. "This is it," he declared as the rest of their group arrived at the tree line.

"The mine?" one of them questioned.

"They will consider this whole area their territory," the ranger explained.

Lonan looked about. "And how exactly are we to lure them back here?"

Merith walked towards the former captain as a shark might survey its prey. "They already know we're here," he reported. "There's no missing the fear in your sweat."

Lonan scowled at the Vorska's back but said nothing, unlike Asher who stepped in beside the pale creature. "Do not mock their bravery," he berated once out of earshot.

"They are just mortals," Merith flippantly replied, coming to a halt on the threshold of the mine. "Sometimes I feel as if I could blink and miss your entire life."

"It's their mortality that makes them so brave," Asher argued. "Braver than you will ever be."

Merith half turned to flash one of his fangs. "Let's see how far that bravery gets them, shall we?" With that, the Vorska melted into the abyss beyond the entrance.

"He cannot be left alone in there," Hadavad hissed. The mage stamped his staff just the once, igniting a halo of flames around the top as if he carried a long torch.

As Hadavad brought illumination to the cave mouth, Lonan made his way to the ranger's side. "I do not like your new friend; he has an ill way about him."

"He's not my friend," Asher said, perhaps a little too quickly. "But he's right. The wolves will have caught wind of us by now. They're likely doubling back as we speak." The ranger gestured for them to follow him inside.

"Why do we have to go in there?" one of the watchmen asked.

"If we get surrounded," Asher explained, "we're dead. Better to have a wall at our back." By the way a few of them looked at the entrance, it seemed they knew a tomb when they saw one.

"If we fight together," Lonan said rousingly, "we will all return home as heroes."

"And if we die," the tallest of the group asked unhelpfully, reminding Asher that every one of them was out of their depth.

Still, proving himself worthy of his former title, Lonan had an answer for them. "Then we will be *remembered* as heroes."

CHAPTER 32
DOWN, DOWN, DOWN

Bearded Dragon - *A sea serpent to rival the mighty King Basilisk.*
These monsters are aggressive, so much so that they have been known to
not only stalk merchant ships but board them.
Think of these creatures in two halves. Their lower half is all tentacles,
and barbed ones at that. Nasty things.
Their top half is always likened to a dragon, with two arms and wicked
claws that can easily dig into the wood of any ship. Their reptilian head
is dominated by strong jaws. It is the tendrils that hang from those jaws
that lend the monster its name.

A Chronicle of Monsters: A Ranger's Bestiary, 12th Edition,
Page 21.

Mendra Falcorn, Ranger.

"Light every torch you can see!" Asher called out, scattering the group.

With the growing flames, it soon became apparent that they had left the meandering tunnels and entered a small cavern, where a further three tunnels had been excavated out of the far wall. Mining tools lay strewn across the ground, dropped where their owners had been standing, and empty carts sat waiting on tracks. It had been abandoned, and at speed by the look of it.

But not fast enough.

The ranger lowered his torch and ran the light over the nearest body. The corpse was in pieces and what remained had mostly been eaten, the bones gnawed. Asher imagined Creed and his band first coming across the mine while under the moon's thrall, the lot of them no better than savage beasts in the wake of Iskander's blood.

"There's more here," Hadavad informed, his staff brought down to reveal two more victims against the wall, each as brutalised as the one at Asher's feet.

"And here," Lonan added quietly, crouching to better see what was left of the man's face.

Standing in the middle of the chamber, Merith raised his chin. "There are dead men in every tunnel," he reported, compounding his strangeness to the others. "A *lot* of dead men," he reported wickedly.

Lonan stood up, his gaze boring into the Vorska. "You do not sound disturbed, sir."

"I've been around a lot of dead men before," Merith replied, as if such a response would be explanation enough.

Asher recognised that he was mocking them. "Ignore him," the ranger instructed. "Derail every cart and begin moving them to obstruct the entrance," he commanded, gesturing to the tunnel that had granted them entry to the cavern. "It won't stop them but it might slow them down, funnelling them to one at a time." While the watchmen got to the task, the ranger pivoted and gripped Merith by the arm. "Stop it," he demanded.

The Vorska's grin only widened. "Worried they'll discover they're barricading themselves in with a monster?"

Asher's grip tightened. "Which way?" he seethed.

Oblivious to the strength in Asher's fingers, Merith tilted his head, eyes shifting to the tunnel on the far right. "That way."

"We hold our ground here," the ranger stated. "If we're over-whelmed, retreat down that passage."

The Blood Fiend turned so that only Asher could see him. "We should go *now*. I know how the key works. I can open the lab and we can *all* take shelter inside. The wolves will likely spend the rest of the night trying to get inside. We could just wait them out."

"You're not going anywhere near that key," Asher told him firmly. "You're going to fight with us here and now or our deal's off." The ranger had already drawn the silvyr blade from over his shoulder, the weapon catching Merith's attention now.

"Haven't we done this already?" the Vorska countered quietly, if amusedly so. "You're no more a threat than they are," he added, throwing his head towards Lonan and his men.

"Do we have a problem?" Hadavad asked, his deep voice cutting through the tension.

Merith regarded the mage's staff, which had been purposefully moved towards his face. "No problem at all," the Blood Fiend assured with a disarming smile. Asher walked away from the wretch only to be halted by the creature's loud voice. "Though, I would ask... What am I to do when your friend Russell arrives, hmm? Should I fight *him* too or should I spare him as you did?"

The questions kept the ranger rooted to the spot. His gaze shifted towards Lonan, who was looking directly at him with confusion and righteous revelation behind his eyes. "What's he talking about?" When Asher said nothing the question came again, more urgently. "Gods damn you, man," he seethed. "You said he was dead this very night!"

"Russell Hobbs *is* dead," Asher argued, keeping his voice considerably lower.

Lonan started forward and thrust one finger into the ranger's face. "Don't!" he snapped. "Don't you lie again! Whatever truth you think you're spilling it's *not*! Why?" he demanded, cheeks flushing to red. "Why would you spare him? He killed Elias! He killed *so* many more in the square I couldn't name them all!"

"That wasn't him!" Asher fumed, exhausted by the repeating argument. "You can't blame him for the wolf! Russell is a good man!"

"He's a *beast*!" Lonan spat. "They all are!"

"Not Russell! He's different. He hates what he is. He wants to do *good*."

Lonan half turned to point at the entrance. "And what will he do when he comes through there?" The answer didn't need giving. "You were supposed to slay him!" the former captain complained, his free hand knotting into a fist. "Not befriend him! And now..." Lonan gestured to his men before shaking his head. "What have you brought us here for? Are we to be the fodder so you might subdue him? Or would you have us kill him because you cannot? Is that it?" he asked again, believing he had secured the right thread. "You are a coward, I say!"

Lonan's rage had built to a tipping point, bringing his sword round in a wild arc. Asher knew from the distance between them that the steel would never touch him, its meaning more an extension of his emotions than any violent intent. Letting him have the moment, the ranger remained still and let the tip of the sword sit directly in front of his face. Behind the former captain, the watchmen acted in accordance with their unofficial leader and brought their weapons to bear.

"I asked you here," Asher finally spoke, his tone flat, "because you've seen a Werewolf up close; you know what to expect. I asked you here because baiting the wolves will save the town—*your* town—and I thought you'd rather die here, protecting your people, than die in the streets with everyone else. I let Russell live because..."

The ranger truly considered his answer, taking into account all that had been debated over the last two months. He wanted to say

401

he let Russell live because he's a better man than him. Though true, that benchmark didn't say much. The real truth then struck him with shameful clarity. Those words, however, were not for any but Russell himself.

"I let him live because I could," he stated boldly, his silvyr blade brushing the man's sword aside. "And it changes *nothing*," he continued, addressing all of them now. "Anything that comes through there we will put to the sword." Hard was the gaze he levelled at Lonan. "There are no cowards in here."

Turning his back on the former captain, the ranger was quickly intercepted by Hadavad. "How exactly," he began, his words hardly more than a mutter, "are you planning on saving Russell?"

"I haven't figured that part out yet," Asher admitted. "My intentions were to single him out somehow, but the peril they have put the townspeople in..." The ranger sighed. "It changes my plan. Russell would understand."

"I suppose he would," the mage agreed with a sympathetic smile. "He is a *good man*, after all."

Asher was glad of the support, surrounded as he was now by those who believed him so wrong, a coward even. Lonan had already turned away, aiding his men in moving more equipment into the narrow tunnel. The ranger was tempted to double down on his argument, renewing their clash of heated words, when he noticed an absence.

"Where's Merith?"

The question saw Hadavad swivel about, his robes sweeping with him. Something akin to a growl rippled from the mage's throat. "I knew the fiend wasn't to be trusted! He's gone for the lab!"

"What's this?" Lonan was quick to interject, looking from ranger to mage. "What's going on?"

"We have to go after him!" Hadavad insisted, oblivious to the former captain's words. "He can't be allowed to get inside, Asher."

Already suspicious of them, and still bristling, Lonan advanced. "What are you talking about? And where's your pale friend?" His questions came out like arrows now.

"Come," the mage bade, the wolves forgotten as his personal quest returned to the forefront of his mind.

Driven to use his weapon, Lonan brought it up to bar Hadavad's way. "What in the hells is going on? Where are you going?" He glanced back at the entry. "They could be here any second! Isn't this why we're here?"

The mage considered the blade in his way before looking to Asher, as if the ranger might give him permission to use force. Indeed, he might have given advice or even put himself between them, in the hope that words alone might calm the situation, but that warrior's sixth sense turned him another way, back to the entry and the dark beyond.

Asher's lips parted to warn them all, but he was too late.

The dark gave birth to a monster that filled the tunnel from side to side. So hideously big was it that the creature was forced to enter on all fours, its thick blunt snout leading the way. Its drool glistened in the torchlight as it oozed between fangs and found its way to the ground in a single strand. Splayed hands with claws like hooks brought the beast into the light. The carts weren't going to slow it down.

And, indeed, they didn't.

Creed, for it could have only been Creed, barrelled through the crates and supplies like a battering ram. One of the watchmen was immediately removed from the fight when the corner of a cart slammed into his head. Another was ripped to bloody shreds of torn flesh when a single swipe of those meat hooks reached out and dragged him down and back, to where the mighty wolf's jaws were waiting. The man's head disappeared in that one bite.

The audible crunch of a human skull was enough to put everyone back a step. As they retreated, the great Werewolf advanced, his weight more than enough to break the spine and every rib in the dangling watchman's body. Asher glimpsed the eager wolves behind it, their amber eyes peering out of the shadows.

Granted the space, Creed rose on two legs and assumed his full height, putting him somewhere between ten and twelve foot, if not taller. His shoulders were as wide as four men abreast, the muscles easily seen despite his black fur. Were Death to choose a form, surely this would be it.

In spite of the space the remaining Werewolves now had, they refrained from entering the cavern, as if Creed was a barrier they dared not cross without express permission. It was the only thing that might save them.

"Run!" Asher yelled, one hand waving behind him to indicate the tunnel Merith had pointed out.

Fear, bravery, or a combination of the two, perhaps, saw one of the surviving watchmen charge in the wrong direction and swing his sword at Creed's right leg. With one hand, the enormous wolf snatched him mid-run, taking him clean from his feet. The sword clattered hopelessly against the ground as the watchman was lifted high, his torso fitting neatly inside Creed's impossible grip.

The man was dead, even if he was currently breathing. They wouldn't waste his sacrifice. "Run!" Asher urged again, his free hand pushing Lonan after Hadavad. In the mad scramble, one of the remaining two watchmen vanished down the wrong tunnel with naught but a torch for company. The ranger managed one last glance over his shoulder, sighting the other wolves pawing at the ground, desperate to pursue.

The lip of the tunnel concealed the watchman from the shoulders up, just as Creed snapped his powerful jaws shut around his head. Still, Asher heard the blood as it spilled on the cavern floor. "Run!" he cried.

Leading their escape was the only watchman in active service to have taken the correct tunnel. In front of Hadavad, however, he suffered from a lack of light, with the flames surrounding the head of the mage's staff meeting the man's back and casting stark shadows before him. Asher didn't even see him fall down the jagged hole in the path. He heard Hadavad call out for him before hearing the man himself shouting as he plunged into a seemingly bottomless abyss.

"Jump!" the mage called back, crossing the hole in a single leap.

After him, Lonan made the same jump and missed a good footing by inches. His left leg slipped back, taking him down to his waist until he found purchase with his hands. To be sure of his own leap, Asher used a portion of the wall at the side of the hole to kick off from. Upon landing, he and Hadavad gripped a wrist each and dragged the former captain to safety.

"Run!" Asher yelled.

They soon heard the wolves.

Padded feet and sharp claws took to the tunnels with rapidity. With impeccable night vision and an even better sense of smell, they would track down the trio in less than a minute. And so, they had only seconds to evade their pursuers.

Every other tunnel opened up into another cavern, each a different size, but each strewn with corpses, the walls splattered with blood. Hadavad appeared to be choosing their path at random, though he constantly had them turning left and right in the hope of taking some of the speed out of the racing wolves.

"We can't keep running!" Lonan panted, though it seemed likely he was talking from a place of exhaustion rather than the need to stand and fight.

Hadavad skidded to a stop before two adjacent tunnels, robbing them of precious seconds. Asher barked the mage's name. "This way!" the older man called, taking them left.

A cool breeze washed over the ranger's skin before he caught the scent of something damp, or metallic perhaps. A moment later, the tunnel opened up to a canyon so vast several blocks of Kelp Town could have nestled between the opposing walls. There was but a single bridge that connected the two sides, and of sturdy build to handle the flow of Demetrium-filled carts that passed over it day and night. Left and right there was only darkness, a curtain of nothingness that knew no end.

"Down there!" Lonan yelled, directing them briefly to a spot of light in the chasm.

Asher maintained his pace while sighting the distant watchman who had taken the wrong tunnel. As he reached the other side of his own bridge, the light of his torch fading, a Werewolf darted out across the wooden planks, its hunt nearing its end. There was nothing the trio could do to help the man and it seemed likely he would be dead by the time they reached the end of their own bridge.

A sharp growl and a separate snarl resounded from behind them, proving they had troubles of their own. Two Lycans burst from the darkness they had left behind and hurried across the bridge. Further still they heard the terrible sound of an almighty roar, a precursor to Creed's thunderous steps.

"Quickly!" Hadavad snapped, the first to reach stone again.

The mage was already pivoting to face the incoming wolves as Asher and Lonan ran past him. In the manner of a lumberjack bringing his axe down to chop through a log, Hadavad wielded his staff in two hands as he hammered it down onto the bridge. A flash of brilliant white light erupted from the staff's end, his magic unleashed.

The spell created a staccato of explosions that rippled across the surface of the bridge, compromising not only the boards but the traversing beams and bracers that kept the bridge fixed between the walls. In seconds, the entire structure was collapsing in on itself and dropping into the abyss. Of the two Werewolves, the slower lost its footing and plummeted with the bridge, its growl transformed into a whimper. The faster, however, managed to leap the remainder of the distance and find purchase with its front claws.

It raked desperately at the ground in an attempt to heave its bulk up and over the lip. A heartbeat was all the time Asher had to think and react. It wasn't much, a fraction of time in which he could do little but rely on his instincts. And his instincts told him the beast was not Russell.

Too small.

The ranger dropped to one knee and plunged his silvyr blade down and through the creature's head until the tip protruded its jaw and dug into stone. There he held it, waiting. The monster was unquestionably dead, its weight pulling against Asher in a bid to slip away from the edge. Still he waited, for he had to know, to see with his own eyes.

Inevitably, the wolf's features faded, retreating to whatever hell it had originally emerged from, and left the human form behind. The weight of the nameless man was a burden Asher could handle, adding to his relief that he had not just killed Russell.

In one motion, he rose from his crouch and withdrew the short-sword, allowing the body to fall away. Asher's skin prickled, turning his gaze back across the way, to the adjacent wall. He narrowed his eyes but failed to perceive anything but shadows. Sensing his unease, Hadavad aimed his staff high into the chasm and released a fireball, banishing the darkness.

There was Creed, partially clinging to the wall, his amber eyes locked on the trio from afar. The hulking beast made no sound, not even a growl. He simply watched. It was unsettling. In a frighteningly fast burst of energy, the massive wolf then took off, scrambling over the face of the wall in search of a way across. In his wake was another of his ilk, and a relatively large one at that.

Russell.

The new pup was sticking close to its pack leader. Asher did a quick head count, noting that two of the six were now dead with one other hunting the stray watchman. Russell and Creed were clawing their way across the chasm. That left one unaccounted for.

"We should keep moving," the ranger voiced, nodding at the mage and his fiery staff to take the lead.

Forging their way through the mine, they crossed other, smaller, bridges, and descended not one, but three lifts that had operated on a counterweight system. It was only then, in those untold depths, that they laid eyes on veins of raw Demetrium.

Asher had never seen the material before, coveted as it was by mages the world round and concealed within their wands and staffs. Seeing it now, the ranger couldn't help but think of it as the mountain's actual veins. It ran like rivers on a map through the stone, a deep red with the faintest of blue speckles scoring its surface.

Hadavad ran a gentle hand over the nearest vein. "It's been centuries since I've seen Demetrium in this form."

Lonan was visibly drained from their escape, but he still heard the mage. "Did he say centuries?"

"He meant years," Asher assured, his eyes trying to pierce the shadows of the next tunnel. The ranger swore. "Merith didn't come this way," he groaned.

"The lifts," Hadavad stated, catching on.

"They were waiting for us," Asher elaborated. "They should have all been at the bottom of their shaft." He swore again. "He lied."

"Of course he did," the mage said, an air of superiority about him. "It's in his nature."

"Who is this Merith?" Lonan questioned, able to stand up straight for the first time. "And where is he going that you would abandon the fight to reach him?" When mage and ranger said nothing the former captain sighed. "You have a lot to answer for," he said accusingly to Asher. "Were I still captain, and we survived this hellish pit, I would throw you in irons and send you to the block."

"We don't have time for this," Hadavad pressed, moving for the next tunnel. "This mine is like an ant hill—every tunnel is connected. We must continue our hunt."

"I thought we were the ones being hunted," Lonan pointed out.

Asher ignored him and moved to join the mage. "He could be anywhere and these mines are old; there's likely miles of tunnels."

"Not anywhere," Hadavad corrected. "*Down*, where the Demetrium is more plentiful. That's where Iskander will have built his lab."

Lonan nearly stopped in his tracks and might have had the light not been with the mage. "Iskander? Who in the hells is that?" he growled. Again, his companions offered naught but silence. "No!" the man fumed, before barrelling into Asher's side and pinning him to the wall. "I'm done with this! I want answers damn you! My men, my *friends*, have died in this wretched place! There is a *pile* of charred bodies outside my home, all of them butchered by these monsters, monsters you were supposed to slay! What. Is. Going. On?"

Hadavad looked to be on the verge of casting a spell until Asher subtly shook his head. The ranger clasped his hand over the one Lonan had pressing into his cuirass. It would have been easy to inflict pain and prise it away, but he understood the man's frustration and would have felt the same way were he in his position.

"Easy," he bade, his tone low and soothing enough to see the former captain back off. "Yes," he admitted, "there's more going on here. More than I can rightly explain with the time we have."

"I'm a quick learner," Lonan replied forcefully.

Asher exhaled through his nose, sparing Hadavad a glance. How could he condense hundreds of years of history and events that were beyond the understanding of a humble watchman? With time against them, however, he had to try.

"Kargon Iskander is a mage," he began. "*Was* a mage. A very bad mage. A lot of his old works are somewhere down here. The wolves—they're drawn to it; that's why they're here. It's also why we're here. Iskander's work needs to be destroyed before Creed or Merith can get their hands on it."

"Among those works is a precious stone capable of bringing nightmares to life," Hadavad interjected, his voice stern. "What we do here, now, is for more than Kelp Town. The Ice Vales and beyond will suffer if our foes succeed."

Lonan blinked. Then he blinked again. "And..." he licked his lips. "And who *is* Merith, exactly? I'm starting to think he isn't a ranger."

"He's a Vorska," Asher said plainly, his response a blunt stroke.

Lonan's jaw fell open. "A... A Vorska?" He licked his lips again. "I always thought they were just a myth."

"No more than Werewolves," Hadavad remarked.

"Or Hell Hags," Asher added. "Make no mistake," he continued gravely, "it's us who live in a world of monsters, not they who live in ours."

"Do you actually *kill* any of these monsters?" Lonan retorted bitingly. "Or do you only aid their wretched existence?"

"That about catches him up," the mage said impatiently, cutting off any potential argument. "Can we be off?"

Asher waited, letting Lonan be the one to answer the question. It seemed he required an extra moment to absorb the brief explanation, though whether he truly had remained to be seen. Either way, he nodded and looked to Hadavad to lead the way.

"Good man," the mage affirmed, turning to leave.

Lonan didn't move after him, his attention flitting back to Asher for a moment. "Whether your lies were for good or bad, you are not absolved. Russell Hobbs should have died in those woods. His victims should have been avenged." That was all the man had to say, not waiting around for the ranger's response.

Asher's feet didn't follow them immediately and the shadows began to engulf him. He restlessly twisted the hilt of his silvyr blade, his thoughts and emotions whirling. He knew absolution was unattainable, for all his sins, and what a long list they made. His was only to *try*.

There in the growing dark, for the first time in his years freed from Nightfall, did he feel content with that.

His determination crystallised, the ranger hefted his weapon and made for the light.

CHAPTER 33
INTO THE PAST

Shadow Dealers - Get a mage. I'll write that again. Get a mage. Aptly named, these monsters crawled out of the Shadow Realm, but it is not what they are or where they came from, but what they do, that is so hellish.

A single bite from these demons will scar you with what can only be described as a void. I've heard mages call them portals. From these wounds, more of their wicked kin are able to claw their way into our world. These nightmarish gateways can only be closed by a mage— killing the poor soul who was bitten will not suffice.

Get a mage.

A Chronicle of Monsters: A Ranger's Bestiary, 12th Edition, Page 421.

Nay Hodden, Ranger.

H adavad stopped in the middle of the passage.

"What is it?" Asher asked, failing to detect any threat.

"The walls," the mage replied, his neck craned. He indicated their surroundings "This tunnel was made by your ancestors," he said, gesturing to Lonan. "But this cavern is natural."

Asher stepped in beside the mage and examined the small chamber, its pointed top lost in darkness. The ranger agreed with Hadavad's assessment, though he couldn't fathom why it caused him to stop.

"*That* tunnel," the mage continued, pointing his staff at the circular hole that bored through the adjacent wall, "was made with magic."

Asher advanced to see for himself, though he was forced to wait until Hadavad's flames caught up with him. The walls inside the new tunnel were smooth, too smooth for the works of ancient miners. Even the edges were rounded before they met the jagged natural stone of the cavern wall.

"We're here," Hadavad declared at no more than a whisper.

"You're sure?" Lonan asked, his first words in some time.

"No tools of man forged this passage," the mage confirmed. "Kargon Iskander himself did this."

Asher tilted his head and inhaled the air. "Smells like..."

"Wet dog," Lonan finished.

"Werewolves," Hadavad concluded grimly.

As one, the trio left the natural chamber behind and entered the smooth tunnel. It curved left and right for a time, weaving through the mountain stone like a snake. They were eventually guided out by light, though not the mage's. At fifty yards lay a flaming torch, the fire more than enough to give some shape to the arching cavern. In that light, the hanging stalactites glistened, reminding Asher of wet fangs.

"By the gods..." It was Lonan who had poured his voice and disbelief into the chamber.

Asher had already spotted Merith, seated on the cold stone

beside the torch. The Vorska was cradling the watchman who had, inadvertently, fled down the correct tunnel and followed in Merith's footsteps. Of course, the man was dead now, his throat in the clutches of the fiend's over-extended jaws. Merith's fangs were deep into flesh and his suckered tongue gorged on the blood, not a drop wasted.

Partially hidden in the darkness was another corpse. His limbs rested at unnatural angles and his naked body bore the lacerations of a sword. At least the damned Vorska had killed *some* of them, the only comfort Asher could take from the gruesome scene. The ranger subtracted one more from the pack, leaving Creed, Russell, and one last unaccounted for wolf.

Merith rolled his head back from his victim's throat with dramatic flair, his thick tongue mopping up any blood from around his lips. "Sorry about that," he said. "I was a little peckish after dispatching that one."

"Monster!" Lonan raged, his sword coming up.

Asher failed to grab him. Holding him back was the only way to save his life but, fortunately for the former captain, Hadavad's reach was made longer by his staff. The flaming end was enough to halt Lonan before his charge picked up any meaningful speed.

Merith, beaming all the while, tossed the watchman's body aside with ease as he stood up. "I have to say, I'm impressed you made it this far; I thought you'd all be wolf food by now."

"And *this* is as far as you go," Hadavad threatened, his staff levelling out at the Vorska.

Merith narrowed his eyes, only the fiend wasn't looking at them but between them. "I think not," he replied smugly.

Some part of Asher's brain realised what was about to happen and urged him into action without thought. He shoved Lonan to one side with enough strength to send him barrelling into Hadavad. As the pair were knocked one way, the ranger dived the other, creating just enough space for the unaccounted for Werewolf to leap between them.

Four sets of claws raked across the cavern floor as the beast skidded to a stop and turned back to face the trio. Asher had already turned his dive into a roll and found his feet again, a fine edge of silvyr raised in one hand. Movement beyond the wolf shifted the ranger's attention to Merith. The Vorska was facing the wall and turning something with his hand—the arrow head! He turned it once and pushed it in until it was flush with the groove that had accepted it.

Asher wanted to watch what happened next but the wolf had determined he was to be its first victim. In a single bound it closed the gap between them, reaching for the ranger with outstretched hands and pointed claws. Asher swiped a backhand while simultaneously dropping into an evasive roll. He barely felt the keen edge of the silvyr as it sliced through the monster's hand, separating four fingers from its grip.

The wolf's roar was malformed by the pain and it landed in a heap of limbs, rolling over itself until it struck the wall. It recovered in no more than a second, only now it knew fury. And it could still kill them all with one hand or the snap of its jaws.

"Hadavad!" Asher yelled, imploring the mage to bring his magic to the fight.

Lonan had got up first, though he appeared unsure where to insert himself. He hadn't, however, run away, a credit something even the bravest of warriors could never guarantee. The ranger gestured with his short-sword for the man to edge round to the right, splitting their foe's attention. The wolf was too quick for such a tactic and simply lashed out with one hand—knocking Lonan off his feet—before charging at Asher.

A strong thrust broke the monster's stride and a second downward stroke scored a red line down its snout. Asher knew better than to employ his hands, feet or knees, for any one of his limbs could be snatched from the air and torn free with brute strength.

Its hand actively bleeding, the wolf roared in his face and swiped with its good hand, bringing five claws down the ranger's cuirass. Two of the claws were able to pierce the hard leather above his hip, dragging him down to deliver a jolt of pain up through his knee. The Lycan then reversed its attack, sending a swift backhand up Asher's face. White hot pain seared into his skin and the impact of solid knuckles knocked his head back and took his body with it.

Another jolt of pain racked his body, this time through his back where he landed on the cave floor. He could already feel blood running down one side of his face where the claws had gashed open his eyebrow and forehead. The taste of blood informed him his lip had been split, though his nose hurt so much he could have blood oozing from his nostrils. He might have made better sense of it all had he not felt so keenly as if his skull had been placed between an anvil and a dwarf's hammer.

Only when the Werewolf towered over him, its amber eyes and drooling mouth bearing down on him, did the impending sense of death sharpen his focus. His right hand squeezed to grip the short-sword that was no longer there. It was to be death then. He could reach up and try to keep those jaws at bay, but he had sense enough to know that he would be crushed beneath the monster's bulk. He chose instead to thrust his hand inside its mouth and choke the wretch before it could bite his arm off. At least he would have, had the wolf not been impacted by a blinding spell.

The ground shuddered as the beast rolled over itself, a smoking crater deforming one side of its ribs. Asher turned his head to see Hadavad slowly advancing. As the beast attempted to rise, the mage flicked his staff from low to high, expelling a wave of water and debris that crashed into the Lycan and twisted it up and round. Again, the ground shuddered upon the fiend's impact.

For many monsters—and certainly any man—that would have been the end of the fight, but Werewolves were no ordinary crea-ture. A low rumble escaped its throat as it rose and squared the mage in its sights, Asher forgotten. Its injured hand didn't slow its explosive bolt forward. Hadavad let loose another spell and missed his target by inches, giving the beast all the time it needed to close the gap. It seemed beyond the old man's responses but still he succeeded in raising a shield about him as the wolf rammed ahead.

Both were taken from the ranger's view in the blink of an eye, the force of their collision sending both across the cavern. Trying to rise so he might aid the mage informed Asher that his head was dragging in ways he couldn't define. Staggering back to the ground, he could only watch the battle out of the corner of his eye, though Hadavad's spells often blinded him.

Merith...

He could see the Vorska clearly, the pale creature still within the light of the fallen torch. The ground shuddered again, but this time it wasn't caused by the wolf. The tremor continued, rattling the small stones that lay scattered about the ranger.

It was when the ground itself began to move that Asher blinked, sure that he was hallucinating.

One by one, slab by slab, the ground dropped, descending even deeper into the mountain. It continued in this fashion, creating a rectangular hole all the way to the wall, where the arrow head had come to rest. Slowed by his knock to the head, Asher only realised after Merith had dropped from sight that the ground wasn't falling away into a chasm but was, in fact, moulding itself into a set of wide steps.

Something of a war cry broke the ranger's attention and turned him back to the fight, which Lonan had now thrown himself into. He hacked again and again at the monster's muscled back, though it barely seemed to notice as it swiped at Hadavad. The mage deflected the claw with his staff and cast destructive spells in between, but the wolf's erratic movements only put Lonan in harm's way. One such spell nearly took the man's head off, forcing him to duck and, subsequently, receive an accidental backhand from the beast.

As Lonan skidded across the cavern floor, Asher picked himself up and called on the power of the gem to make him whole again. Within seconds his wounds were a memory, if a painful one.

Scooping up his silvyr blade, the ranger immediately launched it overarm, his aim more instinct than anything else. The sword found its mark, despite the wolf having moved in the time the weapon crossed the gap. With a length of silvyr buried in its hip, the creature dropped and howled. The pain kept it still just long enough for Hadavad to point his staff and expel his devastating magic.

Something hotter than fire punched the Werewolf in the chest and melted through to its spine. Death was dealt and the beast left in a smoking heap. The mage sighed in relief and leant heavily on his staff for a moment.

"Lonan?" Asher called, seeing the man slowly rousing.

"I'm alive," he reported wearily.

The ranger would have walked over and offered the man a hand, but their problems hadn't ended so much as shifted. "Hadavad," he addressed urgently, though the mage was already aware of Merith's actions and was making his way towards the newly-forged steps.

"What new devilry is this?" Hadavad crouched at the top of the steps as he voiced his question.

Asher tilted his head but was forced to descend a few steps to see what the mage was talking about. The steps connected the cavern to a wide passage that was lined with blazing torches, their light revealing the back of Merith.

Groaning through his injuries, Lonan joined them, his sword handled in the manner of a walking stick. "What's he doing?" the former captain asked, crouching beside Hadavad. "Why's he just standing there?"

Asher frowned at the scene, his sixth sense telling him that something was very wrong. The ancient Vorska was as motionless as the stone around them, as if he had been carved from the rock in the middle of the passage.

"He's not standing," Hadavad pointed out.

Asher reassessed the scene and saw the truth of it—Merith was running. His left foot wasn't even touching the floor and his white-blond hair was frozen in the air behind him. The Vorska's stance wasn't the only thing the ranger noticed now.

"Look at the torches," he directed. "The flames."

The others joined him in scrutinising the fires and soon realised that, like Merith, the flames weren't moving despite casting light into the passage.

"What evil is this?" Lonan questioned, almost accusingly.

Hadavad remained quiet, though he did cautiously descend the steps and plant his feet on the flat stone of the passage. He stood there for a time, contemplating with his back to them. Only when Asher questioned him did the mage move to the wall on his left. He said nothing as he ran one hand over the stone, its surface as smooth as the one that had brought them to the cavern.

"What is it?" the ranger asked, one eye on Merith.

The mage turned around and stared up at him, his expression firm but unreadable. Again, he offered no response but, instead, retrieved one of the stones from the ground. He felt its edges with his fingers before tossing it into the passage, his aim projecting the stone at the Vorska. Asher was dumbfounded when the small rock began to slow mid-flight. Then it appeared to freeze altogether, just as the Vorska had.

"Hadavad?"

The mage's attention appeared lost to the tunnel. "This magic," he began, his speech protracted, "is not known to me. Nor any," he muttered absently. "Come, look at this," he bade.

Asher made his way down the final dozen steps and joined the mage, though he now felt very wary of how far away he was from the bottom step. Hadavad guided him to the wall on their left where the ranger could see that it was not as smooth as he had believed. From top to bottom, the stone had been engraved with glyphs he couldn't hope to understand, not one belonging to a language he spoke, including elvish. The lines ran all the way along the passage, over the ceiling, and down the adjacent wall until they disappeared into the gloom.

"What is this?"

If Hadavad had been awed by the magic at work it was fleeting, for he now looked only disturbed. "This," he replied, gesturing at the glyphs, "*is* the spell. It's a net," he likened. "Any who get caught in it get taken out of their time and frozen in a moment..." The mage trailed off, his eyes intent on the nearest torch planted in the ground. "No," he mumbled. "Not frozen. *Look.*"

Asher had to watch the still flames for some time before noticing that they did move, if excruciatingly slowly. "He's not frozen," the ranger deduced.

"No," Hadavad agreed. "He's just moving very slowly. These torches have been burning for eight hundred years..." Again, the mage trailed off, his thoughts tumbling and darkening by the look in his eyes.

"What is it?" Asher demanded, seeing Hadavad's mouth hanging ajar as he gazed into the passage. "Hadavad!" he thundered, slapping his right hand against the wall.

A great *thoom* resounded from deep inside the mountain, culminating in a torrent of wind rushing from the tunnel and blowing out Asher's green cloak as it escaped up the steps. He shielded his eyes from the strong gust and turned his head away as the others did. Only in its wake did the ranger hear rapid footsteps growing ever distant.

"Merith!" Hadavad growled.

The Vorska was already disappearing round the corner of the passage, just as the mage's thrown rock was tumbling across the ground.

"What was that?" Lonan exclaimed, picking himself up off the steps.

Hadavad swivelled on the spot to face Asher. He scrutinised the ranger, his gaze drifting down to his right hand, where the black gem remained hidden inside his fingerless glove. "I would say the spell was broken," he explained, without actually explaining anything.

Asher subtly raised his hand and examined it as if he could see the hidden ring. The gem protected him from magic, he knew, but its ability to *break* spells was a revelation.

"Come!" Hadavad bade, an urgency about him. "We have a Vorska ahead of us and Werewolves behind us."

Asher looked back just once to check that Lonan was still accompanying them. Proving himself the warrior, the former captain pushed through his wounds and did his best to match their jogging speed. They were soon rounding that same corner and following the torches, though the passage was shorter than the one that had brought them to the chamber. In less than a minute the trio stood on the threshold of a new and vast cavern, its true size hidden by clusters of deep shadow.

Shadow or not, there was no mistaking the cavern for what it was: a mage's laboratory.

Small bridges, some of wood, others of stone, connected various parts of the cavern, criss-crossing to create a web. A surplus of ropes and chains hung from numerous pulley systems, including a makeshift lift in the far corner. Here and there, the natural walls and jutting stone had been hollowed out to create shelving units or tables, all layered with sundries, vials, and books. Veins of red Demetrium wormed through it all, some as wide as a man.

There was no missing the bodies, specimens to a mage perhaps.

Some were human, while others were something else altogether—creatures and horrifying amalgamations that Asher didn't recognise. Most were hanging from hooks and chains while others rested horizontally, limbs and torsos strapped to large boards. They were all in various stages of decomposition and *all* had been cut open in some way, their insides exposed. Whoever and whatever they were, they were all from another time, their corpses having been trapped, like the flames, sealed away from true time for eight centuries.

Between them all were crates, chests, and barrels, their various labels suggesting they were filled with supplies, food, and water. Instinctively, Asher took cover behind a tall stack of crates, where he might assess the environment unseen. It was a pointless exercise, of course, when his quarry was a Vorska.

Merith's voice, indistinct as it was, reverberated throughout the expanse. His individual words, however, were lost to its size, though they were enough to move Hadavad and Lonan behind cover.

"Can you see him?" Asher mouthed.

The mage peered out from behind the crates, his eyes searching high, before shaking his head. Lonan wasn't even looking, his back to a stack of barrels. His face glistened thanks to the sheen of sweat that coated his skin and mingled with his cuts. He was gripping his sword in both hands and tightly so. He was fighting his fear as only a warrior could.

Another voice responded to Merith's, stealing the breath from the sheltered trio.

"There's someone else in here," Lonan hissed.

The blood appeared to have drained from Hadavad's face. "I think I know why Iskander left that key," he uttered.

Asher tried to piece together what he knew but the machinations of mages were beyond him. So far, he had assumed the time spell was nothing more than a way of preserving the work. "It's been a long day, Hadavad; speak plainly."

The mage collected himself and gestured to the wall of glyphs, behind the ranger. "Kargon Iskander carved these," he whispered. "Every single one! Where or how he discovered the magic is a mystery, but this must have taken him years to accomplish. It's meticulous. Detailed. Beautiful in its own way."

"Hadavad." Asher's impatience was growing by the second.

"Think like *him*," Hadavad insisted. "Isn't that what your masters taught you?"

Asher didn't appreciate the call back to his former life, especially in front of Lonan, but his mind did begin to look at the situation from a different perspective, as if the dark mage was his prey.

If he had been Kargon Iskander, hunted by The Black Hand, he would need somewhere to hide. More so, he would need somewhere to hide and continue his work, work that he couldn't give up. The logical conclusion was to wait out those who hunted him, but to do so would inevitably see him die before his work could be finished.

Unless...

Unless there was a way to slow down time.

The ranger moved closer to the glyphs, gleaning some truth behind their unreadable shapes. "Iskander didn't want Merith to find his lab," he breathed. "He wanted Merith to find *him*."

Hadavad was watching him with a hard stare. "Kargon Iskander yet lives."

CHAPTER 34
UNDER THE MOUNTAIN

Three-headed Dread Serpent - If you've read about Hell Hags, you should have an idea how foul and ferocious they are. Hell Hags have nightmares about these serpents.

Dread Serpents will encroach on the swamp of any monster and make it their own. While it is good that they devour other monsters, they themselves are extremely hard to kill. While you might evade one or even two snapping jaws, few can avoid the bite of a third.

I myself shared the reward with a mage. She froze the swamp and I lopped off the heads. We could all do with learning a spell or two.

A Chronicle of Monsters: A Ranger's Bestiary, 12th Edition, Page 333.

Jayms Mellor, Ranger.

A sher took the revelation in his stride—his survival demanding it.

Looking beyond the crates, he tried to spy the dark mage who had cheated death for hundreds of years. The ranger squeezed his right fist, feeling the ring within. The gem would protect him from direct spells, but Kargon Iskander was an unknown quantity, an assassin's nightmare. Ultimately, the mage was a complication in what was already a precarious situation. And he would, of course, divert Hadavad's attention—no meagre thing.

Requiring more information about this new adversary, the ranger crept around the crates and began to infiltrate the lab proper. Hadavad and Lonan naturally fell in behind him, each using the cadavers and workstations to remain concealed where possible.

An acrid smell attacked Asher's nose, turning him to a table of multicoloured chemicals in glass vials. Among them was a severed hand and a decapitated head with the top half of the brain exposed. The ranger crouched to all fours and crawled under the table and out the other side, where a set of curving steps had been carved out of the rock. After a slow ascent, he came to rest before reaching the higher floor, flattening himself to the steps.

The voices now possessed a discernible clarity.

"How long has it been?" Iskander's voice was like old wood creaking in the wind, though it retained an undertone of strength and superiority.

"I last saw you eight hundred and twenty-three years ago, Master."

Asher's view was skewed by his low angle, but he could just make out Merith's back, the Vorska kneeling reverently before the mage.

"Eight hundred and twenty-three years..." Kargon echoed, his words dying off towards the end. "Eight years have passed for me. Eight years under this mountain, talking to myself lest I forget the sound of my own voice."

"I thought you dead, Master."

There was a pause between them, the tension building. "You should have found me sooner," Iskander chastised, his tone sharp and clipped. "I taught you so much, *gave* you so much. I even granted you the power to make more like you. What have you accomplished with your immortality? With your strength and speed?"

"Forgive me, Master," Merith grovelled.

"Centuries," Kargon agonised. "I taught you my ways. Were you so clouded by your hunger? You were to be better than those of your making!" the dark mage growled. "What of my enemies?" he asked, his ire pivoting. "What of The Black Hand? I am assuming you have spent the last eight hundred years vanquishing them."

"They are scattered across Illian, Master. They have become adept at hiding their activities."

"Excuses!" Kargon lambasted, his temper quick to return. "You thought me dead, though you never saw my demise! You failed to discover the key I left for you! And you have allowed those *hacks* to continue their work! *Yet*," he emphasised, "you come before me and demand a cure. A *cure*! As if you are afflicted! You don't need curing, worm, you are precisely as I *intended*."

Silence, again, reigned over them. "*Intended...*" Merith whispered.

"Magic demands balance," Iskander went on, the direction of his voice suggesting he was moving. "By night you walk the earth as a god. There must be a price."

"Then... I am to remain this way for... *ever*."

"How selfish you have grown," Kargon accused. "You find your maker, the only one who ever gave you a chance, and all you can do is bring your problems to my feet."

Merith seemed almost oblivious to his master's words. "Can you undo the curse?" he asked, if not pleaded. "Can you make me... *human* again?"

The Vorska's torment was pouring out, revealing the real Merith beneath the bravado and arrogance. He hated what he was. Or, perhaps, he loved what he was, what he was capable of by night. He just didn't think it was worth the so-called *price*. It spoke volumes about the depth of pain he had endured every daylight hour for the last eight centuries.

A thunderclap cut through the cavern and Merith was hauled from the ground by unseen powers. There he remained, suspended and pulled taut. Asher raised his head ever so slightly and spotted the wand being pointed at the Vorska and the pale hand holding it.

"Curse?" Iskander spat. "You have been in my presence for no more than minutes and you insult me? You will remember your place! You are *my* creature! Mine! You belong to *me*! I made you and *yes*, I can *unmake* you! But, rest assured, I would unmake you one piece at a time!" The wand dropped and Merith with it.

There was a rustle of robes and the sound of boots on the cold floor as Kargon approached his minion. "For eight long years I have awaited your return. I have spent hours, days, watching that passage, wondering whether you were about to walk out of it. And here you are, at last. What a disappointment you are, apparently no more than a shadow of your former self. It matters little, I suppose," the dark mage added flippantly. "In your absence I have continued my great work unhindered by your petty needs."

"Master," Merith beseeched. "I *am* here to serve... I am... I am yours."

"You are here because you sought ultimate power," Iskander corrected. "Ungrateful wretch," he remarked scornfully. "If only you knew what ultimate power really is. Had you returned in the appropriate manner, you might have remained at my side when I reshape the realm."

"Forgive me, Master," the Vorska begged on his knees. "Let me... serve you again."

"I think, instead," Kargon croaked menacingly, "you should live the rest of your eternal days in the light."

The *snap* of magic drowned out the immediate spell that Iskander spouted. Merith's cries of agony only added to that, masking the spell altogether. Asher moved again to see past the table legs, and the clutter that sat around them, to see the Vorska. His beauty had been banished, leaving behind his true and horrifying appearance. With it came his every injury for the last eight hundred years.

The tip of the wand flicked under the Vorska's chin and slowly guided him back up to his feet. He stood hunched, head low with patches of long hair hanging across his marred face. He was managing his pain now to no more than grunts.

"You aren't even worthy to serve anymore," Iskander sneered. "You have naught but demands where you should have offerings."

"I am sorry, Master. I truly thought you dead."

Kargon hissed like a snake and his wand brought more pain to the Vorska, knocking him back into a jutting slab of rock. "I cannot die!" he proclaimed. "Not while my work remains unfinished!" The dark mage paused, catching his breath after the outburst. "They were going to take it from me," he explained, his tone softened and aged now.

The ranger was beginning to see an edge of madness to Kargon Iskander, though whether that was brought on by years of isolation or he was naturally maniacal remained to be seen.

"The Black Hand wanted it all," he continued, his voice growing stronger as his passion rose. "I did what they could not. I *made* it," he whispered with glee.

From his vantage, Asher saw Merith's hideous features break into epiphany. "You actually did it?" he asked incredulously.

"Yes," Iskander purred. "Last year—a *century ago* to you," he specified, his tone hardening again as his mood shifted like the wind. "The power of the Obsidian Stone is *mine*."

Asher looked back and down to see Hadavad and the grave concern that ruled his expression. The ranger flexed his fingers to suggest calm and to keep the mage where he lay partially across the steps. It was no good. Mention of a Skaramangian Stone set a fire within him. Before Asher could do anything to stop him, Hadavad was on his feet and marching up the steps, past him.

"I think *not*," he stated firmly in response to Iskander's proclamation.

With Lonan in his wake, Asher rose from concealment and braced himself for the fight to come. There was no immediate backlash, however, the dark mage content to merely observe the intruders.

Asher assessed the ancient man in no more than a second. He was in his forties, perhaps fifties, and still with a thick mane of black hair that knew only a few lines of silver as it ran down to his waist. Equally long, and just as thick and immaculate, was his dark beard and its single shock of white. After eight years of isolation, the ranger had expected to see someone closer in appearance to a vagabond. Instead, he looked upon an exceptionally tall and well-groomed man.

Between the two sources of hair rested a face that *had* known solitude for eight years. Absent the sun, his skin was deathly pale and so dry as to be peeling around his eyes and across his cheeks. There wasn't much to see of his frame, hidden beneath thick robes of deep green and black, but if his sharp cheekbones were anything to go by he was a slight man. Like most mages, he had come to rely on magic over muscle.

In his right hand, pressed between fingers and thumb, was his wand, a perfectly straight piece of wood that seemed in keeping with his impeccable appearance.

A thin eyebrow arched into the dark mage's brow. "You brought guests, Merith."

"No, Master," the Vorska responded, his pain slowing his rise. "I brought an *offering*." He was looking directly at Asher as he said it.

Of course Merith had known they were there—he had simply been waiting for the opportune time, when *they* might serve *him*.

"That one," the Vorska announced, indicating Asher with a crooked finger. "He possesses an artefact of great power, a power that allows him to defy injury. Perhaps even death."

"Keep your foul tongue behind your fangs, beast," Hadavad warned him, staff at the ready.

"He is *my* beast," Kargon affirmed. "He will do only as *I* bid." With a subtle flick of his wand, Merith was returned to his exquisite features, granting him a vigorous demeanour once again.

Hadavad took his staff in both hands. "You do not stand the

master here, Kargon Iskander. You are a man out of time in more ways than one."

"You have come to kill me then," the dark mage surmised, a coy smirk reshaping his tight lips. "Yet," he continued, "you do not have the bearing of The Black Hand. You are a simple mage, yes? What quarrel do you have with me? After all, I was born *centuries* before your great grandfather."

"My quarrel is with evil, sir. You have unleashed terrible curses upon the realm, ruined good lives. You are not worthy of a Skaramangian Stone."

The fine muscles around Iskander's eyes twitched at the sound of the ancient name. "Even in my time there were few who knew of them, who knew that *name*. Still, like them, you have come to take it from me. Well, mage, here it is."

Kargon stepped aside to reveal a rectangular shelf carved into the stone wall. There, at its centre, sat a small wooden display with what looked like a smooth lump of glistening crystal gripped between iron claws. Its surface was partially concealed by thin veins of Demetrium that snaked around its curves.

"Take it," Iskander challenged. "If you can."

Hadavad didn't move, his eyes shifting between the dark mage and the Obsidian Stone. On the brink of violence, Asher's mind settled into a sea of calm. Obviously the mages would trade spells, neither of which could harm him, though Lonan was ever under threat. The ranger would shove him aside first, pushing him out of immediate harm.

Merith would likely come for him, wishing to take the ring from his finger as a gift for his master. To slow him, Asher decided he would launch his dagger into the Vorska's path. It would give him a second or two, nothing more, but it might be enough to put himself between the Blood Fiend and Hadavad, granting the mage more time to counter Iskander's spells.

From there it would be bloody violence to the bitter end.

"That is no Skaramangian Stone," Hadavad said boldly, his words replacing the predicted violence.

Kargon's mouth contorted, his already hard features taking on a sharper edge.

"'Tis a poor man's imitation," Hadavad continued. "Nothing more."

"I have made my *own* Obsidian Stone," Iskander boasted. "It possesses all the power of a Skaramangian Stone and, what's more, it obeys only me."

"You can't *make* your own," Hadavad protested. "Not with all the Demetrium in Verda can this be done. Whatever powers forged those stones no longer exist on this plane. It cannot be replicated by some *greedy* mage in a *cave*. Nevertheless, I would assume that anything you create is simply dangerous. *Evil*," he added with a glance thrown at Merith. "I will not stand for it. Your great *work* goes no further."

Iskander displayed a wicked smile. "My great work might have something to say about that."

Asher followed the dark mage's gaze out across the expanse where, from their lofty vantage, they could see the entrance to the cavern. Stalking out of the shadows was a black hulking beast of pure muscle and rage, its amber eyes leading the way.

Creed.

Quite impressively, he didn't make a sound as he emerged, and with a smaller Russell beside him. Creed let loose a low rumbling growl that reverberated around the cavern; a wordless threat.

"It has been years since I have laid eyes on one," Kargon said, marvelling as he edged towards the lip of their higher tier. "Even I didn't realise they could get so big. Don't you love it when your creation takes on a life of its own?" he asked, turning back to Hadavad. "And with that," he went on, indicating the black stone on display, "I will continue to remould the world as I have the flesh."

"They'll kill us all before you do anything," Hadavad spoke quickly, his attention now split between the dark mage and the monsters. Even Merith had taken a step back in sight of the towering Creed.

"Is that so?" Keeping his arm low, Iskander slowly twisted his wrist, curling his wand through the air.

Before them all, the wolves began to transform. Bones broke and shrank. Muscles spasmed and coiled. Their skin paled and masses of hair fell away. The beasts howled and roared with pain until their cries became human, leaving Creed and Russell on all fours, sweating and panting.

"You see?" Kargon was beaming with pride. "They are *all* mine." With that, the dark mage flourished his wand and the transformation began anew, filling the cavern with their screams. Taking advantage of the turmoil, Iskander turned to look directly at Asher. "Bring me this artefact," he commanded.

It took the ranger a precious second to realise the order had been for Merith, who was already moving at speed to close the gap. The Vorska was reaching out, strong pale hands preparing to yank his fingers off if that's what it took. For the first time, however, having a companion who knew of the gem and its protective properties worked in Asher's favour.

There was no need for finesse on Hadavad's part, his spell cast broadly and with enough kick to upturn the table, hurl Merith into the air, and even crack a segment of stone wall that gave the rough workshop its shape. No more than Asher's hair and cloak were affected by the magic.

Just as the mage had been quick to act, so too had Kargon Iskander, his wand already levelled at Hadavad. Before Merith had even landed, a staccato of lightning had burst forth from the wand. Who could say whether the power of that spell would have been enough to kill Hadavad, but Asher knew it wouldn't be enough to kill him. A heartbeat, perhaps less, was all the time the ranger had and he used it well. In one smooth motion, he pivoted and roughly pulled the mage into him by his robes. When the lightning reached its end it found only Asher's back.

Iskander was staring intently at the ranger. "An offering indeed," he said absently, a hungry look about him now.

Asher didn't hesitate. The silvyr blade left his hand, launched as he turned to face the dark mage. The weapon's trajectory was unquestionable—Kargon Iskander was going to be impaled through the chest, and with a killing blow. His magic might have saved him had his mind been quicker than the reflexes of an Arakesh.

And yet...

The dark mage was saved by a descendant of his creation. Creed had leapt up in a single bound and barrelled into the space between wizard and ranger. The entire length of silvyr drove deep into the giant wolf's arm. Whether it truly hurt or not, the shock of injury was enough to send the beast off balance. In a bid to regain his footing, Creed threw out his uninjured arm, a massive trunk of muscle that overshot and slammed awkwardly into the stone wall. Five claws, each comparable to butchers knives, raked fresh grooves down the rock.

It only took one claw to disturb the makeshift Obsidian Stone and cast it from the display.

Asher found it hard to make sense of what happened next. There had been a blinding flash and release of energy, perhaps even lightning. The noise, at an unbelievably low pitch, had been just as significant as a blade cutting through flesh as it tore through the expanse and robbed it of all sound. Adding to his disorientation, the ranger was lying face down in a completely different part of the cavern.

His nose was the first to bring him any kind of information he could assimilate. Burning hair. Charred skin. He followed the smell and soon found its source. Creed was thirty yards away and slowly rising from the ground. The wolf's previously uninjured arm could no longer boast such a thing, the limb severely burnt, exposing the muscle as far up as his shoulder. On the same side, where he had been so close to the makeshift stone, his face was smoking and disfigured.

Steadily enough, the ranger's mind put events together. Iskander's stone—a truly unstable thing—had not reacted well to its displacement and exerted a portion of its power. Creed had taken the brunt of that force, so much so that he had likely saved them all from similar burns. His considerable size, however, could not be avoided. Asher looked up at the ledge above, where he had recently been standing, and envisioned the enormous wolf slamming into him, sending them both to their current positions.

What was left of the stone remained to be seen and, though it was not a true Skaramangian Stone, Asher decided its complete destruction was a priority.

The ranger might have retraced his steps and discovered the stone's fate had his path not been blocked. With Creed at his back now, Asher faced the other Werewolf in the cavern: Russell. Though small compared to the anomalous Creed, Russell Maybury was undoubtedly large amongst his kind. On two legs, with no sign of injury and his fingers splayed and claws ready, he focused on the ranger.

Fearing any sudden movements would send the wolf into a frenzy, Asher maintained eye contact with Russell while his right hand moved slowly across his waist in search of the dormant broadsword. The moment his fingers coiled around the familiar leather, the wolf started forward. Despite his human speed being no match against his foe, the ranger continued to draw his sword, his only hope of battling the beast.

The ranger was granted more time, however, as Lonan leapt from the stone steps, sword held high. The edge of his blade bit deep between Russell's shoulder blades and slid down his back, splitting the tough hide to his waist. The wolf howled as if he could see the moon, his throat exposed. What Russell could no longer see was the ranger freeing his broadsword entirely. One clean swing would open the arteries in his neck, a blow even a mighty Were-wolf could not recover from. That would be the end of Russell Maybury.

No time to consider his options with any real thought, Asher acted as he always did: on instinct. He brought the weapon to bear in a two-handed swipe that scored a red gash across his oppo-nent's mottled chest.

Sensing a wild counterattack, the ranger turned his swinging motion into a drop and roll. The manoeuvre saved his life, but not because he evaded Russell's incoming claws. Creed, in all his immensity, had leapt at Asher from behind and crashed into Maybury, taking them both across the cavern in a violent tumble of limbs. Lonan should have been crushed by the ramming power of two Werewolves, a fact he survived only by having still been in a crouch following his jump from the steps. Instead, he was clipped by Russell's legs and taken in by the chaos for no more than a second before being ejected and thrown across the stone.

Iskander's voice cried out from above and Hadavad grunted as more explosions of light and sound erupted between the warring mages. Debris was sent flying in every direction and the ground was shaken by their battle. If only, Asher thought, he could get in the middle of their fight he could use his immunity to extinguish Kargon's threat and free Hadavad to unleash his magic on Creed.

That left one monster from his calculations.

As the ranger made for the stone steps, Merith deftly bounded between the various walls and protrusions of rock to bar his way. The Vorska was absent his familiar smile now, his jaws stretching to reveal fangs. Cold and predatory eyes glanced at Asher's right hand.

No words passed between them, they who collided with steel and grit.

Their dance lasted only seconds, neither scoring a blow, before Creed and Russell fell upon them. While they recognised Iskander's power, the same could not be said of the dark mage's other servants. Merith was forced to dart away and flee just as Asher was. The ranger leapt from the edge of his current level and caught one of the hanging chains while the Vorska dropped and skidded down a slope that had been smoothed after untold years beneath a shallow stream.

Russell peeled away in pursuit of Asher, missing the ranger by inches as he swung his legs to carry him further on the chain. The wolf landed on the floor below but his speed took him through one of Kargon's workstations. The wooden table was reduced to splinters and the numerous glass vials and bubbling pots scattered across the stone. There came a brief but small explosion as the potions mixed and, ultimately, set the remaining pieces of the table alight. The flames were enough to force Russell from his path, granting Asher the much-needed time to reach out and climb over the rail of the bridge above.

Not far away, Merith was weaving between supply boxes, jumping over jutting rocks, and sliding under tables to evade Creed. The burnt Werewolf paid no heed to anything man-made, his strength more than enough to destroy it all and pave his own path. More than once he nearly caught the Blood Fiend with an extended arm, but Merith had centuries of skill to call upon, keeping him just ahead of his opponent.

Inevitably, the Vorska found his way back up and was rushing towards Asher on the same bridge. The ranger was first to lash out this time, cleaving his broadsword high and across. Merith curled his body to the side and narrowly evaded the edge of steel, only to snap back and bring his sword down over Asher's shoulder. With the footwork of an Arakesh embedded deep in his muscles' memory, the ranger was able to dodge the counterattack and respond with one of his own.

Merith's head snapped back as the broadsword chopped up into one side of his jaw and exited via his cheek. Feeling no pain, the Vorska was merely knocked back a step.

"Something to remember me by," Asher remarked, twisting the blade that Iskander had firmly planted in Merith's hopes.

The Blood Fiend sneered even as the wound closed up. He raised his sword to attack but their fight was, once again, interrupted by other monsters. Creed brought the wooden bridge down with both hands, the structure no match for his weight. Merith didn't even try to save himself but, instead, used his fall to lash out with his blade and score a gash down Creed's torso. The wolf roared, a deafening sound that momentarily drowned out the clashing mages.

Asher glimpsed it all as he made his jump back to the same hanging chain. This time, the ranger held on and turned his attention to the stone bridge above. He tossed his broadsword up and began the arduous climb to put more distance between him and Iskander's monsters. Russell attempted a vertical leap to hook his claws into flesh but even his considerable strength couldn't close the gap.

Atop the new bridge, his weapon was soon back in hand, the steel scraping across the stone as he rose to his feet. Looking over the edge, he could see Merith darting in and out of Creed's attacks while simultaneously striking the wolf's legs and hips. The Vorska erred, however, upon scaling the behemoth's back and plunging his blade into thick muscle. Creed growled and shook the Blood Fiend free, where he was then able to snatch the creature from the ground and slam him into a jagged wall.

The gruesome scene couldn't occupy Asher for Russell was his main concern. The young Werewolf was bounding round the cavern walls, circling to where Lonan was still picking himself up. Asher called out to the man in a bid to warn him, but the litany of spells being exchanged between the mages kept his words at bay.

The ranger wasted no time, dropping his sword and retrieving his bow. The limbs snapped to life and the string gladly accepted the arrow he nocked. With his thumb pressed into his cheek, just below his right eye, Asher tracked Russell's progress and, more specifically, his impressive speed. Sure of his aim, he released the arrow to a sharp whistle. He missed by an inch, the arrowhead bouncing off the stone wall beside the wolf's left hand. Still, it was enough to divert the beast's attention and bring it to a halt on one of the natural ledges.

Amber eyes soon found him.

By then, the ranger had already nocked a second arrow and let the missile fly. It penetrated Russell's thigh and shot through to the other side, eliciting a pained roar from the wolf.

"Come and get me," Asher bade, replacing his bow and flicking the broadsword up by the toe of his boot.

Lonan was looking up at him now. "I'm coming up there!" he shouted, his words finding just enough of a gap between spells.

"No!" Asher yelled back, waving his hand to convey his meaning. "Find the stone!" he instructed, pointing at the workstation from which he had been thrown. "Find the stone! We have to destroy it!"

It was too late to say any more. Russell had found an unconventional way up, but a way up all the same. The wolf now prowled along the bridge towards him, wary, perhaps, of the human who had successfully injured it several times. Asher nearly opened his mouth to speak, to try and communicate with any part of the monster that might still be Russell, but what was the use? There was nothing about the man behind those amber eyes, not while the full moon reigned. Not while Kargon Iskander lived to transform them at will.

The wolf barrelled towards him, convinced it had all the advantage it needed. Asher held back his swinging attack and threw the vial from his belt. It struck Russell across the snout and smashed, filling the air around his nose with a cloud of yellow safida spice. In the Lycan form, his sense of smell was magnitudes beyond that of his human self and the wolf inhaled much of it.

The Werewolf skidded and staggered out of its run, head shaking to rid itself of the potent scent. Asher had planned to step in and drive his attack but he was beaten to it. Merith appeared from behind Russell's masking bulk. The Vorska gripped him by wrist and throat and shoved the wolf from the bridge, casting him back to the lowest tier of the cavern.

"I'll be taking that ring now," he stated.

Asher desperately wanted to find Russell below and discover his fate, unsure if such a fall could kill a Werewolf, but Merith was on him, sword whipping high and low. Pushed back, Asher deflected and blocked between his own counters and misdirects. Merith, of course, met every strike of steel, his reflexes and experience superior to the ranger's. This was a point the Vorska drove home when he ran his blade across Asher's thigh, dropping him to one knee, where he then thrust a boot into his face.

"Don't bother getting up," Merith voiced upon his approach. "I'll just take the whole hand and be on my way."

Asher felt a cold hand snatch at the base of his wrist and a strong tug to stretch his arm out. His face already felt swollen from the kick and one of his eyes refused to open. He could barely spy the Vorska even as he crouched over him. Still, he knew roughly where his enemy was positioned and, more importantly, his legs were working.

Like a snake, Asher flicked one leg up and coiled it around Merith's midriff. It was enough to give the creature pause, his blade held high to sever the ranger's hand, but Asher's sudden twist was enough to send them both over the edge of the bridge.

They dropped ten feet before they impacted the next bridge. Being made of wood, the boards instantly gave way and the pair continued their descent amidst dust and debris. Somewhere in the fall, Asher had the good sense to roll his body around Merith's, positioning himself on top of the Vorska. It still hurt like hell when they slammed into an outcropping of rock from the west wall of the cavern. It was a relatively flat plateau, but they had landed so close to its edge that Asher was cast off Merith and sent plummeting once again.

He was embraced by water so cold it could have been mistaken for ice. Its depths claimed him, robbing him of sight and sound.

It was in that darkness that the ranger found clarity.

The Nightseye elixir in his veins was excited by the abyss and so connected him to the cavern beyond. He knew immediately that he was sinking into the depths of a small pool and that he alone occupied it.

He could taste his own blood in the water. It seeped in from his mouth, cuts on his hands, a gash on his head, and the incision to his recently wounded thigh. The temperature of the water kept his pain at bay for the time, though it would undoubtedly return. As he listened to his senses, the ranger closed his right fist and allowed the black gem to fill his body with warm healing.

At last, he could picture the cavern in its entirety. While it rose up from the main entrance, it was also separated from the eastern wall by a chasm at least a hundred feet across. So deep was it that even his enhanced senses couldn't fathom the distance.

He found Merith next, not too far above him. The Blood Fiend was already rising from his fall and healing well. He only had until sunrise, of course, before he felt that impact all over again.

Russell was surprisingly close as well. The wolf was in the

process of recovering from its own fall. How strange it was to hear bones re-forming at speed instead of breaking under pressure.

Lonan's ragged breathing soon gave his position away to Asher. Crouched behind an upended table, it seemed he was observing the duel between Hadavad and Iskander. Not observing. Waiting. Asher could feel the volatile stone in his hand. He had found it! If he was waiting for the opportune moment to hurl it, he was out of time.

Creed too had found him.

The massive Werewolf slowly advanced on two feet, lending him all the terrifying height he had to offer. Lonan naturally began to retreat, his backward steps taking him directly towards the eastern wall, towards the chasm.

Asher kicked his feet and burst from the water. Made whole again, his muscles responded with pain-free ease. His senses returned to that of an ordinary man, he unclipped his soaking green cloak and left it where it fell. The broadsword was gone, lost in the fall and nowhere in sight. The same could not be said of his silvyr blade, the short-sword dislodged from its place in Creed's arm when he rammed into Russell.

The ranger scooped the weapon up as he rounded the jagged rise in the natural rock. There he saw the back of Creed, a wall of dark muscle and charred flesh, as he continued to push Lonan towards the chasm. Russell appeared from behind one of the walls hewn by Iskander's magic, the wolf eager to join its maker and share in the kill.

Asher realised all too late that the cacophony of spells had ceased.

"STOP!" Kargon bellowed, his voice amplified by magic.

The wolves froze.

Lonan halted his retreat, still oblivious to the drop behind him.

Merith was suspiciously absent.

Hadavad was on his knees, beaten, bleeding, and out of breath. Iskander's wand was pointed at his head, the tip pressing into his temple.

Not looking nearly so dishevelled as Hadavad, Kargon levitated his defeated opponent and descended the steps beside him. There was pain in Hadavad's expression, as if the spell that lifted him did far more than simply move him. The two mages joined the others, Iskander sparing the ranger a mere glance before focusing on Lonan.

"You have something that belongs to me," the dark mage stated. "Give it to me or I will have the big one here eat you *feet first*." Asher started forward but Kargon turned his head over one shoulder. "You might be immune to my magic, but this one is not. Another step and your friend here will have an extra hole in his head." By then, Iskander had lowered Hadavad back to his knees, where he might destroy him with no more than a flick of the wrist. "Merith?" he questioned.

On cue, the Vorska seemed to materialise at Asher's side, his blade held at arm's length to rest against the ranger's throat. "I have him, Master."

Asher eyed the Blood Fiend, intending to convey his fury by expression alone, when the ranger noticed something. Merith's fingers, the ones gripping his sword, were slowly decaying, the knuckles flaking, leaving raw bone behind.

Somewhere beyond the deep dark of that hell, the sun was rising.

The revelation turned Asher back to Russell and Creed.

While Creed maintained his imposing and monstrous physique, Russell's Lycan form began show signs of deterioration. It was subtle at first, a hand spasming, a twitch of the head. Then he retreated somewhat from his pack leader. Soon they would be human and Merith would be a quivering wreck, a product of his new wounds. It would be the only advantage they had against Iskander, but Asher knew he would have to act quickly before the dark mage used his power to transform them back.

"Carefully now," Kargon purred, one hand held out to Lonan. "You've seen what happens when it is mishandled. Put it down and I will permit you, and you alone, to leave this place."

Glassy eyed, Lonan was fighting his fear. "You're going to kill us whatever I do," he reasoned.

Iskander dropped his facade. "Put it down *carefully*," he reiterated, tone full of malice, "and you will feel no pain in death. Defy me... and I won't *let* you die."

Lonan looked past the dark mage and found Asher's eyes. The ranger purposefully looked at the stone in his companion's hand before then looking up. Lonan did the same, his brow pinching in thought as he made sense of Asher's command. The ranger was willing him to do it, to do it now before the insane mage lost his sense of calm. Time was also running down for Russell and Merith, the former now leaning against a rock as his body searched for its original shape, and the latter's neck was slowly turning black and red from preserved injury.

The moment arrived when Merith showed the first sign of pain. At the same time, his grip on the sword faltered and the ranger felt the weight of the blade on his shoulder. It was now or never.

Asher exploded into action. He had only to bat the Vorska's weapon aside and the creature lost his grip altogether until he and the blade fell to the ground, his agony undeniable. Before he hit the floor, the ranger had started for Lonan at a sprint. At the same time, splitting the attention of both Iskander and the hulking Creed, the former captain of the watch tossed the makeshift stone into the air, just as Asher had indicated.

Kargon's gaze snapped up to locate his precious stone. Hadavad—ever the opportunist—reacted as Asher had predicted and used the distraction to tackle the dark mage to the ground. By then, the ranger was running past them, keeping himself in line with the descending stone. If it landed, they would all likely die.

But...

If he caught it, Asher could ensure that only one had to die. Like so many times before when dealing with these monsters, speed was his problem. Creed had determined that he was to taste the ranger's flesh and was preparing to leap at him. One bound and he would close the gap before Asher could grasp the falling stone.

It was then that one ranger became two.

Russell Maybury leapt onto Creed's back and managed to wrap his arms around the monster's throat. The enormous Werewolf arched up and back and raked a set of claws down Russell's shoulder and ribs, but still the miner from Snowfell held on. It gave Asher all the time he needed to skid on his knees and catch the falling stone. In the same smooth motion, the ranger threw the stone underarm. His target was hard to miss.

Striking Creed's slab of a chest, the stone reacted violently, sucking all the sound out of the cavern as it ruptured and released the terrible energy Iskander had forced inside.

The resultant light was blinding, but Asher still managed to glimpse both Creed and Russell being expelled from the edge and into the chasm before the shock wave blasted him back. Lonan had maintained enough sense to dive out of the way before Asher had even thrown the stone, and was now blinking hard to regain his vision.

"Russell," Asher breathed, staggering to his feet.

The ranger fell to all fours as he reached the edge. He was already imagining Russell falling into that yawning abyss, claimed by darkness before the inevitable and most sudden stop. And he would have to return to Doran and tell him the worst.

But Russell Maybury was not so easily killed.

"Russell!" Asher blurted, discovering the man pressed against the stone, his fingers pinched on subtle holds.

The ranger didn't ask him if he needed help but simply reached out and grabbed one of his arms. Together, they worked to get him back on solid ground.

Panting, Asher almost laughed in disbelief, if nothing else. His smile dropped away when he noted Russell looking past him, his features hard as stone.

"You..." Iskander's voice was ragged. "You... DESTROYED IT! My life's work went into that! Decades! Years trapped in *here* so I might finish it! I could have used that to change the world!"

Asher was barely listening to him as he found his feet. Instead, he was assessing Hadavad who was struggling even to pick himself up on all fours. Further still was Merith, his limp body quivering on the cold stone.

"You!" Kargon raged, wand coming up to point at Asher. "You should have remained insignificant," he seethed.

"You can't hurt me," Asher reminded him, his silvyr blade twisting threateningly in his grip.

"But he can," Iskander replied smugly, his wand shifting slightly to point at Russell.

The ranger held his weapon firmly now. "He won't even have claws before my blade finds your heart."

Seeing the truth of this, the dark mage shifted his wand again, aiming it now at Lonan. "Then I will turn him inside out," he imperilled. "Drop your sword!" he barked. "Now! And remove the ring," Iskander added, his smile spreading.

Asher's lips parted to give his blunt response, but he decided to wait. After all, he had seen that look in a man's eyes before; the look of quiet and righteous rage. He saw it now in Merith.

The Vorska assaulted his master from behind. One hand twisted his head aside, exposing his throat, while the other grappled the wrist that controlled the wand. Helpless and surprised, Kargon Iskander was no more than prey to the very predator he had created.

Fangs like a viper's sank deep into the dark mage's neck and the Vorska's hideous tongue bathed in blood. So terribly disfigured as he was, the blood ran into the fiend's throat before pouring out of deep gashes, soaking him red. Iskander moaned and thrashed but he was losing blood faster than had he simply been stabbed. He was soon too weak to remain on his feet and Merith crouched with him, gorging all the while.

Rather than drain him of his last drop, the ancient Vorska peeled his mouth away and, with one hand, snapped his master's neck. Like a rag doll, the dark mage fell to the ground, dead.

On his knees, Merith looked up but failed to meet any of their eyes. "Everlasting torment," he whispered. "Those were his... *intentions.*"

Not far from the creature, Hadavad was, at last, on his feet. He had risen with Kargon's wand in hand. "Whatever slight you feel," the mage said. "Whatever life you believe you were cheated of. It does not excuse the atrocities you have spent eight long centuries committing."

Merith tilted his head but could not look directly upon Hadavad. "For once, old man," he rasped, "we agree." The Vorska took a breath, his charred lips moving to speak. "Do—"

He never finished his instruction, not before Hadavad blew his head from his shoulders. So weak and damaged was his skull that it struck the ground as no more than bloody mulch. His headless body followed soon after, finding its resting place on the cold stone beside its dead maker.

"It is finished," Hadavad declared, and he allowed himself to slump against the nearest wall.

"Not yet," Lonan replied.

By his voice alone, Asher knew there was to be more violence, but he was too far away to put himself between the former captain and Russell.

Completely naked, Maybury had naught but his hands to defend himself, though his strength was more than ample to do so. As Lonan came in, his sword swinging from high to low across Russell's head, the Lycan ranger knocked the flat of the blade aside using his knuckles. But Lonan came in again, striking at his chest this time. Russell had managed to step back before the weapon fell upon him but the tip still succeeded in slicing a bloody line down his torso.

Pain was the quickest route to rage.

Maybury growled and advanced, a wall of muscle and fury that Lonan couldn't hope to stand against. With one hand, Russell squeezed Lonan's sword arm until his grip flowered open and the blade clattered against the stone.

"Russell!" Asher snapped, coming to a stop beside him.

By then, the big man had taken the former captain by the throat and lifted him from the ground. The ranger's hand naturally went for the safida spices that were no longer on his belt. Asher swore and placed a firm grip around Russell's arm, though there was definitely no budging it. The arm might as well have been a log.

"Russell," Asher hissed, seeing Lonan's face changing colour.

The ranger was all-too aware of the silvyr blade in his other hand. Being so close, he had only to thrust and Maybury would be dead before he hit the ground. Light as it was, the weight of it was pressing upon him. If he was going to use it he needed to use it now, before Russell killed the former captain. It was one thing to kill as the wolf, but Asher would not tolerate the same from the man.

"Russell!" he growled, the tip of his silvyr blade coming up to point at the gap between his ribs. "Remember who—"

Lonan fell to the ground, his legs crumpling beneath him.

While he lay coughing and rubbing his throat, Russell was backing away, his chest slowly rising with deep breaths. "I know who I am," he said, voice catching. "I know who I am."

"You're a *monster*," Lonan managed. "Nothing can change that."

"Lonan." Asher's tone was a command to silence, but the former captain was beyond rebuke now.

"*You* were supposed to kill him," he rasped, rising unsteadily. "It might be your job to kill monsters, but it's my *duty* to kill them. Captain or not, I swore an oath to protect my people. I took it seriously then and I do to this very day. I even gave up family to uphold the laws of my country. He *must* die."

"Russell is walking out of here with the rest of us," Asher told him. Affirming the ranger's bold position, Hadavad walked over to join him, wand still in hand.

Lonan looked over the three of them. He knew he was no match for any one of them—his expression said as much. But how would he react in defeat? Asher didn't know him well enough to predict his actions beyond that of an honourable man. It seemed now, however, that his honour had taken him too far.

"You're really going to let him live?" Lonan questioned incredulously. "A Werewolf!"

"He's earned his right to live," Asher replied. "He could have killed you. But he didn't. He *chose* not to. That's not a monster in my books."

Lonan's shoulders slumped and he sighed as defeat set in. He looked down at the sword he had dropped. Asher was willing him not to pick it up. There had been enough blood and death for one day. Still, if he had to, he would defend Russell's life by taking another.

The former captain tore his gaze from the weapon. Instead, he walked over to the edge of the cavern and found the abyss that awaited any unfortunate enough to lose their footing.

"Lonan?" The ranger couldn't gauge the man.

"You might be able to live with letting monsters roam free," he said, turning so his heels were flush with the lip of the cavern, "but I can't. And if I can't kill that monster, I'll have to settle for killing another."

Asher frowned in confusion. "Lonan," he said warily.

The former captain raised his left arm and turned it over, revealing a bloody injury. Asher didn't need to inspect it up close to recognise the exact nature of that injury. Lonan had been bitten by a Werewolf.

"I've got what? A month? I've seen what awaits me then. I've seen the victims too. I won't do that—I won't *let* that happen!"

The ranger changed his approach and sheathed the silvyr blade over his back. "Lonan, you don't need to do this," he began, glancing at the chasm beyond. "There are other ways, ways to live with it. You saw Russell, his *control*. You can achieve the same."

"Bandaging a wound doesn't stop it from killing you," Lonan retorted.

"You don't have to do this," the ranger reiterated. "Come away from the edge and we can find a way; all of us, together."

"I swore an oath," Lonan repeated, his head held a little higher. "I would protect the people against any and all... even myself. The men who died here tonight swore the same oath. They were all heroes. I would have them remembered as such." The former captain swallowed, considering his next, if not final, words. "An honourable death is a good death," he said.

Asher had disagreed with Lonan the first time he had said as much, when they had fled Elias's first and only transformation so many weeks ago. The ranger had told him there were no honourable deaths. Whether he still agreed with that statement or not, Asher could see that there was nothing he could do or say to stop the man from doing what he thought was right. And so he nodded, granting the captain whatever form of closure he could.

Lonan let his weight take him back and the void took him in its hold, pulling him down.

By the time Asher reached the edge, Lonan had been wholly claimed by the darkness and taken from sight. The guilt was almost immediate. His intervention had brought the group of watchmen into the mountain. He knew that for years to come he would remind himself that they each chose to accompany him. That they had not been forced into the path of monsters. But they were still dead—all of them—because they had met him.

"Asher." It was Russell's voice that brought him back from the edge; in more ways than one. "He's gone."

"He lived by his oath to the very end," Hadavad commented. "A true warrior of the people."

Asher was sure he would come to see it that way but, right now, his nerves were somewhat raw. The ranger gave no reply on the matter. "Iskander is dead. The stone is destroyed. Let us leave this hell behind."

"I quite agree," Hadavad said. "Though I would not leave it to be found again."

Upon reclaiming his staff, the mage joined Asher and Russell by the entrance. Maybury had discovered the area within the cavern that had been used by Iskander to store crates and chests of clothing. Kargon's impressive height worked in Russell's favour, allowing him to dress not only from head to toe but also don a cloak.

Asher didn't even bother searching for his broadsword—he just wanted to leave.

"Here ends the threat of Kargon Iskander," Hadavad

announced. With that, the mage aimed his staff at the cavern's arching ceiling and unleashed his magic.

The expanse was filled with the sound of cracking stone and raining dust. The trio required no encouragement to run back through the tunnel and escape the cave-in. They reached the top of the previously hidden steps as a great dust cloud rushed out from the tunnel.

Now it was finished.

CHAPTER 35
HOME

Lizard Folk - *I have had to fight hard to have these monsters included in this edition. My fellow rangers believe me mad, delusional. They tell me the heat of The Arid Lands got to my mind.*
I saw them.
Tall as men they were and damned if they didn't walk like us too. There was no mistaking what they were, however. The Lizard Folk of The Narrows are real. Some of them were even wearing clothes I tell you. Long tails dragged behind every one of them and their claws were curved and sharp. I know what I saw. Heard too. They could talk to each other, coordinate and the like. I'm sure as hell never taking a contract that takes me anywhere near The Narrows.

A Chronicle of Monsters: A Ranger's Bestiary, 12th Edition, Page 489.

Old Ned, Ranger.

Covered in dirt and blood, Asher and Hadavad stood before General Crem—a picture of exhaustion. The general had looked them up and down many times during their report, so much of which had been deliberately withheld. The important part—as far as the old soldier was concerned —was the deaths of the Werewolves.

As expected, they weren't compensated nearly as much as the general had promised, citing the lack of any real evidence as his reasoning.

Asher didn't much care. He accepted the coin without protest and immediately turned to Secretary Royce. "See this divided up and given to the families of the watchmen," he instructed. With the exception of Hadavad, there wasn't a man in the room who didn't look surprised at that.

Royce's expression suggested he was reassessing Asher, if not rangers in general, as he accepted the coin. "I will see it done," he assured.

"*Captain* Lonan," Asher emphasised, "died a hero. He should be remembered as such and granted all the funeral rights of his station."

The secretary didn't have the power to agree to those terms and so naturally looked to General Crem, the soon-to-be lord of Kelp Town no doubt. He gave it no more than a moment's thought before nodding his head.

"Then our business is concluded," Asher decreed.

"So it is," Crem confirmed, for only he could dismiss them.

With Hadavad by his side, Asher was happily escorted from Stormwood Manor. He cared nothing for the politicking of men and the schemes of kings, just as he cared nothing for Lord Kernat and whatever fate awaited the man. It would no doubt be a comfortable retirement that few in all of Verda ever enjoyed. The ranger just wanted to put Kelp Town behind him and let The Ice Vales continue as it would.

To his dismay, however, Russell was not where he had left him. The big man should have been seated on the small wall at the base of the manor steps, his frame concealed within his new cloak and face hidden by the hood.

"He can't be seen here," Asher warned.

"Then find him quickly," Hadavad advised. "I will fetch the horses and meet you beyond the entrance."

The ranger handed the mage his stable token so he might collect Hector. "I won't be long," he promised, sure that he knew where to find Maybury.

～

"I thought I told you," Asher said, "Russell Hobbs is dead."

Seated on his old bed, Russell mustered half a smile. "That he is," the big man agreed.

The ranger moved further into the small dwelling, his breath misting the air. "We should go," he insisted. "Kelp Town holds nothing for either of us now."

Russell nodded along. "I know," he replied sombrely.

Asher folded his arms and leant against the same frame in which he had previously discovered the bronze orb. "You did well," he complimented, if quietly so. Garnering a look from his companion, Asher elaborated. "You could have killed Lonan."

"Didn't I?"

"You are no more responsible for his death than I am," Asher replied, though he was still struggling himself with the latter. "Lonan's path was his own to walk. That's what we have to do now."

"Back to Lirian?"

The ranger gave a subtle nod. "Back to Lirian," he agreed.

Russell stood up, the top of his head not that far from the ceiling. "I just have one stop to make first."

Asher's attention was drawn to the small rectangular chest in Russell's hands. "What's that?"

"My savings," he answered. "They didn't find it after all. I suppose they never thought to check the privy," he added with some amusement.

With no further explanation, the big man made for the door, pausing only to fix his hood in place. Asher walked with him, content to follow rather than ask questions. They didn't traverse the town for very long before arriving at the intended destination. Asher knew the house having been inside it himself and hung back to watch from across the street.

Russell placed the small chest at the base of the door. He hesitated. Then he knocked twice. Of course, he was not to be recognised and so, before the door could be answered, Maybury walked away and vanished down the nearest alleyway. Asher observed a while longer, until the door was answered by Saski, the widow of watchman Elias. The ranger glimpsed the rough shape of a child behind her legs but never saw her face. Saski looked around, confused, her eyes darting from passerby to passerby. She eventually picked up the chest and opened the lid no more than an inch. Her jaw dropped and tears welled in her eyes.

Asher had seen enough. He peeled away from the corner and took off in Russell's footsteps. He soon caught up with the man and they walked under the arch of Kelp Town's main entrance. The armoured soldiers recognised them from earlier that morning and let them leave without issue. Further out, they spied Hadavad on the flat icy plain and with the two horses.

"That was a good thing you did back there," Asher told him. "Most would have kept the coin."

"You didn't," Russell pointed out.

Asher considered the statement. "We aren't most men," he reasoned, allowing them to share a brief laugh. His own wording, however, made the ranger think of other ways in which he had clumped them together in his mind. "I owe you an explanation," he began tentatively. They walked side by side a little longer before he was able to voice his thoughts. "I didn't just bring you into this life because I thought you deserved a second chance." The ranger took a breath, battling any vulnerability he might feel. "I thought that, by extension of my mercy, you would do good in the world on my behalf. That you might atone *for* me. That won't make sense to you and it doesn't have to. But it was selfish—dangerous even."

Asher wanted to go on and tell his companion how he had believed they were the same, that if Russell could overcome his monster then so too could he. But without knowing about the life Asher had come from, it would make even less sense than why he might atone on his behalf. Perhaps that was to be a revelation for himself alone. They weren't climbing the same mountain, but that didn't mean they wouldn't reach the top somehow.

Asher didn't know what to do with hope, and so he buried it for the time being and focused on the present.

"I am thankful," he continued, "that despite my failings, you have prevailed. The lives you have saved... the lives you're *going* to save; they are credited to you alone."

Russell took it all in as they crossed the hard ground. "I thank you for your honesty but, regardless of your reasons, you will always have my thanks. How could you not? Your actions speak louder than your intentions. You have fought with me. You have fought *for* me. In return, you can always count on me to do the same."

Asher appreciated the words as well as the brotherly pat on his shoulder.

"Though," Russell added, drawing the word out. "I would know why one so inherently good as yourself needs to atone—if you would share."

Asher almost scoffed. "Inherently good," he echoed, a description he would never assign to himself. Still, he looked up at Russell and saw not a man nor beast but a *friend*. "Perhaps I will tell you on our way home," he decided.

"Home?" Russell questioned, a word he had likely never expected to hear from the ranger.

Asher considered where they were going and what he had in mind for it. "Home," he said.

∽

Lirian was right where they had left it, nestled in the heart of The Evermoore mid-winter. Smoke rose from chimneys and snow fell lightly upon rooftops. After a week on the cold road, it was a welcome sight. Asher bid Russell and Hadavad make their way directly to The Ranch, where Danagarr and Doran anxiously awaited their return.

The ranger had another direction in mind.

Parting ways with them at the first crossroad, Asher rode Hector through the streets wearing the spare green cloak he always kept in one of his saddle bags. It collected snow all the way to the notaries' office, in the north-east district. It was there that he implemented the first stage of his plan.

From there, he made his own journey back to The Ranch, where the others had already reunited and begun to share their tales. Danagarr clapped forearms with him, a beaming smile of relief on his bearded face. Doran managed to limp across the room, refusing to be met sitting down. There came questions as to where he had been but the ranger successfully deflected them all. They were all just happy to be together again. Even the smith seemed to have forgotten Russell's curse.

"'Ere!" Danagarr called, motioning for all of them, though mostly Maybury, to look at the wall directly opposite the front door. "I knew ye was to be comin' back," he said. "I was sure o' it! So I made ye somethin', jus' as I've made these two somethin' in the past."

There, hanging horizontally on the wall, was a pick-axe. Unlike Russell's previous one, this had been forged by a dwarven smith and its wooden haft sat within a snaking vine of steel that connected to the head. It was certainly more weapon than tool.

"I don't know what to say," Russell uttered, bewitched by it.

"Ye don' 'ave to say anythin', big fella. Ye jus' 'ave to use it."

Maybury couldn't take his eyes off the weapon. "That I will," he promised. "Thank you, Danagarr."

"Ye're welcome, lad," the smith said with a wink.

"There'll be plenty o' time for usin' it," Doran remarked impatiently. "There's a few ales in that crate over there, Rus," he specified. "Let's celebrate, eh? We should all be dead given what we've gone through."

There were none who could argue with that logic, though Hadavad waved a dismissive hand. "It's a little early in the day for me."

"On yer own mage," the son of Dorain replied heartily. "There ain' no better breakfast than a Hobgobber's Ale, I say!"

Asher couldn't help but laugh. Gods help him, he had missed the blasted dwarf.

And so they drank and ate, and enjoyed what merriment they could. Barring Danagarr, theirs was a life of peril so who knew when they might next enjoy such company, and under a roof at that. It felt good, and encouraged Asher to enact his plan all the more.

It was a little while later, when the companions had acclimatised to each other again, that Asher found a quiet moment to speak with Russell alone.

"What's this?" Maybury asked, accepting the bound scroll from the ranger.

"It's the deeds to this place," Asher informed.

"The deeds?" Russell glanced at the parchment, somewhat bewildered. "Why are you giving it to *me?*"

"I can't legally *give* it to you," Asher said, repeating the explanation the notary had given him. "You're going to look after it for me. When we have the coin, you're going to turn this place into a *tavern.*"

"I am?" Russell asked, wide-eyed.

"You're bound to this place now," Asher went on, sparing a glance at the door that led down to the basement. "It needs to be more than a prison for you. You need to return here *and* leave here knowing who you are. With enough coin you can make that life you've always wanted. With every notch you put on that," he said, indicating the newly-forged weapon hanging on the wall, "you will get a little closer to making it real. I can help too—I need little coin."

Russell stumbled over any response, his attention flitting between the document in his hand and the man before him. "Asher that's... I cannot repay you... I... I have nothing to offer."

The ranger's warm smile had just the slightest hint of mischief behind it. "I have a few ideas I would see you implement. But that can wait," he reassured. "I would know, instead, what you might call a tavern of your own?"

Russell returned that same smile, his gaze turning to fall upon the pick-axe.

CHAPTER 36
THE ROAD TO LEGEND

Foreword - It has been my experience that these archives are better taken as guidelines and never hard facts. Read every page and read them well, but do not believe the monsters herein can be contained in these words alone.

Never underestimate your quarry. Always assume the monster has the advantage and always plan ahead. Rarely will you find that a good swing of steel will get the job done. Being a ranger requires more than that.

Strategy is everything. Be cunning. Use surprise. Keep your supplies stocked. Ensure your blade is sharp and, more importantly, ensure you have a second blade.

Finally, I would caution the blind belief that everything in this bestiary is a monster. That is to say, not every monster between these pages needs slaying.

Good hunting.

A Chronicle of Monsters: A Ranger's Bestiary, 13th Edition, Page 1.

Asher, Ranger.

. . .

S*ome Years Later...*

Serene was the word that came to mind as Asher made his way through the streets of Lirian. The city was never more beautiful to the ranger than during the spring months. The snows had thawed and the scent of new flowers lingered in the air with freshly-baked bread. On the cusp of summer, with the light of day stretching, the people of Lirian were full of palpable anticipation.

It was most welcome after dealing with the nest of Drayga beyond the city's borders. The vicious beasts had ripped his cloak to ribbons, scored his leathers, and, ultimately, claimed his sword, the blade lost to their swamp. Now, his skin smeared with filth and blood, he made a mockery of Lirian's serenity.

He was given a wide berth by any who caught his odour on the breeze and most looked upon him in horror. There was but one place, however, where he would fit in, a place where his malodour was no more than an addition to the general musk.

He heard it before he saw it.

The high-pitched squeal of a large pig. The smash of glass. The bang of a door as it was slammed open and the internal ruckus momentarily amplified.

"HEAVYBELLY!" Only Russell's voice could create such a *boom*.

Rounding the corner, the ranger spotted the culprit. The Warhog was dashing across the street, back to the stable, with a bottle of beer between its teeth. The sight of it brought a much-needed chuckle to Asher.

"I see some things never change," he remarked at Pig, before leaving Hector in the pen beside it. The Warhog was already lying on its side, lapping up the beer as it poured out of the bottle.

He tossed a coin to the stablehand and crossed the street, pausing only to read the sign that extended from the porch.

The Pick-Axe.

He ascended the steps towards that green door and pushed his way inside. As always, the tavern was busy. Every booth was taken and most of the tables in between were occupied. To his right, a small band were in the middle of setting up their instruments. The bar was lined almost from end to end with patrons, but Asher could still see the pick-axe that hung on the wall between dozens of bottles. He couldn't count all the notches scored into the haft.

It always brought a smile to his face.

"Asher!" Russell called cheerily from behind the bar. "I hate to think what they look like," he observed with amusement, taking in the ranger's ragged attire.

Asher hadn't left any of the Drayga intact, be it their limbs or torso, but he merely nodded in return. "I'll take a bath if you can spare the water."

"Of course," Russell replied. "There is a room too."

"I won't be needing it," the ranger reported, approaching the bar. "Just the bath. And a resupply," he added, thinking of his empty scabbard and ruined cloak.

"Danagarr sent a fresh supply through just last month. Your locker is stocked."

Asher thanked him with a nod and made to leave for the basement.

"Can I tempt you with a hot meal?" Maybury offered.

"Perhaps later," Asher answered, considering his current state.

"Oh no," came a familiar voice, turning the ranger's gaze to the side and down. "Ye're not goin' anywhere before buyin' a round! It's yer turn!"

"You struggle to remember what day it is," Asher countered, "but you can remember it's my round from six months ago?"

"Aye! Only the important things," Doran stated, tapping one finger against his temple. "And I'd hear a tale or two while ye're at it. Ye look like ye've got one to tell."

"Sort that damned pig out, Heavybelly!" Russell yelled over the patrons.

The dwarf waved him away. "The old wolf gets more cantankerous by the day," he opined, before motioning for Asher to follow him. "Come along then. I've got Salim an' a booth over there."

Asher searched beyond the son of Dorain and found the southerner with a cup of steaming tea in hand. They shared a nod of greetings from across the room before Asher began to notice the other rangers. Their numbers had picked up over the years and not all had been brought into the life by his doing.

From where he stood, he could see Kaleb Jordain, a disgraced Graycoat of all things. He had taken to the life of monster hunting with ease, though he might have found it all the easier had he not always carried a bottle of ale into battle.

Then there was Hadavad, of course, seated in the corner with a young woman—his latest apprentice no doubt. The mage caught his eye and offered no more than a flexed finger by way of greeting. It had been years since he had seen the mage, but whenever he did it was always in The Pick-Axe.

Rarely did they speak to each other, both abiding by some unspoken agreement. Asher couldn't put that agreement into words, though he knew it concerned the secrets they held. The mage knew of the black gem and the ranger knew of the Viridian Ruby. It was as if those secrets were better kept if they seldom came into contact with each other.

Seeing Hadavad guaranteed the ranger's thoughts would dwell on the black gem and its mysteries. It was an itch he couldn't scratch. It remained tethered to his first life, before Nightfall, though he couldn't fathom what that was. That didn't stop him from dreaming about it and the younger version of himself that was innocent. He desperately wanted to find that part of himself and knew the gem would lead him to it.

But where to start?

Asher couldn't answer that question and so he relied on the only course he had, the very same he had given himself years earlier, when he set out on the road in search of monsters.

Always forward.

"Glaide's about somewhere," Doran said, bringing Asher back

to his surroundings. "He'll be joinin' us soon. Best get 'im a pint too," he advised with a nudge from his elbow.

That lifted Asher's spirits all the more. He genuinely enjoyed the company of Jonus Glaide, a relatively new member to their unofficial order. "Should I just buy you a *keg*?"

Doran laughed. "I wouldn' complain, lad!" The dwarf waved over to Hadavad and his apprentice. "It's Asher's round! Come join us!"

The ranger could already feel his coin purse becoming lighter. "Why don't you invite the whole damn tavern, Heavybelly?"

"Ye're always breezin' in an' out with ne'er a word. Ye're goin' to join us for a round... an' ye're goin' to pay for it," he added with a hearty laugh.

Though he was somewhat resistant, Asher couldn't help but enjoy the company. Endless months of isolation on the road had once been his way of life, but those days, it seemed, were behind him. Now, like Russell had for so many years, he had a place that drew him back time and time again. And it wasn't always just to resupply.

Untold hours went by before he slipped from the booth and found his way down into the basement. The rangers' lounge, as it had become, was empty save for the armchairs and roaring fire. Passing through, Asher noted that some of the rooms were locked, occupied by rangers taking refuge for a time. It was just as he had envisioned. Thanks to Russell, it was actually better than anything he had envisioned. Now their kind had a safe haven, a base to share resources and recruit allies.

He made his way through the narrow corridor, passing the door that had not one but four padlocks keeping the room beyond sealed shut. For three nights a month, none were permitted to sleep in The Pick-Axe. Under the full moons, it was Russell's domain alone, a decision they had made together years earlier.

The room Asher was looking for was at the end, round the corner. Though not so large as the tavern itself, it was the second biggest chamber on the premises. Barring an alcove that had been covered by a black curtain, the walls were lined with weapons and armour of every variety. They were available to all at a moderate cost, though none held any interest to Asher.

He pushed the curtain aside, revealing his personal locker. There he found four clean cloaks, all the same shade of green. Beside them stood a rack of broadswords, all boasting a spiked pommel and all forged by Danagarr. Crowded in one corner was fresh armour; brown leathers that had never known the touch of a wicked Drayga. And, of course, new boots that didn't squelch with every step. A luxury.

Delayed as he was, and by merriment no less, the ranger ended up sleeping at The Pick-Axe. He had bathed and resupplied, but there had been only one way out of the tavern and that meant getting past Doran and the others. Even the skills of an Arakesh could not see it done. Food, more drinks, and tales had followed and the morning soon became the afternoon.

In the quiet before the summer's evening rush, Russell joined Asher and Doran in their booth. "You've got that look about you," he said, eyeing the ranger across the table. "You're itching to be on your way again, aren't you?"

Doran licked his lips and frowned as he levelled his gaze on Asher. "What's he on abou'? Ye've only jus' got 'ere!"

Asher didn't say anything, though Maybury was right. He had returned to The Axe, a place where the *Ranger* swelled in his heart and the *Assassin* paled to naught but a shadow in the back of his mind. He had only to return here every so often to remind himself who he was. That accomplished, the wilds called to him and the hunt all the more.

"Where are you going?" Russell asked.

Asher took a sip of his beer before responding. "Whistle Town," he answered.

"Whistle Town?" Doran repeated, his opinion of the place easy to read in his dour expression.

"Big monster?" Maybury enquired.

"Big *wolf*," Asher specified, eyeing Russell over the rim of his tankard. "Want in?"

The booth was quiet while he considered it, his attention

briefly wandering to the pick-axe on the wall. "You can handle it," he eventually replied. "Besides, it doesn't matter how big it is— you've definitely fought bigger."

"He also needs to replenish his purse!" Doran chipped in with a laugh from deep inside his chest.

"All thanks to you," Asher quipped, bringing out a laugh from Russell.

The ranger gave in to one more drink before saddling Hector and mounting the horse outside the tavern. Russell and Doran accompanied him, as they always did, so they might say farewell as he took to the road.

"Don't leave it so long next time," Maybury suggested.

"Aye," Doran agreed. "Jus' make sure ye bring back a good tale or two, eh?"

Asher nodded his head with amusement as he guided Hector away. "I'm sure when next I return," he called back dryly, "it will be with a tale worthy of legend!"

Doran barked a laugh. "Either that or yer dead!"

Smiling, he rode on, the *Ranger* quite content.

ASHER'S STORY CONTINUES IN...

THE
ECHOES
SAGA

RISE OF THE RANGER

PROLOGUE

The sound of men dying in battle wasn't unknown to Asher. In the past, he had remained hidden, while his father and brothers had fought against rival clans in The Wild Moores.

The boy had heard the sound of their weapons clash and the noises men made when they died. But he had never heard the sounds that drifted through the open window now, carried in the wake of a hundred war horns. When the elves went into battle, it could not be called a conflict or a skirmish, as it was with the human tribes, but was in fact given another name that was new to Asher.

The elves called it a war...

The cries of the two armies were drowned out by the ominous beating of heavy wings that thundered overhead, delivering deaths by the hundreds across the battlefield below - their fiery breath igniting the sky. The battle outside had spread, breaching Elethiah's great walls and drawing ever closer, the clash of steel against steel echoing through its stone corridors.

Asher dared to steal a glance over the window ledge, only to be terrified by the hulking shadow that flew across the moon, eclipsing its glow with bat-like wings. The boy quickly ducked, hugging the cold stone and scrambling for the safety of the large wooden table in the centre of the room. His nine-year-old body was too gangly for his young mind to control, and he barely registered the pain as his head bumped into the table leg. Asher's heart pounded in his chest at the sound of a roar no man could rightfully stand against. The great flying beasts went by another name that was new to the young boy, and the word felt strange in his mouth. The elves called them dragons!

The door to his right burst open in a splintering of wood, accompanied by the familiar song of swords colliding with incredible speed. From his sheltered vantage, Asher could only see a pair of armoured legs stagger into the room, crashing into the table, as another pair of legs followed him in, clad in a flowing white dress that danced around their foe. The laboured breaths of a man and a woman were matched by the slash and parry of their swords. The armoured legs jumped onto the table as metal scraped against the smooth wood, knocking over Asher's glass and the jug of water, before finally landing on the other side. Water washed over the parchments covering the table and poured over the edge, splashing the boy's hands and face.

The white dress dashed over the table, making no sound at all. Something softer than a sword struck the armoured man and sent him stumbling into a bookshelf. The white dress dropped to the floor once more and met its attacker with a flurry of swords and sparks.

The conflict came to a swift end as one of the swords hit the floor with a loud clatter, and hot red blood spattered against the stone. The armoured feet faltered, until a pair of knees fell to the floor, under the crumpling body of a dark-haired elf. Blood rushed from his throat and mixed with the water, slithering ever closer to where the boy knelt. Asher gasped, trying to crawl backward as the blood moved like a snake towards him.

"Asher!" The white dress wrinkled as the beautiful face of a blonde elf appeared under the table top. Her fair features were marred with concern at the sight of him. Droplets of blood were streaked across her cheeks and golden hair, though they did nothing to reduce her beauty.

With one strong hand, she pulled him out from under the table, careful not to drag him through the blood. She steadied him by the shoulders and quickly checked him over for any injuries, her soft hands gliding over his skin.

"I'm fine." Asher gently reached for her hands and pushed them away.

The boy was always ashamed of his ragged human appearance in the company of such magnificent creatures. His dirty clothes and unwashed skin made him stand out even more than usual next to her perfect complexion and exquisite clothes.

"We need to find your father and brother. You need to get back to The Wild Moores as fast as possible. You will be safer there."

That statement alone was proof of their dire situation. If The Wild Moores were safer than Elethiah, he hated to imagine what was going on beyond this room.

"I don't want to leave you, Nalana..." Asher looked into her crystal blue eyes and knew she would insist.

Nalana was the mother he'd never had and cared for him in a way his father and the rest of his clan never could. She had spent years teaching him the elven language, and countless days had been devoted to helping him read and write. He was the first of many Outlanders the elves planned to take in and teach to be civilised. After just four years of her tutelage, Asher knew he was already smarter than most of his clan, if not the strongest.

"There's no time, young one. You remember what I told you, about Valanis?"

Of course he remembered. Valanis was the tyrannical elf, set on ravaging the whole of Illian like a hungry plague of locusts. His name seemed to strike fear into the hearts of every elf in Elethiah. Asher's father had told him to leave elven troubles to elves, but Elethiah stood on the edge of The Wild Moores, and it seemed Valanis had brought his madness to the Outlanders' home too.

"His army attacks without fear of death. I don't know how long our forces and the dragons can keep them at bay. The eastern wall is already breached and they are swarming the city." Nalana nodded to the dead body behind him. "I will get you as far as the kitchens. Do you remember the door I showed you, our secret door?" He nodded absently, looking past her to the sound of fighting. "Take your family through there and run as fast as you can. Are you ready?"

Nalana took his hand and picked up her curved blade off the table. Asher had never seen her wield a sword before. It was hard to fathom that someone so delicate and gentle could be so deadly. The boy couldn't take his eyes off the sword and its unique shine, as the Outlander had never seen a sword as ornate and well-crafted as this. His own people could do no better than blunt axes and weak spears. The flat of the blade was engraved with runes he had yet to learn, and he once again felt the hunger for knowledge that Nalana had awoken in him.

They made their way through the halls and adjoining rooms as quickly and quietly as they could, Asher by comparison to Nalana sounding like a team of Centaurs. When eventually the choice of direction arose, left or right, Nalana hesitated. Asher had just enough fear to extinguish his excitement at the path the elf chose. They soon passed under a large wooden arch that led into Elethi-ah's grand library, a forbidden place. The race of men was not granted access to the ancient tomes of the elves, for fear of the books being mishandled.

It was everything he imagined and more as the room opened up into a tall oval shape, covered in wall-to-wall books, and with walkways connected by spiral staircases. Every corner was illuminated by a soft glow, emanating from yellow orbs that floated between the shelves. The orbs were a simple creation for any elf with a basic understanding of magic. It was an understanding Asher was decades away from grasping. Long tables of red-brown wood filled the space between the archway and the double doors on the other side. Asher knew that the library offered a shortcut through the main palace and had always hated taking the longer route to reach Nalana's teaching room.

Without warning, the doors were violently thrust open as four elves in dark armour and shadowy cloaks strode into the room.

Nalana pushed Asher back, putting herself instinctively in front of him while raising her sword. "Stay back, Asher."

He did as he was told and clung to the wooden arch at his back.

Nalana calmly walked around the long table and closed the gap between her and the dark elves. Their movements were hard for Asher to keep track of as they advanced on her with great speed, each of their swords angled to remove a limb. Nalana's grace and precision were unparalleled by the dark elves, and she deflected two of the strikes whilst narrowly dodging the others. Metal rang against metal in every direction as the fighters danced across the table top. Nalana looked a true warrior, using her hands and feet to push the dark elves back, whilst knocking a short-haired elf off the table with a strong backhand from her sword.

"Nalana!" Her younger brother, Elym, charged into the library with his dark hair flowing out behind him.

Elym deftly flipped onto the table and charged in with his double-ended spear. Nalana cut down the tallest of their attackers, removing his head and the hand of another elf in one blow. Elym took the advantage and impaled the one-handed elf with his spear, twisting his own body to avoid the blade of the third attacker. Asher watched as the back-handed dark elf rose from the floor, ready to swipe Nalana's legs out. To protect his teacher, the Outlander reacted without thinking and pulled a leather-bound book off the nearest shelf and threw it into the dark elf's face. The surprise blow was all Nalana needed to drop to one knee and drive her blade straight down into the elf's head, burying it deep into his body.

Elym's sudden cry of pain pierced the library, as his blood splattered against the wood. Nalana spun on the ball of her foot and whipped her sword across the final dark elf's chest, slicing through the armour and splitting his ribcage. Nalana paid him no heed as he toppled off the table, instead rushing to the aid of her brother. Asher had met Elym several times over the years, but the young elf had never quite agreed with teaching the wild humans, who had arrived from lands unknown to the elves.

Asher ran to the table, making a wide circle around the dead elves. Nalana held Elym in her arms as blood slowly poured from a gash across his gut. He groaned in pain and clung tightly to his sister.

"I have seen worse little brother..."

"We don't have time." Elym's words came through gritted teeth. "I came from the Hall of Life." The young elf reached into his tunic and tugged at the silver chain around his neck. He presented Nalana with a rugged, black crystal the size of his little finger. "Valanis is here. They're preparing to cast the Amber Spell..." He placed the crystal in the palm of her hand. "He's already killed the king and Lady Syla. We need to keep it safe, Nalana."

She remained silent; staring at the necklace with an expression Asher couldn't read. Elym's pain-filled cry, however, brought her out of the reverie soon enough. Nalana looked from her brother to Asher, gripping the crystal until her knuckles whitened.

"Asher..." Nalana called him closer. "I will stay with Elym. You need to find your family and make for The Wild Moores. Stop for nothing." Nalana rested her brother's head on her knee and quickly looped the necklace over Asher's head. "Take this and hide it deep in the forest. I will come for you when the battle is over." Asher stared at the crystal sitting in the middle of his chest before Nalana tucked it into his ragged top. "Run, Asher!"

With a lasting look at the siblings, he ran for the door.

Asher made for the kitchens, calling his father and brother as he did. Fighting had broken out across the palace, forcing him to search for new ways through the stone corridors.

"Asher!" His father's voice echoed down the hall. Typically, they were already hiding around the kitchens, always looking for food to take back to The Wild Moores. "Where have you been? We were about to leave without you!"

Such were the ways of his people. You either help the clan or you get left behind.

His older brother looked truly scared, clearly having witnessed the elves in combat or one of the winged beasts that swarmed above the city. Asher's father was sweating, no doubt fearful for his own survival while being slowed by his sons.

"This way, follow me!" Asher led them through the kitchens and down into an old tunnel, long abandoned in favour of newer refurbishments.

His brother and father ran on ahead, while Asher closed the kitchen hatch behind them. Their splashing was easy to follow once Asher jumped off the last rung. At the end of the tunnel was an old wooden door that allowed a small grid of moonlight to illuminate the wet ground and moss-covered walls.

"He'll never make it!" His brother's voice echoed through the tunnel as the pair ran full pelt through the doorway.

Their doubt in Asher's ability to survive only spurred him on to run faster.

Both his father and brother ran into The Moonlit Plains, heading straight for The Wild Moores as if the dragons themselves were at their heels. Neither looked back to check on Asher.

Before reaching the door, Asher heard one last roar, this time from somewhere deep inside the palace. He didn't stop, but rather pressed on as fast as his legs would take him. The green fields, which glowed under the moonlight, came into view beyond the door. His father and brother ran for cover under the canopy of a large oak tree.

"Keep running!" his father shouted.

Asher's chest burned, desperate for breath, as he ran for the moonlight. The black crystal around his neck pulled at his attention when it floated out in front of him, still tethered to his neck. The unexplainable occurrence didn't stop him from running through the threshold with all haste.

Asher ran through and felt the cool night air suddenly transform into warmth, as blinding light erupted from all around. Dropping into the field, Asher covered his head, fearing the hot fury of what was surely a dragon's breath. An eternity went by as he waited for the inevitable pain and darkness of death to take him. But when death should have claimed him, Asher instead heard the squawk of a bird overhead and the warmth on his back was nothing but pleasant.

The Outlander opened his eyes to a world he didn't recognise.

A midday sun beat down on a field of overgrown, faded yellow grass. Asher stood up in a daze, his ankles deep in bog water where it had moments ago been hard ground and short green grass. He took a breath, slowly turning to survey his bizarre surroundings. The city of Elethiah remained behind him, where it should be, but as a shadow of its former glory. The stone had darkened and become overgrown with weeds and thick roots, which crawled up the great walls. To his left, were the remains of a demolished tower, lying in ruin where it had fallen. The oak tree, where his father and brother had taken shelter, was gone, a broken rotten stump in its place and his family nowhere in sight.

Beyond the stump, he could still see The Wild Moores in the distance. The forest was over five hundred miles from north to south with incredible depth. Asher gasped for breath, unbelieving of his new reality. Where had the night gone? Where had Valanis's forces and the dragons gone? Where was his family? He cried for his father and his brother, screaming at the top of his voice.

The reply came not from his father or brother, but from the howl of a creature he had never heard before. Asher ducked into a patch of long grass, seeing dark shapes moving through the strands, crouched low to hide their true form. Something slipped out of his shirt and he held it in front of him.

The black crystal...

He didn't have time to think about it before the howls came again, much closer this time. He dropped the crystal back into his shirt and ran for the forest that lay sprawled before him. His clan was surely in there somewhere and they would protect him. The rapid padding of many heavy feet came from behind, but he had no idea of their number.

It wasn't long, however, before he realised the forest was simply too far away. The Outlander would never make it before the predators caught him. Changing course, Asher ran for the collection of large rocks dug into the small hillside on his left. Maybe he could lose them in there.

By the time Asher reached the first rock, he was exhausted. He fell to the grass and crawled further into the outcropping. Rolling onto his back, he saw a lumbering creature climb the rock at his feet and stretch to its full height. Dark green scales covered its sloping leathery head, with two thick arms reaching down to its knees and ending in pointed fingers of sharp bone. Its face was closer to that of a lizard, with several rows of razor-sharp teeth. A screeching howl preceded five more, who appeared from behind the other stones, licking their maws with long slimy tongues.

The first creature jumped off the rock, blocking out the sun as it came to land on top of him - only it never did land, at least not alive. The beast had been struck in the face by an arrow, mid-air. Looking up from his back, Asher glimpsed a stranger charge over his head and dive into the fray, with a short-sword in one hand and a bow in the other. The beasts leaped at their new prey, only to have their limbs removed with every slash of the stranger's sword. His movements were similar to that of an elf but Asher could also see the differences; this was a man.

The fight was over in seconds and the stranger was standing amid a heap of diced monsters.

The stranger turned to Asher, his sword shining under the sun. He wore dark leather armour, engraved with unusual, intricate patterns, and a grey cloak which spread out across the ground, collecting mud. Perhaps the strangest element of his appearance was the red blindfold he wore. He had apparently defeated those beasts without his sight. The stranger proceeded to remove the red cloth from his face, revealing shadowed, brown eyes and curly black hair.

"Gobbers," the stranger stated flatly, wiping the blood off his sword with the edge of his cloak.

Asher had heard Nalana speak of such creatures and was thankful for surviving the encounter.

"And who might you be?" the stranger asked.

Asher's eyes searched the plains for his father once more. "I am... Asher," he stuttered.

"Is that a statement or a question, boy?" The stranger flicked his bow in the air, activating a series of mechanisms and cogs built into the wood. A moment later the bow had folded into itself, before the stranger placed it out of sight, under his cloak.

Had Asher not been too stunned by the events of the past few minutes, he would have marvelled at the bow's construction.

"My name is Asher," he replied more boldly, standing up and wiping the dirty water from his face.

The stranger regarded him curiously. "Is that it? Just Asher? Well, this is no place for a boy to wander; between the swamps of Elethiah and The Wild Moores... You must have a talent for survival." His voice had a foreign twang to it that Asher couldn't place.

The boy nodded absently, trying to make sense of the stranger's words. From here, Asher could see what remained of Elethiah. Its beautiful spires and domed towers were gone, with nothing but decay hanging over the entire land. It was more akin to a swamp now, the splendid Moonlit Plains nothing but a memory. He wrapped his hands around his arms feeling the cold against his wet skin.

The stranger announced, "I am Nasta Nal-Aket, of Nightfall..."

Asher remained silent, unaware of the man's significance or the place he was from.

"Have you never heard of it, boy?"

Asher shook his head slowly.

"I am a spectre, an Arakesh," he stated proudly.

Asher's face dropped at the sound of the elvish word; he knew that word.

"I am an assassin," Nasta Nal-Aket confirmed.

Asher stood his ground, as his father had taught him when facing a bear.

"If I had to guess from your appearance, I would say you're an Outlander."

Asher became self-conscious of the black tattoo, outlining a wolf's fang, below his left eye, signifying he was from a clan of hunters.

"I didn't think your kind strayed beyond The Wild Moores these days. What are you doing out here?" The assassin tucked his blindfold into his belt, letting it hang loosely in the breeze.

Asher noted the assassin steal a look at Elethiah, but he appeared physically disturbed by the landmark and walked further into the hillside as if to gain more distance.

The Outlander looked up at the sun and knew it should be the moon that greeted him. "I was..." Asher didn't know how to explain it. "The elves were fighting and..." He could only look at the ruins of Elethiah.

Nasta looked from the ruins to Asher in puzzlement. "Elves? Are you talking about The Dark War?"

Asher didn't know anything of a Dark War and began to look round for his family once more. They wouldn't be out there looking for him, he had fallen behind. He was alone.

"And what would a young Outlander know of a battle over a thousand years past?"

The gravity of Asher's situation drained the blood from his head, blurring his vision. "A thousand years..?" He spun in every direction, desperate to find something, anything familiar. The landscape began to blur when the colours of the world faded and his vision narrowed. The ground rose up to greet him and the darkness swallowed him whole.

PHILIP C. QUAINTRELL

Hear more from Philip C. Quaintrell including
book releases and exclusive content:

PHILIPCQUAINTRELL.COM

FACEBOOK.COM/PHILIPCQUAINTRELL

@PHILIPCQUAINTRELL.AUTHOR

@PCQUAINTRELL

ABOUT THE AUTHOR

Philip C. Quaintrell is the author of the epic fantasy series, The Echoes Saga, as well as the Terran Cycle sci-fi series. He was born in Cheshire in 1989 and started his career as an emergency nurse.

Having always been a fan of fantasy and sci-fi fiction, Philip started to find himself feeling frustrated as he read books, wanting to delve into the writing himself to tweak characters and story-lines. He decided to write his first novel as a hobby to escape from nursing and found himself swept away into the world he'd created. Even now, he talks about how the characters tell him what they're going to do next, rather than the other way around.

With his first book written, and a good few rejected agency submissions under his belt, he decided to throw himself in at the deep end and self-publish. 2 months and £60 worth of sales in, he took his wife out to dinner to celebrate an achievement ticked off his bucket list - blissfully unaware this was just the beginning.

Fast forward 12 months and he was self-publishing book 1 of his fantasy series (The Echoes Saga; written purely as a means to combat his sci-fi writers' block). With no discernible marketing except the 'Amazon algorithm', the book was in the amazon best-sellers list in at least 4 countries within a month. The Echoes Saga has now surpassed 700k copies sold worldwide, has an option agreement for a potential TV-series in the pipeline and Amazon now puts Philip's sales figures in the top 1.8% of self-published authors worldwide.

Philip lives in Cheshire, England with his wife and two children. He still finds time between naps and wiping snot off his clothes to remain a movie aficionado and comic book connoisseur, and is hoping this is still just the beginning.

AUTHOR NOTES

Having written The Echoes Saga first, this is kind of a weird moment. I've been writing about Asher, living in his head, since 2015—he was my gateway into the fantasy genre. It feels like the end of an era leaving him on that last page.

If you haven't read The Echoes Saga, I'm happy to tell you that Rise of the Ranger picks up right where this book ended (chapter 1, not the prologue) and there's a lot more Asher in your future.

For those of you who have now read both series, all I can say is... Asher will return. One day. Any story he shows up in, however, will be post Echoes and the next saga I'm writing takes place thousands of years before either of these series, so he won't be in that.

I just know that he *will* return.

Speaking of people who have read one or both series, there was an obvious thread in this trilogy that wasn't tied up: the black gem. If you haven't read The Echoes Saga, I'm sorry that you've got to the end of the trilogy with no answers. I'm afraid I just couldn't enlighten you (or Asher more to the point). Get stuck into The Rise of the Ranger though and you won't be disappointed. That's a series that really peels back the onion that is all things Verda.

As for The Ranger Archives, I've had an absolute blast writing them! It was refreshing, if challenging at times, to write a story that had a beginning, middle, and end all tied up between two covers. I was so used to weaving a sprawling saga of numerous story threads that I initially had to reign it in a bit. Once I got into it, though, I really enjoyed it—I think my imagination needed the break. It's definitely had that, I'd say, as I'm currently craving those big sweeping stories again.

Despite the standalone nature of the books, there was a continuing story that moves through the trilogy and that's Asher's character growth. I've found throughout the three books that writing him was all about balance, and what a fine one it was. Obviously, by the end, Asher had to be something close to the man we meet in Rise of the Ranger: still a loner, but also able to make friends and allies. That fine line was always there though, reminding me that I was writing an earlier version of the man. And, being so close to his time as an Arakesh meant always tilting him towards darker places.

That's not to say he's the perfect hero in Rise of the Ranger. The *Assassin* continues to lurk just beneath the surface, but in this trilogy I felt it was important to see it come out in him. I also felt it was important to see him fail. He's not a natural mentor and he's not the best ranger he could be. Nightfall didn't instruct him to be a teacher so the whole thing was a learning exercise for him as much as it was for Russell.

In the end, it was great to see Asher realised his similarity to Russell had nothing to do with fighting the monster within, but having somewhere to return to, where he was welcome and surrounded by friends. It really felt like Asher was taking the first step in a journey that takes him right through all 9 books of The Echoes Saga.

It was also great to introduce the Skaramangian Stones in a little more detail, even if some of those details have been skewed by so much history. A bit like Asher, you haven't seen the last of this particular legend. I don't want to say much more than that right now as the next saga I'm writing will get into it. No spoilers!

And how could I chat on an on if I didn't mention The Pick-

Axe? I so wish I could visit that tavern in real life. It was amazing to be able to get into its origin, something I had wanted to do since Asher and Doran had that particular chat in A Clash of Fates.

I was itching to bring it into the story as early as A Court of Assassins, but, obviously, it couldn't be done. Even then, writing this book, I still couldn't get it in until the end as, like Russell, it needed an origin. As I said, Asher will return and so too will The Pick-Axe in future stories.

As always, if you could find a minute to leave a review on Amazon that would be greatly appreciated. I'm a self-publisher so your opinions on the books go a long way in convincing others to take a chance on them. And if you want to keep up with me and all things writing then look me up on social media or keep an eye on website.

Until the next time...

APPENDICES

Kingdoms of Illian:

1. ***Alborn*** (eastern region) - Ruled by King Rengar of house Marek. Capital city: *Velia*. Other Towns and Cities: Palios, Galosha, and Barossh.

2. ***The Arid Lands*** (southern region) - Ruled by Emperor Faros. Capital city: *Karath*. Other Towns and Cities: Ameeraska, Calmardra and Tregaran.

3. ***The Ice Vales*** (western region) - Ruled by King Gregorn of house Orvish. Capital city: *Grey Stone*. Other Towns and Cities: Bleak, Kelp Town and Snowfell.

4. ***Orith*** (northern region) - Ruled by King Merkaris of house Tion. Capital city: *Namdhor*. Other Towns and Cities: Skystead, Dunwich, Darkwell and Longdale.

5. *Felgarn* (central region) - Ruled by King Uthain of house Harg. Capital city: *Lirian*. Other Towns and Cities: Vangarth, Wood Vale and Whistle Town.

6. *Dragorn* (island nation off The Shining Coast to the east) - Ruled by the four crime families; the Trigorns, Fenrigs, Yarls, and the Danathors.

Significant Wars: Chronologically:

The Great War - Fought during the First Age, around 5,000 years ago. The only recorded time in history that elves and dwarves have united. They fought against the orcs with the help of the Dragorn, the first elvish dragon riders. This war ended the First age.

The Dark War - Fought during the Second Age, around 1,000 years ago. Considered the elvish civil war. Valanis, the dark elf, tried to take over Illian in the name of the gods. This war ended the Second Age.

The Dragon War - Fought in the beginning of the Third Age, only a few years after The Dark War. The surviving elves left Illian for Ayda's shores, fleeing any more violence. Having emerged from The Wild Moores, the humans, under King Gal Tion's rule, went to war with the dragons over their treasure. This saw the exile of the surviving dragons and the beginning of human dominance over Illian.

~

The Gods:
Atilan - King of the Gods
Paldora - Goddess of the Stars
Krayt - God of War
Naius - God of Magic
Ymir - God of the Harvest

Zephia - Goddess of Music
Sebela - Goddess of Marriage
Ibilis - God of Shadows
Athar - God of Agriculture
Mydowna - Goddess of Night and Day
Farg - God of Blacksmiths
Balgora - Goddess of the Afterlife
Atarae - Goddess of Destiny
Oemis - God of the Sea
Fimira - Goddess of Wisdom
Ikaldir - God of the Hunt
Nyx - Goddess of Life and Death
Nalmiron - God of Thunder
Lethia - Goddess of fortune
Vidilis - God of Dreams

A Chronicle of Monsters: A Ranger's Bestiary 12th Edition:

Skalagat - *A mistake of nature to be sure. These monsters are often referred to as forest knights or knights of the wood. They are not so noble as knights, however.*
Their black hides produce a sticky substance that binds whatever they can find to their bodies. Most commonly, they are found to be using bark from the trees, lending their exterior a look something akin to a suit of armour - hence the reference to knights.
It should be noted that Skalagats will use anything they can find, not just parts of the forest. They have been seen to wear the skulls of their victims like masks or even utilise the claws of other animals.
If you can get close enough to bring your sword to bear, they are vulnerable between these makeshift plates of armour. Getting close can be difficult though. Fully grown Skalagats can reach twenty feet in height, a fact that allows them to blend in with the trees.

Margotta Elysabef, Ranger.

Spider - *If you can squash it with your boot, it's not the breed of Spider I'm writing about.*

There are parts of the world where Spiders grow and grow until they could stand side by side with a horse (see A Charter of Monsters, Page 22, for known locations).

If possible, bring a mage into the contract; they're worth their weight in coins when it comes to Spiders. You see, Spiders hate the light, despise it. Now don't be thinking you can just take a torch into a nest - you're going to need a weapon in both hands. A mage can bring light to the hunt and it could mean the difference between life and death.

Your next advantage will be to keep moving. If you remain in one spot, which will be tempting when faced by waves of the fiends, you will be overwhelmed. See below for extensive list of strengths and weaknesses.

The knight with no name, Ranger.

Lech - *To the common folk, these monsters are known as Mudslugs. It's an apt description, though Lech are closer in size to a large dog.*

Typically found in bogs and marshes due to their preference for wet environments. If you can't see through the water and it's past your knees, take a care. The bite on these beasts is almost as painful as it is strong. Once they've got you in their maw, you're going to need fire to make their fangs retract.

Thankfully, they're easy to kill. They have no outer shell or any natural protection beside their ability to blend in with their surroundings. They don't taste too bad either.

Dane, son of Heslin, Ranger.

Stravakin - *So wicked and foul a creature could only have been born of nightmares I tell you. Bone eaters our ancestors called them and rightly so. The first one I came across had left a bear carcass in its wake. Can you imagine finding a dead bear with all but its bones? A more unnatural thing I never saw.*

The bite on these beasts is next to none, their jaws capable of reducing bones to splinters. And, as large as their pointed maw might be, don't bother attacking it - those jaws will blunt your blade. Fire is your best bet. Set your trap and make certain you've plenty of oil about it. Don't hang about to watch it burn, mind you. Something in its gut gives off poisonous fumes when put to fire. Those fumes, however, are the perfect lure for the mate, and Stravakin always have a mate they're paired with until death.

Welek Tysarion, Ranger.

Basilisk - These are likely to be among my last words, certainly my last written words. I have recently returned to Lirian after taking a contract in Longdale.

It's a miracle of the gods that I made it back. I slew the Basilisk plaguing the outer villages, but not before it sank its fangs into my arm. There is no cure for their venom save for a touch of magic perhaps. A simple ranger, I possess no such talents.

I was able to make a small amount of Selvin paste (see Nature's Secrets, A Ranger's Companion, Page 88) with local resources. This helped with the pain and slowed down the deadly venom.

Now for what might help you. I found that luring the Basilisk was made all the easier using a blend of Gorsk oil and sheep fat. If you can also get your hands on a vial of Weet Green, add this to the bait. It will make the monster gag until it spills the contents of its stomach. This will be your moment to—

Amaya Hawkyns, Ranger.

Scudder - Just because you've killed yourself a Lech or two, don't be thinking you can tackle a Scudder. These beasts are faster and far more aggressive than Mudslugs.

And when I say fast, I don't just mean in the water - they're equally fast out of it. And when I say they, I do mean they. These buggers do naught but eat and breed, increasing the size of their nest as they go.

Thankfully, they're prey to a number of other monsters who help to keep their numbers down, but should they encroach on civilisation, they need rooting out as soon as possible.

There's always a female at the heart of the nest and she's the one you want if you're to put a stop to the nightmare. She's no fiercer than the males, though she is somewhat larger.

Now, there's nothing special required to kill the wretches. You just need something sharp and a strong swing behind it. (Read on for known sources of natural bait).

Handor Grain, Ranger.

Werewolf - *'Tis a curse, simply put. How this began is up for much debate, though talking about it makes little difference. Werewolves are real and they are among us.*

Contracts concerning these beasts should be left to the most experienced of our kind. I don't just say that because these beasts are seven feet tall with claws as long as your fingers. I urge the young among our ranks to leave these contracts because a wise ranger knows you don't hunt the wolf. You hunt the poor soul who received the cursed bite. Be warned though, they're still stronger than the average person their human form. It's going to feel like killing a person. A deed like that will weigh on a good man.

Oh, and don't stock up on silver, it's a myth most likely started by a Werewolf. You can kill it the same way you kill anything - with a good swing of steel.

Arnathor (the old hunter), Ranger.

Dragons - *The addition of this creature is a point of contention among my fellow rangers and for more than one reason at that.*

Firstly, no one has seen a dragon since the time of the elves, a thousand years ago. Some say they're extinct, others say they migrated to lands unknown. The truth is beyond this humble ranger.

Secondly, what legends there are speak of intelligent creatures of innate wisdom. Of course, we're still talking about an animal that has the power to level cities and torch entire forests.

Should you meet one, as unlikely as that is, pray to the gods that your death is swift and worthy of history's note.

I would also add that more than one report has come from The Shining Coast in years of late. Rumour has it the mages of Korkanath have one under their spell, a pet of some sort perhaps.

Fenrid Arlvark, Ranger.

Golem - *The first thing to know about these brutes is that they aren't natural. Golem aren't born, they're made out of pieces of the dead. Make no mistake, this is dark magic, necromancy work, crude as it may be. The most important thing to keep in mind is that they cannot be killed. Burn them, break them, cut them into bits - nothing stops them except a command from their maker.*
That leads me to my next point, so be sure to read it twice. You're looking for people, not the Golem itself. Be it a mage, wizard, witch - whatever you want to call them. They're the key. You either trap the monster in something it can never get out of (good luck with that) or you convince the wretch who brought it into the world to stop it.
But be warned; a Golem will protect its master, and most Golems can rip a man in half with their bare hands. Trust me, I've seen it.

Hamish Lancet, Ranger.

Troll - *There exist variants of this creature, both big and enormous (read on for the breakdown of all types). They are brutes all and of limited intellect at that.*
Solitary beasts, they are rarely found in any numbers, though, be aware, their breeding season runs through winter. These areas can be found by following the sounds of recurring landslides.
Weak spots for most variants include the face, in particular their large eyes, and their softer midriff. I would advise using a surprise attack and with a spear, utilising the distance of such a weapon. If possible, coat the tip in Oylish poison (see A Ranger's Guide to Alchemy, Page 97) so that you might slow the Troll down first.

Gallad Corsair, Ranger.

Mer-folk - *The darkest depths of The Adean are said to be home to numerous creatures of intelligence, some even equal to our own (though that's entirely debatable), but it is those who dwell closer to our shores that move my quill this day. They be real monsters.*

Depending on when you are reading this, you may or may not know of Haven Run, a fishing village on The Shining Coast, just north of Velia. The creatures of the sea came in the night, slithering across the beach like snakes. All but myself were dragged from their homes into those murky waters, reducing the village itself to a lifeless husk.

I found no weakness in them other than with the swing of my sword, a skill the fishermen did not possess. Should a contract be posted concerning these monsters, share the coin with your fellow rangers - your only hope is in numbers.

Olav One-Eye, Ranger.

Vorska - *These monsters have gone by many names over the centuries. Your great grandparents likely called them Vampeer or Vampire. Before that, they were Gorgers and Blood Fiends. Whatever you wish to call them, know this: they are the real hunters. They have been preying on humanity since the dawn of time.*

Should you cross them in the light of day, you will see their true appearance and what a monstrosity they are, their nightmarish features forged in the pits of the lowest hell. But, by night, they will appear as the most beautiful person you could imagine. They will charm their victims into seclusion before their beastly tongue drains them of blood.

Silver, my friends. They abhor its touch. Use this to reveal them, then take their head with a good piece of steel.

Dobrin Vansorg, Ranger.

Sandstalkers - *Don't run. Never Run. Sandstalkers are among the most confident predators the world of monsters has to offer. Standing your ground will put them off balance and lend you an edge in the fight. If faced by one on its own - and this is unlikely - seek out the monster's weak spots, the softer flesh between the joints; their chitinous exterior* *can blunt the best of steel. That said, it is more likely you will encounter a nest. In this instance, run. Run until the heat of The Arid Lands beats you into the sand. A nest of Sandstalkers is not to be taken lightly, nor ever alone.*

Jorven Dorn, Ranger.

Gobbers - *Gangly creatures of muscle and claw. What they lack in intelligence I have found they make up for in ferocity, a feature that is amplified all the more by their pack-like behaviour.*
They have speed on their side and you won't see them coming until they have you ambushed. Their scales are tough but not impenetrable - nothing a good axe can't deal with.

Kel Kregor, Ranger.

Wraith - *This foul creature is not of this world, but that of the Shadow Realm, a nightmarish place that only the most experienced mages can access (see Monsters of the Deep World).*
Half in this world, half in another, most folk call them ghosts but, as we all know, there's no such thing. Though, fighting these beasts can sometimes feel like fighting smoke.
Killing the mage who conjured the Wraith won't change a thing; once it's here it's here to stay. Studying Wraiths is near impossible due to their hyper-violent nature, so we have no idea what they crave. We only know that their victims are drained of vitality and life: a painful process from all reports.
While magic is the best weapon against a Wraith, they can be killed with traditional means, including an unusual weakness to salt. For reasons unknown, salt disrupts their ethereal nature and reveals more flesh and blood. Good hunting.

Gudvig, son of Gendervig, Ranger.

Giant - *Not to be confused with Trolls. Their heights might cross over, especially where the Mawclaw Giant and Mountain Troll are concerned,* *but the Giants are, as their name suggests, the largest of Illian's monsters.*

Their level of intelligence varies across the subspecies. Through all my travels and all the contracts I've taken, it is my strong belief that the Ice Giants of West Vengora are the smartest and, therefore, the deadliest. Regardless of the subspecies, however, all Giants appear to suffer from bad hearing. Either that or they can't hear us tiny folk. Keep this in mind when springing your trap or ambush.

Bragen Durth, Ranger.

Rakenbak - *If you haven't come across one of these beasts there's no mistaking them when you do. Imagine, if you can, a hedgehog and a bear brought together by monstrous forces and you have an idea what a Rakenbak looks like.*

They're fiercely territorial and their boundary grows as they do. This becomes a problem when the mother drops a litter close to a town or city, though you'll mostly find them in a woodland environment.

Now, once you've engaged a Rakenbak there's no walking away - or running away for that matter. At a flat-out run, they're faster than any man and they can climb anything you can. So don't attack the fiend until you know exactly how you're going to kill it. Read on for a list of suitable poisons and baits.

Weylan Ganes, Ranger.

Yarxal - *So fair a voice has never been heard, for it is like honey to the ears. How many travellers have fallen prey to this lure I cannot say, but I have discovered Yarxal nests decorated with more human bones than I could count.*

They are proficient predators that kill with admirable swiftness. This is a blessing in disguise I feel, as the beasts don't waste any part of their prey, whether it be devouring the flesh they strip from bone or using those same bones to secure their nests. These monsters prefer to hunt alone, only gathering in significant numbers for breeding purposes (don't even try hunting a Yarxal during this time).

Upright on three legs, they also possess three slender arms, their third limb protruding from their chest. Their grotesque heads will spread like the petals of flower, revealing a combination of suckers and fangs. It is also from where their unusually hypnotic voice comes from. The survivors I have encountered described the voice they heard as a lullaby, though they were all convinced it belonged to a beautiful woman. Now, their skin breaks as easily as ours do, but I have found they suffer greatly when exposed to a particularly high pitch. I would recommend capturing a Banshee first (see page 400) and transporting it to the Yarxal nest. It's a lot of work, but a disorientated Yarxal is an easy kill.

Gelethaine the Grey Knight, Ranger.

Banshee - *Keep your head on a swivel with these noisy buggers. They've well-earned their name and they'll use their wretched screech to disorientate you—make you look one way while they attack from the other, and always from above.*

They live in swarms of up to twenty and prefer high vantages (see A Charter of Monsters, Page 107, for known locations). If you ever come across these pale predators, you'll understand why they're so well-suited to high vantages. You see, they possess a thin membrane that connects their limbs and hooked claws to the main body. Once they leap from their perch, their limbs spread out and this membrane allows them to glide without a sound.

Once they've got their hooks in your back their razored beaks will take chunks out of your head, so don't go blundering into a swarm. Locate them, then smoke them out (add Harlergrayde to the smoke and they'll get drowsy - see A Ranger's Guide to Alchemy, Page 214). Once they start dropping, get to work.

Yurik (The Beast of Bleak), Ranger.

Arkilisk - *A distant cousin of the Basilisk, though, thankfully, much smaller and easier to trap. Having said that, the bite of an Arkilisk has a much faster acting venom and is capable of killing a man in mere minutes rather than the hours Basilisk venom requires.*

You will find these most deadly of creatures in forests, their preferred habitat due to their bark-like hide that allows them to blend in with the trees.

Now, in all honesty, it is going to be rare that a contract comes up to hunt an Arkilisk down. They don't actively hunt humans and they never stray from their woodland domain. As a ranger, however, it is likely that you will share that same domain at some point or another and it's best to know your neighbours when they could kill you with a single bite.

Speaking of their bite, don't even think about an antidote. Even if one existed, you couldn't ingest it before their venom paralysed you, a symptom that begins in the hands of all places. Your only hope is to kill it fast or, better yet, from a distance. Just bear in mind that Arkilisks have six legs and move with significant speed.

The best advice I have for you is this: leave them well alone. If you don't pose a threat to either the Arkilisk or its prey, then it will leave you alone.

Korkali of the Oseki Tribe, Ranger.

Darkling - *The addition of this monster is something of a special case, but the rangers' council has agreed it warrants inclusion. The first thing you need to know when dealing with Darklings is this: they're already dead.*

These abominations are the creations of dark mages and the foulest of magic. From our archives, it appears I am the only ranger to have ever encountered Darklings and I pray to the gods that this will forever remain the truth.

I came across these dark mages in Snowfell. Their insidious cult, whose name I was never able to learn, was in the process of digging up the dead from their graves and breathing new life into them. Only, it was not the life they had known. No, these people were brought back as monsters, fiends who know only their master's command.

They're fast, ferociously violent, and they feel no pain, no fear, and they never tire. Under their master's spell, they hunt in packs and consume the flesh of any poor soul they come across.

Darklings do not return to death idly, and they killed my ward in the time it took us to discover a viable method of destruction. You must take their head or set them alight with fire. Nothing else works. They can lose limbs and take enough damage to drop a Rakenbak, but they will never stop coming for you. So I will say it again. Take the head or set them alight. Better yet, use both methods.

As I said though, these are not naturally occurring monsters. They are products of magic, the machinations of mad men. Though I never got the opportunity to kill one of these dark mages, there is a possibility that their death would end the spell and the Darklings with it.

Omas Ban-Harqen, Ranger.

Praitora - *Also known as the Fisherman's Bane. Praitora are most definitely the creatures that slithered out of the ocean's nightmares. If you've ever spent any time by the sea you probably have an idea about what an octopus is. For the sake of this passage I will assume you have. They are similar in appearance to the more harmless octopus, but they are considerably larger and have no qualms about encroaching on the shore. They hunt in the shallows and often claim nearby caves—the damper the better—as temporary dens while hunting on land.*

Some of the larger ones have even been known to capsize small fishing boats. Now don't even bother hunting these or even the smaller ones if they remain in the water; that's their territory. If one has come ashore, hunt it down or use bait to lure it from the sea if you must (see below for list of appropriate baits).

Logan Hackett, Ranger.

Drayga - *If Scudders and Mud Worms weren't enough to steer you clear of swamps, let the Drayga be the warning you need. These pale beasts move on two legs as we do and even stand with the height of an average man, but they are feral to the bone.*

Their sloped heads are more fangs than anything else but if you look into their black eyes you will see the sickness that lives there. Drayga are one of few monsters who hunt prey for no more than sport. Hungry or not, these creatures will rise from the swamps of Illian and tear you to shreds. They do not, however, cope well out of water. Their ghostly pale hides dry up fast, a fact that causes them pain by all reports. If you can lure them onto dry land, away from their precious swamps, you will stand a better chance of whittling their numbers down. And they will have the numbers. Drayga move in family pods and always attack with every member, no matter how old or young they are.

Not to fear. If you are a competent swordsman these monsters will fall to your blade as easily as any man.

Arthur Penvin, The Dancing Sword, Ranger.

Trakian - *There's nothing in this world more appetising to a Trakian than a dead body, and a human one at that. These fiends haunt graveyards up and down the six realms, disturbing the departed and leaving a ghastly mess in their stead. They might have no interest in the living, but that won't stop them from defending their feeding ground. Best to hunt them by day since they're nocturnal by nature. You can find their warren around the graveyard in question; they won't stray far from it, not even to sleep. Smoke them out and chop down anything that emerges from the den.*
    Varlan Bard, Ranger.

Lumber Dug - *I don't know who named these monsters but lumbering will come to mind if you ever cross one. Hulking beasts of stone they are! At least most of their body is. If you dare face one from the front, and contend with the enormous horn protruding from its face, you could take a swipe at their soft underbelly. I wouldn't advise it though. What they lack in speed they more than make up for by being able to crush every bone in your body with one meaty fist.*
You are better off poisoning their food (a dead deer will do nicely) or using fire depending on the environment.

Sedwig The Trapper, Ranger.

Lewsha - *Of all the monsters you might face during your career, I guarantee you will never come across one so beautiful as a Lewsha. Beware*

496

these creatures, for they will appear to you as one thing when, in fact, they are something else entirely.

The glands in their neck produce a toxin of some kind. It disturbs the air around them like the heat of The Arid Lands. Once you have inhaled this poisonous air, you will see only what you want to see: a beautiful maiden, a lover, even an old relative. With this they will lure you in, revealing their true and hideous nature when it's too late.

If Lewsha are your prey, you must ingest a potion of Hackweed and Lindis Grass. It will rob you of taste and smell but once it is in your gut it will counteract the Lewshas' toxins. Just try not to lose your nerve when you see their true form.

Arnor Grimbold, Ranger.

Howling Matron - What devil gave birth to such a creature I could not guess nor would I care to meet it, for this offspring of evil is wretch enough. It boasts a dozen pincer legs, giving this beast its scurrying speed. Its carapace, sizeably comparable to a horse, is plated like armour and capable of chipping our blades and keeping back our arrows.

And what hellish sight its monstrous jaws are. Upon attack, the largest of the Matron's armoured plates retreats just enough to reveal the six blood-red tentacles that surround a razored beak. It will howl almost continuously, altering its pitch until it finds one that disorientates its prey. Once thoroughly dazed, those tentacles will have you; then there's no getting away from that beak.

All that in mind, you'll be wanting to tackle this monster with a spear—to give those tentacles something to do. Then push the beast back and lever it up to expose its soft underbelly. That said, I would advise bringing another ranger into the contract. If that's not possible, you're going to need more preparation time. First, hunt down a Narkul - you're going to need the natural acid their mushrooms produce as it's one of the few things capable of burning through the Matron's carapace.

Just try not to die extracting the acid from the Narkul first.

Keldrik The Grey, Ranger.

Centaur - *The scourge of The Moonlit Plains, to be sure. Most would describe these creatures as part man, part horse. They'd be wrong. There's no shred of man to be found in these beasts. Now, I know the legends as well as anyone—ancient friends of the even more ancient elves. But whether they were once friends to the elves or not, one thing that isn't a legend is their brutality towards humans. Stray too far from The Selk Road while traversing The Moonlit Plains and it's said you'll meet your end by way of a Centaur. And they would be right. Why the beasts hate us so much has been debated by scholars of The All-Tower for centuries but we rangers know the truth, don't we? Centaurs are like any animal we hunt—they're territorial. The Plains are theirs, it's that simple. But, sometimes, it's they who stray from their territory. In these cases, most contracts for a Centaur will come out of Vangarth or Tregaran. But be warned, they hunt and live in teams of forty or more. They are not likely to be brought down.*

Hadrik Delaney, Ranger.

Humming Swarm - *Twenty-six years. That's how long I've been in this business. That's a long time for a ranger. I tell you this because in all my years on the job, only once have I come across a contract for a Humming Swarm.*
The swarm I was contracted to destroy was on the west coast, not far from Ameeraska. The little buggers prefer a hot and dry climate. They also devour their prey within three to five seconds and they leave naught but nibbled bones in their wake. The closest creature I could compare them to is a piranha fish—if it had wings.
Most mistake them for leaves, and a whole swarm will fill the branches of a fully-grown tree. Unfortunately, each individual Hummer (my preferred name for them) is no bigger than the end of your finger, so your sword, axe, bow— whatever your preference—is of no use with these monsters. You could swing at them for hours and hit naught but air. Not that they'd give you the chance.
The only way to kill the critters is with smoke. Since they sleep at night, I would suggest creeping under the canopy and starting a few fires. Either that or don't take the contract. The latter is probably more sensible.

Arslef, Ranger.

Dopplegorger - *Once you've learnt of these demons you'll have enjoyed your last night in a tavern or upon the cosy bed of some sleepy inn. I thank the gods Dopplegorgers are rare (almost wiped out in the fourth century of the Third Age).*
These monsters will infiltrate villages or towns, lurking on the outskirts until they find a suitable candidate (often a loner with little to no family). Once they do, they not only kill their victim but assume their identity. I am yet to understand how they accomplish their devilry, but it seems they skin the victim and then proceed to wear it. Beyond this, the fiends are able to transform their bodies until their resemblance is flawless.
It is then that the fox is able to walk among the chickens. Should you find yourself hunting one of these monsters, be sure to thoroughly question everyone—leave no stone unturned. Their level of intelligence is only passable in brief encounters; extensive questioning will reveal them. Just make sure your sword is in hand when you do.

Borvun the butcher, Ranger.

Naerwitch - *These be demons of the dark I say. The pitch-black is their home and they know it well. How these cave-dwellers are able to detect their prey remains a mystery but, make no mistake, they will find you. And while you will need fire to hunt them down, the light will not deter them. It's for this reason we believe Naerwitches lack eyes altogether. These creatures move on six legs, though it should be noted that some have been discovered to possess eight or even ten. I hesitate to describe their feet but it is a feature that remains unique to these monsters. It doesn't matter how many legs they have, they all walk on feet that look exactly like human hands.*
Why this is the case remains as much a mystery as their perception. As for killing a Naerwitch, aim for their protruding torso and swing hard—you don't want to get into a prolonged fight while your fire is dying. Once you lose the light, you lose your life.

Anther Grane, Ranger.

Greyking - *Like the Arkilisk, the Greyking is another sub-species of the Basilisk, which is itself a sub-species of the incredibly rare King Basilisk. Firstly, I would like to talk about their size as I'm sure that would be on any ranger's mind when something as big as a Basilisk is mentioned. The Greyking sub-species fits nicely between the dog-sized Arkilisk and the Basilisk which, of course, is comparable to a horse. I believe the largest Greyking on record was just shy of seven-feet in length, so no easy beast to bring down.*
Unlike those of the broader species, the Greyking does not possess a venomous bite. That's not to say its bite can't kill you—it most certainly can. However, depending on the season, the Greyking will either remove your limb with a single bite or implant a number of eggs into your body. I, personally, have come across two victims who believed they had survived their encounter with a Greyking by some miracle. Of course, once those eggs mature they poison the blood, resulting in a deadly fever. Once the victim has died, the newly-hatched Greykings begin to eat their way out.
It is not a sight for the faint-hearted.

Eletta Gelding, Ranger.

Banefisher - *Devils of sea and land I say. They plague the coasts from north to south paying the weather no heed, for neither heat nor blistering cold can bother them. Their outer layer is that of a crab, a natural armour that can also lend them the appearance of a rock should they curl up on the beach. Upon their two feet—webbed claws—they stand at six-feet tall. Now these beasts are fast on land and even faster in the water, so mind your surroundings.*
I've seen the buggers eat, or consume I should say. They have four rows of translucent fangs and an extendable jaw that can fit a man's face neatly inside. Don't let them get that close. You're going to need something with a bit of weight behind it if you're to crack their shell exterior. I would recommend a war-hammer or spiked mace even.

Hamish Harclaw, Ranger.

Red Daliad - At two-feet tall, these monsters might not appear all that
threatening, especially since they seem all legs with an almost indis-
cernible body. But hunt these beasts with caution in your step. Should
you wander into their nest (see A Charter of Monsters, Page 212, for
known locations) they will quietly, almost innocently, approach you
with feigned curiosity. Do not be fooled. They regard you as naught but
prey.
When close enough, the Daliads will leap for you, their hooked legs
fanned out. It is then that you will see their mouths, located on the
underside of their small body. They'll take chunks out of you while their
hooks barb your skin to keep them anchored.
One of my earliest contracts was to exterminate a nest, just west of
Vangarth. There were two of us, in fact, and I was the novice. I watched
my mentor disappear, his body overtaken by these red monsters.
Now, depending on the size of the nest, you can either take your sword to
the task or - as I did - use a portion of the contract money to hire a mage.
If you take the latter route, for the larger nests, insist that the mage uses
a freezing spell. The Daliads have a curious resistance to fire. I will
continue to research the reason for this.

Rogaer the Blueblood, Ranger.

Ghola - If I'm being honest—and I know I've been discouraged by my
peers to voice as much—it would be easier to relocate the village or town
plagued by a Ghola than to kill the monster.
I have checked the records and found only one instance of a ranger
killing a Ghola. The records are limited, however, as that same ranger
died from injuries only moments after defeating the beast.
Luckily for all of us, Ghola dwell solely in the mountains. They rarely
venture beyond them, only doing so if they feel their territory is threatened. Such was the case of Harvest Snows, a small village outside of
Longdale. As you know, this area of the world is nestled well within the
stony walls of The Vengoran Mountains (known colloquially as
Vengora).

As you might not know, Harvest Snows no longer exists. Or, rather, it is no longer inhabited. Should you happen across the village site you will find naught but the shell of a village. From what I can tell of the records from the time, the village was in the process of expanding, soon to become a town in fact. That must have been when the Ghola felt threatened.

Now, the reason I suggest relocation over tackling the monster is their speed. Ghola can only be described as supernaturally fast, despite appearances being likened to a human. Before dying, the ranger who fought the beast described it as no more than a blur with claws.

Folaf Ingerson, Ranger.

Dathrak - In the cities, I have oft heard the pigeons be referred to as 'rats with wings'. If such a phrase was to be coined for Dathraks, it would be something akin to 'a Basilisk with wings'. In truth, one of the strongest theories I've come across actually suggests the Dathraks are distant cousins of dragons.

If the true size of dragons is to be believed, then Dathraks are considerably smaller. That's not to say they aren't large monsters in their own right. The largest recorded possessed a body close in size to a shire horse. Believe me when I tell you, a Dathrak will have no trouble snatching you in its claws and returning you to its high nest (see A Charter of Monsters, Page 112, for known locations).

On two legs, their stance is not dissimilar to that of a vulture's. Their snout is even beak-like, with a razored hook on the end. 'Tis their hide that sparks the debates regarding their relation to dragons. Dathraks are scaled from head to tail and hard it is too, harder than any scales a Basilisk might boast. See below for list of viable poisons and proven traps.

Arn Grawly, Ranger.

Urgal - It is highly unlikely you will ever encounter this creature, but there are two accounts in our oldest archives that detail Urgals, and so I have chosen to make an addition to our growing bestiary.

Having thoroughly read the reports from our long dead colleagues (it should be stated that neither man ever met, with forty years between the death of one and the birth of the other) I can see that their descriptions of an Urgal are identical. And disturbing.

The Urgals were seen north of Snowfell, at the base of The Vengoran Mountains. This alone would suggest that their species inhabits the area. There are local myths and legends about Urgals, though most in The Ice Vales refer to them as Goblins.

At a reported three-feet tall, they are green of colour with large pointed ears. They've sharp teeth and lethal nails on their six-fingered hands.

Now for the disturbing part.

According to both late rangers, the Urgals they encountered could speak and even wore clothes, if a little shabby in their appearance. Furthermore, it was reported by both that the creatures possessed a level of intelligence on a par with a human. It was the creatures who named themselves as Urgals, in fact.

The second ranger to meet an Urgal made note of tools hanging from several belts around its waist, though their purpose was never recorded. Nor was their reason for being around Snowfell.

With that, they remain a mystery.

Elswyn Palona, Ranger.

Harkon - Vicious aquatic hunters, the Harkons could best be described as eel dogs. They hunt in fresh water such as lakes and rivers (see A Charter of Monsters, Page 203, for known locations). They can reach up to twenty feet and weigh up to four hundred pounds.

It's a myth that these creatures possess a venomous bite—as far as humans are concerned that is. To the fish it shares a habitat with, the bite of a Harkon means death within seconds. That's not to say their bite doesn't mean death for a human, for their jaws are extendable and capable of taking a limb, given the opportunity. A fully grown female could snap a man in half.

As with any monster who calls the water their home, Harkons can be difficult to hunt (see below for suitable list of bait).

When it comes to killing them, I would recommend using poisoned bait.
Failing that, you're going to need a spear and a lot of patience.
Good hunting.

Cal Phesto, Ranger.

Fade - *A nightmare of the Shadow Realm, of that there is no doubt (see Monsters of the Deep World). 'Tis a plane of existence that should never have been tampered with, but I could write a book on the arrogance of mages.*
The Fades are either brought through from their world and let loose or they find a way through to our world due to a mistake on the mage's part. Either way, they will seek to create chaos in our world. Fortunately, in most cases, these creatures of the abyss are taken care of by the mages of Korkanath (they don't want magic's reputation to be tarnished after all).
Rangers are called upon when these monsters find people—and they will find people. They seem to be drawn to civilisation, as if we are no more than play things for their entertainment.
Fades are categorised by their appearance: unnaturally tall and thin, cloaked in black, they attack with claws the size of your hand. Unlike Wraiths, kin from the Shadow Realm, salt will not aid you in your fight. It is known, however, that Fades cannot cross iron. Even a fallen sword is as impassable as a stone wall. This makes for subtle traps—use them well.

Kasira Cornwell, Ranger.

Kruid - *A good old-fashioned monster if ever there was one. If you're yet to accept a contract on one of these beasties, perhaps you haven't spent enough time in The Arid Lands, typically Karath. Kruids hail from The Undying Mountains, a place no man can say much about. Adding to the mystery of the mountains is, in fact, the Kruids themselves. It is unknown why they only appear during the summer months, though I would guess it has something to do with their food supply.*
When it comes to slaying these monsters, you would be better off sharing

the contract with another ranger, maybe even two. They're easy enough to kill, but they're big. The best description I can give would be to compare a Kruid to a scorpion, except they can reach twenty feet in length.
Now, as long as you have a sharp enough sword, you'll do just fine. I would suggest assaulting as a team so you can distract the beast, specifically its pincers. Keep them busy, and you can attack from the sides.

Robyn Kobb, Ranger.

Skitter - *Sometimes referred to as Ice Spider. These buggers start out life no bigger than your hand and can grow to the size of a small house. If you come across the latter, leave well alone. No contract reward is worth the risk.*
I should also say, if you come across the smaller ones, there will be hundreds of them and their mother, one of the big ones, won't be far away. Leave them all alone too.
Anything in-between is manageable. They appear to go through a phase in their adolescence that sees them isolate themselves, especially the males. When taking them on, use fire. Their icy hides are so sensitive to heat that even light has been known to burn them.

Elgor Thrice-Bitten, Ranger.

Cruul - *A Cruul, pronounced 'Cruel', is well suited to its name. These monsters—a distant cousin of the Hell Hag—dwell in deep lakes, the darkest depths their home.*
The majority of their bodies are made up of tentacles, and long ones at that. They reach up, towards the surface, and wrap a single tentacle around their victim's leg. Once their human prey is ensnared, they will drag them down and then let go, allowing the person to swim back to the surface. This is by design. The Cruul wants its victim to shout for help, thereby bringing more into the water.
With up to a dozen tentacles, the beast can easily drag down numerous people. There is no escaping it then. There are no records in the older archives that detail any ranger ever killing a Cruul. Most are slain when

the problem is escalated to the local lords or even kings and queens, who have access to court mages.

Suesh Nas-Arteese, Ranger.

Narkul - Known as the Mushroom Folk to some, these monsters do not actively hunt out human prey, though they are more than capable of killing humans.
When left to themselves, Narkuls will simply get on with their lives but, should their territory be disturbed, they will not only protect it but consume those who have wandered into their path.
Their true form is unknown due to the sheer number of mushrooms that protrude from every inch of their bodies. We do know they are capable of standing on two feet and possess two stubby arms.
Their main form of attack is to rear up and burst a number of mushrooms on their chest. The spores and flesh that explode from these mushrooms will melt you to the bone. (If harvested correctly, this substance can be used as a weapon against other monsters).
Killing Narkuls is relatively easy, though it does feel cruel to kill an animal for no more than defending its territory. Still, a contract's a contract.

Wovun Bhear, Ranger.

Wither - Forest dwellers—the darker the better. In fact, a prevailing myth surrounding these creatures suggests they possess some ability to darken the areas they inhabit.
At six feet tall, they are entirely covered in coarse black hair. Beneath all this hair stands a beast not unlike a wolf. This likeness ends, however, when taking into account the ram-like horns on their heads.
Exclusively meat eaters, these monsters have no problem eating humans should they cross paths. Of course, it is not very often the two encounter each other, as most people avoid these strangely dark areas of the forest. When a contract arises though, and they do from time to time, you need to know how to tackle the creatures.
Firstly, they live in groups of male or female. The two only mix when it

*comes to mating season during the autumn. From studies, there seems
no difference between the male and females when it comes to facing
them, but it should be noted that the females are more territorial.*

Galus Kroma, Ranger.

Husk - *These skeletal monstrosities haven't been seen for some time,
though they are worthy of note in our fine bestiary. Their origins is
unknown to our order of hunters and, perhaps, even the mages of
Korkanath. What we can all agree on, however, is that magic had its
part to play.
The beasts do not have brains or working minds as we do—they do not
even possess organs. Their bodies are capable of reshaping its form to
match whatever prey has endured the misfortune of crossing it. They
simply engulf their victim from head-to-toe, wrapping around them like
strips of filthy cloth, and leech every ounce of energy. You see, these creatures are not named for their appearance, but for the manner in which
they discard their prey.
Steel, neither sharp nor blunt, will aid you here. Fire is key when it
comes to destroying Husks. Until fire and flame are required, prey to the
gods that the monsters stay in seclusion.*

Beregor Nine-Fingers, Ranger.

Scelda - *Known as Gremlins to those who call The Shining Coast their
home. Scelda burrow in and out of the white cliffs in the east - excellent
climbers. The people of Velia and Barossh, in particular, have started
many a legend about these small creatures. Most of them are absolute
twaddle, the spindled tales of storytellers with nothing better to do.
Ask any along the coast and they will warn you of Scelda, the baby-
snatchers! 'Tis ludicrous, of course, since these s0-called Gremlins prefer
to eat stone over meat. The only real threat these monsters have ever had
was nigh on three centuries ago, when they displayed a liking towards
the hewn stone of Velia's walls. Small as they are, however - and none
have ever been recorded as being taller than one's knee - it would take
hundreds, if not thousands, to weaken Velia's walls.*

Still, if you piss the little bastards off you can imagine the bite these stone-eaters are capable of. Best kill them quick, eh.

Old Bill, Ranger.

Hell Hags - *You best be having some years behind you before taking on a contract for a Hell Hag. One wrong move—or if you're too stupid to plan ahead—and you're Hag food. These wicked specimens of life call swamps their home, and the worse the better. If you can't see through the water or you feel the trees around you have gathered to defy the light, you're probably right in the middle of their lair.*
Now, I've heard some talk of this evolution rubbish, as if monsters can change according to their environment, but no one can argue that Hell Hags were designed by the very scaled hands of demons themselves. Atilan protect us.
To see a Hag from the shore, you would think you were watching some poor girl drowning in the swamp, even crying out for help, arms flailing. You'd be wrong. And if you dived into the water to save that girl, you'd be dead too. That girl—at least what you can see of her—is the humanoid bait that protrudes from the top of a Hag's back. The spider-like creature that dwells below the surface is a monster you wouldn't soon forget. They vary in size, but I've never seen one dredged out of the water that was smaller than my horse.
You can see below the numerous methods used against Hell Hags over the years but, more than anything, you're going to need a big set of lungs.

Veador Hemsmith, Ranger.

Royal Gobber - *I'm sure you will agree that slaying Gobbers is nothing short of fun for the experienced and exhilarating for the recruits, but—and there is a but my fellow rangers—a Royal Gobber is a completely different beast.*
Coming in at somewhere between seven and eight feet, these behemoths are sheer walls of muscle, rage, and speed.
Not much is known about them, though we believe they are asexual

creatures and responsible for hatching the lesser Gobbers that trail them. Like I say, we believe. This is only a theory and there are there credible theories where these beasts are concerned. I've heard it said that the Royal Gobbers serve to impregnate some kind of Queen Gobber, though there has never been any proof that such a monster exists.

When it comes to killing these things, well, you just need to know your way through the beats of a good fight. They don't go down easily, known for taking a damn good beating before giving it up. Personally, I found a nice heavy axe to the skull did the trick. On the third swing.

Mosef Gibbs, Ranger.

Cruxta - Wherever the dead have fallen, these monsters will be sure to follow. They move in small packs of three or four, all with a nose for the stench of rotting flesh. Make no mistake, though Cruxta prefer the taste of the dead, they will settle for the living and they have the claws to see it so. If there is a big enough battlefield, where chaos reigns, they have even been so bold as to begin feasting amidst the fighting. It should also be known, if the battle goes on and on it is likely more packs will arrive. This can be advantageous as the packs will consider each other rivals and fight amongst themselves.

I have to say, in most cases, we rangers are not called upon in these circumstances. The last contract I accepted for a pack of Cruxta was in an old crypt just outside of Kelp Town. This is more typical for our line of work.

If it's possible, I would recommend hunting them during the day, while they sleep in their nest (see A Charter of Monsters, Page 301, for typical locations).

Don't however, think that light and dark will have a part to play beyond their natural sleep periods. Cruxta have no eyes but rather a whole face of nostrils. And a mouth. A very big mouth in fact. I should probably have mentioned the mouth earlier. Anyway, back to the nostrils. Always approach from up wind.

Kalem Bifson (oldest ranger on record).

Dhisha - *I have no intention of dying by the fang or claw of any monster but, if I had to choose one of their foul kind to end my days, it would be a Dhisha.*

I am fairly confident in stating that there is no other creature in the realm that kills its prey quite like one of these beasts. You can see from the crude drawing below what they look like, but it does nothing to explain how their unique venom works.

Dhisha will always attack their prey while they sleep (they have not mastered lock and key but they have no trouble opening doors). When they do attack, a pair of retractable fangs, so fine as to be mistaken for strands of hair, will sink into the victim's skin and do a number of interesting things.

As the venom is not powerful enough to paralyse a person, it instead seeks out the mind, working its way into their very thoughts. Those who have survived these attacks state that same thing. They are all-consumed by their dream-like condition to a point that the mind chooses not to wake up. The victims also stated that this was accomplished through some shadowed figure in their mind, a figure who grants them three wishes. They are then able to play out their greatest fantasies while the Dhisha drains them of life.

I don't know about you, but I know what my three wishes would be.

Ryfe Fenlock, Ranger.

Broxon - *A bullish monster that enjoys the taste of cattle over a human. That said, the loss of cattle is often the catalyst for a contract to be drawn up. Thus enters the ranger.*

My first description was, perhaps, deliberate as Broxon resemble bulls. That is in shape and by the horns on their head. All else is quite different. For starters, they are twice the size of any bull. Their hide is difficult to look at, well, at least it is for those unaccustomed to the musculature of any animal. You see, Broxon hide is the deep red of muscle, as if the beasts have been stripped of their skin. That would certainly explain their bad temperament.

There are a number of ways to slay a Broxon, some easier than others. By far the easiest way is to poison the beast with suitable bait, but I would

advise killing the monster the old-fashioned way. Granted this comes with greater risk, but doesn't such a thing always come with greater reward?
A fully-grown Broxon can feed a village for a week. They taste like pork of all things. Now, if you can put the beast down with steel instead of poison, you can then sell the carcass and add the coin to your reward.

Fenley Klum, Ranger.

Dredling - *A parasite to be sure. These squid-like creatures will secure themselves to travellers who wander through bogs and the like, finding purchase under the concealment of clothing. Most prefer a nice juicy calf. Once they are attached, they will immediately begin to poison the mind of the host, turning them violent and mad. This usually results in several deaths before the Dredling is discovered.*
There have been numerous cases of Dredlings injecting their eggs into their host and forcing the victim to seek out civilisation before the offspring slither out of their mouth to find hosts of their own.
There are signs to look out for, of course, before the violence begins. The eyes of the host are always extremely bloodshot for the first few days. Then they begin to turn black. By this stage, madness will have its firm hold. Other signs include a slight tremor in the hands, loss of appetite, paling skin, and muttering to oneself.
If you can identify a Dredling host before their eyes turn black, there is a chance you can save their life, though you must sever the limb. This, however, might result in their death anyway.

Selene (the maiden of Snowfell), Ranger.

Jaxyl - *A monster of cruel design and, in my opinion, further proof that some thing truly wicked has put monsters on our fair Verda. You will know a Jaxyl when you come across one or hear of their description. In fact, I have never met a witness who didn't tell me they had seen a creature of wolf and ram. 'Tis an apt description. To put it simple, they possess the head of a very angry ram (with four eyes mind you) and the body and claws of a wolf.*

Something drives these beasts to rage and I have seen as much on my hunts. They roam the wilds with a very particular look on their four golden eyes. Yo've probably seen that look, in a tavern or pub, before a fight breaks out. It's as if the Jaxyls go looking for trouble, and not always fr sustenance. They just like to kill, as if they've something in them that must be unleashed.

Killing them is just as easy as swinging your sword into the right body part, just be sure to avoid those horns though—even at a short charge a Jaxyl will break your legs.

Sabine The Red, Ranger.

Fraedan - Perhaps it's my age, but I was raised to call them Imps or Sprites. Regardless of their name, the best word to describe these little creatures is mischievous. I've never seen one taller than my hand but it's their size that lends to their vexatious behaviour. They can get into everything and, thanks to their nimble fingers, I've even seen one reach into the keyhole of a door and undo the lock.

Who can say what drives these wicked beasts? I say it is no more than boredom, though I have heard others—of the religious sort—claim they are sent by the Goddess Atarae to keep our individual destinies on track. I'm sticking with my theory. You're free to make your own and add it to the next edition of this bestiary.

You will know a Fraedan when you see one. The homunculi look strikingly like us, with all the features you would expect to see in a human. There are some added features, such as their small horns and mouse-like tail. They're also a deep purple, though I have seen a few with red skin. When they're not setting mills alight or leading several thousand rats from tavern to tavern, Fraedan sleep together in one big pile. This pile will be inside the largest bird nest you have ever seen and high up a tree. If you catch them sleeping, a flaming arrow should do the trick. If you tackle them while they're awake, they'll likely swarm you.

Just look for the nest.

Osmand The Mute, Ranger.

Khalighast - *Easily identified by the three thick tendrils protruding from the back of their head and shoulders. Here's a monster that can take to the water as swiftly as it does the land. I've hunted these beasts in both and, honestly, they're a bugger to kill in both. They're fast runners, fast swimmers, and damned fast killers. They move prominently on four legs but they can stand on two if they wish - this puts them somewhere between six and seven feet.*

Their grey hide is that of a rough leather, not dissimilar to a Gobbers, if a little tougher. In fact, after you've brought the Khalighast down, I would recommend turning them into a good saddle.

When it comes to distinguishing between the sexes, you need to get a good look at those tendrils I mentioned. The females' are longer and darker than their male counterparts. You might be wondering why you need to know the difference—a monster is a monster. But, when it comes to Khalighasts, targeting the right one can make all the difference to your hunt. Due to the fact that they live in a female hierarchy, if you can identify and kill the matriarch first, the pack loses its cohesiveness. When these creatures aren't working together they're more mindless animal than dangerous predator. That's when you wade in with your sword, but I'm not going to teach you to suck eggs.

Agnes Stone, Ranger.

Creeper - *You'll never hear them coming. It doesn't matter the terrain, Creepers move like the silent hand of Death. I've seen the needle legs walk through snow, forests of fallen leaves, and caves littered with puddles. By the time you realise one has crept up on you, it will be too late.*

At four feet tall, they can also be something of a pain to see. Adding to that, their arms and legs are such fine points of bone that there isn't that much to see of them.

Of course, you will know about it when they are upon you. If they don't impale you with their needle arms they will clamp their jaws around a limb and they will not let go. I saw a fellow ranger stab a Creeper in the back repeatedly and it never once relented its bite. It a tactic of the

males, used to slow you down until the females can attack. Nasty
buggers.
If you do find yourself with a Creeper's jaw wrapped around your leg or
arm, use fire to free yourself. It's the only thing that will make the crea-
tures retreat.

Trantor Vane, Ranger

Luxun - *I have been laughed at for this comparison, but the resem-*
blance between a giant tortoise and a Luxun is most certainly there.
Rather than being housed inside a hard shell, Luxun find safety inside
their shells of jagged stone. In fact, when head and limbs are retracted,
these creatures are often mistaken for boulders. I myself have walked
right past a family pf Luxun while on the hunt. I can tell you quite
humbly, it is damned embarrassing to drive your spear into no more
than a large rock, only to discover the real thing is slowly flanking you.
Now, there are obvious differences between a tortoise and a Luxun—
besides their shells. The head and neck of one of these beasts is closer to a
snake. It will slither out of its stony shell and spit venom at its prey (their
spit has been known to reach ten feet).
Thankfully, killing Luxun is as simple as cutting off their slimy head.
You just need to lure them out of their shell first. Oh, and avoid the
venom, of course.

Renley Killenger, Ranger

Ydrit - *The White Bears our ancestors called them. If only they were as*
easy to kill as a bear. Ydrits are suited to cold environments, the harsher
the better. Most are found north of Longdale and around The Shards.
The common myth is that they prefer the mountains, but they are more
commonly located near to water—typically the sea.
On two feet, Ydrits stand at nine foot and, let me tell you, they make for a
tower of muscle and white fur you've not seen. If you find yourself in the
shadow of one of these beasts, you had better be at the top of your game.
Their flat faces are partially hidden behind curtains of fur, but their
large lower fangs can't help but stand out. And don't be looking in their

black eyes for they'll be sure to rob you of your courage and leave you in a
puddle of your own making.

Their two arms are comparable to logs, thick and strong, with five
wicked claws. One swipe will send you to the next world so keep your
distance.

Now, they usually hunt fish and the like with little interest in the taste of
humans. That doesn't mean they can't be persuaded. In the winter,
when the ice is thick and the fish harder to come by, they have been
known to turn their sights on Longdale's outlying villages.

Isold The Hook Hand, Ranger

Nefaris - These pale walkers hail from the Shadow Realm, a dimension
of fangs and claws that should remain behind lock and key. Sadly, the
magic users of our fair realm have learnt of dark and twisted paths that
lead to that hellish abyss.

One such creature that has been unleashed from that other place is
known as a Nefaris. On two feet, they move like a man and even stand at
our height, but they possess four arms, the upper pair of which are so
long as to reach their knees. The arms protruding from their skeletal ribs
are smaller, designed for shredding the flesh of any prey pulled in by
those stronger, outer arms.

Their head is, in effect, a mouth, capable of opening from forehead to
chin to reveal several rows of teeth.

Thankfully, there is nothing fanciful required when it comes to slaying
the nightmarish beasts. A good length of steel or even a well-placed
arrow will bring them down. If you ask me, it's the mages who should be
hunted down and made to answer for the monsters they unleash on our
world.

Royce Wiggins, Ranger

Grodel - I used to like birds. I thought they were exquisite animals and a
reflection of the gods' beauty. I don't anymore. Not after meeting a
Grodel.

How best to describe this monster of the sky? Even my worst nightmares *could not conjure such a thing. Alas, I shall do my best to detail the creature.*

On four scaly legs, a Grodel stands at around seven feet and can reach up to twelve feet in length when fully matured. Halfway up, black feathers conceal the rest of its hideous form and spread out across its impressive wingspan. Its head is that of an enlarged crow, though I have met rangers who state they encountered a Grodel with an eagle's head. I cannot vouch for that.

Just below their throat, you will find a pair of arms no longer than your own. Should you find yourself on your back, a Grodel looking down on you, they will use these arms to pin you and disembowel you with their beak.

Keep moving. Stay on your feet.

Red Radigan, Ranger

Draugur - *Monsters breed legends and legends breed monsters—this is the way of things. Draugur have a particular myth about them that has always stuck with me. It is said that Draugur were made by the elves during the Second Age, though it could easily have been during the First Age, as we know the elves called Illian home in that time. I believe this myth is part of the reason Draugur are also referred to as Forest Witches, just as their creators are referred to by some as the Forest Folk.*

If this is true, I could not begin to guess at the reason for their creation. What I do know is that these creatures form considerable nests in the heart of forests, often manipulating the surrounding environment to blot out the sun. After that, everything begins to die. These monsters are the definition of blight and must be eradicated as soon as possible. The decay that spreads from them can have detrimental effects on nearby civilisation.

Tarwen Evensin, Ranger

Ghost - *My fellow rangers and I feel it prudent to include mention of ghosts in this edition of our fine bestiary. Let me tell you why. Should you be hunting some monster out there and you decide you're chasing a*

ghost, you're going to turn to this book for advice. You would then discover that there is no advice concerning ghosts and would, perhaps, wonder if your predecessors had failed to collect an accurate library of the beasts that prey on our world.
Well here it is, the advice you are looking for.
There are no such things as ghosts.
Whatever it is you are hunting, it is not the spirit of the departed. It is something else inside this book. Try harder.

Melinda Shadow-Born, Ranger

Harpy - *What beautiful critters these monsters are. At only a foot tall, bodies like the bark of trees, large doe eyes, and wings like lush summer leaves, they will lure you in with the innocence of a child—even their smile is a twisted mimicry of our own. Whether this appearance is by evil design or unfortunate coincidence is unknown.*
Make no mistake, Harpies know exactly what they're doing when it comes to us humans. Woodland dwellers, one or two will make contact, appearing as playful things to lower defences. If you are foolish enough to follow them back to their forest nest, you will be set upon by thirty or more of the buggers. Then you'll see their teeth.
It's not typically our way, but I would advise donning a suit of armour before tracking them down. They'll bite through leather as easily as they do flesh, but iron will give them something to think about.

Tobias Noon, Ranger

Ghoulist - *I have transcribed the passage from the eleventh edition of A Chronicle of Monsters: A Ranger's Bestiary, despite the fact that no ranger has identified a Ghoulist in over a hundred years. I know from experience that just because a thing hasn't been seen for a long time doesn't mean it can never be seen again. So I warn you not to skim over the details but commit them to memory, as you might be the first to cross a Ghoulist and, as you have probably learnt by now, facing any monster unprepared is a good way to lose your life.*
If you are reading this, my fellow ranger, then I say well done to

you. It would take even the most learned of men some time to reach this page, which means you must have many a monster under your belt.

If you must add another, pray to the gods it is not a Ghoulist. With six legs and the musculature of a horse, you can bet they are bigger, stronger, and faster than yourself. Should you manage to stay on your feet long enough to actually fight it, beware its twin-tails, each ending in razored bone. Then there's its head, a hideous thing. If you have ever come across a Scudder, that's exactly what their head and neck look like. Wicked beasts.

I only survived because the damned thing was more interested in devouring my horse.

Harndel Goft, Ranger (transcribed by Barnwen, son of Farngorn)

Vogan - *Now here's an interesting creature for you, dear learner. Though these little beasts do not directly hunt humans, they are undoubtedly a threat should the two ever meet. Vogan can be typically found in the wake of Giants. Not always, I should say, but their presence is not uncommon.*

These beasts come in at no taller than the average man's waist with a naturally hunched back and long arms that aid in their movement. On their own, any Vogan is easily killed by even an amateur swordsman but, due to the numbers they travel in, they can overwhelm a person or potentially a group if motivated enough.

As I said, however, they trail Giants, preferring to pick clean whatever they leave behind. There's nothing fancy to be done here—there's no bait or poison to employ. If you take on a contract regarding a Giant, it's always good to be aware of these creatures lest they surprise you. It's rare to see a contract come up specifically for the Vogan but should one arise, be mindful that the Giant they're following is likely dead, leading to the Vogan creating trouble for humans directly. If the Giant is dead, you have to wonder what could kill it. There's always something worse out there.

Rogan Vane, Ranger

Mergossa - *The trees that eat, my mother called them. There are many myths surrounding the Mergossa, and from many cultures and times, but they all agree that these beasts have a taste for human flesh. Personally, having observed them in the wild, I have seen no such propensity. I have witnessed the devouring of everything from baby rabbits to bears, depending on the size of the Mergossa. I cannot say what power put them on our fair world or how it came to be that they are able to so closely mimic the trees around them, though I would wager there is evil at work within them.*

I also cannot say where the myth came from that Mergossa are static creatures. Perhaps it is because of their likeness to the trees they live between. I can tell you for a fact, my fellow ranger, that Mergossa can move as they like, and swiftly too. I believe, however, that they choose not to move so often because of the great noise they make, their heavy legs thundering into the ground.

Nathaniel Crawly, Ranger

Triffid - *A four-winged bat would be a better name for these creatures, but I suppose it doesn't roll off the tongue quite so well. Still, there is not better description for these flying monsters. Worse still, they are equal in size to a fully-grown hound and perfectly capable of lifting a man from the ground. What happens to the man thereafter I leave to your imagination, dear ranger, but rest assured, it does not end well.*

These nocturnal hunters can be found in deep caves (see A Charter of Monsters, Page 110, for known locations), though be warned, their colonies number in the hundreds. I say this so you do not take the contract likely. A monster hunter you may be, but some jobs are simply beyond the skills of an individual or even a group. Should a colony of Triffids pose a real threat, escalate the job to whomever rules over the threatened. You're going to need an army.

Hadrian Bossem, Ranger

Wretch - *This might be the twelfth edition, but these monsters have featured in every iteration of our fine bestiary. It's as if these creatures*

*have accompanied us from the very hands of the gods. There might be
some truth in that, as our oldest legends would suggest we humans came
from The Wild Moores. A humble ranger cannot say. What I can say is,
be it the damned Outlanders or the Wretches that blend in to the trees,
don't go anywhere near The Wild Moores without expecting a fight.
As for the Wretches themselves, they can blend in with their environment. You're going to need Dovun Dust, let me tell you. Throw it high in
the air and let the beasts move through that red cloud. No missing them
then. Swing true and victory will be yours.*

Balor Ved, Ranger

Hell Spores - *If you've got this far into the bestiary, you're probably
expecting another monster with claws or talons and a hide of scales or
spines. Not all monsters are so easily identified, nor do they hunt as you
would expect.*
*Hell Spores are often found near damp caves (See A Charter of Monsters,
Page 86, for known locations). They also like to grow around tasty
mushrooms. Some poor soul comes across the mushrooms, picks them,
and ends up breathing in the Hell Spores. What follows ain't pretty.
It might take seconds or hours but the end is the same: death. In death,
the spores really get to work. They appear to take control of the body and
violently attack anyone and anything to spread more spores. Don't
worry, you'll know an infected person when you see one. They're wild
and covered in what can only be described as fungi.*
Burn them. Burn them all.

Cal Vornan, Ranger

Clackers - *What interesting creatures these beasties are. Rare too. I say
that with a prayer of thanks to Atilan. Clackers are blind monsters who
rely on sound to find their prey. It is my belief, though, that they also use
their incessant clacking to understand their environment as we might
use our eyes.*
*As for the threat they pose: it is extreme. They move in nests of at least a
hundred, but you will find just one Clacker is fight enough.*

Nessa, Ranger

Ratikan - *Who can say where these monsters came from. Some would point at mages and their magic and they might be right. Mages have been known to conjure wicked fiends and lose control. But, Ratikans could just as easily be another monstrous part of the natural world. Whatever their origin, it does not change the fact that they are dangerous. Growing to eight feet and capable of standing on their back legs, Ratikans will easily tower over their prey. And their name is well earned thanks to their rat-like appearance. There are numerous legends surrounding them, as there are for all things, I suppose. The prevailing mythos, though unproven, is that Ratikans are men by day and monsters by night. I see no truth in this, but we already know of other monsters who are bound by similar laws.*

Do Harcken, Ranger

Marrow Wolf - *Easily identified by their hard exterior of bone. It's this same exterior that makes them quite hard to kill. They're as fast and agile as a wolf and they each possess a keen predatory mind, so striking true with axe or blade can be difficult enough without hitting that natural shielding.*
My recommendation, dear ranger, would be the use of poison. That said, I am yet to find a poison potent enough to actually kill a Marrow Wolf. Ghast Gut or Hyron's Bane, however, is powerful enough to slow the beasts. Once sluggish, you can move in and locate one of the gaps between its bony armour and put it down for good.

Kat Orteeze, Ranger

Weadle - *Fascinating creatures! And proof that not all monsters require a blade to deal with them. Weadles, on the whole, are not to be feared, though I caution against getting in their way. At twelve foot tall and with a jagged exterior akin to mountain stone, these lofty walkers will squash you without care.*
It should be archived that this is not done maliciously. From observa-

tions, it seems Weadles simply don't notice humans, as if we are just another part of the mountain environment in which they live.

They spend their days walking across the highest slopes of The Vengoran Mountains doing no more than moving boulders around, as if they are curating the mountains themselves. Who can say why they do this. Like everything else about these lithe creatures, it is a mystery.

Maynar Phal, Ranger

Hook Hands - Aptly named I should say. The skin about their arms narrows to a bony protrusion that rounds into sharp hooks. So too do their four legs. These hooks are perfect for disembowelling their prey, so they might feast on the preferred organs (liver and kidneys), but the hooks are also excellent for lending these fiends great speed and agility. Like Sandstalkers, you will find subtle variations of these creatures in different environments (See A Charter of Monsters, Page 101, for known locations).

Personally, I have always found the ilk that dwell in caves harder to kill than those which inhabit woodland areas. Be that as it may, every variation of the Hook Hands species is vulnerable to bright light. Combine this vulnerability with fire and you have the perfect weapon.

Horis of The Vales, Ranger

Ice Troll - I am aware that the bestiary has an archive regarding Trolls and their various breeds, but I feel it prudent to give the Ice Troll its own piece of parchment.

Unlike its kin, the Ice Troll possesses a unique exterior that makes them much harder to kill. Most would describe it as jagged ice but, on closer inspection, it is something more akin to crystal. This strange armour seems to grow quite naturally from their skin and is entirely random, creating a distinct appearance for each Troll.

With most believing it to be ice, the majority of hunters have brought fire to tackle the beasts. Do not rely on fire. Their crystal-like hide will not melt to flame.

They have but one universal weak spot: their face. No Ice Troll has *ever been seen with the natural armour on their face. A well-placed arrow, if you have the skill, could put the monster down in a single shot.*

Leah Norst, Ranger

Pixlet - *Where the name came from I cannot say, for these little buggers are better known as Kilits in The Arid Lands, where they originate. Still, the name has stuck amongst us northerners.*
Now, the first thing you're going to do is underestimate a Pixlet. No taller than your knee and relatively rotund, they are seemingly harmless. Do not be fooled. Their jaws are capable of over-extending and when they do, you won't be able to count all the fangs inside. If you come across one on its own, you might be able to cut it down before it inflicts serious harm, but seldom are they alone. Their packs number in the dozens and they will strip you to the bone.

Han Gorson, Ranger

Skab - *Once referred to as the children of the forest, Skabs are impish creatures that move about the forests via burrows. It has been pointed out to me by my fellow rangers that the latter is merely a theory. Though burrows have been found near Skab sightings, they have never been seen to use them.*
There are few reports of these little beasts harming folk. More often than not, travellers complain of belongings being stolen and farmers report missing livestock. Having seen Skabs up close, I am thankful they do not require the blade, for they bear an uncanny resemblance to human children.

Delken Phen, Ranger

Tilly Wig - *These monsters are located in the north east, specifically Longdale. These are the only beasts known to have ever been domesti-cated. Where they used to be a danger, they are now used to plough fields and cart goods about.*

You'll easily spot them, being slightly larger than a bull. That and their horn, a protrusion that shapes most of their head.
It's rare, but these can go wild. When they do, it's guaranteed someone will die. Most of the time, the folk up there know how to deal with them but, just in case, see below for the best traps.

Hestor, Ranger

Crownling - *No larger than a dog, these beasts might seem hardly a challenge, but beware ranger for, with jaws like a warthog, their bite can break bone and sever limbs. With that in mind, it will only take a single bite to take you out of the fight. If you can't defend yourself, the rest of the pack will descend and tear you to pieces.*
Since their back is lined with jagged rock, you will have to target their sides but don't rely on arrows for they tend to annoy them more than anything.
See below for known poisons and traps.

Baigan Ruun, Ranger

Xigerat - *A reptilian beast to be sure. They stalk rivers, preferring fresh water, though some claim to have seen them in The Adean.*
From head to tail you're looking at a monster of ten feet. They aren't a common threat, living mostly on a diet of river life, but they have been known to wander beyond the banks and attack humans.
They can do so on four limbs but be warned, when it comes to challenging them, they rear up like a bear on their back legs. That's a wall of muscle, claws, and razored teeth in your face.
There are no known poisons or even traps that lure them in. I'm afraid this is a good old fight with an equally good length of steel.

Sham-Vet, Ranger

Moss Fiends - *Irritating buggers, though irritating is perhaps too harmless a word. Do not get me wrong, for a single Moss Fiend is* *capable of killing a man. It's just that such a man would have to be uninitiated in the ways of the sword.*

These creatures prefer to hide in forests, though some have been found in fields and across the plains of Alborn. You won't even know you're looking at one, and especially from afar. The bulk of their body is covered in some kind of false moss that lends them the appearance of a small and natural mound.

When close enough, they will explode from their apparent hiding place on six pale legs and spit venom from their spider-like head. The venom isn't deadly to humans but it will still irritate your eyes and even blind you for a time.

Personally, I have found it quite satisfying to use flaming arrows from afar while they remain in 'hiding'.

Old Carduune, Ranger

Smilers - *Disturbing are these monsters of shadow. In truth, they are creatures of the Shadow Realm, a land of darkness that should never have been tapped by foolish mages.*

Standing like a man, they mirror many of our features—if you can imagine a man who wears his skin inside out. Worst of all our similarities, these beasts wear a permanent expression; the very same that has lent them their name.

They are simple monsters, seeking flesh for sustenance. It would seem, however, that they seek to induce fear in their prey first. Some have theorised that it makes us taste better.

Callum Forgson, Ranger

Thindle - *These scrawny monsters might not look like much, being skin and bone and with a head of thick hair that conceals their everything from the neck up, but they're vicious little blighters. They lurk around swamps mostly but that don't mean they're confined to such.*

Now, if you consider yourself a strong but slow hunter, these aren't the contracts for you. Speed is required to tackle a Thindle's agility. And never let them get a single swipe in. Their nails carry disease that will spoil your blood and put you in the ground within days.

Authen Madwell, Ranger

Oligort - *Sticky buggers—literally. I fought one only ten days ago in Whistle Town. It decided one of the outlying barns was its territory and it guarded it so.*
In their natural position, they're no taller than your waist. This is due to their six legs always being bent. When they spring for you, their length is considerably more.
These are the first monsters I've ever crossed that possess a mouth on both the upper and lower part of their bodies. Truth be told, I'm not sure they have a right way round. What they do have is an awful amount of sticky fluid across their entire body. They secrete all their life and this can often be used to track them.
Interestingly, and most fortunately, this same fluid is rather flammable.

Caleb Moore, Ranger

Wyvern - *Said to be extinct, the rangers of old have continued to include Wyverns in every edition of the bestiary.*
If you were to compare these creatures to anything it would be dragons. They looked exactly the same save for their number of legs. Wyverns have but two hind legs, using their wings in the manner of front legs, much like a bat.
It was also said that they were smaller than dragons though far more agile. And instead of breathing fire they were capable of spitting some kind of acid. If it is to be believed, they were made extinct by the dragons themselves.

Norm Bronson, Ranger

Berserker - *Another foul abomination from the depths of the Shadow Realm. I hate to imagine what that hellish plane of existence truly looks like. Going by the monsters brought forth, it would make a man go mad.*

The Berserker is no exception. We have to assume some devil beyond understanding gave this beast life. 'Tis a man made flesh with a scorpion. They possess three scorpion tails and arms that end in hideous claws. Their head can only be described as a man's split in half and peeled over the shoulders.

At ten to twelve feet in height, these behemoths aren't easy to kill. See below for known traps and baits.

Benjamin Cawl, Ranger

Kraken - You likely don't need to be reading this to know that The Hox is the domain of a beast so terrible no kingdom dare set sail across it. That monster has gone by many names, I don't doubt, but folk in these parts refer to it as the Kraken or sometimes Leviathan.

We have decided to include it in this edition of the bestiary due to its undeniable nature, but don't be thinking you can fight it. The last time a sighting was reported—by my grandfather's generation—it was seen taking down a whole vessel in minutes, dragging it down to the depths.

There were reports of tentacles and a mighty tail but little else. Besides that, we know nothing of the monster. Well, that's not strictly true, I suppose. We know it won't let any ships cross that sea.

Varys Nad, Ranger

Trappers - Experience you'll need, Ranger, if you're thinking of taking on a contract concerning these beasts. They've been known to dwell in both deserts and muddy plains—wherever their prey believes they walk on solid ground.

While underground, these monsters have a unique way of vibrating their bodies and liquifying the hard earth. The next thing you know, you're sinking into the world and the hungry maw of a Trapper.

Balen Stone, Ranger

Gilgamorg - You've likely heard of the demon, no more than a myth to most; a bedtime story. But more than one ranger has sighted the creature and lived to tell of it, so we will continue to pass on what we know.

It is said the Gilgamorg came into being during the first civil war, when Gal Tion's kingdom fractured into six. His court mage enacted a terrible spell in the middle of a heated battle. The nature of that spell remains unknown, but the devastating consequences were felt by all that day, to be sure.

One by one, the dead littering the field were brought together into one nightmarish fiend. So massive was it that all could see the terrifying creature wrought from dead limbs and severed heads. Imagine a beast with a thousand hands and a sword in each.

It's enough to keep me away from The Vrost Mountains.

Craegor the Long-lived, Ranger

Razor Hog - The history of this beast has been passed down from our very first edition and those most earnest of rangers who had dealings with the dwarves of Dhenaheim.

According to them, the dwarves ride on mounts called Warhogs, brutish animals that make the children of the mountain all the more formidable. The Warhog, however, is not the monster in question. It is the monster from which they are bred.

The Razor Hog is said to be equal in size to a shire horse and roughly the same in appearance as an average hog. The exception is its numerous tusks and trio of horns that line its head.

Should you cross one of these behemoths, I would simply recommend running in the opposite direction.

Liam Kelin, Ranger

Witchweavers - There has been much debate whether these fiends are of our realm or the Shadow Realm. I personally believe they hail from that dark place but there is no proof.

Witchweavers favour forests for their skill comes from their ability to weave walls from twigs and branches, creating corridors that force their prey in a particular direction.

By wailing and screeching, they terrify people, inducing such fear that they flee into these 'natural' corridors and get lost in a hellish maze. From there, any and all are easy pickings for the spider-like witches.

Roy Clement, Ranger

Sirens - *There are plenty of sailors around Velia's port and the like who will swear blind that Sirens exist. They'll recount sightings and tell tales of men hearing the sweet and hypnotic song of these creatures.*
They don't exist.
If they did, we would have killed one by now. It is unanimous amongst our order of hunters that Sirens are no more than fairy tales.

Neave Gladwell, Ranger

Skulldiggers - *Imagine, if you will, a butterfly the size of your hand and with teeth like a beaver. Oh, and an appetite for human brain.*
At speed, one of these critters will fly directly into your face and immediately begin digging through flesh and bone until it's situated inside your skull.
If you see a swarm—hide. If you're hunting a swarm, stock up on salt; they hate the stuff. I would also recommend smoke, to make them drowsy first.

Haylin Nord, Ranger

Blatenwik - *A brute of a monster, and an angry one at that. If you must hunt one of them, surprise will be your greatest weapon. If your surprise attack fails and you're face to face with it, best be having your affairs in order, because running isn't an option.*
With the rounded horns of a goat and a head that could only be compared to a Gobber's, it's a creature born of nightmares. Its hideous face and tusks aside, the danger posed by a Blatenwik comes from its strength. There's no fat on these creatures, just muscle. Trust me when I tell you, they will use that muscle to tear your arms off.

APPENDICES

The Blacksmith, Ranger

Greyfang - *I have to say that these beasties are dangerous because they've been known to kill plenty of folk, but, I also have to say, they're really not. At least, they're not that dangerous if you know anything about using a sword.*
Big black eyes and big sharp claws make them look more formidable than they really are. Their bodies are more bone than anything else. With little muscle, they rely on their claws to deliver damage. They're so easy to cut down it's almost fun. If nothing else, they're good for sword practice.

Bru Vane, Ranger

Unicorn - *I understand that we live in a world of monsters, in a world of things. But Unicorns are just for children.*
Move on.

Ankar Tor, Ranger

Bearded Dragon - *A sea serpent to rival the mighty King Basilisk. These monsters are aggressive, so much so that they have been known to not only stalk merchant ships but board them.*
Think of these creatures in two halves. Their lower half is all tentacles, and barbed ones at that. Nasty things.
Their top half is always likened to a dragon, with two arms and wicked claws that can easily dig into the wood of any ship. Their reptilian head is dominated by strong jaws. It is the tendrils that hang from those jaws that lend the monster its name.

Mendra Falcorne, Ranger

Shadow Dealers - *Get a mage. I'll write that again. Get a mage. Aptly named, these monsters crawled out of the Shadow Realm, but it is not what they are or where they came from, but what they do, that is so hellish.*

A single bite from these demons will scar you with what can only be described as a void. I've heard mages call them portals. From these wounds, more of their wicked kin are able to claw their way into our world. These nightmarish gateways can only be closed by a mage— killing the poor soul who was bitten will not suffice.
Get a mage.

Nay Hodden, Ranger

Three-headed Dread Serpent - *If you've read about Hell Hags, you should have an idea how foul and ferocious they are. Hell Hags have nightmares about these serpents.*
Dread Serpents will encroach on the swamp of any monster and make it their own. While it is good that they devour other monsters, they them-selves are extremely hard to kill. While you might evade one or even two snapping jaws, few can avoid the bite of a third.
I myself shared the reward with a mage. She froze the swamp and I lopped off the heads. We could all do with learning a spell or two.

Jayms Mellor, Ranger

Lizard Folk - *I have had to fight hard to have these monsters included in this edition. My fellow rangers believe me mad, delusional. They tell me the heat of The Arid Lands got to my mind.*
I saw them.
Tall as men they were and damned if they didn't walk like us too. There was no mistaking what they were, however. The Lizard Folk of The Narrows are real. Some of them were even wearing clothes I tell you. Long tails dragged behind every one of them and their claws were curved and sharp. I know what I saw. Heard too. They could talk to each other, coordinate and the like. I'm sure as hell never taking a contract that takes me anywhere near The Narrows.

Old Ned, Ranger

CPSIA information can be obtained
at www.ICGtesting.com
Printed in the USA
LVHW010246160723
752602LV00006B/91

9 781916 610200